Hornblowe[illegible]gacy:

BREWER'S LUCK

A SEA NOVEL

BY

JAMES KEFFER

Hornblower's Legacy:

BREWER'S LUCK

BY

JAMES KEFFER

www.penmorepress.com

Brewer's Luck by James Keffer

ISBN-13: 978-1-942756-26-2(Paperback)

ISBN -978-1-942756-27-9 (e-book)

BISAC Subject Headings:

FIC014000FICTION / Historical

FIC032000FICTION / War & Military

FIC047000FICTION / Sea Stories

Editing: Chris Paige

Cover Illustration by Christine Horner

Address all correspondence to:

Michael James

Penmore Press LLC

920 N Javelina Pl

Tucson AZ 85748

CHAPTER I

Lieutenant William Brewer looked around the quarterdeck of His Majesty's frigate *Defiant* and could scarcely believe his good fortune. In this year of our Lord, 1821, peace reigned in the world. While this would normally be considered a good thing by most people, for a King's officer in the Royal Navy it meant a decided reduction in opportunities for employment. To put it plainly, the peacetime Royal Navy needed only a fraction of the ships that it did in wartime, and fewer ships require fewer lieutenants to man them. Those low on the seniority list, or unlucky enough not to secure a place on a ship, were put ashore to fend for themselves.

Brewer was one of the lucky ones. When the Napoleonic wars ended in 1815, his ship, the *Dreadnought*, survived the wholesale paring of the fleet that guarded England's overseas commerce, and Captain Tyler had asked Brewer to stay on. He had worked hard, and in early 1817 was rewarded when he was called into the Captain's cabin and given his opportunity.

"Sit down, Mr. Brewer," the Captain had said. "I have something to tell you. I have received new orders from the Admiralty. I am being relieved of command of HMS

Dreadnought and will be given command of HMS *Agamemnon*. I am permitted to take two lieutenants with me, one of whom will be the first lieutenant, naturally. I would like the other to be you, Mr. Brewer."

"Sir," Brewer had said, "I can't thank you enough for thinking me worthy of this honor."

"Nonsense, Mr. Brewer," Tyler had said. "You've earned it, sir; do not think otherwise. The decision is entirely yours; if you should wish to stay aboard *Dreadnought*, I will not think less of you. But, before you make your decision, let me inform you of our mission. *Agamemnon* is to carry the new governor to St. Helena and will lead the squadron guarding Napoleon Bonaparte!" Brewer recalled how proud Tyler had looked at that moment. "I tell you, Mr. Brewer," Captain Tyler had continued, "if there is the smallest chance of meeting or even seeing the Corsican, one would be a fool to let it pass by!"

Then, just two weeks before they were to sail, a new captain came on board with orders from the Admiralty relieving both Captain Tyler and the first lieutenant. The new captain was William Bush, who had made his name as Commodore Lord Hornblower's first lieutenant during the war. Bush struck Brewer as a solid, no-nonsense sort of captain, the kind that brought his crew home alive without flogging someone daily to set an example. That was Captain Tyler's great weakness, in Brewer's opinion; the captain felt the crew needed to fear him, and when he thought they did not, he would flog whoever committed the next offense, no matter how minor it was, simply to inspire fear, and through fear, obedience. The word on Bush was that he had learned differently under Hornblower, and no one had ever heard of excessive floggings when Bush commanded *Nonsuch* in 1812.

Brewer found he was to remain as second lieutenant.

The new first was named Gerard; he, too, had sailed under Hornblower. When they were introduced, Gerard had flashed Brewer a brilliant smile and given him a warm handshake. Brewer thought hopefully that he would prove a good one to work for. It was Gerard who told him about their special passenger.

"Captain Bush told me on the way here," Gerard had said, "Lord Horatio Hornblower himself has been appointed governor of St. Helena. We will be transporting him to the island along with his wife, the Lady Barbara, and their son. Wait 'til you meet them!"

That voyage was the best time of Brewer's young life. Both on watch and off, a sailor could listen to stories of Hornblower's adventures around the globe. Like everyone else on board, Brewer hung on every word. But the best was yet to come. Not long after their arrival at St. Helena, the captain passed the word for Brewer to report to his cabin.

"Mr. Brewer," the captain had said, "you are being detached for a temporary assignment. Pack your sea chest and report to the governor right away."

"Aye aye, sir," Brewer had replied. "May I ask, what sort of duty, sir?"

Bush looked up at him and smiled. "The governor will explain further," he said, "but I daresay you'll enjoy it."

And so the greatest adventure of his life began, as Brewer spent the rest of his time on St. Helena as Hornblower's private secretary. His organizational skills were tested by his duties in running the governor's office, but Brewer rose to the challenge. By far the best part of his job was his contact with the former emperor of the French, Napoleon Bonaparte.

Brewer remembered the many times he had greeted the Corsican when he came to the governor's office. Bonaparte was unfailingly polite, occasionally pausing to chat with Brewer on his way out. Brewer smiled as his eyes scanned the *Defiant's* gun deck, remembering the one lapse in the ex-emperor's courtesies. It was during the escape crisis, right after Governor Hornblower ordered increased security around Napoleon's house at Longwood. Bonaparte had stormed into the office, and, upon learning the governor was out, vented his wrath on Brewer. Brewer's chin rose slightly in pride at the memory of how he stood toe-to-toe with the greatest military mind since Charlemagne, or even Caesar himself, and did not flinch. Governor Hornblower later told him that Bonaparte was impressed by his presence of mind and self-control during the incident, telling the governor those were the very qualities that he sought when making a man a Marshal of France.

Leaving his post on St. Helena and returning to the decidedly less-exciting duties of a second lieutenant was the hardest thing he had ever done, but Brewer had been determined that neither Captain Bush nor Lord Horatio Hornblower would find any fault in his performance of his duties.

Brewer had spent much of the voyage home to England speculating on his future. Rumors in the wardroom said *Agamemnon* would be laid up when they reached Portsmouth. Soon after they'd left St. Helena, Captain Bush invited Brewer to dine with Hornblower and himself.

After the dinner was over, the three men sat in Bush's cabin smoking cigars and drinking wine brought from St. Helena. The main topic of conversation was their late charge.

"What an extraordinary man he was," Hornblower said.

"I wish I could have known him better," said Bush. "Although I daresay, the one time I did meet him had more of hospitality than what he intended for us back in France! Wouldn't you say, m'lord?"

Hornblower smiled at the thought. "Absolutely, captain! Still, it amazes me that after all these years he remembered us, Bush. He recalled the circumstances of our escape and even told me the fate of the captain of our guard. What an intellect! Who knows what good he could have done for France had he been satisfied to rule instead of desiring conquest!"

Captain Bush looked thoughtful; Hornblower smiled and turned to Brewer.

"And what did you think of Bonaparte, Mr. Brewer?"

Brewer's eyes snapped up, surprised by the question. "I'm not sure, m'lord," he said. "He wasn't at all what I expected. He seemed... kinder, more human somehow; I'm probably not saying it right. I imagine he was brought down by his circumstance—that probably made him seem a shadow of what he was. I'm sorry, m'lord, but words seem to fail me. All I can say is, I doubt I shall meet his like again."

Hornblower nodded his agreement. "Well said, Mr. Brewer. Captain, do you have that bottle of port I asked you to hold for me?"

Bush called for his steward. In a few minutes the man appeared with the port and fresh glasses. Hornblower uncapped the decanter and poured each of them a generous portion.

"Mr. Brewer," he said, "will you kindly render honors?"

As the junior officer present, it fell to Brewer to toast the King's health. As solemnly as he could, Brewer raised his glass. "Gentlemen, the King." The others raised their glasses in salute, and all drank the King's health. Hornblower set his glass down and leaned one arm on the table.

"Now, Mr. Brewer," he said, "may I ask if you have any plans for your future?"

Brewer looked from Hornblower to Bush, unsure how to answer without seeming to beg or boast.

"You may speak, Mr. Brewer," Captain Bush said, "just say what's in your heart."

Brewer flushed. "Well, my lord, I would like to stay in the navy if at all possible. All I ever wanted was to serve on a King's ship at sea."

Hornblower nodded while Bush sat back and smiled.

"An admirable ambition, Mr. Brewer," Hornblower said.

"I felt the same way ever since I was a midshipman." Hornblower glanced at Bush, who merely nodded, then he regarded Brewer.

"Mr. Brewer, I have had the great fortune in my career of attracting the notice of officers of influence who aided me, and I promised myself I would return the favor whenever I could. It has been my pleasure to be of some small benefit to Captain Bush and Lieutenant Gerard on occasion over the years, and now I would like to do the same for you."

Brewer was astounded, hardly believing his good fortune. "My lord, I don't know how to thank you."

Hornblower held up his hand. "No need for that. You've earned it, Mr. Brewer; don't think otherwise. I only ask two things of you: continue to do well in your duties, and let me hear from you from time to time. Remember, the double-edged sword about patronage is that it can be withdrawn as quickly as it is granted. As for hearing from you, I want you to write me at Smallbridge when you get the chance. These are to be personal letters, Mr. Brewer, not reports; I'm sure I will get enough of those from Captain Bush."

"Indeed, my lord," Bush said with a conspiratorial smile.

Hornblower nodded and sat back in his chair. "As it should be. Well, Mr. Brewer, what do you say?"

Brewer lowered his eyes. "My lord, I am deeply honored. I won't disappoint you."

Hornblower smiled and stood. Brewer and Bush rose as well, and Hornblower shook Brewer's hand.

"Congratulations, Mr. Brewer," Bush said when it was his turn to shake Brewer's hand. "Now you'd best turn in and get some rest before your watch."

"Aye aye, sir," Brewer said. "Good night, my lord. Good night, Captain."

Brewer was true to his word, and Hornblower never regretted his patronage. After docking in Portsmouth, *Agamemnon* was decommissioned. Hornblower arranged for

Bush, Gerard, and Brewer to be reassigned to the frigate *HMS Lydia* with orders to join the Mediterranean fleet and fight the Barbary pirates. Over the next two years, Brewer distinguished himself in several battles with the pirates, once taking command of the badly damaged *Lydia* after Bush and Gerard were both seriously wounded, and nursing the frigate successfully back to Gibraltar for repairs. The action earned him a promotion to first lieutenant.

Brewer was also faithful in writing to Hornblower often, mailing his letters when in port or when the *Lydia* met with a courier. He was surprised to receive replies from Hornblower, full of advice and encouragement, but occasionally with a timely warning. Brewer always heeded Hornblower's advice and had yet to regret it.

Finally, the old *Lydia* was ordered back to England to be decommissioned. Captain Bush told Brewer he would be retiring when they reached England. They had taken several prizes during their cruises, so Bush and Brewer each had a decent amount of prize money to fall back on.

"What will you do with yours?" Brewer had asked Bush.

Bush considered for a moment before answering. "Do you know, I believe I'll buy an estate outside Smallbridge for my sister and myself. It sounds like a nice, quiet place to live. And you?"

Brewer thought about it. "I'm not sure, sir. I am supposed to meet Lord Hornblower in London. If I can get another ship, then I'll invest the money for safe keeping. If not, well... I'm just not sure."

Brewer's meeting with Hornblower resulted in orders to report to *HMS Defiant* as first lieutenant. Hornblower had been promoted to Rear Admiral of the Blue and was sailing immediately to take command of the West Indies squadron. *Defiant* would follow within the month and join the squadron after stopping at Boston, New York, Washington City, and Savannah to pick up any news. Brewer could hardly wait to get under way for America.

Just forty-eight hours ago, Brewer had arrived on board, met at the entry port by a handsome officer nearly as tall as he was.

"I am Lieutenant William Brewer, come aboard to join."

"Welcome aboard, sir," the officer said. "I am Benjamin Greene, the second lieutenant. Mr. Johnston! Take the First Lieutenant's dunnage down to the wardroom, if you please, and see that Creighton stows it for him."

"Aye aye, Mr. Greene!"

Greene watched the sailor pick up Brewer's sea chest and go below. He turned to Brewer and said, "The Captain's not here, I'm afraid; he's in London at the Admiralty. We expect him back in two or three days."

Brewer nodded and shook Greene's hand. "That's fine. I can use a couple days to settle in and learn the ship."

"Of course, sir," Greene said. He turned and called, "Mr. Peters, you have the deck! I shall be in the wardroom with the First Lieutenant."

"Aye aye, sir!"

Greene turned to Brewer. "If you'll follow me, sir?"

Greene led the way below decks. Brewer had tried to learn all he could about the *Emdiyon* class frigates like *Defiant*, but even so he was impressed by the sheer size of the ship. You could almost fit his old ship inside her hull! They walked past the midshipman's berth, and Greene opened the screen door to the wardroom. He led the way in and then closed the door behind Brewer.

Brewer took in the table dominating the center of the room and the ten chairs surrounding it. A young officer—Brewer at first mistook him for a midshipman—who was sitting in one of the chairs reading, jumped to his feet when Brewer entered the room.

Mr. Greene stepped around Brewer and saw the young officer standing at attention. "Oh!" he said. "My apologies, Mr. Phillips; I did not see you there. Mr. Brewer, may I present Lieutenant John Phillips, *Defiant's* third lieutenant. Mr. Phillips, this is Lieutenant Brewer, our new first lieutenant. "

Phillips made a small bow. "Welcome to *Defiant*, sir."

Brewer nodded. "Pleased to make your acquaintance, Mr. Phillips. Please take your seat; I did not mean to interrupt whatever you were doing."

"Thank you, sir," Phillips said as he sat back down and resumed his reading.

“This way, sir,” Mr. Greene led the way back to the corner cabin on the starboard side and opened the door. “Here you are, Mr. Brewer.”

Brewer entered his new home and discovered that, like everything else on *Defiant*, it was bigger than its counterpart on his old ship. He also found a middle aged man, who reminded Brewer very much of a bookseller he had met in London, unpacking his sea chest. When Brewer stepped in, the man looked up from stacking some of Brewer’s books on his desk.

Mr. Greene made the introductions. “Mr. Brewer, this is Creighton, the wardroom steward. Creighton, this is Lieutenant Brewer, our new first lieutenant.”

The steward bowed. “Welcome to *Defiant*, Lieutenant.”

“Thank you,” Brewer said.

Creighton placed his hand lovingly on the books piled on the desk. “If you would like, sir, I can have the carpenter fix you up a shelf here, with a lip to keep the books in place when we’re at sea.”

“Thank you,” Brewer said. “That would be most kind.”

“I’ll see to it immediately, sir, don’t you worry about it. I’ll return later, if you like, to finish stowing your things, sir.”

Creighton bowed and left the cabin.

"He's a good steward, Mr. Brewer," Greene said. "He likes to make a good impression."

"I'm sure he is," Brewer said as he set his hat on the desk and looked around the room. "Call me William, if you wish; of course, it should be 'sir' in front of the hands."

"Of course," Greene agreed. "I'm Benjamin." The two men gazed about the room. "Would you like a glass of wine, or would you like some time to settle in?"

"I think I'll settle in first," Brewer said. "That is, if you don't think I'll offend Creighton."

Greene smiled. "He should be fine, sir, as long as you don't put a bookshelf up."

Brewer laughed. "I won't, then. I'll see you on deck later, Benjamin."

Greene saluted. "Aye aye, sir."

When Brewer was alone, he looked around his cabin and marveled at his good fortune. His cabin wasn't a palace, but it was bigger than the one on his old ship, and he was inordinately pleased that he didn't have to share it with a gun. He was first lieutenant of a frigate at the tender age of twenty-one. He wondered if he would get his own ship before he was thirty.

He stepped back out into the wardroom, only to find it empty. He was about to go up on deck when the screen door opened and a man entered. He was a head shorter then Brewer, and his disheveled appearance and bulbous nose gave him the air of someone who is addicted to drink. His eye was clear, however, and his speech distinct when he spoke.

"You must be the new first lieutenant," he said.

"Yes," Brewer answered and put out his hand. "William Brewer."

The other gave him a hearty hand shake. "Adam Spinelli.

I'm the surgeon."

"Pleased to meet you. I look forward to getting to know you better, Doctor, but right now I'm on my way topside."

"Aye aye, sir," the doctor said with a grin. Brewer chuckled and went out.

When he got on deck, he did not see Mr. Greene. A fresh sea breeze bit into Brewer's cheeks and reminded him of why he loved the sea. It had called out to him ever since his family made a visit to the seaside when Brewer was six. Brewer's father was a prosperous farmer in Kent, and his roots ran as deep in the Kentish soil as the roots of one of the great oaks his son loved so well. When Brewer left home at fifteen to join the navy, his father refused to give his blessing. He wanted Brewer, as the eldest son, to take over the family farms and be an important man in the county. Brewer still felt a pang of shame whenever he remembered the argument they had that night and his father's final words to him.

"You are practically a man, William," his father had said, "and if your heart is set on this foolish venture, then I cannot stop you. But know this: your home is where your heart is. If you decide to leave, then you have no home here. It is for you to choose."

With those words, his father had turned and left the room, and Brewer had not seen him since. He'd packed his sea chest and left the house before dawn. He kissed his tearful mother and sister goodbye before shaking his younger brother's hand.

"Take care of the land," Brewer said to him, "and Father."

"I will," he said.

Brewer had walked away from the family estates and not gone back since. He'd made his way to Portsmouth, where a family friend was able to secure him a post as a midshipman in the old *Ulysses*. His mother and sister wrote to him faithfully, and he answered as often as he could. Because paper is at a premium at sea, his letters were quick one or two paragraph notes hastily scribbled between the time the courier boat was sighted and when it joined his ship to pass over reports and supplies and collect reports and mail. Brewer congratulated himself on his decision to bring a large amount of paper with him aboard *Defiant*.

A midshipman ran up and saluted. "Lookout reports lighter approaching, sir."

"Very good, Mr.—?"

"Tyler, sir."

"Really? Any relation to Captain Tyler?"

"Don't think so, sir."

"Very well. Report to the master's mate of the watch, and pass the word for the purser."

"Aye aye, sir!" The midshipman saluted and went off to complete his tasks.

Brewer looked up to confirm one more time that *Defiant* was fully rigged and ready for sea. His practiced eye saw nothing amiss. The boatswain was occupied drilling new recruits, but otherwise the hands were busy stowing supplies so the ship could sail with the morning tide as scheduled.

Brewer looked around *Defiant's* deck again and suddenly could not wait to get her under sail. She was a ship of the *Endymion* class, originally completed in 1813 as a forty gun frigate, but upgraded in 1817 to fifty guns in response to the larger size and greater firepower of the American frigates. Brewer wondered if they would see action, possibly in the Caribbean. If so, Brewer pitied any ship that crossed her—*Defiant* carried twenty-eight 24-pounders backed up by twenty 32-pounder carronades as her main punch, and two long nines in the bows. Still, it would be nice to get a look at one of the American giants.

Brewer's thoughts were interrupted by the arrival of the purser. Mr. Barton was a small, squirrelly sort of character, the very picture of a miser. *Still,* Brewer thought, *he seems to take good care of the crew.* Any new officer on a King's ship learns two things very quickly from the crew: how the ship sails, and what the purser is like. So far, in his short tenure aboard, Brewer had heard next to nothing bad about Mr. Barton.

The purser came up and saluted. "You sent for me, Mr. Brewer?"

"Yes, Mr. Barton. What stores are we short on? We sail on the morning tide."

The purser reached inside his shirt and pulled out a notebook. "Let me see... yes, here it is. We finished stowing the casks of salt pork and beef this morning. Water is being stored as we speak, and the rest of the fresh fruit and livestock should be aboard by nightfall."

"What sort of livestock?"

Barton consulted his book, turning pages until he finally found what he was looking for. "Two bullocks, five sheep, ten goats, and fifty chickens. I'm going to try a new way to feed the chickens."

Brewer was surprised. "How so?"

"By feeding them the weevils we shake out of the ship's biscuits. A friend on the *Dauntless* says hens love 'em. You shake the biscuits while they're still in the sack, you see? Not hard enough to break the biscuits, but enough to get the buggers to come out. They fall to the bottom of the sack. Then you just pour them out for the hens to eat, and you end up with lovely fat chickens ready for roasting."

Brewer smiled. "Mr. Barton, I look forward to it. Now, the captain will be back aboard soon. Is your report ready for him?"

"Yes, Mr. Brewer," the purser said. He flipped back a couple pages in his book. "As I said, provisioning will be complete by tonight. We should reach the American coast long before the weather turns nasty, depending on how long we stop in Newfoundland."

"Newfoundland?"

The purser smiled. "Sorry, lieutenant; I forget this is your first voyage with Captain Norman. The captain loves seafood, you see, especially fish from the North Atlantic, so we always stop at Newfoundland whenever we are in the area to see what the fishing fleet has fresh to offer."

"Really?"

"Yes, sir!"

Brewer nodded and dismissed the purser. After the man was gone, he considered what the purser had said. He knew nothing of his new captain. On his way to the ship, he had stopped at several public houses to see if he could learn anything, but came up empty. *In a way, that's good,* Brewer thought. *Perhaps that means Norman doesn't have a bad reputation.*

Brewer had written to Bush as soon as he was assigned to *Defiant* to see if he had heard of Captain James Norman. Bush wrote back to say he believed Norman had been a lieutenant in *Victory* at Trafalgar. According to Bush, there was a rumor that, when he saw Nelson fall, Norman grabbed a musket from a dead marine and shot the French marksman who had killed his admiral. Bush also wrote that he had heard neither good nor bad about Norman as a captain.

Brewer's thoughts were interrupted by the voice of the lookout.

"Deck, there! Captain's boat approaching! Two points off the larboard beam!"

"Very good!" Peters, who had the deck, answered. He looked around and spied young Mr. Tyler. "Mr. Tyler!"

"Sir?"

"The captain's boat is approaching. Muster the appropriate honors. Do you remember the procedure?"

"Yes, sir!" Tyler said as he saluted.

"Off with you, then, Mr. Tyler! You don't want to be late!"

Tyler saluted again. "No, sir! I mean, aye aye, sir!" Brewer smiled as he watched the young midshipman run from the quarterdeck, barking orders for the honor guard to fall in at the starboard entry port.

Brewer took up his position just as the captain's boat reached the ladder. Mr. Greene and Mr. Phillips were also there, probably notified by Peters. The bosun's mate piped the captain on board as the officers and Tyler saluted.

Captain James Norman stood five feet, seven or eight inches to Brewer's six foot two, but there was no doubt as to who was in charge. Brewer and the officers held their salutes and watched the captain salute the quarterdeck and then the marines of the honor guard before acknowledging them. This was a man who was clearly comfortable with himself and confident in his own abilities. The hair beneath his hat was completely white, but the grey eyes held a fire that banished all thought of old age. Norman was not a powerfully built man—in fact, his build was rather slight—but Brewer got the definite impression of an iron will and strength of character that could produce astounding results when called upon. The captain's uniform was immaculate, and the amount of gold bullion on the coat and hilt of the sword told Brewer that Norman either came from a wealthy family or had been lucky with prize money.

Norman stepped up and returned the salute of his officers.

"Carry on, Mr. Tyler," the captain said.

"Aye aye, sir."

"Mr. Greene, Mr. Phillips, it is good to see you again. Is all going according to schedule?"

"Yes, Captain," Greene said. "We will be ready to sail on the tide."

"Excellent," Norman said. He turned to Brewer. A quick look in his direction told Mr. Greene to make introductions.

"Captain James Norman," Greene said formally, "may I

introduce Lieutenant William Brewer, newly come aboard as your First Lieutenant. Mr. Brewer, this is Captain James Norman, captain of HMS *Defiant*."

Brewer saluted, and after a pause during which the captain assessed his new officer, Norman returned it. "Welcome to *Defiant*," he said. "Excuse us for a moment."

"Of course, sir," Brewer said.

Norman conversed privately with Mr. Greene and another man Brewer did not know. Norman seemed to be making some point rather emphatically, the other two men nodding in agreement. Norman turned back to his new first lieutenant.

"Mr. Brewer," he said. "Come with me to my cabin."

Brewer followed his captain aft. The sentry outside the cabin came to attention as Captain Norman passed him and opened the door. Brewer was surprised to see that Norman's cabin was huge for a frigate; perhaps it had been expanded during the refit. Large windows across the stern lit the space with warming sunlight. The furnishings were well appointed but not extravagant (there were no silk pillows) and gave Brewer the impression that the occupant was used to being surrounded by such quality. Either that, or his wife decorated the cabin for him.

Captain Norman handed his hat and sword to his servant and turned to Brewer, who properly tucked his hat under his left arm.

"Well, Mr. Brewer," Norman said, "might I offer you some wine? Bring the Madeira, Jenkins. Now, Mr. Brewer, how are you getting settled in?"

"Yes, very well, thank you, sir," Brewer said, as he took the chair indicated by his captain. He waited until Norman was seated behind his desk before continuing. "The purser reports victualing will be completed today, sir, and water is being stowed."

"Yes, I saw the lighter as I came aboard." Norman

paused as his servant reentered the cabin with the wine, placing the decanter and two glasses in front of the captain before withdrawing. "Don't worry about Mr. Barton. He'll get the provisioning done, and on time, too. Been with me almost ten years; he's the best purser in the fleet, as you'll soon find out. The crew loves him."

Norman sampled the Madeira before pouring them each a generous portion and handing one to Brewer. "Oh, I know you were only doing your job, Mr. Brewer, and it speaks highly of you. I'm just letting you know you can depend on our Mr. Barton to work with a minimum of supervision."

"As you say, sir." Brewer tasted his wine and was pleased to find his captain stocked a quality Madeira.

"Good," Norman said as he sipped his own, and Brewer wondered whether the comment was meant for him or referred to the wine. "Now to our orders. Are you aware of them?"

"Only the basics, sir. We are to sail for the American coast, stopping at various ports before joining Admiral Hornblower in the West Indies. After a stop in Newfoundland, I understand."

"What?" Norman's glass stopped halfway to his mouth, and for a moment Brewer thought he had overstepped his bounds. He was relieved when the captain smiled and took his sip. "Mr. Barton told you about that, did he? Well, it's true. A little weakness of mine, I suppose you could call it. Best fishing in the world is right off Newfoundland, and I simply cannot bring myself to pass it up. Once, back in 1808, I think it was, we took three French privateers as prizes off Newfoundland while we waited for the fishing fleet to return!"

Brewer hid his smile by taking another swallow of his captain's excellent Madeira. He found himself liking James Norman more and more, but a little voice in the back of his mind wondered if he weren't missing something.

Norman set his glass down and leaned back in his chair. "We will stop at Boston, New York, Washington City, Charleston, and Savannah on our way south to join Admiral Hornblower. At Washington City, I will go ashore to meet with our ambassador and deliver into his hands certain dispatches I carry from London. At the other ports, I intend to stay only a night or two, sending various officers ashore—two or three together, mind you, never alone—to visit various establishments and see what tidbits of information they can pick up.

"It is also possible we may run into an American warship in one of the harbors. If so, we will offer to entertain our American brethren. I expect them to jump at the offer, as it would be their first look at one of our upgraded fifty-gunners. I am hoping they will be suitably impressed with either our ship or our wine—quite possibly both—to give us some juicy information. The Admiralty has heard rumors of a 120-gun three-decker to be built at Philadelphia. If the Americans do build her, it would require us to keep either a first-rate or two second-rates on that side of the Atlantic. I can tell you that is money the Admiralty does not want to spend."

"But why should the Americans build such a ship now, sir?" Brewer asked. "Seems a trifle late in the game, if you ask me."

Norman looked up at him. "Late?"

Brewer drained the last of his Madeira while he organized his thoughts. "What do they want with a 120-gun first-rate, sir? They've already got three 74s they've no use for. Their major interest now is protecting their merchant vessels and dealing with pirate activity off Florida and in the Caribbean. That's a job for sloops and frigates. The only thing a first-rate is good for is the line, to beat an enemy's three-decker and control a patch of ocean. They needed to build something like that ten years ago, sir, not today. We're on the same side now, more or less, so they can't feel the need to use it against us. Why spend all that money on one three-decker instead of three frigates, which would help them more?"

Captain Norman nodded his approval. "Well said, Mr. Brewer. Your reasoning is sound. That is precisely what the Admiralty wish us to find out. But let us leave that topic for now. Do you have any other questions?"

"What's the crew like, sir?"

"Most have been with me since the war ended. Besides yourself, Mr. Spinelli, the surgeon, is new, along with both the second and third lieutenants. Have you met them yet?"

"Mr. Greene met me when I reported on board, sir. I met the third lieutenant and the surgeon in the wardroom."

"Good. They are all having dinner with me tonight. I presume you'll be free to join us?"

"Of course, sir."

"Very well," Norman said as he rose. Brewer stood also, his hat again under his arm. "Off with you, then. I'm going up on deck, so you may take your ease. Be back in an hour for dinner."

"Aye aye, sir."

Brewer passed the sentry outside the door without seeing him as he followed Norman out of the cabin. When they reached the stair, Norman ascended to the deck, but Brewer stopped and watched his captain. He looked back down the passageway at his captain's door before going down the stairway to his own cabin. He needed to think.

Chapter 2

Brewer was just finishing a letter to his sister when he heard the ship's bell and knew he only had a half-hour to get ready to join the captain. He signed the letter and sealed it before setting it beside the one for his mother. The captain should send mail ashore before sailing, and Brewer did not want to miss the call.

He pushed back his chair from the desk and stood, careful as always not to ram his head into the deck beams above. His cabin was spartan, the furnishings being his bunk, the desk and two chairs. He only carried with him two things of value—to him, anyway. One was his portable writing desk, bought in London with his prize money from *Lydia*. The desk top opened to reveal compartments where he could secure inkwell and quills, plus another for paper, and the whole thing sealed tight against wetness and locked. Brewer was very proud of it. The second was his library, which he stored on the shelf above his desk that Creighton had asked the carpenter to install. Brewer had been amazed to find it already on the wall when he'd returned from the deck that first day, and it held his books very well. A dozen volumes were all he ever took with him at a time, and he was careful to hold them in place with a length of twine. His books were his prized possessions, and the pride of his collection was always his Bible. It had been given to him by his mother the day he left home. She had made him promise to read it daily so God would protect him; and, barring battles, he had managed to keep his promise all these years. He had nine volumes by Shakespeare, Bacon, and Locke, and two new books he'd bought for this voyage. The first was Gibbons' *Decline and Fall of the Roman Empire*, a favorite of his mentor that Brewer had finally decided to try. The second was a novel by Sir Walter Scott just published the year before, called *Ivanhoe*.

Brewer picked up his hat and stepped out of his cabin. The sentry came to attention as he approached the captain's door, and Brewer nodded to him as he knocked.

"Enter."

Brewer opened the door and stepped through, allowing the sentry to close the door behind him.

"Ah, Mr. Brewer," said the captain, "there you are. Come in, man, come in. I believe you know everyone."

Brewer shook hands with the surgeon and nodded a greeting to the two lieutenants. He accepted a glass of claret from the captain and took a sip. It was excellent, just like the Madeira.

"Gentlemen," Captain Norman said, "if you will take your seats, Jenkins will serve dinner."

Brewer moved with the others to find his place at the table. The captain sat at the head of the table, with Brewer on his right and the surgeon Mr. Spinelli on his left. Green sat next to Brewer while Phillips sat next to Mr. Spinelli.

A rich tomato soup was brought first, and Captain Norman filled each officer's bowl and passed it down. Brewer tasted it and found it delicious and hot. Poor Mr. Phillips was not as cautious and burned his mouth when he swallowed a large spoonful. As each officer finished, Jenkins appeared at his elbow to remove his bowl and spoon and replace it with a china plate. Brewer noticed the captain made no attempt at small talk during the first course.

After clearing the captain's bowl last and then the tureen, Jenkins brought two meat dishes, two vegetable dishes, and a large bowl of steaming potatoes with a gravy boat alongside. He refilled everyone's glass, again pouring the captain's last.

"Thank you, Jenkins," Norman said. The servant bowed and withdrew two steps. "Mr. Phillips, feel free to help yourself to that steak-and-kidney pie in front of you. That other is a ragout of pork. Mr. Brewer, I trust you will do the honors?" Brewer accordingly rose and began carving slices off the roast in front of him.

"Mr. Spinelli, feel free to try some of those potatoes before you. You, too, Mr. Greene, help yourself. Everyone, dig in and pass it around!"

Brewer took generous helpings of everything, and when he dug in, he congratulated himself on his wisdom. Everything that touched his lips was nothing short of heavenly. The ragout of pork was juicy, the pie delicious, the potatoes were perfect, and the cauliflower and carrots were just tender. The best was the gravy, and Brewer was happy to follow his captain's example and pour generous dollops over his potatoes and steak-and-kidney pie.

Mr. Spinelli looked up from his plate. "I say, Captain, this man Jenkins is an absolute wizard! Wherever did you find him?"

"I went looking for him, sir!" the captain said proudly. "I knew about him from a dinner party he catered on *Pluto* back in 1812. So, when I heard *Pluto* was to be laid up in 1816, I sought him out. He was just about to sign on with another ship when I found him and persuaded him to join *Defiant* as my steward. I am happy to say I have never had cause to regret my decision, and I pray you haven't either,

Jenkins!"

"Never once, Captain!" Jenkins replied. Brewer noticed he had not stirred, and guessed this was not the first time he had been praised in this fashion.

The food was passed around the table until nearly every serving dish was empty and every belly filled. At a signal from the captain, Jenkins and two other stewards quickly cleared the table; then, wine glasses were refilled, and cigars passed out and cut.

The captain picked up his glass. "Mr. Vice, the King."

All eyes turned to Mr. Phillips, who as the junior officer present was responsible for toasting the King's health. Brewer was impressed to see a steady hand and hear a strong voice as Phillips raised his glass and said, "Gentlemen, the King!"

"The King!" echoed the men seated around the table as they raised their glasses and drank.

Captain Norman lit his cigar and leaned back in his chair to blow a large cloud of smoke at the ceiling above. "Relax, gentlemen. Smoke, if you wish." Brewer was the only one who puffed his cigar into life.

"Gentlemen," the captain said, "I want to welcome you aboard *Defiant*. I know we are in an unusual position, with the officers all being new to a veteran crew. I trust you will be quick in getting to know the men in your divisions. The midshipmen are all young—I believe Mr. Tyler is senior at sixteen—but they all have at least one or two voyages under their belts, and the petty officers have all been with me for a while now, so you may rely upon them to know their jobs. Mr. Phillips, I believe, is only newly promoted, is that not so?"

"Yes, sir," Phillips said. "It will be two months tomorrow."

"This is your first voyage under commission?"

"Yes, sir."

Norman smiled. "Enjoy it, Mr. Phillips. I still have fond memories of my first cruise as a junior lieutenant, and you most likely won't have to worry about anyone shooting at you!"

Laughter rose from the table, and Phillips had the good sense to look hopeful but say nothing. Brewer's estimation of him rose.

Captain Norman continued, "Take the opportunity to learn your duties well, Mr. Phillips; remember, the men will look to you for leadership. Gentlemen, I know of you all from your service records and recent reports from your former captains. I look forward on this voyage to hearing of your adventures in the South Seas, Mr. Greene, and your exploits with Captain Bush on the *Lydia*, Mr. Brewer, and also, perhaps, of your time on St. Helena?"

"I am at your disposal, sir," Brewer said. Captain Norman nodded his thanks, and Brewer saw the look of shock and awe in the faces of the two junior officers and sighed inwardly. He had been unpleasantly surprised to discover that his actions on *Lydia*, combined with his time on St. Helena, had elevated him to near-legendary standing among the junior officers and midshipmen. On occasion, this got in the way of his work in one form or another.

"Excellent," the captain said, and he sat forward again. "As I said earlier, gentlemen, I hope to get better acquainted with each of you during the days ahead. But, in the meantime, allow me to lay down a few... guidelines, shall we say? Please do not take anything I say personally, gentlemen; I am throwing no stones at any officer here or anyone's former captain." Norman made eye contact with each of them to emphasize his point. Brewer was the last, and he thought the captain held his gaze a little longer. He wondered if the captain may have heard some stories of Captain Tyler; surely it couldn't be anything about Captain Bush? But Norman went on, and Brewer forced himself to concentrate on his captain's words.

"I am simply letting you know what I expect on my ship." Norman paused to puff his cigar and tap off a bit of ash. "I don't like floggings, gentlemen, so I ask you to reserve that punishment for the most serious of offenses."

"Here, here!" said the surgeon.

Norman silenced him with a look. "I also will not tolerate any officer to be drunk aboard ship, either on or off duty. Take this as your only warning, gentlemen; the consequences will be severe."

"Aye, sir," came from the lieutenants. Brewer noticed Mr. Spinelli did not answer. Norman went on.

"A ship of war in peace time is a dangerous place, gentlemen. Standards can grow lax, training and discipline tend to slide because the Articles of War are not strictly enforced. I have seen it on other ships since the wars ended, and it always results in higher casualties when those ships are brought to action." Norman leaned forward, tapping the table for emphasis. "That will not happen on *Defiant*, gentlemen. The crew must be kept in a readiness to win when called upon to fight. As much as possible, I expect standards of gunnery and sail handling to be held to wartime standards."

"Aye, sir!"

"The crew, as I said, is veteran for the most part and used to my standards. The petty officers will see to the new recruits and bring them up to speed rather quickly. Gentlemen," Norman said as he stood and raised his glass for a toast, "I give you *Defiant*, once and future best frigate in the fleet."

Brewer and the others raised their glasses and toasted the ship.

"Thank you, gentlemen," Norman said. "I will bid you good night now. We sail with the morning tide."

The room was filled with "Good night" and "Thank you"

as the various officers filed out of the room. By unspoken agreement, Brewer remained behind with the captain. When they were at last alone, Norman turned to Brewer, still seated at the table.

"Well?" the captain said as he picked up a decanter of claret and refilled both their glasses.

Brewer nodded his thanks. "Sir?"

Norman took his seat. "What do you think of them?"

Brewer grinned. "Sir, I would like to know more about them before answering your question."

"But from what you've seen of them this evening?"

Brewer held his captain's eyes long enough to know the other was genuinely asking for his assessment. He sighed and drank the claret.

"Well, sir, at first meeting they all seem very personable, although it is too early to tell if that is due to caution or just a quiet confidence in their own abilities."

Captain Norman's eyes narrowed over his glass. Brewer wondered if he had just gone up or down in his captain's estimation. He went on.

"Mr. Greene seems to carry himself well enough. I don't believe I heard him say anything that would give me cause to question him. I'm sure he will reveal himself in short order, sir, but my first impression was generally a good one."

"I agree," Norman said. "Let's find out what our Mr. Greene can do. Have him take the ship out when we leave tomorrow."

"Aye aye, sir."

"And Mr. Phillips?"

"Seems a bit young for a commission. What is he—sixteen?"

"Barely," Norman said. "He was promoted because all the lieutenants in his previous ship were killed in action against the Barbary pirates, and he was the senior midshipman alive. The captain thought he did well enough to ask the Admiralty to confirm his appointment after the ship docked at Spithead."

"I see," Brewer said. "Well, that speaks highly of him, if the captain asked for his appointment to be confirmed. He will need to be taught how to give orders, but he seems a good enough sort, and he's already been bloodied and come through. I have high hopes for him."

Norman nodded and stared into his drink. "And Mr. Spinelli?"

"Haven't heard anything around the fleet. Appears to be addicted to drink, as most surgeons are. I hope he's not the typical butcher, but I suppose we'll see. Do you know anything about him, sir?"

The captain shook his head. "No, nothing. His last ship was put in ordinary, and the Admiralty assigned him to *Defiant*."

"Well, sir," Brewer paused for another taste of claret, "do you have any other questions for me?"

"Just one, Mr. Brewer," Norman replied as he rose. "Did you really stand toe-to-toe with Napoleon Bonaparte and make him back down?"

Brewer stood, tucking his hat under his left arm.

"That depends, Captain."

"On what?"

Brewer smiled. "Did you really pick up a musket and shoot the Frog who got Nelson?"

A grin broke out on the captain's face, and Brewer quietly breathed a sigh of relief.

"Good night, William," Norman said as he stuck out his hand. "We'll make a ship of her."

Brewer shook his hand. "Yes, sir. Good night."

Brewer left the captain's cabin, passing by the sentry as he made his way to his own cabin to write another quick letter to his mother.

CHAPTER 3

The morning dawned with a fair wind blowing as Brewer appeared on deck. Lieutenant Phillips had the watch, and he saluted Brewer as he approached.

"Good morning, sir."

"Good morning, Mr. Phillips. What have you to report?"

"*Defiant* is ready for sea, sir," he said. "All personnel are accounted for. Mr. Barton reports all supplies are aboard, and Mr. Shelby says all are secured."

"Thank you, Mr. Phillips. Pass the word for the midshipman of the watch, then you may send the hands to breakfast."

"Aye aye, sir." Phillips saluted and passed the order.

Brewer was casting a wary eye over the lines and shrouds when Mr. Tyler appeared and saluted.

"You sent for me, sir?"

"Yes, Mr. Tyler. My respects to the captain. Tell him *Defiant* is ready for sea and that I have sent the hands to breakfast."

"Aye aye, sir!" Tyler saluted again and was gone.

Mr. Greene approached. "Good morning, sir."

Brewer looked at him and nodded. "Good morning, Mr. Greene. Are you ready to put to sea?"

"Yes, sir. All guns are secured, powder and shot stowed and checked. Any idea when I can begin drilling my gun crews?"

"Second or third day out, I should imagine. I want to speak with the captain first to see if he has any preference as to the scheduling of drills."

"Aye aye, sir," Greene said, his eyes scanning the shore.

Brewer noticed and smiled to himself. He recognized the nerves that came with joining a new ship.

"Ever been to America, Mr. Greene?"

"No, sir. My only posting was on *Reliant* in the South Seas."

"See any action?"

"No, sir, just patrols and convoy escorts, that's all."

"I see."

At this moment, Captain Norman appeared on deck. He automatically cast his eyes aloft, taking in the stays, shrouds, and yardarms at a glance before walking aft.

"Good morning, gentlemen," he said.

"Good morning, sir," Brewer and Greene replied as they touched their hats.

"Ready to get under way, Mr. Brewer?"

"Aye, sir," Brewer answered, "when you are ready. I've ordered the mail collected to be sent ashore. Do you have anything, Captain?"

"No, Mr. Brewer. Please signal for the guard boat to take the mail ashore, and let's get under way."

"Aye aye, sir," Brewer said. "Mr. Greene, mail goes ashore at once. Mr. Tyler! Signal the port admiral and request permission to proceed!"

"Aye aye, sir!" Green said. "Get the mail to the guard boat and cast it off!"

"Ready, sir!" Tyler said. "Port admiral's reply: *Permission granted. God speed.*"

"Mr. Greene! Get the ship under way, if you please!"

"Aye aye, sir! Stand by the capstan! Loose the heads'ls! Hands aloft to loose the tops'ls!"

Brewer went to stand beside his captain, and together they watched Lieutenant Greene put to rest any doubts they had about his seamanship. As the anchor broke loose, *Defiant* began to move. As soon as they had steerage way, Greene ordered the wheel hard over and sent the hands to the braces. The head came around slowly, and *Defiant* was soon gliding out of Portsmouth harbor and into the open sea.

Captain Norman turned to Brewer and said, "I'd say he knows his business, eh, Mr. Brewer?"

Brewer smiled. "I'd say so, sir."

Norman looked again at his second lieutenant and smiled before turning back to Brewer.

"Mr. Brewer, once free of the harbor, set a course to clear the Isle of Wight. I shall be in my cabin. Call me if I'm needed."

"Aye aye, sir," Brewer said, and saluted.

It took less than an hour for *Defiant* to clear the harbor entrance, and once she was free Brewer ordered the change of course. This was accomplished by Mr. Greene efficiently, and Brewer was pleased. He looked over at the sailing master, a man named Sweeney who was rumored to have been master on Cook's first voyage. The master just looked back at him and nodded, and Brewer was grateful to know he was not alone in his judgment.

A midshipman approached him and saluted. "Sir."

Brewer looked down at the boy, forcing himself to keep a stern look on his face. "Yes?"

"The captain sends his compliments, sir, and would you please join him in his cabin?"

"Thank you, Mr.—?"

"Short, sir. William Short."

"Age?"

"Thirteen, sir."

"First voyage?"

"Second, sir."

Brewer nodded. "Very well, Mr. Short, I will attend the captain at once. You may carry on with your other duties."

Brewer left Greene in charge of the deck until Mr. Phillips relieved him at the turn of the watch and went below to see what the captain wanted. The sentry came to attention as Brewer approached. Brewer nodded to him and knocked on the door.

"Enter."

Brewer opened the door to find his captain seated at his desk, writing in his logbook. He glanced up as Brewer closed the door behind him.

"Ah, Mr. Brewer. Thank you for coming. Just give me a minute or two to complete this entry, and I'll be with you directly. Please be seated."

"Aye, sir," Brewer said as he took the seat indicated by the captain. While he waited, Brewer enjoyed the view out the stern gallery, watching the coast of England slide past.

Norman finished his entry and closed his logbook. "Now, Mr. Brewer, what do you think of *Defiant*?"

Brewer was mildly surprised; he had not expected this. "She seems to sail very nicely, Captain. It's as if she were grateful at being freed from the harbor."

"Yes, I quite agree," the captain said. He looked wishfully out the gallery as well. "I feel like that myself, sometimes." He shook his head, as though rousing himself from a dream. "My apologies, Mr. Brewer, my mind was wandering. Have you studied the watch bill?"

"Yes, sir."

"I believe we need to reorganize it just a bit. I only

suggest this because, being new to the ship, you will not yet be familiar with crew performance. I think we can safely move one or two of the more experienced hands from Mr. Greene's watch to Mr. Phillips'. I believe we are both rather reassured as to Mr. Greene's ability to handle the ship?"

"Yes, sir," Brewer said. "I believe Mr. Sweeney is also breathing easier."

Norman smiled at the thought. "Yes, I can well imagine. You'll get used to Mr. Sweeney, William; he learned his trade under Captain Cook himself. He tends to get a tad nervous when I allow 'youngsters', as he calls them, to conn the ship. His signature on a lieutenant's record carries weight at the Admiralty, let me tell you. Mr. Sweeney's presence aboard is one of the reasons I agreed to take young Mr. Phillips on. I've already spoken to Mr. Sweeney, and he will make sure Phillips knows his ship-handling and navigation. But until we are sure of him, I would like you to keep a close eye on Mr. Phillips, William. I don't mean that you should necessarily stand watch with him, but take him under your wing, as it were. He's an officer now, no matter how he came by his commission, and it would be wrong to put him back in classes under a master's mate along with Mr. Tyler and the other midshipmen. That leaves me with you to make sure he knows what he is required to know. Mr. Greene and Mr. Sweeney will assist you, of course. Remember, Mr. Phillips never went before a commissioning board as you and I did. Your job is to prepare him anyway."

"Aye aye, sir."

Norman rose. "Very good. I know it's not what you expected to be doing as a first lieutenant, William, but I have every confidence in you. And when the time comes, you and I shall be his unofficial board."

Brewer rose. "He will be ready, sir. I will speak to Mr. Phillips to gain an idea of what he has already learned, and then I will consult with Mr. Sweeney."

Norman nodded. "Thank you, Mr. Brewer. Please keep me informed."

"Aye aye, sir."

Brewer left the cabin with his hat still under his arm. He paused at the bottom of the ladder and planted it firmly on his head before going up on deck.

Defiant was riding a strong sea breeze under tops'ls and jibs. Mr. Phillips had the watch, and Brewer nodded as he touched his hat by way of salute. Mr. Sweeney was standing behind the wheel, so Brewer walked over to him.

"Mr. Sweeney," Brewer said, "I have just come from speaking to the captain."

"About young Mr. Phillips?"

"Precisely," Brewer said, as both men turned to look at Mr. Phillips, who was standing with his back to them as he spoke to Mr. Tyler. The two were watching the topmen as they went through exercising aloft.

Sweeney nodded. "Aye, the captain spoke to me about him. Wants me to keep an eye on him and such. Captain says he's just sixteen, and he was a midshipman less than three years before he got his commission."

"Yes," Brewer said, his mind lost in thought.

Sweeney turned and looked aloft. "Makes you wonder how he did it."

"Did what?"

"That voyage home that got him his commission, all the lieutenants dead and the captain wounded? Had to be a frightening experience for the lad, wouldn't you think? Captain makes him a lieutenant before being carried from the deck. Lucky his wounds were slight. Even so, the boy must have held himself together well for the captain to request his commission be made permanent at sixteen."

Brewer looked at Sweeney and then back at Phillips. It was more or less the same story the captain had told him, but now he heard the question behind Mr. Sweeney's tale. What did that voyage do to young Mr. Phillips, and what would he be like now? Third lieutenant or not, the lad was only sixteen years old. *Well,* Brewer thought, *the captain put me in charge of his schooling, so I need to find out.*

"Mr. Short!" Brewer called.

The midshipman jumped down from the shrouds, where he had been watching the horizon, and came over to Brewer and saluted. "Sir?"

"My compliments to Mr. Phillips, and ask him to join me in my cabin at the end of his watch."

"Aye aye, sir!"

Brewer walked down the companionway to his cabin. He was just taking *Ivanhoe* from its place on the shelf when he heard a knock at his door and smiled. *I must make a note to get Mr. Short a watch!*

"Enter!" Brewer said as he replaced the book.

Mr. Phillips came in, hat properly tucked under his left arm. He approached Brewer's desk and asked, "You sent for me, sir?"

"Yes, Mr. Phillips. Please, be seated. I wanted to talk to you. Before we start, let me say that I would like to ask you some questions; please do not take any of them personally or as a slight to your honor."

"Understood, sir."

"Who did you leave in charge of the deck?"

"Mr. Sweeney, sir."

Brewer nodded. He took out a piece of paper and wrote Mr. Phillips' name at the top.

"How old are you?"

"Sixteen, sir."

"And you have had your commission for two months now?"

"Yes, sir."

"And how long were you a midshipman before that?"

"Almost three years, sir."

"What ship?"

"*Retribution.* Captain Styles, sir."

Brewer nodded and wrote some notes on the paper. "And that was the ship in which you were commissioned?"

"Yes, sir."

"I understand all senior officers were lost. That must have been an ordeal, Mr. Phillips."

"Well, sir, we were sent to the Barbary Coast with orders to deal with the pirates. We were off Tunis when we were attacked by two pirate sloops. I was aloft with the topmen. Captain Styles outmaneuvered them both, sir, putting broadsides through the stern of one and raking the deck of the second. But then the wind shifted, sir, and they had the advantage of us. We were dead in the water, you see, but they could still row across our stern. We took broadside after broadside. Then the wind shifted again, and we could maneuver. Two broadsides into one of them and she exploded, and then the captain dismasted the other. We left them smoking and settling in the water.

"I had no idea of the condition of the ship until I returned to the deck. I wanted to report to a lieutenant, only I couldn't find one. I saw the captain leaning on a railing aft, so I went to report to him. When I reached him, I saw blood running down his left arm. That was when the captain told me all the lieutenants were dead, and since I was the senior surviving midshipman he was promoting me to lieutenant for the rest of the voyage. Right after that, the captain collapsed, and I detailed two men to take him below to the surgeon."

Brewer nodded. "How badly was the ship damaged?"

Phillips didn't answer right away. Brewer saw him look down at his hands and then over at the wall, and he swallowed at the memory.

"It was horrible, sir," he said as his voice cracked.

"Blood, bodies or pieces of bodies everywhere. It was hard not to slip and fall on the bloody deck. We lost the top foremast and several of the guns were out of action."

Brewer made notes as Phillips told his tale. The occasional break in the voice reminded Brewer that he was dealing with a boy.

"Did you set working parties to repair the damage?"

"No, sir," Phillips said. "The work was already starting. The captain must have given the orders before I found him."

"Yes, of course," Brewer said as he made more notes. "Did you set course for Gibraltar or Malta?"

"The sailing master recommended Gibraltar, so I told him to do so. It was slow going, let me tell you. The carpenter came up to report water in the hold and to request hands for the pumps, so I told him to take anyone so long as they were not working on the new foremast or tending to the wounded. An hour later, I had to detail some men from the wounded to relieve the men on the pumps."

Brewer nodded again, and more notes went on the paper. When he was done, he looked back to Phillips. "Mr. Phillips, how would you rate your skills at navigation?"

Phillips looked confused. "Sir?"

"Navigation, Mr. Phillips. How do you rate your knowledge of spherical trigonometry?"

Phillips shifted in his seat. *Another sign of his youth,* Brewer thought.

"I would say not too bad, sir," Phillips said weakly. "I may be a bit out of practice, but I assure you I'll get right back into it, sir!"

"I'm sure you will, Mr. Phillips. How are you with a sextant?"

"I can handle one, Mr. Brewer."

"I see," Brewer said. He set down his quill and leaned back in his chair. "Let me tell you now why I asked you down here, Mr. Phillips. Normally, a young man of your age and experience would be a midshipman who would have perhaps two or three more years of study and learning to go through to get ready to go before the commissioning board for lieutenant. Due to your special circumstances, you missed those years. The captain wants to make sure you get that study and training under your belt."

Phillips blanched. "You mean I am to be a midshipman again, sir?"

Brewer waved the lad's fear aside. "You have your commission, Mr. Phillips, rest assured, but we still have to teach you what you did not have the chance to learn as a midshipman. The captain has asked me to see to that. You are not being punished, John; the captain is doing you a favor. He is giving you a chance to learn what you did not have the opportunity to learn, instead of expecting you to know it already based on your commission. Mr. Sweeney will tutor you privately in navigation and ship-handling, and the rest of your schooling will fall primarily to me."

Phillips looked crestfallen and stared at his hands, folded in his lap.

"Don't look so down, John," Brewer said. "You're not in any trouble, and I can assure you the captain is not doing this because he saw something wrong in your work."

Brewer saw he wasn't getting anywhere with the boy, so he brought his chair around the desk and turned Phillips so they sat face-to-face.

"Look at me, John," Brewer said in his best big-brother voice. "What I told you before is true; you are *not* being punished. In all my years of service, John, I've never seen someone in your situation. You were a young midshipman who was thrust into a job he should not have had to face for another four or five years. And you did well. Usually when a midshipman is promoted under circumstances like yours—it happened frequently during the wars—the promotion only lasted until the ship made it back to port. New lieutenants were brought in, and the midshipman went back to his old duties.

"But somehow, John, you impressed your captain so much that he asked the Admiralty to confirm your commission, despite the fact that you were only sixteen. But John, you don't know everything that Greene knew when he was commissioned, or what I knew when I got mine, because you did not have those last three or four years as a midshipman to learn it. All we are doing here is giving you the tools that every other Lieutenant already has. Tools you will need to save your ship or the lives of your men."

Phillips looked at him with a glint of hope in his eye. "Honest, Mr. Brewer?"

Brewer patted him on the knee. "Yes, John. Honest."

Phillips smiled. "Thank you, sir. I can't tell you how thankful I am. I've been trying to pick up things by looking over people's shoulders or watching Mr. Greene or Mr. Sweeney."

"Good," Brewer said, "I'm glad you see my point. From now on, Mr. Phillips, anytime you have a question, either come and ask me directly, or if you can't leave, send a midshipman for me and I'll come to you."

"Aye aye, sir," Phillips said, his confidence as a lieutenant somewhat restored.

Brewer returned to his desk. "Do not be surprised to see myself or Mr. Sweeney or even the captain on deck during your watches. We will be observing you, and we may give you specific tasks to see how you do. Don't get nervous—use these opportunities to prove yourself. And don't be discouraged if you are called aside and corrected for a mistake; use the chance to learn how to do the task properly and master it. Your goal should be that when you are asked to do it again, you do so well that they can only smile at you and nod."

"Aye aye, Mr. Brewer. I won't let you down!"

"Good man," Brewer said. "You may return to your duties."

Brewer watched his young lieutenant as he rose and left the cabin. He smiled and shook his head, and then he reached for *Ivanhoe*.

CHAPTER 4

Defiant glided effortlessly through the waves as she approached the southern coast of Ireland. In the time *Defiant* had been at sea, Brewer and Sweeney had begun implementing their program for the education of young Phillips, and the boy seemed to be taking it very well. Of course, it was impossible to conceal such an undertaking completely from the crew and especially from his watch, but Phillips was amazed to find his watch wanted him to succeed even more than Mr. Brewer did. Brewer sat back and watched the petty officers assist their officer. Soon Phillips learned he could take one of them aside and ask how to do something and why, and trust their answer. In the weeks that followed, Brewer would be pleased to note that Phillips sent for him less and less; Mr. Sweeney likewise reported young Phillips to be making adequate progress in his lessons as well.

Brewer came on deck to find *Defiant* sailing under full sails. Mr. Phillips was in charge of the deck during the forenoon watch. Brewer smiled and turned aft.

"Good morning, sir," he said to Captain Norman, who was talking to Mr. Sweeney.

"Good morning, Mr. Brewer. Mr. Sweeney and I were just discussing putting the ship about on the larboard tack and heading for Newfoundland."

"Indeed, sir? Excellent."

"Mr. Sweeney," the captain said to the sailing master, "do you think young Mr. Phillips could mark our position and work up a course?"

Sweeney scratched his chin for a moment as he considered the captain's question. "Aye, sir, I think he could. Might take him a while, though, but I think he could do it."

The captain nodded. "Very well. Mr. Brewer, you will please take over the deck and reduce sail. Use the opportunity to exercise the hands aloft. I want you to keep us in this basic area until our young Mr. Phillips gives us our next course to steer."

Brewer smiled. "Aye aye, sir." He turned to a midshipman and said, "Pass the word for Mr. Phillips."

Phillips came up to the group and correctly saluted the captain as the senior officer present. "You sent for me, sir?"

"Yes, Mr. Phillips," the captain said. "*Defiant* has reached the point when we need to change course for the next leg of our voyage, which will take us to Newfoundland. I want you to do that for me."

"Me, sir?"

The captain smiled. "Don't worry, Mr. Phillips. This is a test for your schooling. Mr. Sweeney believes you can do it. I want you to calculate our current position first, and then come up with a course. Mr. Sweeney will be here to assist you, should you need it. Work up the position and course, and let me know when we are ready to implement it."

"Me, sir? Uh, what about my watch?"

"Mr. Brewer will take over the deck, Mr. Phillips. Take all the time you need."

"Aye aye, sir," Phillips gasped. Brewer almost pitied the boy; he looked like he had the weight of the world on his shoulders.

Norman nodded. “Very well. Mr. Brewer has the deck. I shall be in my quarters.”

They all said, “Aye aye, sir,” and saluted the captain. After he left the deck, Mr. Sweeney patted Phillips on the back.

“If you will excuse us, Mr. Brewer, Mr. Phillips has some brain work to do. Come along, lad.”

Brewer grinned. “Of course. Carry on, Mr. Phillips.”

Brewer strolled forward until he found Mr. Greene standing near the foremast watching some hands doing their work. Greene saw him approach and saluted.

“Good morning, sir,” he said as he touched his hat.

“Good morning, Mr. Greene. Fine day, isn’t it?”

“Aye, sir, so far it is.”

“Mr. Hobbs!” Brewer shouted to the nearby bosun’s mate, “Would you be so good as to have the hands take in sail? We’ll run under tops’ls and the jib for a while.”

“Aye aye, sir,” he said and began bellowing orders.

“When sail is set, put the ship about,” Brewer said. “Mr. Greene, you have the next watch, correct?”

“Yes, sir.”

“Will you please join me in my cabin after you come on watch? I’m sure Mr. Tyler can take the deck for a short time.”

“Aye aye, sir,” said Greene, now thoroughly confused and wondering what he did wrong.

Brewer turned away to hide the smile on his face. *Let him wonder,* Brewer thought. *It’ll be good for him, keep him on his toes.* Brewer thought about Mr. Greene; he remembered informing him of the training program for young Phillips.

Brewer had come below deck after he was relieved from watch just days after beginning Phillips’ lessons and gone to the wardroom looking for his breakfast. He’d entered to find

Lieutenant Greene still sitting at the table sipping on a cup of coffee.

"Good morning, Mr. Greene," Brewer had said. "Creighton!"

The steward stuck his head out of the pantry. "Sir?"

"Breakfast for one."

"Aye aye, Mr. Brewer."

Brewer sat down at the head of the table. Within minutes, Creighton brought out Brewer's breakfast and refilled Greene's coffee.

Greene set down his cup. "William, may I ask you a question? Is something going on with Mr. Phillips?"

Brewer looked up. "Phillips? Has the captain spoken to you regarding Mr. Phillips?"

"No, sir."

Brewer nodded and sat back in his chair. "I thought not. Let me tell you what we are doing. I know there hasn't been much talk in the wardroom about his service before he came to *Defiant*. You may, however, have heard Mr. Phillips say in the captain's cabin that he had only held his commission for two months when we sailed. Do you know how he got promoted? No? You should ask him to tell you some day, it's a fascinating tale. For now, suffice it to say he received a temporary promotion from midshipman to acting lieutenant at the age of sixteen after less than three years in the midshipman's berth. Somehow, he impressed his captain so much that the captain asked the Admiralty to confirm the promotion in spite of the lad's age, and their Lordships did so."

Greene stared wide-eyed at the first lieutenant. "That young? You mean he's never been before..."

Brewer smiled. "You begin to see part of the problem, Mr. Greene. Being promoted so young and never having gone before a Board of Examination, he does not know either by education or experience what you or I knew when we were commissioned. It is the captain's desire that we remedy this deficiency by means of tutoring. Mr. Sweeney is working with him on navigation and ship handling, and I am supposed to instruct him on everything else he will need to know."

Greened chuckled. "How can I help?"

Brewer leaned forward and slapped the table. "I'm glad to hear you put it that way, Ben. I may need your help from time to time, but mainly I just wanted you to know what was going on. Young John is going to need a... big brother of sorts, especially for things he would not feel comfortable bringing to his first lieutenant. That's how you can help."

Greene said nothing for several minutes, and Brewer sat back and let him think. He hadn't thought Greene the thinking kind. *Another plus for him,* Brewer thought.

Greene was silent for a total of perhaps seven or eight minutes before Brewer finally heard him sigh. Greene looked around the wardroom for a moment, and Brewer thought he was trying to fight off a bad memory. *Oh, well,* Brewer thought, *there's something to be found out later.*

Greene turned back to him, and Brewer was surprised to see that he wasn't smiling anymore.

"Is something wrong, Mr. Greene?" he asked.

Greene's eyes snapped to his, and Brewer saw something behind them, but before he could decide just what it was, Greene's control reasserted itself, and it was gone. Brewer frowned inside.

"What?" Greene said. "Oh. Nothing, sir."

"Any problems?"

"No, sir. I'll do whatever I can to help."

"Very good, Ben. Thank you."

Not for the first time, Brewer wished it were possible to peel back layers of people as you would an onion to see what lay beneath. *Oh, no,* he thought, *that would be too easy, wouldn't it?*

Greene returned at the change of watch, and Brewer turned over command of the deck. Greene saluted, and then he turned to Mr. Tyler.

"You have the deck," he said. "I will be in the first lieutenant's cabin if you need me."

Tyler saluted. "Aye aye, sir."

Greene followed Brewer below, and he hesitated for a moment after Brewer entered the cabin.

"Come in, Mr. Greene," Brewer said as he slid behind the desk. "Have a seat. I called you down here for two reasons. I imagine you're wondering why I took in sail? Yes, I thought you might be. The captain wants to stay in this area for the moment."

"I see, sir," Greene said doubtfully.

"I don't think you do," Brewer said evenly. "Let me give you a free piece of advice, Mr. Greene; you speak plainly with me, and we shall get along marvelously."

"Yes, sir."

"As I said, that one was free. The Captain wants us to stay in the area for a while."

Greene looked confused, and Brewer smiled.

"Mr. Phillips is working out our position prior to coming up with a course for Newfoundland."

"Ah! I see now." Greene said. "How's his schooling going?"

"I think he's doing well," Brewer answered. "Something still seems to be buried beneath the surface, but I can't figure out what it is. Has he said anything to you?"

"No, nothing," Greene said. Brewer was surprised to find his friend's face change to an unreadable mask. What was Greene trying to hide?

"Well, let me know if he does," Brewer said. "Thank you, Mr. Greene."

Greene saluted and left the cabin without a word.

Brewer sat behind his desk for some time, rubbing his chin with one hand and trying to figure out what he had seen in the lieutenant's eyes. *When I first mentioned Phillips' schooling to him, Ben was fine until I mentioned acting like a big brother to John. Yes, that was when he changed. Now he became unreadable when I asked whether Phillips had confided in him. I wonder what his family life was like.*

Brewer sighed and leaned back in his chair. He knew he was not the one to question anyone's family past. His eyes drifted up to his library and came to rest on the Bible his mother had given to him. He wondered if he would ever be able to go home again. He tore his eyes away, surprised as he always was that it still could hurt so badly. He rose from his chair and thought about pacing to help him think, but he was frustrated by the confines of his cabin. He picked up his hat and headed for the captain's quarters.

The sentry snapped to attention as always at his approach. Brewer nodded to him as he knocked and was granted admittance to his captain's sanctuary.

Brewer found Captain Norman standing with his back to him, hands clasped behind his back, looking out the great stern windows at *Defiant's* wake. Brewer stood for a moment, hat tucked correctly under his left arm, unsure what to do.

"Yes, Mr. Brewer?" Norman said without turning around. "Is Mr. Phillips finished already?"

Brewer cleared his throat. "Not that I know of, sir. I've been in my cabin with Mr. Greene."

Norman turned and looked at his first lieutenant. "I see," he said. He walked over to the couch. "Won't you sit down, Mr. Brewer?"

"Thank you, sir."

"Something to drink? Jenkins!"

The servant appeared from the pantry.

"You called, sir?"

"Coffee for myself and the First Lieutenant, please."

"Very good, sir," he said, and retreated into the pantry.

"Now, Mr. Brewer," Norman said, as they sat on what Brewer decided was a very nice settee, "what can I do for you."

"It relates to our project with Mr. Phillips, sir," Brewer said. "I have spoken to Mr. Greene about it. I thought he should know, if only to be watchful if Phillips should need a friend. The first time I spoke to him, he was all for it until I mentioned something about his being a sort of big brother to the lad. Then he suddenly closed up on me. He still said he would do whatever we asked him to, but he honestly seemed to resent it. His enthusiasm and joy were gone. Today, I got a similar response when I asked if Phillips had said anything to him."

Norman thought it over while Jenkins reappeared with their coffee, placing one steaming porcelain mug on the low table in front of each man before silently retreating.

"Thank you, Jenkins," Norman called to the pantry door as it closed. "Now, to Mr. Greene. It certainly seems a strange way to behave. Probably some family history to account for it, no doubt. I haven't seen it affect his duties, have you?"

"No, sir. I had hoped I was wrong about it, but I believe something is there."

Norman grunted. "Well, keep an eye on him. Let's hope we haven't awakened a sleeping dog."

Brewer tasted his coffee, strong and sweet. Just what he needed after the episode with Greene. He took another swallow and felt the tension begin to drain from his neck.

"William," the captain said as he settled comfortably back, "I hope you won't think me forward, but I cannot help myself, I have to ask: what was it like, meeting Napoleon Bonaparte?"

Brewer smiled as he set the cup down. He figured this would come up, sooner or later. It wasn't that he minded talking about it; it still seemed almost like a dream somehow. He leaned back on the settee and took a moment to organize his thoughts.

"It was incredible, sir," he said. "I don't know that words could do it justice. A cross between what it would be like to meet Nelson and the King. He was kind, for the most part, and he gave me some good advice."

"That hardly sounds like the tyrant who came within an inch of conquering Europe."

Brewer shrugged. "He was very different by the time I met him, sir. He was beaten and spent most of his time causing trouble for the old governor and making England look foolish into the bargain. That's why Lord Hornblower was sent to the island in the first place."

"Yes, I remember," Norman said. "And what was this advice he gave you?"

"He said I must be ready to seize an opportunity when it arises, because they rarely come twice."

Norman stared at him. "That's all?"

"Yes, sir, basically that was it. I'm afraid he spent a lot more time speaking to Governor Hornblower than to me."

Norman seemed disappointed. "Yes, well... Still, something to tell your grandchildren, isn't it? Thank you, Mr. Brewer. Have Mr. Phillips report to me when he has completed his task."

"Aye aye, sir," Brewer said as he stood, recognizing the dismissal. He left the Captain's cabin and went up on deck. He paused as he passed the chart room; Mr. Phillips was working out calculations on the small table with Mr. Sweeney looking over his shoulder and making an occasional comment. Sweeney looked up, saw Brewer, and gave him a wink and a smile. Brewer decided that meant the calculations were progressing satisfactorily, if slowly, so he proceeded up on deck. He turned forward and saw Mr. Greene talking to two midshipmen by the mainmast.

Brewer thought about what happened in the captain's cabin. He hated lying to the captain, but he found it was usually the easiest tack when he spoke about his time with Napoleon Bonaparte. The reason he did so was simple—no one had ever believed him when he told the truth, especially about that last interview.

He remembered being so engrossed in getting his paperwork caught up for the new governor's aide that he paid almost no attention when someone entered his office, automatically saying that he would be with him in a moment. He had realized his mistake when he heard that unmistakable voice answer.

"Take your time, Mr. Brewer."

Brewer had dropped his papers and jumped to his feetto look straight into the amused eyes of the former Emperor of the French.

"I'm sorry, sir," he had stammered. "I did not realize it was you. The governor is not here at the moment, and I'm afraid it may be some time before he returns."

"Quite all right, M. Brewer," Bonaparte had reassured him. "I am not here to see the governor. I am here to see you. Fear not: The governor knows of my mission today, and he already gave me permission to speak to you."

Brewer remembered the confusion he had felt. "Me, sir? I don't understand."

"Please, sit with me here, M. Brewer," Bonaparte had said, indicating two chairs in a corner of the room in front of the office's small, empty fireplace. Brewer had thought about it for a minute before stepping around his desk and taking his seat across from Bonaparte.

The ex-emperor did not speak for a moment. He had appeared to be looking Brewer over, and that had made Brewer nervous. Over the months he had served as secretary to the governor, he had grown to admire this man and had developed a deep respect for what he had accomplished. Brewer remembered taking a deep breath and holding it, sure he was about to be dressed down for the insubordinate way he had stood toe-to-toe with Bonaparte prior to the escape attempt.

"Mr. Brewer," the words had come in English, much to Brewer's surprise, "I have asked the governor his permission to speak to you, and he graciously granted my request. I have watched you closely, *mon ami*, and you have impressed me. You remind me very much of my stepson Eugene, who was Viceroy of Italy and commander of an army corps, and whom I should have put forth to be put on the Swedish throne. It is nothing I say lightly, Mr. Brewer, but I think you are wise enough not to let it go to your head."

Brewer had sat dumbfounded, finally managing to nod his head in understanding.

"Mr. Brewer, I believe you have it in you to do great deeds," Bonaparte had said. The words had come slowly, whether from deliberate choosing or the Frenchman's broken English, Brewer could not tell. "My advice to you is this: opportunity is likely to knock at your door only once, *mon ami*. You must be ready to seize the day when it presents itself. Half measures will not do; you must be ruthless and go for the throat like the wolf. Do not worry about what happens to others. You can best help them by being victorious. Beware whom you trust, monsieur; men of smaller minds often have a lesser vision and lesser ambition. They will hold you back. Listen to them, and the moment may well be lost."

Brewer nodded again. "I understand, sir."

Bonaparte had smiled and stood. Without another word, the Corsican had waited for Brewer to stand, kissed him on both cheeks after the French manner, shook his hand after the English, and walked out of the office without looking back, closing the door behind him. Brewer never saw him again.

Brewer shook his head as he watched the hands scramble aloft to put the ship about again. Bonaparte's words were burned into his memory, and more than once they helped him decide on a course of action. He could never understand why people did not believe him after they begged him to tell the story, so he came up with the simplified version that he'd told the captain. That was all he would say about Bonaparte to anyone. Some people may not understand it, but it was just easier for him.

Brewer's memories were interrupted by enthusiastic cries of "I've got it! I've got it!" He turned just in time to see Lieutenant Phillips rush past him toward the companionway with sheets of calculations in his hands. After he disappeared down the ladder, Brewer turned to see an amused Mr. Sweeney strolling toward him.

"I take it we have success?" Brewer asked.

Sweeney grinned. "Aye, Mr. Brewer, success indeed. 'Course, it took him four tries to get our position right, but once he got that, the course came easy. Would you believe it, on his first try, he had us south of the Falklands ready to round the horn!"

Brewer and Sweeney enjoyed a good laugh at that. "I remember once," Brewer recalled, "on the old *Dreadnought*, I was a midshipman working out a similar problem. The captain looked at my equations and congratulated me on placing the ship just outside Sydney harbor."

"And?" Sweeney prompted.

"We were in the Med at the time."

Sweeney threw his head back and roared with laughter.

Brewer sighed. "And you, Mr. Sweeney? Come now, be honest; surely the great Captain Cook caught an error or two when you were learning your trade?"

Sweeney squinted at the first lieutenant, then stared at his beloved sails while he stroked his chin. Finally, Brewer heard him chuckle, and Sweeney leaned in close and said in a low voice, "Well, not exactly, Mr. Brewer. Let's just say that, if he had corrected my calculations more often, he would not have discovered half of what he did." Then he winked and stood there placidly.

The two enjoyed a fresh sea breeze for a few minutes before the noise from the companionway drew their attention. Mr. Phillips came bounding up on deck. He stopped just long enough to look around before steering straight for Mr. Sweeney. Sweeney gave Brewer a wink and a grin before stepping away to meet his student. Phillips rushed up to Sweeney and showed him the papers he had taken below. Sweeney's head bobbed up and down as he listened to his young apprentice and scanned the papers. They spoke together quietly and then headed for the wheel.

Brewer watched them go, the master and the student, and he wondered how Sweeney did it. He made a mental note to speak to Sweeney about how he taught youngsters so successfully; maybe Brewer could learn some tricks that would come in handy when teaching midshipmen and younger lieutenants.

Hearing a foot upon the companionway, Brewer turned to see Captain Norman ascending to the quarterdeck. Brewer saluted as the captain approached.

"Captain," Brewer said.

"Mr. Brewer," Norman said, nodding to acknowledge the salute. "Have we tacked yet?"

"Not yet, sir. Mr. Phillips is conversing with Mr. Sweeney."

"Ah," Norman said with a nod. "Well, Mr. Brewer, I'd say it's time to find out how our young lieutenant handles a ship, eh?" He gazed at Sweeney and Phillips, and Brewer wondered what his captain was thinking. Sweeney appeared to be explaining something, and Phillips was listening intently. Overhearing their conversation was impossible at this distance; the wind carried their voices away. But Captain Norman made no effort to walk over to them; he just stood beside Brewer and stared at them through narrowed eyes. Brewer came close a couple of times to asking what the captain was thinking, but he stopped short each time. It was a question Bush would not hesitate to ask Hornblower, Brewer knew. He himself would have asked Bush on the old *Lydia*, but he could not do it today. He did not have that kind of relationship with Captain Norman; he wondered if he ever would.

Phillips came over to them and saluted. "Request permission to alter course for Newfoundland, sir."

Captain Norman smiled and nodded. "Mr. Greene! Mr. Brewer has the deck!"

"Aye aye, sir."

Brewer looked at his captain, and then turned back to his young lieutenant. "Permission granted, Mr. Phillips."

"Thank you, sir," Phillips said, and gave off a loud command. "Helm a-lee!"

"Helm's a-lee, sir!"

Brewer was surprised to hear the voice of the sailing master himself answer. He turned to find Mr. Sweeney standing beside the wheel. When Sweeney noticed him, he simply smiled at Brewer and shrugged.

"Raise tacks and sheets!" Phillips cried. Brewer saw he was now standing by the mizzenmast. Someone had given him a speaking-trumpet. Brewer could see him studying the sails, trying to time his commands to keep the ship from missing the stays and coming to a complete stop. Brewer glanced at the captain and found him watching Mr. Phillips intently.

Phillips raised the trumpet to his lips again. "Off tacks and sheets!"

Brewer moved forward to where he had a good view of the foresails as well as the main. He glanced back to see Phillips had taken a few steps forward himself. Brewer turned back in time to see the jib go slack against the wind, and he wondered what Phillips was waiting for. He looked back and saw Phillips looking from mainsails to foresails to jib and back again, desperate to get the timing right. Brewer sighed and shook his head. He remembered his first maneuvers under the eye of the captain and first lieutenant, and he did not envy Mr. Phillips just now. Just as Brewer decided to walk over and help Mr. Phillips, he saw the boy raise the trumpet again.

"Mainsail haul!"

Brewer held his breath as he watched the hands swing the great yards of the mainsails around to try to catch the wind. He felt the ship shudder and looked at Mr. Phillips. Without taking his eyes from the yards, the third lieutenant gave the order to put the helm a-weather, and the ship started to come around. Brewer looked past Phillips to see the relieved look on Mr. Sweeney's face as he relayed the order to put the helm over.

As soon as Phillips saw the *Defiant's* after sails fill, he tore his hat from his head in triumph and raised his trumpet. "Let go and haul!"

Brewer watched as the sails slowly filled and the ship came around. He looked at Phillips, standing there in triumph, his hat still in his hand. Phillips looked over his shoulder at Sweeney, who was now stationed at the ship's compass. When the ship came around to the proper heading, Sweeney nodded. Phillips immediately turned and raised his trumpet.

"Hands to braces!"

Brewer smiled and nodded to himself as he strolled aft. All-in-all, Phillips had done well executing the maneuver. Perhaps he hesitated a moment too long before hauling the mainsails, but that would come with practice.

Brewer touched his hat in salute as he approached the captain. "Not too bad for one so young, eh, sir?"

Norman did not answer him. In fact, he said nothing at all. He did not move, his eyes darting to Brewer for a moment before moving back to Phillips, who was now on his way to report to the captain. Brewer glanced over at Sweeney and was surprised and puzzled to see a pinched look on his face, as though he knew a storm was approaching. Brewer was about to step over and ask Sweeney about it when young Phillips arrived and presented himself.

Phillips saluted smartly. "*Defiant* on course for Newfoundland, sir."

Norman nodded and looked at his third lieutenant for a minute before pursing his lips and looking at the deck.

"Mr. Phillips," Norman said in a low, cold voice, "how would you rate your performance on the maneuver?"

Brewer held very still, only his eyes flashing first to Phillips and then to Sweeney. Phillips looked as though he had been slapped in the face; Sweeney merely closed his eyes and hung his head.

Phillips stood there in shock at his captain's attitude and question, and he had no idea how to answer.

The captain's head snapped up, and Brewer saw a fire in his eye. "Well, *Mr*. Phillips?"

Brewer felt sorry for Phillips, but he dared not interfere, even as he knew Sweeney would not. Phillips was casting about desperately with his eyes, looking for an answer or help, and finding none.

"Sir, I..." Phillips stammered. "I did well enough to keep her out of the stays and on to the new tack, sir."

"You got lucky, Mr. Phillips," the captain said. "You were flopping around like some ignorant *young gentleman*. I must say it appears Mr. Brewer is a very patient man. You should be thankful, Mr. Phillips, that he had the deck, and not I; I would have relieved you the moment you hesitated to haul the mainsails."

Phillips looked at the deck, crushed by his captain's scolding. "Aye, sir."

"I shall expect a better performance next time, Mr. Phillips," Norman said.

"Aye aye, sir."

"Very good. Carry on, Mr. Phillips. Mr. Greene has the deck."

"Aye aye, sir," Phillips looked up and saluted his captain, tears streaming down his face.

Brewer saluted and watched his captain retire down the companionway to his cabin. He could hardly believe the scene he had just witnessed. Phillips stood in shock in front of him, eyes once more cast down as he silently wept at his public scolding. Brewer looked past Phillips to Sweeney, who was looking at Phillips from across the deck. As soon as he noticed Brewer watching him, Sweeney shook his head sadly and turned his back on them.

Oh, no, Mr. Sweeney, Brewer said to himself, *you're not getting off that easily. We will talk about this, I promise you.* His attention turned back to Phillips, and he sighed. *But first things first.*

"Mr. Phillips," he said in a low voice so no one would overhear, "get hold of yourself. No matter what has happened, you are a King's officer, and I expect you to conduct yourself as such. Now stand up straight and take a deep breath."

Phillips inhaled deeply as he complied as best he could. "Aye aye, Mr. Brewer."

"That's better," Brewer said as he stepped in closer. "You did not do so poorly, John; the only time *I* questioned you was when you hesitated to haul the mains'ls, but you acted in time. Never fear; in time you will be able under normal conditions to tack by the feel of the ship without having to watch the sails. It's just a matter of practice, of getting a feel for the ship. It will come, I promise you."

"Thank you, sir," Phillips said.

"That's better," Brewer said. "Now, please excuse me, Mr. Phillips. Carry on."

"Aye aye, sir," Phillips saluted.

Brewer walked past Phillips to where Mr. Sweeney still leaned over the weather rail. Brewer walked up and leaned on the rail beside him.

"Mr. Sweeney."

"Mr. Brewer."

"Would you mind explaining what just took place with the captain?"

"If you want an explanation of the captain's actions, sir, then I suggest you go ask the captain himself."

"I intend to. You knew this was going to happen, didn't you?"

Sweeney said nothing, instead turning his head away and looking out over the waves.

Brewer turned to face him. "You knew, didn't you?"

"I hoped it wouldn't this time."

"But you let it—?"

Sweeney turned on him. "What would you have me do, *Mr.* Brewer? He's the *captain*, for God's sake! If he did it to a hundred midshipmen and young lieutenants, who's to say anything about it? I'm not the boy's bloody nursemaid."

Brewer stood his ground. "Are you telling me he's done this before? How many times?"

Sweeney shrugged. "I've seen him do it a few times. Takes a minor mistake and rakes 'em over the coals for it. Devastates the younger ones, and destroys the soft. And before you ask, no, I don't know why he does it. Now if you want to know any more about it, you'd better ask the captain."

Sweeney turned his back on Brewer and walked forward, leaving a puzzled first lieutenant behind him. Brewer leaned on the railing again and tried to make sense of the whole thing. It was like having Captain Tyler back, with his sadistic ways.

CHAPTER 5

Brewer descended the companionway and turned towards the captain's cabin. He nodded to the sentry and knocked on the door.

"Enter."

Brewer opened the door and stepped inside. He found Captain Norman staring out the stern windows, hands clasped behind his back.

"What can I do for you, Mr. Brewer?"

Brewer was surprised by this, as he had given no indication it was he who had entered the room. He cleared his throat and took a deep breath.

"Well, sir," he began, "I was hoping to inquire regarding your treatment of Lt. Phillips up on the deck."

Norman turned. "You think I was unduly harsh on the lieutenant?"

"I'm just trying to understand your reasoning, sir."

Norman said nothing as he made his way to his desk and sat down behind it. He looked at Brewer for a moment longer before silently indicating the chair on the other side of the desk. Brewer obediently sat down and waited.

"Mr. Brewer," the captain said, "it is my intention to keep this ship as highly trained as it was required to be when we were fighting Boney instead of just visiting him. Mr. Phillips barely avoided missing stays and having to do the whole maneuver over again. I'm not about to pat him on the head for that."

"Sir," Brewer said, "it is still early in the training program you ordered, and, well, he *did* complete the maneuver successfully, sir."

Norman rubbed his chin. "Do you deny you were one second away from ordering Mr. Phillips to haul the mains'ls?"

Brewer sighed and looked out the stern windows for a moment before looking back to the captain. "You're right, sir. I was about to... *remind* Mr. Phillips. But, sir, the point is I didn't have to. He got it done in time."

"Barely," Norman said. "I expect more from my officers."

"He's still a boy, sir," Brewer said, "in a lieutenant's uniform."

"Exactly my point!" Norman snapped. "*In a lieutenant's uniform!* However it happened, Mr. Phillips wears a *lieutenant's uniform!* And as long as he does, *that* is the standard to which he will be held on this ship! Do I make myself clear?"

"Clear, sir," Brewer said, but he still had no idea why the captain was so hostile. Then a thought struck him—what was it the captain said a few minutes ago? Something about 'fighting Boney instead of *visiting* him'? 'Fighting', as Norman had done, as opposed to simply 'visiting' Bonaparte, as Brewer had supposedly done at St. Helena?

He looked at the captain. "But sir, surely we can attribute his hesitation at least partly to his being watched by his captain and first lieutenant? Surely he did it several times after he was promoted at sea?"

"One would think, Mr. Brewer," Norman leaned forward

on the desk, "but who can know? I have no idea what happened on that voyage, do you?"

Brewer sat back. "No, sir. I asked Phillips about it once, but he was very vague. I can understand why he got the promotion, but I have no idea why or what he did to merit his captain asking the Admiralty to confirm it."

Captain Norman leaned back in his seat again, his eyes narrowing for a moment as though he was trying to decide whether Brewer was lying or not. He looked out the stern window and rubbed his chin for a while.

Brewer waited, determined to discover what was behind his captain's outbursts. He hoped he was wrong, that the captain was not so petty, but that hope was fading fast. Captain Norman seemed lost in thought, gazing out the stern windows. Brewer's thoughts drifted back to the question that had gnawed at him ever since he joined *Defiant*: How often in peacetime does a captain need to replace *all* his officers *at the same time?*

Norman turned back and gazed about the cabin. "That is precisely the question I wish to have answered."

"I take it there was nothing in his record, sir?"

"Nothing worthwhile. There was the captain's official request to confirm the temporary promotion to acting lieutenant, and the Admiralty countersign at the bottom for confirmation. The captain must have made his case in person to their lordships."

Brewer's brows furrowed at that. It was quite unusual.

Captain Norman seemed to read his thoughts. "It is a mystery, Mr. Brewer, and I don't like mysteries on my ship. The trouble is, if I ask him, who knows what I would get out of him? How would I know if it be the truth or not?"

"Yes, sir, I see what you mean."

"Find out, William," Norman said. "I don't care how you do it, but I want to know what it was that persuaded the lords of the Admiralty to confirm a commission for a sixteen year old boy with only three years as a midshipman."

"Aye aye, sir," Brewer said quietly. He did not like the order. What difference did it make anyway? No matter what Brewer managed to pry out of him, the fact was that Phillips had his commission. Norman would have to level serious charges to justify stripping the commission, especially one signed by their lordships.

"One more thing, Mr. Brewer," Norman said. Brewer turned back to his captain. "It is regarding the reason you came in. To 'inquire about my treatment of Mr. Phillips', I believe you said? Let me make one thing clear, sir: you are responsible to me for the conduct and training of every officer and man aboard this ship. If I need to take someone to task for an error in their duties, the blame will ultimately be laid at your feet. Do I make myself clear?"

"Perfectly, sir," Brewer said, his face set like a flint so as not to give anything away.

"William," Norman said as he leaned back in his chair, his tone softening a bit, "as I said before, you are new to the ship and to me, so there will, of course, be a period of adjustment, your learning how I want my ship run, and my learning what kind of officer you really are and whether or not you deserve your reputation."

Brewer held his captain's eyes and said nothing.

"Is there anything else, Mr. Brewer?"

"No, sir, nothing." Brewer rose and saluted, and then he turned and left the cabin without another word.

Captain Norman gazed at the closed door long after his first lieutenant had left. He leaned back in his chair and sighed, rubbing his chin absently, deep in thought. He wondered what kind of an officer Brewer would turn out to be. There was no denying he and Sweeney had done good work so far with young Phillips, but this man had a large reputation within the fleet, and so far Norman did not see it was deserved. Bush, Brewer's previous captain, was rumored —as was Hornblower before him—to get the crew to worship him. What if Mr. Brewer had learned that same skill?

Norman stood in exasperation and strode over to stand before the stern windows. It was his favorite pose for thinking, standing before the great windows, hands clasped behind his back, allowing his mind to take a problem or issue apart while his eyes focused on *Defiant's* wake. Just now the problem he was trying to dissect was William Brewer. Would he be the kind of officer Norman could work with? His predecessor certainly had not been, and Brewer's mission just now had Norman wondering whether he was of the same cut. Time would tell, and they had plenty of time before the ship joined Admiral Hornblower in the West Indies. Norman hoped Brewer, or perhaps Greene, would fit the bill; he would have a hard time explaining to the Admiralty why he needed to replace all his officers a second time.

Brewer went down to his cabin and closed the door behind him. He walked over and stared out his quarter light, watching the sea roll past and considering over and over again his interview with the captain. He knew from experience that Captain Bush would never treat an officer so in public, and from everything he knew of the man's character, he very much doubted that Hornblower did. But according to Mr. Sweeney, Norman has been doing this for some time, despite his not-so-veiled threat about blaming Brewer. Brewer wondered idly if that was what happened to his predecessor—had Norman broken him or put him on the beach over such incidents as had just happened with Phillips?

Several things were clear to Brewer as he turned from the window and went to his desk to start a new letter to his sister. First, he would have to have a private chat—possibly several—with Mr. Sweeney. Second, he needed to accelerate the training program for young Phillips, as well as taking a more personal role in his education. Third, he had to make a more concerted effort to get to know the warrant officers in the ward room. Some of them had sailed with the captain for years and may be able to give him some good advice which could help the ship run smoother. Brewer sat down and opened his writing desk, taking out from various compartments the inkwell, quill, paper, and blotter before closing it up again. He arranged the articles around him just so, then he dipped quill in ink and began.

> Dear Eunice,
>
> I am so glad to be able to scribble a few lines to you before I am called away again. HMS *Defiant* is on her way west to America before heading south to the Caribbean, where we will join Admiral Hornblower's squadron. I hope to have a chance to visit with him, but of course that depends on what duties we are given once we arrive.
>
> I am slowly getting used to the new ship, dear sister, but it is harder than I'd imagined it would be. *Defiant* is a frigate like *Lydia*, but it is so much bigger that it's almost up to a ship of the line. The captain and crew have sailed together for a while, but all of the officers are new. This makes my job a little harder, but I will adjust.
>
> How is it at Morningvale? I trust spring is as beautiful as I remember. What do Father and Ben have planned this year?

A knock at the door interrupted him. Brewer looked up as the wardroom steward stuck his head in and announced that dinner was served.

Brewer put down his pen and walked out to his place at the head of the wardroom table. The other attendees stood behind their seats, awaiting his arrival. When they were all seated, the stewards served dinner. Brewer was surprised to see a meaty stew follow the customary soup.

"What's this?" he asked.

Lieutenant Johnson, the marine subaltern, spoke up. "Some of my men were practicing this morning, and a couple of large birds were unlucky enough to come within range. The men were able to save them, and they gave one to me for the wardroom!"

Brewer clapped his hands in appreciation, and there were choruses of "Here! Here!" and "Well done!" echoing around the table. Soon each man was digging in to the fare before him, and Brewer was surprised at how tasty it was.

"Well, gentlemen," Brewer said to the table at large, "I understand we will be looking for the fishing fleet as we pass Newfoundland. I love a good fish as much as the next man. What should I expect when we arrive?"

Mr. Barton, the purser, leaned in. "That depends entirely on where the fishing fleet is when we arrive, and what their most recent catch was."

Brewer chuckled. "I take it the captain has a preference?"

Barton smiled. "Atlantic salmon is the preferred choice, but cod is a close second."

Brewer nodded. "Never had cod, but I love Atlantic salmon. Does the wardroom partake?"

"Not nearly as much as we would wish," Johnson said.

"Mr. Barton?" Brewer looked to the purser. So did everyone else at the table, which made the purser squirm a little.

"Ah, well," Barton stammered, "the subject hasn't really come up until now. The previous first lieutenant wasn't very keen on fish, it seems."

"Well, the new one is," Brewer said. "What do you say, men? Everyone chip in, and we'll see what the good purser can do for us?"

There was a chorus of agreements, and Brewer turned to the purser.

"I'm sure I can be of service, Mr. Brewer."

"Wonderful! Thank you, Mr. Barton."

The stewards cleared the dishes, and Brewer rose, signifying the end of the meal. As he stepped away from the table, he was approached by Mr. Spinelli, *Defiant*'s surgeon.

"Good to see you, Doctor. Where have you been hiding?"

"In my sickbay, Mr. Brewer," the surgeon said quietly, "going over the latest medical journals I picked up in London. I was also getting over my usual bout of seasickness."

Brewer looked surprised. "You're seasick, Mr. Spinelli?"

The surgeon looked embarrassed. "Aye. It happens whenever I spend time on land between cruises. It usually takes a week or two for me to regain my sea legs. I got tired of the jokes and ribbing, so for the last several cruises I've taken to hiding out in sickbay until it passes."

"And how are you now?"

Spinelli shrugged. "Today is the first day I've felt like eating something substantial. I'm glad I was here; Creighton's stew was magnificent! Now I'm hoping my stomach behaves itself. Let me ask you a question, Mr. Brewer."

"Yes?"

The surgeon looked up at the taller first lieutenant and smiled. "Do you play chess?"

Brewer smiled as well. "Lead on, Mr. Spinelli."

Spinelli led the way forward to the sickbay and directed Brewer to one of the chairs beside a table while he got his chess set from a cabinet. Brewer was surprised to see the surgeon come over to the table with a canvas bag. He set it on the table and untied the knot, then he pulled out a cloth chess board folded in quarters. He flattened it on the table and began pulling the pieces out and setting them on the table. The black pieces were stained a rich mahogany color. Brewer picked up a light pine wood rook and examined it. The piece showed a fair amount of use, which made Brewer wonder if he was about to get a thrashing from the good doctor.

Dr. Spinelli sat down in the other chair, and they drew for white. Brewer won, and they arranged the pieces.

"I must warn you," the surgeon said, "I'm not very good."

"That's all right," Brewer replied as he moved his king's pawn to open, "neither am I."

Brewer smiled when he saw the doctor's eyebrow rise as he brought his queen's knight out in reply, and the battle was joined. Neither man spoke as they focused their energies and concentration. At different times, each man sat back in his chair and stared at the board in confusion or amazement before leaning forward again to rejoin the fray. Finally, well over an hour into the match, Brewer moved a rook and sat back with a triumphant sigh.

"Checkmate," he said.

Dr. Spinelli studied the board intently for a few moments before looking up.

"Outstanding, Mr. Brewer!" he cried. "I can't remember when I've enjoyed a game so much!"

"Nor I," Brewer said, extending his hand, "and the name's William."

"Adam," the doctor said, and the two shook hands. "Another game?"

Brewer nodded. "Yes, I've got time."

They reset the board, and the doctor led off this time. The pace was much more sedate this time around, almost friendly. Not quite, but almost.

"Glad to see you're feeling better," Brewer said as he moved a pawn. "Have you had a chance to look round the ship, meet the crew?"

"A little," Spinelli said as he made his move. "I went up

on deck during the middle watch a couple of times. I got to say something to the second and third lieutenants."

Brewer nodded and made a casual move. "And what are your opinions?"

The doctor looked up. "Of our lieutenants?"

Brewer nodded.

Spinelli sat back in his chair and sighed. He seemed to forget the game as he tried to decide if Brewer had an ulterior motive in asking. Deciding he did not, the doctor drew a deep breath and blew it out slowly while he gathered his thoughts.

"Well," he said slowly, "they seem capable, Mr. Greene especially so. I must say, Mr. Phillips seems a bit young for his responsibilities."

Brewer hesitated, staring intently at a rook before castling.

"Adam," he said slowly, "may I confide in you? Rely on your discretion? I need your assistance."

The doctor looked at him quizzically and said, "Of course, William."

Brewer smiled and told the surgeon all about Phillips, from his temporary promotion to his public dressing-down by the captain earlier that morning. Spinelli listened without interrupting the first lieutenant, the chess game forgotten by both men.

When Brewer finished, the surgeon said, "And you say the captain had no cause for the rebuke?"

Brewer shrugged. "He is the captain, Doctor. That gives him sufficient cause to do whatever he wishes."

Spinelli nodded thoughtfully and said, "What is it you want me to do?"

"Just be a friend to him, Doctor. He may want someone to talk to. That's all you need do. That, and let me know if you think he's heading for trouble."

"I am your man, sir," the surgeon said as both men rose

from the table. "Do you know if he plays chess?"

Brewer chuckled. "No idea."

The doctor clapped his hands once and rubbed them together. "I shall have to find out. Always on the lookout for fresh, um, *victims*, shall we say?"

Brewer laughed and bid the doctor farewell. He went up on deck to find Mr. Greene with the watch.

"Good afternoon, sir," Greene said as he saluted.

"Good afternoon, Mr. Greene. How are we doing?"

"On course, Mr. Brewer. At last cast of the log, our speed was seven knots. I can taste that good salmon already. I say, do you think the captain would mind if we stopped around Maine to see if we can get some fresh lobster?"

Brewer shrugged. He'd never had lobster. "I will speak to Mr. Barton about it."

"Thank you, sir," Greene tipped his hat and went to attend to his other duties. Brewer watched him go and wondered if he would be able to get the second lieutenant to loosen up a bit.

Brewer walked over to where Mr. Sweeney was standing by the lee rail.

"Sir," Sweeney nodded in greeting.

"Mr. Sweeney. I hope all is well?"

"Very well, sir."

"Let me ask you a question, Mr. Sweeney. What happened to the previous officers on this ship?"

Sweeney looked up at him. "Sir?"

Brewer leaned over and rested his elbows on the railing. "A question has been floating around my mind, Mr. Sweeney, and that is, why would a frigate in His Majesty's navy have to replace all the officers and the surgeon at the same time in peacetime? I can understand it in time of war, but it seems deuced odd in peacetime. So, I am asking you, what happened to the previous officers?"

Sweeney shrugged. "Nothing special, Mr. Brewer. The third lieutenant took sick and died during our last voyage, and I'm not sure about the others. If you're curious, why not ask the captain?"

Brewer turned to face him. "You're not sure, Mr. Sweeney?"

Sweeney faced him, meeting the unspoken challenge. "Aye, sir, that's what I said."

Brewer held the master's eyes for a moment before turning away and leaning on the rail again. Sweeney did the same, and the two stared at the North Atlantic swells rolling past the ship.

"I was just curious," Brewer said at length. "I trust if you do happen to remember anything that you will let me know?"

Sweeney said nothing. He stared out over the open sea, ignoring the first lieutenant completely. Presently, Brewer stood up and straightened his coat.

"Good day, Mr. Sweeney," he said.

"Mr. Brewer," the sailing-master nodded.

Brewer walked forward, pleased with the ship but vaguely uneasy about Sweeney's silence and what it might mean. The ship's bell rang six bells of the afternoon watch, and Brewer was surprised the day was so far spent already. He wandered forward to the mainmast and stood there watching Mr. Greene exercising the forward batteries of the starboard broadside. He was pleased to see that Greene was not the sort of officer who screamed at the men and berated them. Instead, Brewer saw him talk to the gun crews, instructing them and correcting their mistakes. Brewer noted that the shooting of each gun improved over the course of the hour's exercise, the number two gun crew shooting particularly well. When the exercise was done, Brewer walked up to congratulate both Greene and his crews.

"Well done, Mr. Greene!" Brewer said. "Well done, men! I wager the French are glad the war's over!"

The men cheered, and Greene said, “Thank you, Mr. Brewer. I was about to ask the captain for an extra ration of grog for these men for their obvious improvement.”

“By all means, Mr. Greene. In fact, I will do it myself, along with an extra ration of tobacco for the crew of the best gun. Which would you say that was?”

“Number Two, sir.”

“Yes, that was my judgment as well,” Brewer said. “I will ask the captain for an extra ration of tobacco for the crew of gun number two, Mr. Greene. Again, well done! You men pay attention to your officer when he instructs you in how to do your job better. Mr. Greene’s trying to keep you alive and make sure you kill the enemy before he can do as much to us. The captain will be proud of you! You may carry on, Mr. Greene.”

“Thank you, sir,” Greene said as he saluted. The crews cheered their good fortune.

Brewer went below and spoke to the captain, who authorized the extra grog and tobacco Brewer requested. He came back on deck and informed Greene. Eight bells sounded, and Mr. Phillips came on deck with his larboard watch to relieve the watch on duty, which was dismissed below for the supper. Phillips did not see Brewer until after he had been briefed by Mr. Greene and had taken the deck. He came aft as soon as he noticed Brewer standing by the wheel.

“I’m sorry, sir,” Phillips said as he saluted. “I did not know you were on the deck.”

“Quite all right, Mr. Phillips,” Brewer said. “So, how are you getting along?”

“Well enough, I expect, sir,” Phillips replied.

Brewer nodded. “And your schooling?”

Brewer was pleased to see the boy was not embarrassed by the question, and he took heart. Perhaps the lad would not be crushed or destroyed.

"Pretty well, I think, sir," Phillips said. "Mr. Sweeney congratulated me for working out our position earlier, and he does not seem like one to throw away a compliment. The petty officers on my watch are very good about helping me out, too, sir."

"Glad to hear it, Mr. Phillips." Brewer began to stroll forward around the deck, and Phillips fell into step with him. "I wanted to talk to you about your philosophy for leading men."

"Leading men, sir?"

"Yes. In action, everything depends on how readily the men will follow an officer's commands. If it's an officer they hate, discipline may well give way to panic. The day will be lost, and many men will die."

"I see, sir."

Brewer smiled at the young lieutenant. "No, you don't, but one day you will. The difference as to whether or not the men will follow you will depend in large part on your philosophy of leadership, meaning what *kind* of leader you decide to be and *how* you decide to treat your men.

"In my experience, Mr. Phillips, I have found that under normal circumstances officers usually fall into one of two categories. I call them the teachers and the abusers. Let me deal with the abusers first. These are officers who have decided to rule by fear. Sometimes they scream at the men and berate them at every turn. They rely on the rope's end, the cane, and the cat to inspire the necessary fear in the men to get them to obey their orders. While they inspire fear and a degree of obedience, the focus of the men is all too often not on what they *can* do, instead they are worried about making sure they do *nothing* to earn themselves a beating or an appointment with the cat. Do you see, Mr. Phillips? The focus of the men is on *self-preservation*, not on the good of the ship or defeating the enemy."

"I see, sir," Phillips said thoughtfully.

"Teachers, on the other hand, take the time to teach their men how to do their jobs with the greatest efficiency. Wherever possible, mistakes are corrected instead of punished, and achievement is recognized and rewarded rather than ignored. Make no mistake, Mr. Phillips, to be a teacher is not to ignore discipline. Sometimes you run into a man who, for some reason, simply refuses to come around, and in that case, well, you do what you must. The foundation, the bedrock of command, must always be that your orders will be obeyed. That goes without question.

"I hate the cat, Mr. Phillips, and I try to avoid using it whenever possible. Unfortunately, there are some times it is unavoidable. Personally, I would rather teach a man to think and to do his duty than to beat and frighten him into obedience. If the men believe you are looking out for them, they will move heaven and earth for you, Mr. Phillips."

Phillips nodded. "I think I understand, Mr. Brewer." They strolled past the foremast and glanced at one of *Defiant*'s twenty-four pounders. Phillips paused and said, "But where do you draw the line between looking out for the men and being their friend? Someone told me after the... I mean, on the old ship, the *Retribution*, sir; they told me never to let the men think I was their friend. They said it would cause me nothing but trouble."

"Good question," Brewer said as they started walking again. "It's not too difficult; you just have to maintain a degree of separation. For example, if you have occasion to reward the men with an extra ration of rum, you don't drink with them. I don't think they would expect you to, but if they should ask, you would simply decline politely, saying it's for them because they earned it. Remember, mistakes can be corrected, but disobedience must be dealt with in no uncertain terms. If you are unsure, ask me, and if he deserves it, we'll place the offender on report and bring him up before the captain."

Phillips nodded but still looked uncertain.

Brewer stopped and turned to the young lieutenant. "One of the best ways to learn, John, is to watch officers you think are good officers and use their methods yourself. Just today, I was able to watch Mr. Greene exercise the guns, and he calmly but firmly corrected the mistakes of his crews. The men listened, and as a result every gun showed improvement by the time the hour was over. You might want to see if you can watch next time he holds a gun drill, then perhaps you can ask him a few questions afterward."

They were back at the companionway stairs. Brewer looked around and turned to Phillips.

"It's your deck, Mr. Phillips," he said. "Carry on."

"Aye aye, sir," Phillips said and saluted.

Brewer nodded to him and disappeared below deck. His feet guided him unconsciously, he was so deep in thought that he was almost unaware of the passage. His mind was on the one bit of information he had gleaned from Mr. Phillips—that someone on his old ship told him never to let the men think he was their friend, that it would bring him "nothing but trouble."

Brewer closed the door to his cabin and sat down at his desk to think. What had happened to Phillips on that ship? Brewer was convinced something happened on that voyage to Gibraltar, and sooner or later he would have to ask Phillips point-blank what it was.

Brewer turned to his window and sighed. It was going to be a long voyage.

CHAPTER 6

Defiant continued on her westward track. The weather was good and the wind strong, and the ship showed all the best characteristics of her class when it came to speed. Once when he was off duty, Brewer climbed to the main top and sat there awhile, enjoying the sailing of the magnificent ship. A noise from above him pierced through the shrieking of the wind in his ears and made him look up. To his surprise, about twenty-five feet above him, Brewer saw young Mr. Tyler. He had lashed his left wrist to the main topmast shrouds, and the boy was leaning outward as far as he could, enjoying the wind and shouting at the top of his lungs for the joy of the experience. Brewer sat back against the mainmast and sighed. He shook his head and laughed at the enthusiasm of youth—how he missed it!

Defiant sailed on without incident, day turning to night and back to day again. The entire crew settled into a routine, officers and men alike. The only diversions were the weekly concerts put on by Carslake, a gun captain in Mr. Greene's watch who played the fiddle, and Miller, the marine fifer. Sometimes they would play by themselves and produce melodies that were both haunting and sweet. The entire crew turned out to hear them perform. Even more popular were the nights when they allowed someone to sing with them. Sergeant O'Bannon, a Royal Marine marksman, had a particularly fine and powerful tenor voice, and his performances were greatly anticipated events. Sometimes, Carslake would gather the ship's boys into a choir and lead them in some traditional songs and choruses.

Lieutenant Phillips' education continued. Brewer and Sweeney schooled their young student in their respective specialties, and both were pleased with his progress. Captain Norman usually came up on deck once a week for the specific purpose of having Phillips put the ship through a particular maneuver. Brewer watched these unscheduled examinations with increasing concern, as the problems the Captain presented to young Phillips seemed to be more and more beyond the lad's experience and position. This came to a head one day when the captain emerged on deck. He studied the sails for a moment, glanced out over the ocean waves as they passed, and then walked over to join Brewer and Mr. Sweeney.

"Good morning, sir," Brewer said as both men saluted.

"Good morning," Norman said. "Where is Mr. Phillips? Is this not his watch?"

"It is, sir," Brewer replied. "He asked that I relieve him for a moment, so he might fetch something from the wardroom."

"I see," Norman said. "Mr. Brewer, will you kindly pass the word for Mr. Phillips?"

"Aye aye, sir," Brewer turned and repeated the order to the midshipman of the watch. When he turned back, he thought he saw something in his captain's eye, a look that did not bode well, and he wondered what James Norman had in mind.

Lieutenant Phillips appeared quickly and saluted. "You wished to see me, sir?"

"Yes, Mr. Phillips. I trust you were able to complete your business below successfully?"

Brewer saw that Phillips was nonplussed by his captain's remarks. Phillips looked past the captain to meet Brewer's eyes, and Brewer tried to give him an encouraging look. Brewer looked for Mr. Sweeney and saw that he had moved to the other side of the quarterdeck; the look on the sailing master's face confirmed Brewer's fears that a storm was brewing.

"Yes, sir," Phillips stammered. "I'm sorry, sir, I only stepped below for a minute. I asked Mr. Brewer to—"

"Yes, Mr. Phillips, I'm well aware that Mr. Brewer had the deck while you were below," Norman said. There was a scowl on his face that Brewer didn't like, but he could only watch helplessly as Norman went on. "How goes your schooling, Mr. Phillips?"

"My schooling, sir? I'm getting along fairly well, I believe, sir. That is, Mr. Brewer and Mr. Sweeney seemed pleased with my progress."

"They are, are they?" Norman turned to look at his first lieutenant and then at his sailing master. "They must have you nearly ready for your examination, then."

Norman spun on the unfortunate lieutenant. "Then tell me this, Mr. Phillips: You are officer of the watch, and you hear a cry of 'Fire!' from the foc'sle. What action do you take?"

Brewer could not believe his ears! He looked to Sweeney in time to see the sailing master close his eyes and lower his head in disgust. What was going on? Did Sweeney know or at least suspect this was coming?

Phillips was totally unprepared for the captain's questions. "Fire, sir? Ah, I'm not—"

Norman showed no mercy. "Come now, Lieutenant. The foc'sle's on fire! What do you do?"

Phillips hesitated and turned in Brewer's direction. That

was a mistake, for it drew the captain's ire.

"Don't look to Mr. Brewer, sir! You are the officer of the watch!" Norman shouted. The Captain watched the lieutenant struggle for an answer, and a condescending smile crept over his face. "Well," he said in a softer voice that Brewer thought had a hard edge to it, "it seems your education is not as far along as you may have thought. Very well, Mr. Phillips, how about this: You are sent in a ship ordered to be fitted out, the Captain not having appeared; the lower masts and bowsprits are in but not rigged. What part of the rigging goes first over the mast heads?"

Phillips looked even more wretched and lost than before. "Ah, sir, I'm not sure..."

"Not ready there either, Mr. Phillips? Very well, let's try a little navigational problem. You are officer of the watch beating up channel with Beachy Head under your lee when the wind veers six points and you are taken aback. What orders do you give?"

Phillips began to squirm under the captain's assault. "Beachy Head, sir?"

"Not familiar with it, Mr. Phillips? Well, I suppose you are a bit *young* and may not have traveled as widely as others. How about this: Upon receiving orders to sail from Spithead with a south-east wind, at what time of tide will you begin to unmoor that you may have the advantage of it in plying down to St. Helens?"

Phillips looked utterly defeated. "I don't know, sir."

Norman looked at his lieutenant with what appeared to Brewer to be a look of total contempt. "Mr. Phillips, what have you been learning in your time aboard *Defiant*? We may as well give your commission to one of the powder monkeys. Can you at least answer me this: Your sails are still all set; the wind beings to freshen. What sails will you take in first?"

Brewer was in anguish for his young pupil, but he was

unable to intervene. Then something happened. He saw Phillips' head snap up at the captain's powder monkey remark, and Brewer saw rage in the lad's eyes.

When Captain Norman put out his last question, Phillips looked up at the sails for a moment, and when his gaze fell back to the deck, it happened to hit on the first lieutenant, and Brewer saw a light dawn in the younger man's eye. Phillips excused himself to his captain and made straight for Brewer.

Phillips saluted his first lieutenant and said, "Mr. Brewer, the Captain has given me a problem, and I do not know the answer. I am sent in a ship ordered to be fitted out, the Captain not having appeared; the lower masts and bowsprits are in but not rigged: What part of the rigging goes first over the mast heads? Can you help me, sir?"

Brewer automatically looked over Phillips' shoulder to see a shocked look on Captain Norman's face. That was all he needed. "Of course, Mr. Phillips. This is what you do."

Brewer proceeded to explain the commands and the order in which they had to be given. Phillips repeated the procedure to make sure he had it right, then he marched over to the captain, saluted, and repeated the procedure to him.

Captain Norman barely saluted his third lieutenant, and Brewer saw the captain's face was a flint as he said, "Carry on, Mr. Phillips." Phillips returned to his duties with new found confidence.

Norman watched him go through narrowed eyes. He turned to Brewer and said, "Mr. Brewer, will you please join me in my cabin?"

Brewer saluted. "Of course, sir," he said as the captain walked past him. Brewer looked over to Sweeney, and the other nodded to say that he would watch over Mr. Phillips. Brewer followed Norman to the captain's cabin, and the sentry closed the door behind them. Captain Norman set his hat on his desk and went over to stare out the cabin's stern windows. Brewer stood just inside the door and waited for his captain to speak.

Norman stared out at *Defiant's* wake for several minutes before taking his seat behind his desk. He looked up at Brewer with a withering stare.

"Mr. Brewer," he said. His voice was quiet and cold. "Do you mind telling me why you interfered in the problem I gave Mr. Phillips?"

"Interfered, sir?" Brewer said. "I don't understand."

"Do you deny it?"

"That I interfered? Yes, sir, I deny it."

"Then what do you call it, sir?" Norman shouted.

"I call it doing my job, sir," Brewer said, struggling to keep his voice level. "You gave him a task which he could not do, sir, so he did what he should do, what he was *taught* to do—came to me for help. I gave it to him."

"I wanted Mr. Phillips to do it!"

"Sir, it was beyond him, as it is beyond almost every third lieutenant in the fleet, especially those who have only held their commissions for less than six months! But instead of standing there looking lost, the lad acted to discover what he did not know and solved the problem! Isn't that *exactly* what we want him to do, sir?"

Norman sat there, saying nothing and simply glowering at Brewer with rage in his eyes. Suddenly, an idea dawned in Brewer's mind, and he stared wide-eyed at his captain.

"I don't understand, sir. Why did you do it?" Brewer asked. "You deliberately gave him a task you knew he could not do. You *wanted* him to fail!"

Norman's silence spoke volumes.

"For God's sake! Why?" Brewer cried.

"I do not need to explain myself to you, Lieutenant."

"Begging your pardon, Captain, but I'm trying to understand. You ordered me to bring Mr. Phillips up to speed, to teach him what he did not have the chance to learn, and to get him ready to face a commissioning board. Mr. Sweeney and I both agree Mr. Phillips is doing very well. Now you give him a task that *no one* of his rank and time in grade would be able to complete! I don't understand, sir!"

Norman stared at Brewer and remained silent. Brewer held his captain's eyes as he had once held the Corsican's. Finally, Norman blinked and looked out the stern windows. After a few more minutes, Brewer heard him sigh.

"Sit down, Mr. Brewer. Jenkins!"

Brewer sat down cautiously as the pantry door opened and the captain's steward entered with a tray holding two glasses and a decanter. Jenkins set the tray on the desk and poured the wine before retreating into the pantry and closing the door. Norman picked up his glass, saluted Brewer, and downed its dark contents in a single draught. He stared at the empty glass for a few moments before setting it gently on the desk.

"You are correct, Mr. Brewer," Norman said. "I wanted to see if Mr. Phillips would throw up his hands in despair and give up. That was what the exercise was supposed to teach him, to go to someone and find out rather than stand around and cry about it." He grunted and reached for the decanter. "It appears I underestimated our Mr. Phillips." He toasted Brewer again. "Perhaps he'll make it after all. He certainly has a good teacher."

Brewer sat back and watched his captain quaff his wine. Brewer picked up his own glass; it turned out to be the captain's excellent port. The two men drank in silence as Brewer, for his part, tried to understand his captain's reasoning. Norman intended to deliberately humiliate Phillips publicly in order to teach him something which, while important, could certainly be ingrained in a different manner.

Brewer studied his captain over his glass, trying

unsuccessfully to get inside his head. He could not understand why it was necessary to humiliate a junior officer in order to teach him. He silently thanked God that, whatever his faults, Captain Tyler was not that way with his junior officers, and Lord knows Captain Bush and Lord Hornblower *certainly* were not like that. Brewer sighed inwardly; there was no understanding that kind of cruelty. He just hoped the captain didn't take it too far.

"Well, Mr. Brewer," the captain said as he set down his glass, "it seems Mr. Phillips' training is proceeding quite nicely. I am still concerned about his ship handling skills should one of those North Atlantic gales suddenly appear. Therefore, I would appreciate it very much if you would find it convenient for the next three days to be on deck whenever Mr. Phillips has the watch. Just in case any problems arise, you understand."

Brewer could hardly believe his ears. "But sir," he said, "surely Mr. Phillips could simply send for me—"

Captain Norman interrupted him, a flash of anger on his face. "By that time, sir, we may well be dismasted!" Both face and voice softened. "I would really prefer you to be on deck. It's only three days," he paused and caught Brewer's eye, "this time."

Brewer was sure of it now, he was being punished for aiding young Phillips. It was a severe action for a captain to take against his first lieutenant, but there was nothing Brewer could do about it.

Brewer set his glass on the table, holding his captain's eyes the whole time. "Aye aye, sir."

"Excellent," Norman said with a condescending smile. "I'm glad we understand each other. Dismissed."

Brewer stood, saluted, and left the captain's cabin without another word. As soon as the door closed behind his departing first lieutenant, Norman's smile disappeared. His hand automatically rubbed his chin in contemplation as he stared at the door. He had come close to telling Brewer the truth, that the exercise was a test all right, but it was a test of Brewer, not Phillips. Norman knew Phillips would not be able to do what he had asked of him; Norman had wanted to see what Brewer would do. Would he help Phillips, or would the warning he received the last time they spoke be enough to make him leave Phillips hung out to dry? It was true that Phillips had surprised the captain; he never expected the boy to have the presence of mind to go to Brewer and request the help he needed. And Brewer had done exactly what Norman hoped he would do: help the subordinate who needed it. Norman smiled again, but this time it was an honest smile. Maybe Mr. Brewer deserved his reputation after all.

Reputation. The word made Norman's smile disappear. It reminded him of what Brewer said the night of the dinner party. *"Did you really pick up a musket and shoot the Frog who got Nelson?"* Where did Brewer hear about that? Norman had been trying to leave that behind for fifteen years now. It was disturbing to have it come up again, and he felt the old familiar shame welling up inside.

His reputation had gotten him command of *Defiant* in 1812. Norman wished now he had told the truth at once, but he had been too surprised and too embarrassed at the time to tell Captain Hardy, Nelson's flag captain on *Victory*, that he had been mistaken. Norman had left his duty station to report to Hardy, and he had been on deck and had seen Nelson fall. In a fury, Norman had snatched up a musket and taken aim at the French marksman, but the marksman was taking aim right back. Norman saw this and froze in terror. Fortunately for him, the marksman was shot out of the rigging by one of the marines on *Victory* before he could fire. Hardy had seen Norman pick up the musket and aim, and he saw the marksman fall, so he naturally assumed Norman had been the one to avenge Nelson's death. Norman had almost spoken up as soon as he heard that Hardy was including the incident in his official report, but he hadn't, and, as a result, he had spent the last fifteen years alternating between living up to his reputation and living it down.

Norman stood and went to look out the stern windows. What was he going to do with Brewer? He appeared to be a very good officer who would make a fine addition to *Defiant*, but what would happen when he found out that his captain's reputation was founded on a lie?

Mr. Brewer was, at that moment, ascending the companionway steps to the deck. Mr. Phillips was forward, talking to the sail maker as he watched him and his mates at work, Mr. Short beside him, listening just as intently. Brewer smiled; at least Phillips didn't appear bothered by his run in with the captain.

Brewer turned to walk aft and was brought up short by the sight of Mr. Sweeney staring at him, arms folded across his chest and leaning against the stern railing, shaking his head. Brewer strolled over to him.

"Mr. Sweeney," he said, leaning on the aft rail beside him.

"Mr. Brewer," the master replied. "I see you survived."

Brewer grunted. "Did you think I wouldn't?"

Sweeney smiled as he glanced up at the driver billowing above their heads. "It has been known to happen," he said. "What did he give you?"

Brewer shot him a look. "What do you mean?"

The sailing master pushed himself off the rail. "Will you walk with me, Lieutenant?"

The two walked forward down the starboard side, away from the wind. When they passed the mizzenmast, Sweeney glanced over his shoulder, then leaned toward Brewer. "You never know when he's got the stern windows open," he said in a low voice. "As for your question, you walked out on the deck alone, so he didn't arrest you and confine you to quarters. On the other hand, nobody who gets called to the captain's cabin under such circumstances gets away scot-free. So, what did he give you?"

Brewer paused to inspect the lashings on one of the twenty-four pounders. He turned to face the sailing master and said, "Three days extra duty."

Sweeney shot him a quizzical look through squinted eyes, and Brewer wondered if his punishment was heavy or light. Sweeney's grunt gave him his answer.

"I take it I got off lucky?" Brewer asked.

Sweeney shrugged again. "I guess he likes you."

Brewer shook his head as the two men resumed their walk toward the forecastle. "You've seen this before." It was a statement, not a question.

Sweeney shrugged. "Of course, but you knew that already after our previous conversation. Or did you think you were the first?" He sighed. "Well, at least you didn't argue with him publicly." Brewer looked surprised, and Sweeney scowled. "The last officer who confronted him was arrested for gross insubordination and court-martialed."

Brewer looked straight ahead. "My predecessor?"

Out of the corner of his eye, he saw Sweeney nod once.

"He received a reprimand," Sweeney said casually, "which will be more than enough to ensure he never gets promoted. He was transferred to the flagship at the next rendezvous."

The two men turned and started back down the larboard side. Brewer paused for a moment to enjoy the sea breeze in his face, but Sweeney stepped in front of him.

"Look," he said in a low voice, "I've heard you have the ear of our new admiral, but don't count on Hornblower to protect you. You would be broken and transferred before *Defiant* ever set foot in the Caribbean. And it would be wise to avoid the topic of Hornblower when you're around the captain."

"Why is that?"

Sweeney looked around before edging even closer to Brewer and turning him to face the sea. "Because the captain would take it amiss, that's why. Like you were loyal to Hornblower and not to him."

Brewer could not believe what he was hearing, but the look in the sailing master's eyes told him it was all the truth. He shook his head and stared out to sea. Finally he sighed and nodded his head. *So be it,* he thought. *I will do my job to the best of my ability.*

Mr. Sweeney stood back and watched his words work on the first lieutenant. He saw the younger man stare out at the rolling waves and wrestle with what he had just learned. What would he do? Sweeney thought Brewer was a good officer; it was only right that he know what the captain was like so he could keep himself, and hopefully young Mr. Phillips, out of trouble. Finally, a sigh blew from the first lieutenant's lips, catching the sailing master's attention. He watched with renewed interest as he saw a glint of steel creep into Brewer's eye, and when Sweeney saw him nod, he knew he had the real thing here.

"So, Mr. Brewer," he said, "what's it going to be?"

Brewer turned to face his friend. "Thank you for telling me, Mr. Sweeney; you may rely upon my discretion. I am much better equipped now to give the captain the kind of smooth-running ship he desires. We'll make *Defiant* the best frigate in the fleet!"

Sweeney smiled and nodded, and both men turned to finish their walk.

Brewer actually enjoyed his three days of extra duty, even though being on deck whenever Mr. Phillips had the watch in addition to his own duties meant he was on duty for twenty hours out of every twenty-four. Brewer devoted much of that time to teaching Phillips how to lead men. He was careful to always have a midshipman stay within sight when he was instructing Phillips; this was a precaution so that if the captain heard that Peters, the leading petty officer on Phillips' watch, had the deck and tried to accuse them of shirking their duty in some way, they would have a witness to verify they were indeed about their business and never left the deck.

On the second night, in the middle watch, the wind was gusting fair and the stars were bright. Brewer took Mr. Phillips and their midshipman chaperone, Mr. Short, to the weather rail of the quarterdeck.

"The most important thing," Brewer said as he leaned back against the rail, "is to train yourself to think under extreme pressure instead of freezing in panic. If you can keep your head and think, then you can act. It doesn't matter if a French seventy-four is throwing grape and solid shot at you, or if the captain is giving you a good scolding for a mistake, you must be able to avoid panic and think."

Phillips spoke up. "But what about when a superior puts his nose in your face?"

Brewer smiled into the darkness. "Let me tell you a story. When I was on St. Helena with Governor Hornblower, the governor ordered a security crackdown that required anyone entering or leaving the French compound at Longwood to be searched, and when you-know-who heard about it, he wasn't exactly pleased."

Short whispered, "Napoleon?"

"In the flesh," Brewer said. "He burst into the office while the governor was out and demanded an explanation for the added security. I tried to tell him the governor was out and asked if he would like to wait, but he just got madder and louder. He even pounded on my desk with his fist and demanded that *I* answer his question."

Phillips voice betrayed a wicked smile. "So, did you put old Boney in his place, sir?"

Brewer's voice carried a strong warning to the young lieutenant. "Are you serious, Mr. Phillips? Defeated and an exile, he was still Napoleon Bonaparte, former Emperor of the French and conqueror of most of Europe! That is not someone you speak wrongly to."

"Sorry, sir," Phillips said, suitably chastised.

"So what *did* you do?" Short asked.

Brewer leaned back and enjoyed the breeze for a moment. "I was terrified all right, let me tell you, but I was determined not to let him see it. I stood to my feet and faced him. He continued to demand an explanation, and every time I told him he would have to ask the governor."

"What happened next?" Short asked.

"Fortunately, the governor arrived and handled the situation. But the governor told me later that Boney said he was impressed by the way I handled myself." He turned to Phillips and said, "Look at me, John. We have figured out that the captain is going to give you these tests of his from time to time, and believe me, his aim is to make you a better officer by training you to react under stress. When you fail—and you will, sometimes, but don't worry, it's not the end of the world—and the captain calls you up on it, you stand to attention. Don't give him the satisfaction of seeing you scared. Don't misunderstand me: he *is* the captain, and you are duty-bound to respect the rank and position. You speak respectfully when spoken to, and do what you're told without question. But you don't break! Determine to learn from mistakes so you don't repeat them!"

Phillips nodded and swallowed hard.

Brewer softened his voice, remembering that he was talking to a sixteen-year-old boy. "Look, John, some captains consider it their duty to see if a junior lieutenant or a senior midshipman is fit for a commission by trying to break them, make them cry, if you will. The theory is if they cannot control themselves when the captain of their own ship is getting on them, what will they do when a French seventy-four or a Caribbean pirate is throwing grape at them? You see, we are all working for the same end, really; it's just that the methods are different. But I know you can do it, John! You *stand*, like a man, *take* whatever he wants to throw at you, and, by God, you will earn his respect! Now, I will say it may take a while, but it will happen, I promise you!"

Phillips nodded, a smile tugging at the corner of his mouth. Brewer could just make it out in the moonlight and laughed.

"Good lad," he said. "Now, tell me the procedure for getting underway. In the proper order this time, if you please."

Phillips sighed and hung his head while young Mr. Short snickered under his breath, and the rest of the watch was given over to lessons of a different sort. Phillips recited from memory procedures for doing everything from leaving harbor to reefing the mainsail during a hurricane. When Mr. Greene appeared on the deck just before the turn of the watch, Brewer patted Phillips on the shoulder.

"Well done," he said. "Just remember what I said."

"I will, sir," the younger man said. "Thank you."

Brewer nodded. "Carry on, Mr. Phillips."

Phillips saluted and went to speak to Peters before turning the deck over to Mr. Greene.

The morning watch was traditionally the province of the first lieutenant, so Brewer remained on deck. Mr. Greene came over to present himself after accepting the deck.

"Good morning, sir," he said as he saluted.

"Good morning, Mr. Greene," Brewer said and immediately had to stifle a yawn. "Please excuse me, Benjamin; it's been a long couple of days, and I still have one more to go."

"You seem to be doing well so far. Did the captain come

up last night?"

Brewer shook his head. "No, not since the last dog watch."

Greene shook his head. "That means we're almost certain to see him before the turn of the watch. I hope he's in a good mood."

And so he was. Captain Norman appeared on deck just as dawn was breaking. Brewer and Greene were busy with the log and did not notice until he joined them.

"Sorry, sir," Brewer said as they both saluted. "Good morning."

"Quite all right," Norman said, "and good morning to you both. So, what is our progress?"

"Better than eight knots, Captain," Greene said. "Nigh on to eight-and-a-half."

"Excellent!" Norman said as he rubbed his hands together. "Getting closer to that good Atlantic salmon every hour!"

"We should set our final course during the afternoon watch today, sir," Brewer said. "Do you want Mr. Phillips to do the maneuver?"

Captain Norman looked at Brewer and thought for a moment. "Is that his watch?"

"No, sir," Brewer said.

"Then never mind, Mr. Brewer; I'm sure our young prodigy will get plenty of practice on our way south. Do you like salmon, Mr. Brewer?"

Brewer smiled. "Love it, Captain."

"I knew you were a man of good taste!" Norman said with a smile. "What about cod?"

"Never had it, sir."

"Never mind," Norman said. "If you like salmon, you'll take to cod quickly enough."

"Tell me, sir, how did you ever find such a gold mine of

good fish?" Brewer asked.

Captain Norman smiled at the memory. "Would you believe, we came upon one of the fishing boats that had been dismasted by a sudden gale? That was, let me see... the summer of 1814, I believe. We were homeward bound from the West Indies. Anyway, we towed the ship back to St. John's, and their captain rewarded us with 250 pounds of fresh salmon and cod. Ambrosia, let me tell you! Ever since then, anytime I find myself anywhere in the area, I make it a point to stop and stock up. Well, now that I know how you feel, I can well imagine the wardroom will be very glad you are here."

"Why is that, sir?"

Norman looked out over the rolling Atlantic swells as a faint smile grew on his face. "Let's just say your predecessor neglected the wardroom during our stopovers. It seems he didn't like fish."

Brewer grinned. "Yes, I've been told."

Norman looked up in surprise. "Oh?"

"Yes, sir," Brewer said. "The subject came up during dinner a few days ago."

The captain smiled. "I can well imagine. Was Mr. Barton in attendance?"

"Yes, sir."

"And what did he say?"

"We took up a collection, and he said he would do his best for us."

Norman nodded. "I'm sure he will do well by the wardroom. He takes very good care of the crew. Let me know if he needs more money."

"Thank you, sir."

"Not at all, glad to do it," Norman looked around to make sure everything was in order. "Very well, Mr. Brewer, all looks good. I have paperwork to catch up on. Call me if there is something that needs my attention."

"Aye aye, sir," Brewer said. They saluted, and Captain Norman went back to his quarters.

"Well," Greene said, "that went better than I thought it would. Tell me, Mr. Brewer, have you figured him out yet?"

Brewer looked over in surprise. "Excuse me?"

"The captain. One day he's vicious to Phillips, and the next he's nice as pie to us. It's almost as if he were two different people."

"He's the captain," Brewer said, somewhat sternly, "that's all we need to know. As for Mr. Phillips, you already know what's going on there. Has he said anything to you about it yet?"

Greene shook his head. "He came around yesterday and watched me exercise one division of guns, but he didn't say anything to me."

"Very well, Mr. Greene. You may carry on."

Greene saluted and left Brewer to consider his captain again. A captain who could range from being cruel to smiling and cheerful so easily and seemingly without provocation could turn out to be difficult to please, but he was still the captain.

CHAPTER 7

"Masthead!" the captain called, "let's hear you!"

The lookout peered through the mist for several minutes scanning back and forth across the harbor. They hadn't run into a fishing boat at sea before now, which was not really unusual, but it meant that the captain would have to put in to the harbor. Finally, he was satisfied and leaned over to make his report.

"Looks like they're in port, sir!"

"Well, that's a start," Norman said to no one in particular. "Now to find out if we have to wait."

Brewer scanned the harbor and saw dozens of large fishing boats at anchor. The *Defiant* was about to enter the harbor at St. John's, Newfoundland. Brewer noted the captain had sent one of the senior hands to the maintop to spy out the harbor. Normally, senior hands would consider it a punishment to be sent to such duty, but Brewer noticed that the hand jumped to it quickly enough.

"Very well, let's get on with it," Captain Norman said. "Mr. Phillips, take us in." At the same time, he shot a warning look at Brewer, and the message was clear—Stay out.

But Brewer wasn't worried. For the past two weeks, Mr. Sweeney and he had been going over this procedure again and again until poor Phillips was afraid of saying the steps in his sleep. This was Brewer's first visit to the New World, but Mr. Sweeney knew these waters like the back of his hand and so was able to prepare young Phillips for whatever he might face. In the end, Mr. Phillips learned his lesson well, for *Defiant* glided gracefully to the anchorage assigned her and dropped anchor. Captain Norman turned to Brewer and Sweeney standing off to the side.

"Well done, gentlemen," he said. Both men nodded their thanks as Mr. Phillips came up to report.

"Ship secure at anchor, sir," he said as he saluted.

"You are progressing well, Mr. Phillips," the captain said. "I have been watching you, and I am very impressed with how quickly you have become proficient with your duties. I know how hard the first lieutenant and Mr. Sweeney have been driving you, and it is a testament to your strength of character that you have not only survived but excelled. You're entrance into this crowded harbor was well done; I doubt I could have done any better myself. The only fault I might find with the whole thing was that you were a little slow about it."

Phillips looked a bit shocked to hear this after all the praise his captain just heaped on him. "Slow, sir?"

"Yes," Norman said as he nodded toward the fishing boats. "You were keeping me from my supper." Then he looked at the boats again and raised his eyebrows in resignation and said, "At least, I hope to purchase it here, anyway."

The officers smiled in relief, and Phillips let out the breath he was holding.

"Mr. Tyler!" the captain called. "Signal as many of the fishing fleet as necessary to see if anyone has some fresh salmon or cod to sell."

"Aye aye, sir!" Tyler ran off to carry out his task. Fifteen minutes later he was back.

"Eleven replies so far, sir, all saying about the same thing. The fish remaining on the couple that have any left is several days old. The fleet is due to sail again tomorrow."

Norman frowned and sighed at the unwelcome news. "Just our luck," he muttered. "Any boats still out?"

"Two, sir," Tyler said. "They became separated from the others in a squall."

"Well, let's hope they return soon," Norman said. "Mr. Brewer, please have the cooper bring the water casks on deck for filling and tell Mr. Barton he may proceed with his usual duties in port."

"Aye aye, sir," Brewer said and touched his hat. He turned to Mr. Greene. "Would you please call the bosun and cooper and see that they comply with the captain's wishes?" Greene saluted and left.

Captain Norman looked back through the harbor entrance and across the open sea beyond. "Let's keep our eyes open for those two ships. If and when they appear, we want to be their *first* customer."

"Aye aye, sir," Brewer said. "I'll note it on the log board while we're in port."

"Yes, do that," Norman agreed. "I'm going to my cabin, Mr. Brewer. Call me if I'm needed."

"Aye aye, sir."

Brewer posted two lookouts to the mizzen top to watch for those ships and then went to his own cabin. They were very close to the main British base in this area at Halifax, so there was an excellent chance of being able to send letters back to England. Brewer had several ready, and he wanted to fetch them and give them to the captain's clerk, who acted as the unofficial postman on board. Once this was done, Brewer returned to his cabin again, this time hoping to catch a few hours sleep before dinner. He was foiled by a stifling heat that seemed to come out of nowhere. He tried to read, hoping the combination of a good book and the gentle rocking of a ship in harbor would do the trick, but after an hour he had to close the book and admit defeat. He heard the ship's bell ring eight bells in the forenoon watch, so he stepped out to the gun room for dinner. Everyone was there with the exception of Mr. Barton, who was ashore trying to get fresh supplies for the ship.

"Any sign of the missing ships yet?" Brewer asked as the soup course was served.

"No, sir," repled Mr. Phillips.

"Mr. Sweeney," Brewer queried, "if we should have to wait for these vessels to return with their catch, how long are we looking at?"

"No more than a week, I should think," Sweeney said. "We stayed for a month once, during the wars, but I don't think the captain would try that nowadays. Let's hope we run into one of them quickly."

Brewer sighed. "Well, we'll just have to hope for the best. At least we don't have to worry about the French anymore."

Johnson looked up. "What about pirates?"

That caught Brewer's attention. "Pirates?" he said. "This far north? I've never heard of any."

"It's rare," Sweeney answered, "but it has happened. Edward Teach—Blackbeard, remember?—he used to come up occasionally to try to catch a British packet sailing alone, but usually pirates don't venture any farther north than the coasts of the Carolinas."

Phillips looked up. "What happens if we meet one?"

Brewer smiled. "We blow it out of the water." The grins around the table told him he was not wrong.

There was a knock at the wardroom door, and Mr. Short came in.

"Pardon me, sir," he said to Brewer, "but Mr. Tyler sends his respects. There's a sail on the horizon, and it appears to be heading for the harbor. Could be one of the missing fishermen, sir."

"Very well," Brewer said. "My compliments to Mr. Tyler. He is to watch the sail and inform me as soon as he's sure."

"Aye aye, sir," Mr. Short saluted and was gone.

The meal ended without much more conversation, and one by one the participants rose and filtered out until there remained only Brewer and Mr. Phillips at the table.

"Well, Mr. Phillips," Brewer inquired, "How is your schooling progressing?"

"Well enough, sir," Phillips answered. "Mr. Sweeney says I'm getting better at ship handling."

"I agree, you are improving by the day. Just be careful not to lower your guard, John, you must be watchful every second."

Phillips nodded. "I will take care, Mr. Brewer."

Brewer smiled. "Fine, Mr. Phillips. Is there anything you need to speak to me about, regarding your schooling, I mean? Any questions?"

Phillips shook his head. "No, sir."

"Very well," Brewer said. He began to rise when there was another knock at the door, and Mr. Short entered.

"Beg pardon, sir," the midshipman said. "Mr. Tyler's respects, sir; he says he believes the new sail is one of the missing fishermen."

Brewer rose. "I will come up immediately. Inform the captain, Mr. Short. Mr. Phillips, you're with me."

Brewer and Phillips managed to make it on deck and sight the new sail before the captain arrived.

"Where away, Mr. Brewer?" Norman asked as he accepted a glass and brought it to his eye.

"There, sir. Still hull-down."

The captain took a moment to focus. "We may be in luck, gentlemen. The sails look right, but it's hard to tell at this distance."

An hour later, the vessel was confirmed as one of the missing boats. Signals flew back and forth between *Defiant* and the fishing boat as Captain Norman dickered and haggled to get the best price for the freshest catch. Brewer and Greene stood off to the side, watching for the first time what the veterans of *Defiant* were no doubt used to: Captain Norman with the glass to his eye, watching the fisherman approach, Mr. Tyler racing to raise the captain's signal and then hurrying back with the reply. Finally, the captain lowered the glass and nodded, and from the look on Tyler's face as he ran off, Brewer knew the deal was done.

Captain Norman handed his glass to a sailor to put up for him and walked over toward Brewer and Greene with a look of intense satisfaction on his face. Brewer hoped it meant good news for the gun room as well.

"Success, sir?" Brewer asked.

"Yes, Mr. Brewer," Norman said as he rubbed his hands together in anticipation. "I have sent word for the cook and his mates to be ready; we dine on North Atlantic salmon tonight! Don't worry, gentlemen, I instructed Mr. Barton to make sure the gun room gets its fair share."

"Thank you, sir," Brewer said. He noticed that Greene looked relieved.

The captain hardly had to give an order when the fishing vessel dropped anchor barely a cable's length away. Two boats from *Defiant* were in the water and pulling toward the new arrival quicker than Brewer had ever seen it done. The first arrival back at *Defiant* was greeted with cheers, and nobody had to give the order for the first barrels to be taken straight to the cook. *Defiant* bought slightly more than half of the vessel's haul. As the purser was still ashore, Brewer sent Greene over on the last run to buy two additional barrels for the wardroom with money he had collected from the various officers.

That night, after supper, Brewer went up on deck to take a stroll before turning in. Everywhere he looked, he saw a happy, contented crew, apart from the occasional oddity—the sailor who did not like fish for his supper. It was one of the marvels of peacetime, he decided, that the crew of a King's ship could relax in a friendly port after filling their bellies with a favorite meal provided by their captain's beneficence. He hoped it wasn't the last time he would get to see it.

Defiant stayed three days at St. John's before putting to sea. They put in at the British base at Halifax, Nova Scotia, to drop off mail and see if there were any dispatches needing to be transported. A fast packet had passed through two days before, and there was mail for *Defiant*. Brewer got two letters from his mother, four from his sister, and one from Captain Bush. There was also a diplomatic packet which Captain Norman had to sign for to be delivered to the British ambassador in Washington City.

Brewer just had time to dash quick notes off to his mother, sister, and Bush saying he was well and that he would write back soon. He barely got the letters to the boat in time before the captain ordered *Defiant* under way. Mr. Phillips was called to warp the ship out of the harbor, which he did in a very acceptable fashion, thanks to practice and coaching by Brewer and Sweeney. Captain Norman congratulated Phillips publicly on his maneuver, and then he turned to Brewer and smiled.

"And congratulations to you as well, Mr. Brewer," he said.

"What for, sir?"

"It seems you have learned to play the game quite well, Mr. Brewer," he said as he stepped past the first lieutenant. "Set course for Boston, if you please. I will be in my cabin."

"Aye aye, sir," Brewer said, a bit confused, until he looked up to see Mr. Sweeney grinning from ear to ear, and then he smiled as well. "Mr. Greene, set course for Boston."

Brewer went down to his cabin, eager for a chance to read his mail. The letters from his mother and sister were pretty much what he had come to expect. They spoke of the farm, the town folk in their part of the county, and reported that his father was in good health. His mother wrote that his younger brother Benjamin was doing very well running the farm and that they expected to get a good price for their crop this year. She also wrote of how proud she was of Brewer, keeping them safe and the sea lanes open. His sister wrote that their father still forbade any mention of his name and how she hoped he would find a way to come home one day to be reconciled with him before he died. She also mentioned a certain young man from the village, lately hired as a laborer on the farm, who was paying her a great deal of attention. Brewer shook his head at the news; he would have to warn her to be careful.

Bush's letter was a revelation. He mentioned that he had purchased a cottage on the outskirts of Smallbridge, where Lord Hornblower was the local squire. He reported Lady Barbara Hornblower and her son Richard to be in good health.

Most of Bush's letter was a recounting of a recent visit to the Admiralty in London, where he had several friends on the staff. He stopped in to see them and found one, a man named Stamford, on duty and with a moment to spare, so Bush asked him about one Captain James Norman of His Majesty's frigate *Defiant*. Stamford went and checked Admiralty files for Bush, and he came back with an interesting story to tell. Norman was indeed assigned as a junior lieutenant aboard *Victory* at Trafalgar, but the file contained no confirmation that Norman avenged Nelson Bush asked about this in particular. Stamford thought it unlikely; Lt. Norman's action station was the lower gun deck. Norman had assumed command of *HMS Defiant* in

December, 1812, since which time he'd acquitted himself well in action against Napoleon's forces, taking several prizes over the years.

Before this current voyage, Bush wrote, *Defiant* was brought in for a scheduled refit minus the first officer, whom Norman transferred off the ship. Norman was called to London for an explanation, and while there he arranged for his second lieutenant, surgeon, and chaplain to be transferred off as well. No explanation was noted in the file, which meant that verbal arguments made by Norman to the Admiralty were persuasive. There was, however, a note in Norman's file about a medical report filed by the discarded surgeon, but Stamford was unable to produce the report.

Bush concluded his letter by telling Brewer what he already knew—to be on his guard around Norman. Bush also asked to be remembered to Admiral Hornblower when *Defiant* reached the Caribbean.

Brewer sat back and considered Bush's letter carefully. If nothing else, it confirmed his opinion that Norman could be extremely dangerous in the wrong circumstances. Brewer dropped the sealed letter on his desk and stared out the window. There was probably more than one man who sat around the gun room table who could tell him the whole story of the previous officers—Sweeney, for example, knew more than he was telling—but Brewer doubted he could ask any of them publicly without drawing the ire of the captain down upon himself as well as on them. He would have to be very careful to probe discreetly.

A knock at the door interrupted his thoughts. "Enter," he said.

Young Mr. Short opened the door. "Mr. Sweeney's respects, sir, and would you please come up on deck?"

"Yes, I'll come," Brewer said. He picked up his hat and followed the midshipman on deck. He saw Mr. Sweeney standing by the lee rail talking with Mr. Greene and headed over to join them.

"Good morning," Brewer said. "You wanted to see me, Mr. Sweeney?"

"Yes, sir," the master said. "This is your first trip to American waters, isn't that so, sir?"

"Yes, that's right."

Sweeney nodded. "There are certain, shall we say, peculiarities in dealing with the American coastline that are found nowhere else in the world. I propose to call both Mr. Greene and especially Mr. Phillips every time we encounter one so they can learn how to deal with them."

"Agreed," Brewer said. "Call me as well, Mr. Sweeney; I need to know, too."

Sweeney smiled. "I was hoping you'd say that, sir."

Mr. Greene saluted. "If you'll excuse me, sir, I would like to exercise the men aloft."

Brewer nodded. "Carry on, Mr. Greene."

Sweeney watched Mr. Greene make his way forward. "So," he said quietly, "it looks like you might finally be in the captain's good graces, eh?"

Brewer did not look at him. "What do you mean?"

"The captain's congratulations."

"On playing the game well?"

"Exactly."

"Is that what this is, a game?"

"Of a kind, Mr. Brewer, of a kind, and one that your predecessor either could not or would not play. It cost him his position and quite possibly his career. You, on the other hand, accepted the challenge and met it. That's the kind of officer that James Norman can respect and deal with. Just remember one piece of advice: don't lower your guard, no matter what happens, and not for a single instant."

Brewer sighed. "Sound advice, Mr. Sweeney."

CHAPTER 8

Boston, Massachusetts, presented itself as a town on the verge of becoming a major metropolis as *Defiant* glided into the harbor and rendered her salute. After the usual health clearance check, a pilot was sent out to guide the big frigate to a berth and afterwards stayed aboard for a drink or two at the captain's table. Brewer watched as Captain Norman brought him back on deck and saw him off. The captain looked lost in thought as he wandered over to where Brewer was standing with Sweeney and Greene.

"Well," the captain said after they saluted, "that was a waste of good port."

"How so, sir?" Brewer asked as the others smiled.

"That gentleman knew nothing of the American navy," Norman said. "All he could tell me was that *Constitution* pulled out three days ago, but he had no idea where she was going. A bloody genius! Mr. Tyler!"

Tyler came running and skidded to a halt in front of his captain. "Yes, sir?"

"Do not run so, Mr. Tyler. Find Mr. Short. I want the two of you in the tops. I want to know every warship in harbor. Take a glass each."

"Aye aye, sir!" Tyler saluted and went off, calling for Short and grabbing two telescopes along the way. Brewer watched him go and tried to remember a time when he had that much energy.

"Mr. Brewer," the Captain said, "I must go pay my respects ashore. As soon as I return, how do you feel about a little scouting trip?"

Brewer smiled. "I was hoping you would ask, sir."

"Good. Take Mr. Phillips with you. Be back aboard by midnight. Both of you can breakfast with me tomorrow and give me your report, although, if our good pilot is anything to go by, I don't know that there's a lot to learn!"

And so, after Captain Norman returned from what he called "a thoroughly boring waste of time ashore", Brewer called away the launch and was soon sitting in the stern sheets beside Mr. Phillips, as the coxswain manned the tiller and guided the craft through a maze of merchant shipping toward the dock. Brewer was surprised at how busy the port was; he stopped counting ships after seeing large merchantmen from ten different nations. He wasn't sure what he expected from Boston, but it wasn't this. He'd always pictured Boston as one of the small fishing villages he was familiar with along the coast of Kent, but this place was close to rivaling Plymouth or Southampton!

The boat reached the dock, and Brewer and Phillips walked down the wharf and into the town. They turned into a tavern called The Red Lion Inn and took a booth in the corner. The proprietor ambled over to greet them.

"Greetings, gentlemen," he said.

"Give us two pints of your best ale," Brewer said.

"Coming right up, Lieutenant," he said and was gone.

"They seem friendly enough," Phillips said.

"Friendly?" Brewer said. "What did you expect? Savages?"

Phillips blushed as the innkeeper returned with their

drinks.

"Sir," Brewer said to the innkeeper, "my friend and I have a problem. We have just come across the North Atlantic on a King's ship, which as you might imagine is not renowned for the quality of its cuisine. We are in desperate need of being reminded what good food tastes like. Can you help us?"

The patron grinned broadly. "Lieutenants, you have come to the right place! You are a little early for the dinner hour, but I think we can take care of you. You stay right there and let me remind you!"

Brewer took a drink of his ale and sat back to await his meal. Phillips just looked from the retreating proprietor to Brewer and back again, not really sure what was going on or what to expect. Brewer winked at him, so Phillips just sat back, drank his ale, and waited.

The innkeeper returned in a few minutes with plates and silver for both of them. He begged a few moments more indulgence and disappeared again into the kitchen. He returned barely thirty seconds later, a platter on one arm and a large tray in the opposite hand with three large, steaming bowls on it. He set the tray on the edge of the table, and Phillips' eyes opened wide when he saw the bowls contained peas, carrots, and potatoes. Then the proprietor set the platter down, and Brewer saw it was heaped with thick veal chops covered in brown gravy. It smelled absolutely heavenly!

"This should do for a start, eh, lieutenant?" he said. "You just signal when you want something more. Tell me, did you just arrive from merry old England?"

"Yes, we did," Phillips answered. "Why do you ask?"

"Be right back," he said and ran off.

Phillips looked at Brewer and shrugged.

He came right back with two tall glasses of lemonade. "I was in the navy during the last war," he said, "and I remember what scurvy can do. Drink up, gentlemen, you can never have too much!"

Brewer lifted his glass, and young Phillips did the same. Together they toasted their host and drank down the lemonade in a single draught. The proprietor nodded and left them to their meal.

The two officers dug in with abandon, helping themselves to huge servings of everything. The meal was as good as anything either had ever tasted, even at the best inns in Plymouth or Portsmouth. They were just finishing off the last of the chops and potatoes when the innkeeper appeared with a loaf of bread, which both men used to sop up the excess gravy and juices left on their plates.

The next time the innkeeper appeared, he brought two more pints of ale as well as a platter that held a huge roast of beef and a roast chicken along with another loaf of bread. Both men cut generous portions for their plates and dug in with renewed gusto. When their plates were empty, both officers sat back and sighed, satisfied as they had not been for many months.

The proprietor walked up to them with a smile on his face. "I see you remember now, eh, lieutenant?"

Brewer sighed. "In truth, my good man, I do not *ever* remember eating a finer meal in my life!"

"Hear! Hear!" said Phillips.

"Thank you, sirs, thank you," the innkeeper said as he bowed. "Always glad for compliments from a navy man."

Brewer spoke up. "So, where is the American navy? My brother was rescued by one of your frigates when his ship went down, and I wanted to say thanks."

Phillips knew this was a lie, but he listened carefully.

"Which frigate?" the innkeeper asked.

"*Constitution.*"

"Oh, you just missed her," the innkeeper said. "Went out looking for more pirates, I wager."

"Pirates?" Phillips said. "This far north?"

"Sure," the innkeeper said. "Why, three of 'em was just executed a week or so ago."

"I had no idea," Phillips said. "We must tell the captain!"

Brewer silenced the young lieutenant with a look, and then he said to the innkeeper, "I'm sure they can do the job."

The two men settled the bill and walked out into the street. Brewer noticed the ale was making young Phillips a bit unsteady on his feet.

"You'd better return to the ship," he said. "I want to find a bookseller before I return."

"Aye aye, sir," Phillips said and turned toward the wharf.

Satisfied that Phillips was well on his way back to the ship, Brewer decided to explore the town in search of a bookseller's shop. He ran into a peddler who was kind enough to give him directions to one just a street or two over, and after thanking the man with a coin he set off in search of his destination.

Brewer strolled down the street and was mildly amused at the reactions he drew from the various passers-by. Those who were old enough to have lived during the American Revolution looked at his uniform with disdain and edged away from him whenever possible. To the younger men he was a curiosity, while the younger women looked at him like something out of a dream.

He found the bookseller right where the peddler said it would be, and after perusing the selections in the window, Brewer went inside. The bookseller spoke cheerfully to him as he closed the door behind him.

"Always glad to see the Royal Navy!" he said. "What can I do for you today, *left*enant?"

"Good day to you, my good man," Brewer said. "I understand there is a biography of George Washington that was recently published. I am hoping to purchase a copy, if I may?"

"You're in luck, Leftenant," the bookseller said as he slapped the counter, "we just got that shipment in yesterday."

He retrieved the volume from the back room, and Brewer paid him for it. Brewer thought the price was a trifle high but decided not to say anything. More customers entered the store, and the bookseller went to assist them, leaving Brewer to look over his purchase.

"Are you an admirer of General Washington?"

Brewer turned to find an old man standing beside him. He was stooped by the years, and a pair of spectacles was pushed high on his forehead. He had a serious look on his gnarled face, and his head was almost tilted sideways as he looked up at Brewer with squinted eyes. Brewer wondered if the squint was due to the old man's age or his own uniform.

"Yes, yes I am," Brewer said. He turned to the old man and put out his hand. "Lieutenant William Brewer, first lieutenant on His Majesty's frigate *Defiant*."

The old man eyed him for just a moment before taking Brewer's hand in one of his gnarled ones and pumping it once.

"Pleased to make your acquaintance," he said. "I was not aware that General Washington was held in such high esteem by our British cousins."

Brewer colored a bit. "I could not say, sir; I understood him to be a man of integrity who persevered against impossible odds and not only won his nation's independence but also went on to mold a nation out of thirteen individual colonies. To my mind, such a man, and the others who did it with him, should be studied and imitated by all."

The old man looked at him with a different attitude now, and Brewer wondered if by chance he may have known Washington. The old man nodded and smiled.

"Very true," he said. "I agree with you, sir. Men like General Washington should be studied and imitated by all who aspire to greatness."

Brewer looked at him and asked, "Pardon me, sir, but did you by chance know General Washington?"

The old man smiled. "Yes," he said, "I knew General Washington—quite well, in fact—and he was every inch the sort of man a young man like yourself should study and emulate."

Brewer bowed. "Sir, it is indeed my honor to meet you. Were you among the men who helped the general?"

The old man nodded with a cryptic smile, as though reliving a private joke. "Yes, you could say that. I was there, in the Congress, when he was appointed commander-in-chief of the continental army. I visited him several times at his army headquarters, and I was there when he was inaugurated as the first President of these United States."

Brewer's eyes grew wide, which seemed to amuse the stranger even more. "Sir," Brewer said, "I wish I had the time to hear all about it!"

The old man's eyes narrowed. "And why should a First Lieutenant in His Majesty's Royal Navy be interested in hearing about General Washington?"

Brewer sighed and looked around for a moment to gather his thoughts. He did not want to start an argument with this old man; if Washington actually did even half of what was claimed, he should be honored and toasted by history. Finally, he turned back to the old man.

"I fought against Bonaparte's forces as a midshipman. Later on, when I met him, I thought he might not have been as terrible a despot as I'd always heard, but of course he was. From what I've heard, Washington was everything Bonaparte was not. Washington fought for liberty and then led his nation as president, not dictator. That's why."

The old man's eyes narrowed still further, as though he was trying to decide whether Brewer was being truthful or not. Then a grin broke out across his face, and he smiled.

"Good answer, Lieutenant. When do you have to be back aboard ship?"

"Midnight. Why do you ask?"

They were interrupted by the arrival of another man who was roughly Brewer's age.

"Father, are you ready to..." the new arrival stopped as he realized what was going on. "Oh! I'm sorry, Father!"

"My son, Thomas," the old man said by way of introduction. "Thomas, this is Lieutenant Brewer of the Royal Navy. I was just about to invite him to join us for supper."

"A wonderful idea, Father!" Thomas looked to Brewer. "The inn where we are staying is just around the corner."

Brewer nodded. "I accept."

"Excellent!" said the old man. "Thomas, do you have our books?"

"Right here, Father," Thomas said as he led the old man out. Brewer followed right after them.

"What books did you get?" Brewer asked.

"Actually, the same as you," the old man said as he set out at a healthy pace that belied his age. *Obviously a man used to taking walks,* Brewer thought.

"Why would you do that when you knew him so well?" Brewer asked.

"To see if this author knows what he is talking about," the old man said over his shoulder. "General Washington is no longer around to protect his own reputation; therefore it falls to those of us who remain alive to do it for him, if necessary."

Brewer nodded and prayed God would grant him friends like this after he was gone.

They walked into the inn and sat down at a table in the corner of the dining room. The waiter came over immediately.

"I'm sorry, sir," he said to the old man, "but there will be a very slight delay with supper. Would you care for coffee while you wait?"

"Yes, thank you, George," the old man said, and the waiter hurried away and returned carrying a tray with three steaming cups. After the waiter departed, the old man leaned forward and tapped the table with a stubby forefinger.

"Pardon me, Lieutenant, but I want to make sure I understood you. Did you say you actually *met* Bonaparte?"

Brewer savored his coffee before replying, "Yes, sir."

The old man's eyes narrowed again. "May I ask where?"

Brewer set his cup on the table. "On the island of St. Helena."

"Ah," the old man said as he sat back and nodded. "In what capacity?"

"I was secretary and personal aide to the governor, Lord Horatio Hornblower."

"I see," the other said as he leaned forward to take up his own steaming cup.

Brewer leaned forward to seize the initiative. "Tell me about General Washington. What made him different? What enabled him to succeed against such overwhelming odds?"

The old man leaned back and looked off into the distance, obviously reliving an earlier time of great glory. "What made him different? I have often tried over the years to put my finger on exactly what it was that made General Washington different from the rest of us, but I fear I have never quite succeeded in nailing it down. Certainly he had certain physical attributes in his favor. He was always the tallest, most imposing figure in the room. Exposure to smallpox when he was young left him immune to that disease that carried off so many of his troops at Valley Forge and other places. His physical strength itself was formidable.

"But somehow when I consider all these assets, they do not explain what made the man what he was. And the more I think it over, the more I come to the conclusion that it was simply the character of George Washington that allowed him to do what he did. He had a faith and convictions that he lived by, and he lived by them with an iron will. Once he made up his mind, that was it. But to be fair to him, he would change his mind if he was presented with compelling arguments to do so.

"Faith, sir," the old man said, tapping the table with his finger for emphasis, "faith and convictions, and the fortitude to follow them."

The old man sat back and smiled. The waiter took advantage of the moment to bring their meal. Brewer was pleased to see a wonderful vegetable soup followed by a roast chicken and corn, and for desert a peach cobbler, which the old man pointed out was the specialty of the house. They ate more or less in silence, with the old man or his son occasionally asking a question about his service during the wars or life at sea in general. Thomas asked one about his time on St. Helena with Bonaparte, but Brewer dodged it by taking interest in a chicken leg.

When the meal was over, the waiter cleared the table and brought more coffee. The old man relaxed in his chair and pulled a cigar from a pocket inside his waistcoat. He offered it to Brewer, who accepted graciously, and pulled another out for himself. As if by prior agreement or long-standing custom, Thomas rose and excused himself.

"Forgive me, Lieutenant," he said, "but I must make sure all is in readiness for our trip back to Quincy in the morning. It was a pleasure meeting you, sir." Thomas bowed to Brewer and turned to his father. "With your permission, I shall be in our rooms."

The old man nodded. "Thank you, Thomas. I shall be along presently."

Thomas kissed his father on the head and nodded to Brewer as he left the dining room and went up the stairs to their rooms. Brewer watched him go and turned to the old man.

"A good son, that," he said.

The old man nodded. "The strength of my old age."

Brewer nodded and lit his cigar. He inhaled deeply and leaned his head back to blow clouds of lovely blue smoke at the ceiling. He looked down to find the old man watching him.

"So, tell me," Brewer said, "what's it like to build a nation?"

The old man puffed on his cigar. "What do you mean, sir?"

Brewer smiled. "I don't imagine General Washington did it alone."

The old man laughed, and blew a large cloud heavenward. He took his cigar between his first and second fingers and pointed at Brewer with it.

"You are right, sir," he said. "The men who assembled at the Continental Congress and then at the Constitutional Convention were walking a road never before traveled in human history. To create a republic! Ideas were debated, and men reasoned with each other and compromised in order to form a new government. General Washington was the glue that held it all together in the early days, that is true. We wanted a government of laws, not men, and we have one, now. Washington guided us through getting the constitution written and putting it into practice."

"And were you there then?"

"You mean while the constitution was being written? No, I'm afraid I was out of the country at the time."

Brewer drank coffee while his companion puffed on his cigar, each lost in his own thoughts. Finally, the old man tapped the ash from his cigar, looked at Brewer, and smiled.

"Did you really meet Bonaparte?"

Brewer smiled behind his coffee cup and said not a word.

"What was he like?"

Brewer looked at the old man and sighed. *Well,* he thought, *I do owe him for supper.*

Brewer sat back in his chair and told the old man all about meeting Bonaparte. The old man responded in kind by telling Brewer all about personal audiences he had with Louis XVI and George III. Brewer found himself totally carried away by the stories his companion told, and he was surprised when Thomas reappeared and told his father it was nearly eleven.

"Bless my soul, so it is," the old man said after checking his pocket watch. "Lieutenant, I'm afraid I must bid you a good night. I must get to bed, it seems, and you must return to your ship. I very much regret we are leaving for Quincy at first light; I should love to tour your ship otherwise."

"Perhaps in the future, sir," Brewer said with a nod. The old man and Thomas bid him good night and farewell, and Brewer watched Thomas help his father up the stairs to their rooms.

On his way out the door, the innkeeper bid him farewell, and Brewer took the opportunity to ask the identity of the old man.

"You don't know?" the innkeeper said in surprise. "That was John Adams! He signed the Declaration of Independence, he was our ambassador to France and England, and elected the second President of the United States!"

Brewer stared wide-eyed at the staircase. John Adams! No wonder he knew so much!

"Good Lord," Brewer murmured, as he walked out into the night.

"Amen," said the innkeeper.

CHAPTER 9

Brewer was only mildly surprised the next morning to find Lieutenant Phillips waiting for him outside the captain's door when he arrived for their scheduled breakfast appointment. The boy leaned against the corridor wall, completely ignored by the marine sentry.

"Good morning, Mr. Phillips," he said.

"Good morning, sir."

"Ready?"

The boy nodded and straightened his uniform.

"Right," Brewer said. He nodded to the sentry and knocked on the door.

"Enter" came from within.

Brewer opened the door and entered. Phillips followed and closed the door behind them. Captain Norman was sitting at his desk, writing in his log. Across the room, Brewer noticed the table was laid with service for three.

"Please bear with me, gentlemen," the captain said without looking up, "but I wish to finish this entry. Be with you in a minute."

Norman's pen scratched across the page for another

minute or so before he stopped. He blotted the entry and closed the book. He rose and came round the desk to shake hands with his two lieutenants, and he led the way to the table. The lieutenants sat as soon as their captain was settled.

"Jenkins!" the captain called, and the servant appeared in the pantry door. "We are ready to begin."

The servant disappeared back into the pantry, and Captain Norman turned back to his companions.

"Well," he said, "I hope you gentlemen had a productive time ashore yesterday."

"I'm afraid we'll have to settle for 'interesting', sir," Brewer said. "We checked several taverns but gathered almost nothing in the way of useful intelligence. We were able to confirm that *Constitution* went to sea a few days ago, probably to hunt for pirates."

Norman was surprised at that. "Pirates, Mr. Brewer?"

"Yes, sir. One innkeeper told us three men convicted of piracy were executed less than a month ago."

Norman sat back to consider this as Jenkins and his mates placed several bowls on the table and poured coffee for each officer before withdrawing.

"Begin, gentlemen, please," the captain said as he leaned forward again. "After you left yesterday, I sent Mr. Barton ashore with orders to lay up for us a typical American breakfast. Those are scrambled eggs before you, Mr. Phillips. We also have rashers of bacon, sausages, ham steaks, and potatoes, along with cider, which Jenkins will be bringing us shortly. Good health to you."

The three partook with relish of the food before them, and every man had seconds. Brewer decided the silence that reigned during the meal was proof that the Americans knew what they were doing where breakfast was concerned.

When the meal was over, the stewards cleared the plates away while Jenkins poured them more coffee. Captain Norman sat back in his chair at the end of the table, deep in thought. As Jenkins finished and withdrew, the captain lspoke.

"I've been thinking about the intelligence you brought back," he said. "The execution of those pirates. It certainly explains why three frigates have been through this port in the last month."

"Three?" asked Phillips.

"*Constitution, President,* and *United States*," said the captain.

Brewer turned to the captain. "That's a lot of firepower this far north for just pirates."

"My thoughts exactly, Mr. Brewer," Norman said. "After you left, we scanned the harbor, but the only military craft belonged to the harbor patrol. The harbor master's office didn't know anything, either—about those three frigates, anyway."

"So," Brewer asked, "what's our next move, sir?"

Norman sighed. "At this moment, Mr. Greene is ashore with Mr. Short to try his hand at snooping, as it were; they have orders to be back aboard by noon. Unless they bring me something substantial—and I think this unlikely—*Defiant* will sail with the evening tide. It seems the packet we picked up at Halifax is too important to delay for long. In fact, I was given orders not to stay at Boston longer than three days."

"Aye aye, sir," Brewer said.

"By the way, Mr. Brewer," Captain Norman said, "what happened to you after you sent Mr. Phillips here back to the ship to... *sleep it off*, shall we say?"

Phillips turned a dark red, and Brewer jumped to his defense. "I assure you, sir—"

Norman waved them both off. "At ease, *Lieutenant*; I know what you did, and I know why you did it, and believe it or not, I approve. Now get on with what happened to you afterward."

Brewer shot Phillips a look meant to reassure him, then

he looked back to his captain. "Not much, sir. I got directions to a bookseller's shop, because I wanted to get a biography of their General George Washington that's recently been published. Whilst I was there, I fell into conversation with an old man who claimed to be an acquaintance of Washington's. Said he was there when he was appointed to head their army during their revolution and that he was also there when Washington was made president. He told me of audiences he had had with George III and also Louis XVI. I did not find out who he was until after he had gone up to bed. The innkeeper told me it was John Adams, who was among other things Washington's successor as second President of the United States."

Captain Norman stared at Brewer as he finished his tale. *How like Brewer,* he thought, *to actually meet one of the great men of the American Revolution. Probably told him all about Bonaparte. Why him?*

Norman finally looked away and said, "Too bad he didn't know anything about those frigates."

Brewer was on deck when Lieutenant Greene arrived back aboard only minutes before noon and went immediately to the captain's cabin to report. Within minutes, Brewer heard his name being shouted across the deck. He turned to find Mr. Short running toward him. He managed to skid to a halt without injuring himself or anyone else. Mr. Sweeney turned to inspect the waves so the boy would not see him smile.

"Mr. Short," the first lieutenant said, "young gentlemen are expected to conduct themselves as officers. We do not run across the deck, and we do not shout so."

"I'm sorry, sir," Short saluted. "The captain presents his compliments, and could you please come to his cabin, sir?"

"Of course, Mr. Short," Brewer said. "Carry on."

Brewer went directly to the captain's cabin. He found Greene standing at ease, and the captain looking out the stern window. He turned when he heard Brewer enter the cabin.

"Ah, there you are, William," Norman said. "Our Mr. Greene brings news."

"About those frigates or the pirates?" Brewer asked.

"Neither," Norman said as he moved to his desk. "Sit down, gentlemen. Now, Mr. Greene, tell Mr. Brewer what you just told me."

"Well, sir," Greene said, "Mr. Short and I were walking along the docks when we overheard a snippet of a conversation, something about 120 guns, sir. We stopped and turned to find three men sitting off to the side, sir, one with a peg leg. Peg leg sees us and says, 'That's right, you limeys! I said *120 guns!* I guess that'll make you think twice on going to war with us again!'"

Norman turned to Brewer. "This is the first confirmation we've had of the rumors of the 120-gun first rate. Did peg-leg or his friends say where the ship was being built, Mr. Greene?"

Greene shook his head. "No, sir, not a word."

Norman thought for a moment. "Rumor has it at Philadelphia. I will inform our ambassador in Washington City to send a man up there to confirm it. In the meantime, William, we sail with the evening tide."

"Aye aye, sir," Brewer said as he stood, recognizing the dismissal in his captain's tone. Greene didn't catch it himself and hurried to stand as well. Both men had turned to go when the captain's voice stopped them.

"Mr. Greene?" Norman said. "Well done."

"Thank you, sir."

The two officers went up on deck. The afternoon sun threatened to make it unpleasant very soon. Brewer dismissed Mr. Greene to his duties and went to find Mr. Sweeney. He found him by the foremast, observing as one of his mates taught the midshipmen a class on spherical trigonometry. Not very successfully, either, from the looks on the students' faces.

"Trouble, Mr. Short?" Brewer asked as he walked up.

The young midshipman grimaced. "Two plus two is five, sir."

Brewer chuckled. "My advice to you, Mr. Short, is to lower your head and run as fast as you can into the mainmast. The resulting crack will bruise your brain so much that monstrosities like spherical trigonometry will make sense. At least, that's what did it for me." Brewer saw the shocked look on the boy's face and laughed. "Never fear, Mr. Short; I was only kidding. Stick to your studies and let the mainmast alone. Mr. Sweeney, may I speak to you for a moment?" The two men turned away, leaving some very relieved midshipmen behind them.

"The captain wants to sail on the evening tide," Brewer said as he walked alongside the sailing master, hands clasped behind his back.

Sweeney looked up at the flags flying from *Defiant*. "Wind looks like it will probably cooperate. Destination?"

"South. Washington City."

Sweeney nodded and looked straight ahead. "Mr. Phillips?"

Brewer halted, and the two men faced each other, volumes passing between them as they held each other's eyes.

"Possibly," Brewer said. "He has the first dog watch tonight."

Sweeney nodded and looked up at *Defiant's* yardarms. "I will go over the procedure with him this afternoon."

Brewer nodded. He looked both ways before leaning in close and lowering his voice. "Tell me something, Mr. Sweeney. What is the captain likely to do if Mr. Phillips continues to pass his little tests?"

Sweeney's eyes narrowed. "What do you mean, sir?"

Brewer stepped in close. "Oh, come along, man! You know exactly what I mean! What might the captain do? Pick a new target? Go after Phillips harder, or perhaps try to trick him into a display of anger? Come now, sailing master, you know the captain. *What might he do?*"

Sweeney looked hard at the first lieutenant. Brewer could see the muscles in the other's jaw clenching and unclenching as he tried to decide how to answer. Finally, Sweeney sighed and took a step back.

"I don't know what the captain will do, Mr. Brewer," he said in a voice that was low but nonetheless contained a hard edge. "I have enough to do keeping my own head out of the fire sometimes. Take it from me, so do you; I guarantee the captain hasn't forgotten how you helped Phillips before. I've been on this ship since she first commissioned, Mr. Brewer, and I honestly thought I had the captain figured out. But then *you* came along. You are the fourth first lieutenant since I've come aboard, and you're the first one I've ever heard the captain compliment as he did you with that 'playing the game well' comment. I have already warned you never to let down your guard. Now, that's the best I can do for you! Ask me no more, for I shall not answer!"

Brewer looked the sailing master hard in the eyes for a minute, then he looked away and sighed. "Very well, Mr. Sweeney, we'll let it go—for now, at least. You may carry on with Mr. Phillips."

Sweeney saluted stiffly and strode off without another word. Brewer watched him go and wondered if he had gone too far. Well, no matter now; the next few days would tell for sure.

The *Defiant* warped out of Boston harbor on schedule. Captain Norman came on deck, but he made no mention of Mr. Phillips. When it was reported that all hands were present and all was in readiness, the captain turned to his first lieutenant.

"Take her out, Mr. Brewer," he said, "if you please."

"Aye aye, sir," Brewer said. He was a little surprised by the captain's order but did his best not to show it. He turned to catch Mr. Sweeney's eye, and the sailing master shrugged. Brewer smiled and began issuing the orders that would take the ship out to sea.

The voyage south to Washington City was a period of intense training for all on board. The presence of pirates so far north forced Captain Norman to step up the gunnery and repel-borders drills much earlier than he had originally planned, and the crew of the *Defiant* responded marvelously. Competition between divisions became fierce to see who could reload the fastest or who was the quickest to clear for action. Brewer kept a close eye on both his junior lieutenants, but in the end there was no need. Lieutenant Greene performed well, and performance by his division rose steadily. Lieutenant Phillips was quickly catching on, and Mr. Peters kept his eye on him as well. The men under Phillips command seemed to know what was going on and discreetly let him know through Peters when something went amiss. Brewer smiled to himself and wondered how long their good luck would last.

It ended on their fifth night out of Boston. It was the middle of the night when Brewer was awakened by a knock on his door. A marine private opened the door and stuck his head in.

"Begging your pardon, sir," he said. "Mr. Peters sends his respects, and would you please come up on deck?"

Brewer sat up in his bunk. Peters? Where was Mr. Phillips? He briefly considered asking the private, but instead he decided to find out for himself.

"Yes, I'll come," he said, and the private retreated.

As soon as he set foot on deck, he was met by Mr. Peters. The petty officer was in a state of nearly overpowering anger mixed with severe anxiety.

"Thank God you've come, sir!" he said.

"Mr. Peters?" Brewer said. "What is going on? Where is Mr. Phillips?"

"That's why I sent for you, sir," Peters said. "Mr. Phillips found Johnston drunk on duty, sir, but when he went to write him up, Johnston threatened him, sir."

"Threatened him?" Brewer said. "Are you sure, Mr. Peters?"

"Well, no, sir, I'm not; I wasn't there. That's the way it was told me. Johnston said something like 'no wet-behind-the-ears brat is going to write me up' and then said something about putting Mr. Phillips over his knee and using the cane on 'im!"

Brewer frowned. "But you did not hear any of this yourself, Mr. Peters, is that correct?"

The petty officer nodded. "That's right, sir."

"Go on," Brewer said as both men moved forward.

"By this time, I heard the commotion and came running to find Lt. Phillips on the deck near the mainmast with Johnston standing over him. I ordered Johnston restrained and checked on Mr. Phillips."

Brewer turned at the pause. "And?"

Peters hesitated a moment more, then said quietly, "He didn't seem hurt, sir. He was sort of cowering down on the deck, all covered up, like. He was shaking something awful, and he kept whispering 'Not again. Not again' over and over. That's when I sent for you, sir."

Brewer nodded. "Show me."

"This way, sir," Peters said as he led the way to just forward of the mainmast. There Brewer found Johnston unconscious on the deck with McCleary, a big, brawny Cornishman, standing over him. Phillips was curled up on the deck over by the lee rail.

"What happened to Johnston?" Brewer asked.

"Well, sir," Peters said, "I told you I ordered Johnston restrained, but as McCleary was restraining him, Johnston resisted, and in the course of being restrained got his head run into the mainmast, sir. He was very cooperative after that."

Brewer turned to the big Cornishman. "McCleary?"

The sailor looked sheepish and shrugged. "Sorry, sir."

"It's all right," Brewer said as he bent down to examine Johnston. He found a big lump on the top of his head but no blood. "McCleary, take Johnston below and place him in irons. Then get Mr. Spinelli out of bed to look at that lump on his head."

"Aye aye, sir," McCleary said. He bent down and lifted the unconscious drunk over his shoulder without a second thought and took him below.

Brewer walked over to young Phillips and knelt down on one knee beside him. He was curled up and shaking, his eyes squeezed shut as thought he was trying to get control of himself.

"John?" he said. "How are you?"

Phillips opened his eyes at the sound of Brewer's voice. "Mr. Brewer?"

"It's me, John. Can you stand?"

Phillips nodded, and Brewer helped him to his feet. When Brewer decided he would stay there, he turned back to Peters.

"You have the deck. Send someone to wake up the wardroom steward and tell him to bring a pot of strong coffee to my cabin. Find Mr. Spinelli and ask him to come to my cabin after he's finished with Johnston. I also want the names of anyone who actually heard what went on or what Johnston said."

"Aye aye, sir."

Brewer took Phillips by the arm and led him below to his cabin. He sat Phillips in the chair in front of his desk while he sat on the edge of the desk next to him and looked down at the young man. The incident had obviously shaken him badly; Phillips sat there with a blank look on his face. There was a single knock on the door, and Brewer turned to see the door open and Mr. Spinelli stick his head in. Brewer waved him in and walked over to speak to him.

"How's Johnston?" Brewer asked as they shook hands.

"Awake, now," the surgeon said. "Claims he doesn't remember any of it. Otherwise, he should be fine in a day or two."

Brewer nodded and turned towards Phillips. "Do you know what happened?"

"Yes," Spinelli said. "Mr. Peters told me all about it."

"Good," Brewer said. "Take a seat on my sea chest and listen."

Spinelli nodded and took his seat as Brewer took his seat on the desk in front of Phillips. The boy did not move.

"John?" Brewer said. "John, look at me."

Phillips blinked a couple times and looked at Brewer.

"John, what happened?"

"What hap—?" Phillips whispered. "Johnston—drunk, he... he said... no, not again! I can't do it again!" He squeezed his eyes shut again to block the memory.

"John!" Brewer said, taking him by both shoulders. "John! Get hold of yourself!"

Phillips buried his head in his hands and rubbed his eyes. There was a knock at the door, and the steward entered with a pot of hot coffee and three mugs on a tray. He set the tray on the desk and withdrew without a word, and Brewer made a mental note to thank him later. Brewer poured a cup and handed it to Spinelli, who was now watching young Phillips with great concern. Brewer poured a second cup and held it out toward Phillips, who ignored it completely.

Brewer kicked the chair. "John! Here, drink this."

Phillips took the cup and looked at it as though he'd

never seen one before. Brewer poured himself a cup and raised it in a silent toast in an attempt to get the young lieutenant to drink. Phillips looked from Brewer's cup to his own and back again before finally raising his own to his lips and taking a swallow. The heat and strong coffee taste seemed to bring the boy to his senses.

"Sorry, sir," he said and hung his head.

"Tell me what happened, John," Brewer said softly.

Phillips took another gulp of coffee to steady his nerves, then drew a deep breath and let it out slowly. "I'm not sure, to be honest, sir. I found Johnston drunk on duty. I've never had any trouble out of him before, sir. I ordered him aft so I could write him up per the captain's orders, and he refused to go. Said he ought to put me over his knee and whip me for being insolent to the adults. Then I couldn't help but remember the last time. I couldn't do it again, Mr. Brewer! God help me, I don't think I would do it again."

Brewer and Spinelli looked at each other in mutual bewilderment. Brewer looked back to Phillips.

"Do what again, John? What happened?"

Phillips looked straight ahead and whispered a single word.

"Mutiny."

Brewer and Spinelli looked at each other again, more confused than ever. Brewer raised an eyebrow in question, but Spinelli shook his head to indicate he had heard nothing, no hints of sedition on board.

Brewer looked back at Phillips. "What mutiny, John? Is *Defiant* in danger?"

Phillips shook his head. "Not *Defiant*. *Retribution*."

Brewer sat back and sighed. He looked up to see the question on Spinelli's face, so he stood and motioned for the surgeon to join him by the door.

"What's going on?" Spinelli asked.

"I'm not sure yet," Brewer said. "*Retribution* was his last ship. It's where he was promoted to lieutenant when all the officers but the captain were killed. It was that captain who petitioned the Admiralty to confirm the promotion despite his age."

"Why did he do that?" Spinelli asked as he watched Phillips carefully. "He can't have been ready for it."

"No one knows. According to the captain, there is nothing in the boy's admiralty file, which means the captain pleaded his case to their lordships in person and orally."

"He must have made a pretty good case," Spinelli said. "So, what do we do with our young lieutenant here?"

Brewer looked back at Phillips and sighed. "We find out what happened on that ship."

They rejoined Phillips, and after a moment's quick examination Mr. Spinelli left the questioning to the first lieutenant.

"John," Brewer said, softly but firmly, "I need you to sit up and listen to me. I need to ask you some questions, and I need you to answer me. It may be difficult for you, and I apologize if it revives some painful memories, but I must have answers to my questions. Do you understand?"

Phillips sat up in his chair, took a deep breath and exhaled loudly. He closed his eyes for a moment before opening them and nodding.

"John, I want to know what happened on *Retribution*. You told me all the officers were killed in action against pirates, and the captain was badly wounded but not mortally in the same action, right?"

Phillips nodded.

"And after the action, the captain promoted you to acting lieutenant, before retiring to his cabin due to his wounds. Correct?"

Another nod.

"And you sailed for Gibraltar on the advice of your sailing master. You also said the mates and hands had already begun making what repairs they could to the ship. All right so far?"

Another nod.

"John, what happened on that voyage?"

Phillips was silent for several minutes, his eyes staring into space, then flashing to meet Brewer's for just a moment before staring at nothing again. Just when Brewer thought he might have to prompt him again, Phillips blinked and sighed, and when he looked at Brewer, his eyes looked sad and exhausted.

"We were making only two or three knots toward Gibraltar," Phillips said. "The carpenter advised against trying to use any more sail until he was able to plug some of the holes we had below the waterline. We had pumps going round the clock, and after a few days of that I ordered some extra rations of rum.

"Some of the hands got drunk and decided they had done their duty and wanted out. They got hold of some cutlasses I'd failed to secure after the battle and went to force the captain to turn back to the African coast and let them off. I begged them not to do it, but they took me and made me kiss the gunner's daughter." Brewer saw Mr. Spinelli flinch at the term used to describe when a midshipman was forced to lay across a cannon while his backside was beaten with a cane.

Phillips drew a deep, ragged breath and continued. "They laughed at me, Mr. Brewer. After they dumped me on the deck, they started for the captain's cabin again. I ran below decks and returned with two braces of pistols. I caught up with them right as they entered the captain's cabin. I ran past the lot of them and stood between them and the captain, who was too ill to rise from his bunk.

"I cocked the two pistols in my hands and told them they were under arrest. They laughed again and said I needed another go-round."

Phillips' voice broke for a second, but he quickly

regained control. "I shot the one who said it in the chest, and shot the one who whipped me on deck in the face, killed them both. I dropped those pistols and pulled the other two from my belt and cocked them. I asked if anyone else wanted to die today. They looked at each other and dropped their cutlasses. Right about that time, the last five marines we had on board arrived to take custody of them. The captain ordered them taken below under guard to work the pumps until we reached Gibraltar."

Brewer looked to Spinelli for help, but the surgeon was staring with his mouth hanging open. Brewer sighed and put a reassuring hand on the boy's shoulder.

"When they were gone," Phillips said, "I lost control of myself. I dropped the pistols and fell to my knees and cried. Right there, in front of the captain! And do you know what he did? He put his hand on my shoulder and thanked me for saving his life! But I'm the one who caused it in the first place! Then today, Johnston was drunk, and it all came back to me... I couldn't bear to kill anyone else, Mr. Brewer! Not again!"

Phillips dropped his head into his hands again and sat there trying not to cry. Brewer sat back on the desk and thought about what Lt. Phillips had said. So, now he knew why the captain fought so hard for Phillips' confirmation. He owed the boy his life, no doubt about it.

He looked back at Phillips and shook his head in disbelief. Stopping a mutiny single-handed and saving his captain's life at, what, fifteen? *No wonder he was haunted by the memory,* Brewer thought as he looked at the boy in the chair in front of him. *But how do I get him past this, and what am I going to tell the captain in the morning?*

CHAPTER 10

Brewer looked toward Mr. Spinelli for help, but the surgeon was also at a loss. He looked from the boy to Brewer and shook his head helplessly. Brewer looked back to Mr. Phillips and sighed. The young lieutenant sat there unmoving, elbows on his knees and his head cradled in his hands, not making a sound. Brewer knew he had to do something to restore the lad's confidence, but he had no idea how to go about it.

That wasn't his only problem. What happened tonight had to be reported to Captain Norman in the morning, and Brewer did not want the captain to use it as an excuse to persecute the young officer again. Brewer looked to the surgeon again and saw that he, too, was trying to figure this problem out.

Brewer suddenly realized he had another problem. He knew the story behind Phillips' promotion. He was sure Captain Norman would ask about it sooner or later. Brewer could well imagine the Captain cruelly twisting Phillips' heroism and defense of his captain, but he could not worry about that now. Brewer looked over at young Phillips again. The boy was sitting in his chair, head in hands, an occasional ragged sob escaping his lips. Brewer knew the signs; he had seen it before in many officers over the years, and it was never good.

Brewer steeled himself for what he was about to do. He knew what was on the line and what the consequences would be for Phillips should he fail.

"Mr. Phillips," Brewer said, "John, look at me."

Phillips slowly lifted his head to look at the first lieutenant. Brewer could tell from his eyes he had been crying.

"Tell me what you're thinking."

Phillips sat back in his chair and sighed. "I don't know, Mr. Brewer; maybe that I'm not cut out to be an officer. I can't even control one drunk seaman on my watch without falling to the deck and cowering!"

"John, listen to me," Brewer said. "Like it or not, you're still a growing boy. A drunk like Johnston is real brave to attack a boy, but I'd like to see him be so foolish by the time you are twenty and have your muscles!"

Phillips looked dubious, but Brewer pressed on.

"Mr. Phillips," he said, "you have reached the point in your career where you need to make a decision. You need to decide whether you will continue in the King's service or not. Most don't reach it as early as you have, but it is here nonetheless. You see, Mr. Phillips, every officer runs up against something that causes them to question their calling. For most, it's the carnage they experience during their first battle. For you, it is this matter of what happened during the mutiny on *Retribution*, and specifically circumstances like tonight that remind you of it. In my opinion, if you quit now you will be depriving the King of what will be a very good officer. The decision is, however, up to you."

Phillips sat up and sighed. He pulled a handkerchief from a pocket inside his coat and unashamedly wiped his eyes. Afterward, he sat quietly as he wrung the cloth in his hands.

"All I've ever wanted" he said softly, "is to be a King's officer. Ever since I was a little boy, I wanted to go to sea. But now? I'm just not sure anymore, Mr. Brewer; I just don't know if I can do it or not."

Brewer sat back and considered what to do next. He remembered from watching Captain Bush that they were entering a critical phase in the process. If Brewer was not extremely careful, he could easily drive young Phillips out of the service rather than getting him to stay. Brewer closed his eyes as he desperately tried to recall Bush's rule of thumb for such circumstances. He smiled and looked at Phillips when it finally came to him.

"As I said, John, the decision is up to you. If you want to abandon the King's service for reasons of your own, then I wish you all the luck in the world. But if you are considering quitting because of drunks like Johnston and those lowlife cowards on *Retribution*, then you are not the man I think you are. I think you have the potential to be a great officer, but if you let others push you into doing what you don't want to do then you're better off farming. So, Mr. Phillips, what's it to be? Are you a King's officer, or a farmer?"

Brewer sat back and watched the flurry of emotions fly across young Phillips' face; embarrassment, uncertainty, anger, and indignation followed one another with astonishing speed. Brewer looked over to Mr. Spinelli, but the surgeon looked by no means certain that the ploy would succeed. Brewer didn't blame him at all; if Bush could not make it work, Brewer was by no means confident himself. He looked back to see Phillips staring at nothing, his eyes darting back and forth in a desperate attempt to find an answer to his dilemma. Brewer resisted the temptation to try to steer Phillips on his journey; if he was going to stay, it had to be of his own choosing.

Brewer was just about to change his mind when Phillips

suddenly sat straight up in his chair. His face was hard, the look in his eye was one of cold fury, and Brewer took heart.

"Well, Mr. Phillips?" he said.

Phillips raised his eyes to meet Brewer's. The gaze never wavered. Phillips stood to his feet.

"Mr. Brewer," he said, "I want to be a King's officer."

Brewer nodded. He glanced past the young lieutenant's shoulder to see Mr. Spinelli smiling, and he looked back to his charge.

"Very well, Mr. Phillips," Brewer said. "If that is your decision, then the first thing you must do is resume your duties. Take charge of the deck and finish your watch. As soon as you are relieved, I want you to write out your report of the incident. The captain will be wanting it first thing in the morning."

"Aye aye, sir," Phillips said with a grim smile. He nodded to Mr. Spinelli as he left the cabin.

Brewer heard a sigh escape the surgeon. "Well," Spinelli said, "do you think he'll stay?"

Brewer still looked at the cabin door and nodded to himself more than the surgeon. "He'll stay," he said. "I'd hate to be the next man who gets drunk on his watch."

Spinelli smiled and sighed. He turned to say something to Brewer, but stopped when he saw the look on his face. Brewer was leaning back on his desk looking out the window. His face was drawn and firm, almost angry. Spinelli stood and took a step or two in his direction.

"William?" he said. "What's wrong?"

Brewer's eyes went to the surgeon briefly, and then studied the floor for a bit. Finally, he sighed and looked up. "Nothing's wrong, Adam," he said. "I'm fine. If you'll excuse me, I too need to write a report for the captain; as a matter of fact, so do you. I would appreciate it if you confined your report to Johnston. I'll see you at breakfast."

Spinelli opened his mouth to say something but thought

better of it. He nodded to his first lieutenant and left the cabin.

Brewer watched him go. He hated lying to his friend, but it was probably for the best. He did have to write a report for the captain, but he also had to decide what he was going to tell the captain about Phillips and the mutiny on the *Retribution*, and he didn't want to make the surgeon a possible target for the captain's wrath. Brewer turned back to the window. *What am I going to tell the captain?* he wondered. *If I tell him the truth, will he try to use it against Mr. Phillips in some way? I can always simply not bring it up, but what if he asks me directly? If I don't tell the truth under such circumstances, he can have me charged and broken.* He considered asking Mr. Sweeney for his advice, but he thought it entirely possible that the sailing master would refuse to answer in order to protect himself. Brewer shook his head in disgust at the thought, but then he sighed. He couldn't blame Sweeney for trying to keep himself safe.

He sat down behind his desk and began a very detailed report for the captain. Three pages of tightly-written script later, he had arrived at the interview in his cabin, and he paused and set down his quill. After a moment, he made up his mind: he completed the report with Phillips' decision to remain in the navy. He said nothing about the mutiny on the *Retribution*.

After he was relieved from the morning watch, Brewer collected the written reports from Phillips, Peters, and the doctor in addition to his own and headed for the captain's cabin. He also had a list from Mr. Peters with the names of witnesses to the incident, should the captain wish to question them himself. He nodded to the sentry as usual and knocked on the door.

"Enter."

Brewer opened the door and went in. Captain Norman was just finishing his breakfast.

"Good morning, Mr. Brewer," the captain said. "Would you care for some coffee?"

"Good morning, sir, and yes, that would be greatly appreciated."

Jenkins brought the coffee, and Brewer thanked him for the steaming brew. After his long night, the heat alone helped to revive him. Norton motioned for Jenkins to leave the pot, and the servant withdrew.

"Now, Mr. Brewer, what can I do for you?"

Brewer set his cup down. "Sir, I must report an incident that occurred last night. Mr. Phillips discovered Johnston drunk on duty, and when Phillips went to write him up for your review, Johnston threatened him."

Norman's eyebrows went up, and he was instantly alert. "Threatened a King's officer? Did Johnston touch Mr. Phillips at all?"

"I don't believe so, sir."

Norman settled down a little. "Tell me about it."

Brewer sat back and told his captain the entire story. He finished with Mr. Phillips leaving his cabin, and Norman looked out the stern window as he digested the tale.

"Sir," Brewer said, "I have here my written report of the incident, as well as those of Lt. Phillips, Dr. Spinelli, and Mr. Peters. I also have a list here from Mr. Peters of those who were eyewitnesses of the incident, should you wish to question them yourself." He handed Norman the stack of papers.

Norman took the papers and set them aside. "Thank you, Mr. Brewer; I shall read these carefully before they are included in my report to the Admiralty on the incident. I shall, of course, wish to interview the witnesses myself, along with Mr. Phillips. If, as you believe, Johnston didn't touch Lt. Phillips, he may get off with a visit from the cat, but if he struck him, he may well hang for it. Sentry!"

The sentry opened the door and saluted. "Sir?"

"Pass the word for Mr. Phillips."

"Aye aye, sir," the sentry saluted again and closed the door.

"Please stay, Mr. Brewer," Norman said. "Kindly sit over there." He indicated a couch over by the corner of the stern windows.

"Of course, sir," Brewer said as he moved to the corner. He wondered what the captain was going to do. Whatever it would be, he prayed Phillips would be able to stand it.

Mr. Phillips arrived within a few minutes and saluted his captain. He looked as firm and resolute as he had when he left Brewer's cabin. Brewer hoped that was a good sign and not just bravado.

"Mr. Phillips," Captain Norman said formally, "Mr. Brewer has reported the incident from last night and presented me with your written statement. I have not had a chance to read it yet, but I want you to tell me in your own words what happened. You may stand at ease."

Phillips relaxed and told the captain all that happened during his watch. He paused for a moment, then he told the captain how Brewer talked to him in his cabin and how he had decided to remain in the King's service. Norman's eyes flashed briefly to Brewer, and Brewer knew there would be questions about that conversation later. Phillips finished his tale and stood before the captain.

"Mr. Phillips," Norman said, "I have some preliminary questions. First, did Johnston at any time strike you in any way?"

"No, sir," Phillips said. "He lunged for me, and I stumbled backward and fell to the deck, but he never actually touched me, sir."

"I see," Norman said, "and at any time did he raise a weapon to you?"

"No, sir, he just reached for me, like."

Norman nodded and stood. "Very well, Mr. Phillips. You

are dismissed."

"Aye aye, sir," Phillips saluted and left the room.

Norman sent for and interviewed the three sailors whose names were on Peters' list as eyewitnesses of the incident, and all three tales agreed with Phillips' in all the major points. All verified that Johnston did not touch Mr. Phillips, or raise a weapon to him. Mr. Peters was called, and he related to the captain what he had done from the time he arrived on the scene until Brewer arrived on deck and took over. Norman listened intently to each testimony, and after Peters left, he sat silently, his chin in his hand, considering. Brewer watched the entire proceeding and patiently waited.

"Seems fairly cut and dried, doesn't it?" Norman said. "I'm satisfied as to what happened. Tell me, Mr. Brewer, what was Mr. Phillips like when you took him to your cabin?"

Brewer stirred a bit. "Badly shaken, sir. Very unsure of himself. Scared."

"Understandable, I suppose," Norman said. "Tell me, did you find out what he meant when the witnesses heard him say 'Not again'?"

Brewer looked out the stern window before he answered. He sighed and turned back to his captain. "Yes, sir. He was remembering an incident on his former ship."

Norman nodded. "I thought as much. Did you find out what happened to make his captain want his promotion confirmed?"

Brewer sighed. "Yes, sir, I did, but it took a while." Then he leaned forward in his seat and told his captain the whole tale of how Phillips single-handedly put down a mutiny on *Retribution* and saved his captain's life in the process. Norman listened in silence, his only reaction being to raise his eyebrow when Brewer told how Phillips shot the two mutineers down to save his captain. When he finished his tale, Brewer sat back in his chair and looked out the stern window at *Defiant's* wake.

Captain Norman, too, was looking out the stern windows. Whatever he thought he would hear about what happened to Mr. Phillips during that voyage, it certainly wasn't this. A mere boy, publicly humiliated by drunken mutineers, but who still reacted to avenge himself and save his captain's life. *Good touch,* Norman thought, *shooting in the face the one who beat him. I bet that made an impression on the rest of them.* Norman frowned and looked at his cup, now sitting empty on the table, and he picked up the pot to refill both cups. Norman picked up his cup and stared at the clouds rising from the steaming hot coffee, but they brought him no peace of mind. *It seems that there is much more to Mr. Phillips than appearances led one to believe,* Norman thought. *A man who would only be pushed so far, and one who would resort to action if pushed too far.* Norman's eyes narrowed. *A dangerous man, a man who must be watched.*

His eyes went to Brewer, who was still looking out the stern windows. Brewer could possibly be the best first lieutenant in the fleet, and he was undeniably a vast improvement over his predecessor. *But where do your loyalties lie, Mr. Brewer?* Norman wondered. *Would you side with me, or would you defy me if the opportunity arose and trust your precious Admiral Hornblower to protect you?*

"Well, Mr. Brewer," Norman said, "as I said, fairly cut and dried. Is that how it seems to you?"

Brewer stirred and considered. "I believe so, sir. Johnston was undeniably drunk on duty, and multiple witnesses heard him threaten Mr. Phillips. The only question now is punishment. Will you speak to Johnston first?"

Norman nodded. "Yes. No matter how bad it looks for him, he is still entitled to have a chance to speak in his own defense."

"Will you want Mr. Phillips to be present?" Brewer asked.

"I think not," the captain said, "unless Johnston is such a fool as to contest the charges and demands the opportunity to face his accuser. In any case, let's have him in."

Brewer rose from his seat and went to the door of the cabin. The sentry snapped to attention when he opened the door.

"Pass the word for the marine guard to bring the prisoner to the captain immediately," he said.

The sentry saluted, and Brewer shut the door. As he turned back to the room, he caught a look on the captain's face that chilled him to the bone. It was gone just as quick, but Brewer wondered as he retook his seat just what it meant for the future of *Defiant* and all aboard her.

Less than five minutes passed before there was a single knock at the door. The marine sergeant of the guard opened the door. Norman and Brewer rose to their feet.

The sergeant saluted. "The prisoner Johnston to see the captain, sir!"

"Bring him in," Norman said.

The sergeant turned back to the door and nodded, and Johnston was led into the captain's presence. Brewer had seen prisoners before, and it never failed to surprise him how different they looked when they were brought up before the captain from how they did when they were committing their crimes. Johnston shuffled into the room. He was manacled hand and foot, and the look on his face spoke of both the massive hangover he had as well as the pain he felt from his sudden meeting with the mainmast. His clothes were disheveled, and he stank. The captain looked him up and down with disdain, and Brewer thought he saw Johnston cringe.

Captain Norman picked up a paper from his desk. "Seaman Johnston," he said, "you are charged with the following offenses: being drunk on duty, and making to attack a King's officer. What do you have to say for yourself?"

Johnston shifted pitifully in his chains. "Don't remember none of it, sir."

Norman set the paper down on the desk. "Are you saying you didn't do it?"

Johnston flinched under the captain's word and lamely shook his head. "I don't remember, sir."

Norman leaned forward, resting his fists on the desk. "We have sworn statements from Lt. Phillips as well as from three eyewitnesses, Johnston. Are they all lying?"

Johnston shifted pathetically from foot to foot and shook his head. 'I don't remember, sir."

Norman stood. "Seaman Johnston, as captain of *HMS Defiant*, I find you guilty of being drunk on duty and threatening an officer with bodily harm. I sentence you to six dozen lashes, sentence to be carried out tomorrow at seven bells in the forenoon watch."

Johnston shook his head from side to side and looked as if he would burst into tears, and Captain Norman ordered him taken out. Johnston collapsed as the marine guards took him by the arms and dragged him out of the captain's cabin. Norman stood as he watched him go, then he sat down and looked over at Brewer.

"I hope we won't have any more trouble from Mr. Johnston," he said. Brewer highly doubted it, even if the man survived his punishment. Norman went on. "Mr. Brewer, I want you to keep a close eye on Mr. Phillips for the foreseeable future, just in case this episode comes back to haunt him as well."

"Aye aye, sir," Brewer said. He had already decided to keep a close eye on Phillips, but for a very different reason. The look he saw in the captain's eye bothered him more than he could say, and he was determined to stick close to Phillips —as the captain said, just in case.

Chapter 11

When Brewer came on deck the next morning for his watch, he could feel the tension in the air. There were no secrets in a world as small as one of His Majesty's frigates, and word had spread rapidly of Johnston's conviction and sentence. The sailors he saw working the deck looked sullen, like they were looking over their shoulder to see if someone was coming after them. Brewer couldn't really blame them; the sentence on Johnston was a harsh one. Brewer wondered if Captain Norman was one for severe punishments after all. What was it that Bush's letter had said? Something about the previous surgeon and a medical report that could not be produced. Brewer looked around the deck and could not help but wonder what was in that report. He stared out over the passing sea, lost in thought.

"Good morning, sir."

Brewer looked up, a little startled. "Good morning, Mr. Phillips," he said. "How are you holding up this morning?"

Phillips shrugged and looked out over the passing waves. "Okay, I guess, sir," he said.

Brewer stepped in close. "Something on your mind, John?"

Phillips shrugged again. “I don’t know, Mr. Brewer. Sometimes I think that it’s partly my fault that Johnston’s getting flogged today.”

Brewer looked at him. “*Your* fault? What makes you think that?”

“I don’t know,” Phillips said. “Maybe I could have done something...”

“What could you have done?” Brewer asked. “Shot him?”

Phillips flushed and flashed Brewer a cold look. "That's not funny, sir."

"John," Brewer said, "I'm sorry, but none of this is your fault. Did you get Johnston drunk? Did you make him threaten you?"

Phillips shook his head and looked lost. Brewer decided to switch tactics.

"Lieutenant Phillips," he said, in his best first-lieutenant's voice, "get hold of yourself. Discipline must be maintained for *Defiant* to function. If you cannot agree with punishment when it is justly deserved, then I suggest you resign your commission at the end of this voyage. You did nothing to provoke Johnston, and you are not responsible for his punishment. The captain takes this very seriously; a fact for which you should be very grateful."

"Yes, sir," Phillips said.

"We are each of us responsible for our own actions, Mr. Phillips. You do not control Johnston’s actions any more than you control mine."

"Yes, sir."

Brewer nodded. "Remember it, then. Your job is to lead men, not to be their friend or their bloody nursemaid. You may carry on with your duties, Mr. Phillips."

"Aye aye, sir." Phillips saluted and went forward.

Brewer checked the log and did a quick inspection of the deck. Finding everything in order, he strolled aft to lean on the rail and watch the sunrise. His mind gave him no rest. It kept going back to his conversation with Mr. Phillips, and he wondered if perhaps he was too young for his commission after all. Yesterday, when Phillips walked out of his office resolute and committed, he would have bet all his prize money from *Lydia* that Phillips would stay, but now he was not sure.

Brewer became aware of someone leaning on the rail beside him and turned to find *Defiant*'s sailing master beside him. Brewer smiled and shook his head and wondered how someone as large as Mr. Sweeney could move so softly.

"Good morning, Mr. Brewer," the master said.

"Good morning, Mr. Sweeney," Brewer said. "Ready for today's event?"

"No, sir, I'm never ready for a flogging."

Brewer turned to him. "Seen a lot of them on this ship, have you?"

Sweeney leaned one elbow on the rail and smiled. "What makes you think that, Mr. Brewer?"

Brewer smiled back. "Just curious."

Sweeney looked out to sea. "Johnston's getting what he deserves."

Brewer said nothing as he watched the sailing master for a moment. "I found out what happened to Mr. Phillips on his old ship."

The sailing master pursed his lips. "Did you tell the captain?"

"Yes."

"And what was his response?"

"He told me to keep a close eye on Mr. Phillips, in case this incident haunts him as well."

Sweeney was silent, and Brewer began to feel very uncomfortable.

"It's not good, is it, Mr. Sweeney?" Brewer said.

Sweeney stared out over the passing waves.

"Tell me," Brewer said, softly but firmly.

Sweeney gazed out at the sea for several minutes, and then he closed his eyes for a moment before turning to face Brewer. The look on his face was one of weariness, like he was tired of fighting a particular battle over and over again.

“Will you walk with me, Mr. Brewer?” he asked.

Brewer nodded, and the two men turned to stroll forward. Brewer decided to wait the sailing master out, so he walked with his hands behind his back and his head down, studying the deck before him. As they passed the mainmast, Sweeney spoke. His voice was soft, and Brewer had to strain to hear everything he said.

“I don’t know what will happen,” the sailing master said, “but in all likelihood, Johnston will die today. That’s usually how he does it, so the crew will know who’s in charge.” Sweeney paused as they passed the sailmaker and his mates, taking advantage of the cool morning to work on deck. “On our last voyage, two men died under punishment, and those were the only two floggings of the entire cruise.”

Brewer was stunned. What Mr. Sweeney was describing was unheard of in the peacetime Royal Navy. He leaned toward the sailing master, careful to keep his voice low.

“Two men? In a single cruise? But how? Didn’t anyone say anything? What about when he turned over his logs at the end of the cruise? Nobody at the Admiralty questioned him about the dead men?”

Sweeney’s silence as they walked told Brewer everything.

Brewer couldn’t believe it. “But *how*? How does he get away with it?”

The sailing master stopped and turned to face the first lieutenant. “Because he’s the man who avenged Nelson, that’s how. No one in London wants to be the one who has to break the man who avenged England’s greatest naval commander.”

Brewer could not believe what he was hearing. Talk

about riding on one's reputation! For a brief moment, it occurred to him that Mr. Sweeney might be pulling his leg, but a quick search of the sailing master's face told Brewer this was no joke. Brewer lowered his head and stared at his feet for a moment as he tried to order his thoughts. When his head came up again, he leaned in closer to the sailing master.

"And what happens to Mr. Phillips?"

Brewer saw Sweeney flinch at the mention of the boy. The sailing master studied the deck for a moment and then motioned for the first lieutenant to follow him forward. When they reached a place of relative privacy by the lee rail, Sweeney stopped and faced his friend.

"I honestly don't know what will happen to Mr. Phillips," Sweeney said. "As I told you, I thought I had the captain figured out, but then you came aboard, and now I'm seeing the captain doing things I've never seen him do before. However, based on the story you told me, I would expect the captain to go to one extreme or the other. Either he will be so impressed by Phillips' actions that he will leave the boy alone for the rest of the voyage, or else he will consider the boy a threat and deal with him accordingly."

Brewer's eyes narrowed. "And just what does *that* mean?"

Mr. Sweeney looked the first lieutenant in the eye and said, "Honestly, Mr. Brewer, your guess is as good as mine." And he turned and walked away.

The morning grew bright and fair as the sun rose high in the clear blue sky. HMS *Defiant* sailed along smoothly over gently rolling waves. At the appointed hour, Captain James Norman appeared on deck. His face was stern and unreadable as he approached his officers and saluted.

"Good morning, gentlemen," he said.

"Good morning, sir," the officers said. There was a moment of awkward silence before the captain turned to his first officer.

"Very well, Mr. Brewer," he said, "let's get on with it."

"Aye aye, sir," Brewer said as he saluted and turned away from the captain and addressed the bosun. "Bosun, have all hands lay aft to witness punishment."

"Aye aye, sir," the bosun said. "All hands lay aft to witness punishment!"

The crew of the *Defiant* gathered aft. Brewer noticed the slow pace of a crew who knew what was coming and wanted no part of it. Once the crew was gathered, the master at arms led Johnston out and stood him before the captain.

"Seaman Angus Johnston," Norman said in a loud, clear voice, "you are charged with being drunk on duty and threatening an officer with bodily harm. Do you have anything to say for yourself?"

Johnston stared at the deck in front of him. "Don't remember nothing, sir."

Norman's eyes hooded in disgust. "Is there anyone who will speak for him?"

Nobody moved nor said a word.

"Johnston," Norman said, "I find you guilty and sentence you to six dozen lashes."

The miserable seaman was tied to a grating that had been set up for the purpose. Brewer stood at his place beside Captain Norman and waited while the boatswain brought out his red bag and withdrew the hated cat from it. He waited for the captain's order.

Norman nodded to him. "Bosun's mate, do your duty."

The mate saluted and took position behind Johnston. Brewer looked to his side in time to see Mr. Spinelli step to the front of the crew and then make his way over to the side. His attention was ripped back to the matter at hand by the sound of the cat cutting into Johnston's bare back.

It was a sound that Brewer had never got used to; he tried not to flinch every time the cat came down. He kept his eyes glued to a spot on the horizon and recited poetry very loudly inside his head. It was a trick taught to him by a wise old petty officer on *Dreadnaught*, and it had served him well all these years. He did notice Captain Norman had no problem watching every blow of the cat, but his face was like stone and gave no indication whether he was enjoying it.

After four dozen lashes, the mate hesitated.

"What are you waiting for?" Captain Norman asked.

"Begging your pardon, sir," the mate said, "but he looks like he's going to die if I continue."

The captain sighed and looked around for Dr. Spinelli. "Doctor, will you kindly examine the prisoner and determine if he is fit to continue?"

Spinelli looked hard at the captain for a moment before stepping over to Johnston. He examined the wounds on his back and looked in his eye. He looked over the wounds again, and he turned to the captain.

"Sir, I have examined the prisoner," Spinelli said loudly, so the crew would be sure to hear, "and in my opinion, he will die if you permit his punishment to continue."

"Thank you, Doctor," Norman said. "Bosun's mate, continue the punishment."

"What?!" Spinelli cried. "Sir! Didn't you hear what I said? This man will die if you continue!"

"I heard, Doctor," Norman said calmly, "and I have decided not to follow your recommendation."

"In that case, sir, you will be responsible for this man's death!"

Norman took a step forward. "Doctor, I am responsible for every life on this ship, including yours. Now step aside, or I shall have the master at arms put you under arrest."

Brewer could not believe his eyes. Going against the surgeon's recommendation was tantamount to murder, but there was nothing that could be done about it short of a mutiny. From behind the captain, Brewer caught the doctor's eye and motioned with his head for the surgeon to back off and stand by the crew. Spinelli stared at the captain for a moment more before reluctantly moving away.

Captain Norman watched him go and then nodded to the bosun's mate. The man sighed and moved into position to resume his duty. Brewer watched the captain, but there was no indication on his face of what he was thinking. When the last lash fell on the bloody mess that was once a man's back, the bosun's mate turned to the captain.

"Punishment completed as ordered, sir!"

"Very well," Norman said. "Cut him down."

The boatswain turned and nodded to two of his mates, and they cut the ropes around Johnston's wrists. Johnston collapsed onto the deck. The boatswain examined him, and he turned to the captain again.

"He's dead, sir."

Only one man moved at the announcement. Dr. Spinelli took a step forward, his outrage and fury plainly written on his face. From behind the captain, Brewer shook his head emphatically, and Spinelli closed his mouth and left the scene, pushing his way through the crowd.

Brewer's eyes flew to the captain. His face did not change; it was still set like stone. The captain nodded to the boatswain. "Take him below."

The boatswain saluted and immediately began directing his mates to get Johnston to the sick bay. The captain turned to Brewer and said, "Dismiss the hands, Mr. Brewer. I shall be in my quarters."

"Aye aye, sir," Brewer said. As soon as the captain was gone, he turned to Mr. Greene and said, "Dismiss the hands. You have the watch now, don't you? The deck is yours, then. I shall be in sick bay. Be sure to have this deck swabbed. Get rid of this mess."

Brewer made his way forward and below decks. When he entered the sick bay, he saw Spinelli sitting in a chair looking at Johnston's lifeless corpse lying on the table.

"This was murder," Spinelli said without looking up. "Murder, plain and simple."

"You did what you could," Brewer said. "Adam, what are you doing?"

"I have to write a death report for the captain," the surgeon said automatically. "That's standard procedure in cases like this. But I am also going to write a second report, which I shall put into Admiral Hornblower's hand when we reach the squadron. Someone must know about this."

"I agree, Adam," Brewer said. "Write your reports. But make a copy of the second report and give it to me for safekeeping. And say nothing about the second report to anyone."

"Very well," Spinelli said, "I won't tell anyone; it will be our secret. And thank you, William."

Brewer nodded. Just then there was a knock at the door. It was two of the sailmaker's mates.

"Begging your pardon, sir," one of them said, "but we was directed to come get the body and sew it up for burial."

Brewer looked at the men. "Already? Who gave the order?"

"Word was passed from the captain, sir."

Brewer and Spinelli looked at each other. Brewer thought the Doctor's report should make very interesting reading.

"Very well," the surgeon said. "You can take him."

The two men picked up the body and carried him to where he would be sewn up in a canvas coffin with a couple of solid shot at his feet to make sure the body sank. After they were gone, Brewer stepped over and patted the surgeon on the shoulder.

"Be careful, Adam," he said. "You must hold your tongue from now on."

The surgeon nodded, and Brewer left him to write his

reports.

He went up on deck. He noticed that the blood on the deck where Johnston fell had already been cleaned up. Brewer looked around for Mr. Sweeney.

The sailing master standing by the wheel.

"Mr. Sweeney," Brewer said.

Sweeney merely nodded. "Sir." Brewer noticed that he looked upset about something.

"Anything wrong?" Brewer asked.

Sweeney shook his head.

"Well," Brewer said, "it seems you were right about today."

Brewer saw the sailing master's eyes flash, and he knew he had hit the mark.

"So," Brewer said, "what happens next, Mr. Sweeney?"

The older man's eyes narrowed and he flushed, and Brewer wondered for a moment if he had gone too far.

"What do you *want* from me, Mr. Brewer?" Sweeney hissed. "You've seen the captain for what he is now. What can you or I or anyone else short of the bloody Admiralty do about it? Now *leave me alone.*"

Brewer went back to his own cabin for a moment to sit down and think. Obviously, Mr. Sweeney was right. James Norman was a manipulative monster who cared nothing for the lives of his men. The troubling thing was, there was nothing Brewer could do about it. Even Hornblower, when they joined his squadron, would be hard pressed to remove Norman based on one death under punishment. It was clear to Brewer from what Mr. Sweeney had told him and what he had seen with his own eyes that Norman sacrificed one or two of the men each voyage to maintain his control over the crew. The question was, what—if anything—could he do about it?

CHAPTER 12

The naval yard at Washington City was peaceful and nearly deserted when the *Defiant* sailed in just after dawn. They had picked up the pilot as they entered the Potomac River, and he guided them efficiently but (to the chagrin of Captain Norman) silently up the river to the city and their berth in the middle of the harbor. Captain Norman thanked the pilot as he left the ship, and Brewer walked over to stand next to the captain as they watched his boat pull away.

"Did he say anything, sir?" Brewer asked.

"Not a ruddy word," the captain said. "I wonder if they cut out his tongue before they gave him the job."

They turned away and watched as the crew of the *Defiant* went through the various routines which had to be carried out whenever the ship entered port. After a few moments, Norman turned to Brewer and said, "Mr. Brewer, you had better come with me to see the ambassador. Be ready to leave at six bells, if you please."

"Aye aye, sir."

Norman nodded. "Very well. I'll be in my cabin if I'm needed. Please pass the word for any mail that needs to go ashore."

"Aye aye, sir," Brewer said as he saluted. Norman turned and headed for his cabin. Brewer watched him go and marveled. The man had made no reference to the flogging or Johnston's death, and to Brewer's knowledge he had not so much as appeared on deck during Phillips' watch. He wondered whether the captain had given up his special interest in Mr. Phillips, or was he simply planning his next move? Brewer decided he had better keep an eye on Phillips a little longer, just to be on the safe side.

That same thought was on Brewer's mind as he sat in the stern sheets of the captain's gig being rowed ashore. He glanced over at the captain sitting beside him, the sealed diplomatic packet on his lap. Brewer wondered whether the hard look on his captain's face spelled trouble for the ambassador—or for himself.

A short carriage ride brought them to the ambassador's residence. Brewer knew that his countrymen had taken and burned the city in 1814, and he was surprised at the shape of what was rising from the ashes. It was far too... provincial for Brewer's taste. Not at all what he considered proper for the new capitol of an up-and-coming nation. He expected more grandeur in the architecture. Ah, well, perhaps when they finished their capitol building.

They pulled up to the ambassador's residence. Captain Norman walked past the footman who opened the carriage door and marched up the steps. Brewer nodded to the footman and followed his captain. The two officers were shown into a parlor and told that the ambassador would join them shortly.

Norman handed the packet to Brewer and began to pace along the far side of the room. Brewer wondered what was bothering his captain, but he pushed it aside for the present and turned his attention to the room. It was obviously a place for holding visitors. It had two settees facing each other in the middle of the room, a decorative fireplace on the far wall, and a table against the wall on the right with a small statue of Poseidon on it. The left wall was dominated by a large window looking out over the street. Brewer eyed his captain, but he was still pacing with his head down. Brewer hid a smile by walking over to the window to watch the passers-by.

After a quarter-hour of pacing, Norman suddenly stopped in front of the fireplace and stared at the closed door. It was plain to Brewer that the pacing had not improved his captain's mood. "It would appear the ambassador has forgotten us," he said.

"So it would seem, sir," Brewer answered.

At that moment the door opened and a man strode in to the room.

"Forgive my delay, gentlemen," he said. "I am Stratford Canning, his Majesty's ambassador to the United States."

Brewer bowed, and as he did so, his eyes went automatically to his captain. To his shock, Norman stood there staring wide-eyed at the ambassador. It took a moment, but a look of recognition also appeared on the ambassador's face. It quickly changed to a sneer.

"James Norman, as I live and breathe!" the ambassador said in a mocking voice.

"Hello Stratford," Norman said, and Brewer noted the sarcastic use of the ambassador's first name and wondered what bad blood there was between these two. "I thought you were in Istanbul."

"I've been paroled, old boy," the ambassador said. "But don't worry, I shan't be locked up in this dirty little backwater very long. A little time in purgatory is good for the soul, they say."

Norman sighed. "Mr. Brewer," he said, motioning for Brewer to hand him the packet. He turned back to the ambassador and said, "Your Excellency, I was charged at the naval base at Halifax to deliver this packet into your hands."

"Thank you, Captain," the ambassador said formally. "I'm sorry, but I have a meeting to attend that will take the remainder of the day. Please return tomorrow for instructions."

The ambassador bowed and left the room without another word. Brewer stood there with his eyebrows raised, astonished at this breech of diplomatic protocol, let alone good manners. He looked over at his captain. Norman stood there silently fuming at being dismissed so casually. Brewer was trying to think of something to say when Norman picked up his hat and stormed from the room. Brewer sighed and followed.

Out on the street, Norman eschewed the carriage and instead walked in the general direction of the navy yard. Brewer walked silently beside his captain and waited for him to say something. After three blocks, Captain Norman sighed and slowed his pace.

"I'm sorry you had to witness that, Mr. Brewer," he said. "As you might guess, the ambassador and I have met before."

"Really, sir?" Brewer said.

Norman threw him a wry grin. "Stratford Canning was a lieutenant with me in HMS *Victory* at Trafalgar and afterward. I was given *Defiant* over him, and he's never forgiven me. Since then, he has tried to stab me in the back on several occasions, but without success."

Captain Norman was silent for the rest of their return to HMS *Defiant*. Brewer wondered what was going through his captain's mind, but every time he looked, the captain's face gave away nothing. Norman said nothing as they reboarded the ship, barely saluting as he swept past the honor guard and made his way to his cabin. Greene and Phillips both looked to Brewer for an explanation, but he had none to give. Brewer carried on as best he could, but his mind was not on his work. He was thinking about Norman and Canning, and whatever it was that was still between them. In the wardroom, he successfully avoided the topic of their visit to the ambassador's residence by changing the subject, but he knew he couldn't get away with that for very long. During the evening watch, Brewer paced the quarterdeck and wondered, but he found the empty speculation maddening.

He thought he might get his questions answered when Mr. Short came up to and asked him to please come to the captain's cabin. Brewer hurried as fast as dignity would allow and was only slightly out of breath when he knocked and entered the captain's domain.

Norman was sitting at his desk, writing in his log again. "Please sit down, Mr. Brewer," he said without looking up. "I shall be with you momentarily."

Brewer sat in a chair opposite the captain's desk and waited. Inevitably his gaze was toward the great stern windows, and he lost himself in the view—at least until the captain slammed his log book closed.

"Trouble with the ambassador, sir?" Brewer said.

Norman looked up at him in surprise. "Is it that obvious? I will admit to you that I could have sailed the rest of my life without seeing Stratford Canning again, and I would not have missed him."

Brewer laughed. "He did seem to have a rather high opinion of himself, sir."

Norman grimaced. "You don't know the half of it. Of course, it helps if your brother is the head of the Foreign Office. When he didn't get command of *Defiant*, Stratford resigned his commission. His brother got him into the Foreign Service and has been cleaning up his messes ever since. And now he expects *me* to be at his beck and call—"

Norman stopped in mid-sentence and stared out into space.

Suddenly, Brewer knew what was coming, and he didn't like it one bit.

"William," Captain Norman said, "I want you to go

ashore in the morning and receive whatever our dear ambassador has for us. I'll be hanged if I'm going to give that second rate diplomat another chance to ridicule me."

"Aye aye, sir" Brewer said. He saluted and left the captain's cabin. He was not happy at being thrown into the middle of one of his captain's petty squabbles. Brewer sighed as he entered his cabin and closed the door. Sleep would not come easy tonight.

The morning found Brewer again in the stern sheets of the gig, being rowed to the wharf. No carriage awaited him this time, so he walked to the ambassador's residence. The same sour servant showed him into the same side room and again told him the ambassador would be with him shortly. Brewer shook his head and again passed the time at the window watching the people. He had no idea how long he stood there before he heard the door open and turned to see the Ambassador himself enter the room. Brewer turned to him and bowed.

“Mr. Brewer, wasn't it?” he said. “So, James sent you in his stead. How typical! Well, Lieutenant, follow me!”

Canning turned and marched out the door and down the hall, leaving Brewer to catch up as best he could. Brewer noticed the portrait of the Duke of Wellington that hung in the hallway opposite the grand staircase and wondered what Napoleon Bonaparte would say if he could see it. Brewer smiled; he was sure Boney's first words would be to ask for a razor.

The ambassador finally slowed and turned into an elegantly furnished office dominated by a huge oak desk in the corner. A portrait of the King hung on the opposite wall. The ambassador went straight to the desk and sat behind it. He picked up a pen and dipped it in an inkwell. He thought for a moment before putting the pen to paper. Brewer stood there, feeling vaguely as though he was being deliberately ignored and angry that there was nothing he could do about it. He noticed off to the side of the desk the packet that he and Captain Norman had delivered yesterday; it lay unwrapped, its papers tossed carelessly on top of the wrapping.

"Lieutenant," the ambassador said as he continued writing, "this packet you have delivered to me confirms certain rumors I have heard concerning renewed pirate activity all along the American coastline. I want HMS *Defiant* to take a copy of the packet along with this addendum I am writing to our naval base at Bermuda at once."

"Mr. Ambassador," Brewer said, "*Defiant* is scheduled to join Admiral Hornblower in the Caribbean Sea with all dispatch."

"Admiral Hornblower can wait an extra week or two," Canning said curtly. "Our ships in the central Atlantic need this information immediately."

"We are under Admiralty orders, Mr. Ambassador," Brewer said.

"I don't care," Canning said as he looked up at Brewer. "My orders take precedence in the short term, and your captain knows it."

Brewer was glad that Norman had decided to remain on *Defiant*, a remark like that would have caused him to explode.

"Sir," Brewer said, "might I request that a message be sent to Admiral Hornblower informing him of the delay in our arrival?"

Canning stopped writing and looked up at Brewer, the look on his face similar to something one would give to an irritating child.

"Lieutenant Brewer," he said slowly, "by the time I could do that, your ship would pull into the harbor within 72 hours at most after the message, so I don't think that Admiral Hornblower—"

The ambassador stopped, and a look of confusion crossed his face. He looked at the packet again, then briefly at the portrait of the king before his eyes settled back on Brewer. His eyes were wide, as though recognizing Brewer for the first time.

"Mr. Brewer," he said, almost in a whisper. "Of course. Why didn't I put it together before? You were with Hornblower on St. Helena, weren't you?"

"Yes, Mr. Ambassador."

"Mr. Brewer," the ambassador said as he rose from his desk and walked around toward him. "I would like to hear about your experiences there, if you don't mind?" He took Brewer gently by the arm and led him to two overstuffed leather chairs before the fireplace. He picked up the bell that was on the table in between and rang it. A servant appeared in the doorway.

"Coffee for two," Canning said, and the servant disappeared. "Please, Mr. Brewer, sit, be comfortable. Tell me about Napoleon Bonaparte. I understand your Admiral very nearly became...*friends* with the old boy."

Brewer bristled at the implication that Horatio Hornblower could fall under the influence of the Corsican like that. "I assure you, sir, that the governor—"

"Yes, yes, of course," Canning said, brushing Brewer's protest aside. "Privately, I will confide in you that Hornblower did an incredibly good job under very difficult conditions. He literally had nearly the entire world against him, don't you know. Too many people simply wanted Bonaparte dead."

Brewer was shocked. He sat back in his seat and stared at the empty fireplace. And yet, he knew what the ambassador was saying was correct, one need look no further that the Austrian and Prussian courts or the Bourbon regime in Paris to find any number of royals that would give their entire fortunes to see Bonaparte dead, the slower and more painfully, the better.

Canning paused when the servant returned with the coffee and set the silver service down on the table. The ambassador poured them each a cup and sat back in his chair with his. Brewer picked up his cup and saucer and tasted the steaming beverage. Not surprisingly, it was quite good.

"I suppose Captain Norman knows about your time on St. Helena?" Canning asked.

Brewer nodded.

Canning nodded in sympathy. "That can't make your job any easier, I imagine. James Norman never could stand having anyone around who could outshine him."

"But why should that matter to him?" Brewer said. "His reputation is secure."

Canning looked up in surprise. "Don't tell me he's told you the story of shooting the Frog who got Nelson?"

Brewer was confused. "No, he didn't tell me, but I've heard the story from other sources."

Canning sat back and shook his head. "Bless my soul, every time that story comes up, I'm surprised that Norman hasn't been called on it yet."

Brewer couldn't help himself. "What do you mean?"

Canning smiled. "It's quite simple, Lieutenant: James Norman has made a naval career based on the assumption that he picked up a musket and shot the French sharpshooter who killed Lord Nelson on the deck of HMS *Victory* at Trafalgar in 1805." The ambassador paused to drink coffee. "He did no such thing."

Brewer just stared, not trusting himself to say anything. Finally, he took a sip of coffee while he gathered his wits. "And may I ask how you know this?"

Canning sat forward. "I was there, Lieutenant. On the poop of HMS *Victory* when Nelson was gunned down. Oh, Norman was there as well, although *why* is a mystery that was never investigated; Norman's action station was on a lower gun deck. Nelson was between myself and Norman, so I saw the whole thing. Nelson cried out and fell, and several men ran to him. I clearly saw Norman across the deck standing next to a Royal Marine. The marine raised his weapon and fired, taking out a French sharpshooter in the rigging of the French ship. He was immediately gunned down. Captain Hardy looked up from where Nelson had fallen, saw Norman holding a gum, and anointed him as the avenger of Lord Nelson! He wrote a report to that effect, and the career of James Norman in His Majesty's navy was assured. And Norman let it happen; he never said a word to Captain Hardy, even in private, to say that it wasn't him but the dead marine who did it."

Brewer sighed and gazed at the portrait of King George IV. So, that was it, the reason why Norman was the way he was. His reputation was a lie. Fifteen years trying to live up to a lie, all the while afraid that the truth might come out. Brewer shook his head; it would be more than enough to derange the sanest of men. Of course, a man of character would have confessed to Hardy then and there aboard *Victory* before his report left the ship.

Brewer sighed again and shifted in his chair. Beside him, he could see the ambassador savoring his coffee and enjoying his discomfort.

"If what you say is true," Brewer said, "it was one error in judgment fifteen years ago. Almost anyone in his position might have done the same."

"Really?" Canning said. "Can you picture Horatio Hornblower remaining silent?"

Brewer looked into the fireplace. Blast him, the fool was right; Hornblower would have gone to Hardy privately at the first opportunity and set things straight.

Canning smiled and nodded in triumph. "I can see you know I am right about it. But enough of this; Lieutenant, I wish to hear of your experiences on St. Helena."

Brewer's mind was only half thinking about what he was saying, so he told Canning the whole story about his interactions with the former Emperor of the French, including their last meeting days before he left the island. Canning listened intently, occasionally interrupting with a question to clarify something, and when Brewer was finished, Canning sat back in his chair in astonishment.

"I say," he said softly, "what a tale." The ambassador rose and returned to his desk where he picked up a bell and rang it. Brewer rose as well and turned to watch what was going on. When the servant appeared in the doorway, Canning picked up the addendum he had been working on and handed it to him.

"Include this in the packet for Bermuda and seal it," Canning said. "Bring it here to me along with the receipt as soon as it is sealed."

"Pardon me, Mr. Ambassador," Brewer said, "but I would like your orders in writing, if you please."

Canning looked at Brewer for a moment and then smiled. He looked at the servant and nodded.

The servant bowed and disappeared into the outer office. Canning picked up another report from his desk and proceeded to ignore Brewer completely until the servant returned with the packet and receipt, which he handed to the ambassador, along with another document which the ambassador scanned briefly before signing.

"Sign here, Mr. Brewer," the ambassador said as he indicated a line on the receipt. Brewer signed, and the ambassador handed him the packet. "Thank you, Mr. Brewer. Here is the packet for Bermuda, and here are your written orders for the journey. Good luck to you; Lord knows, working for James Norman, you're going to need it."

"Thank you, sir," Brewer said as he took the packet and left the ambassador's residence. He walked back to the wharf, his mind staggered by the ambassador's revelation about Captain Norman. It went a long way toward explaining the captain's actions. After all, someone whose career was based on a lie might feel the need to compel the crew's obedience with a heavy hand. Brewer shook his head in disgust. *What a waste,* he thought. *Other than the brutality, Norman seems to be a good officer. What might he have been if he didn't have this hanging over him? And yet, he has a good record as captain, with a number of prizes taken. Bloody shame, this—*

Brewer suddenly stopped as the ambassador's last words came ringing back through his mind. *He said, 'Good luck to you; Lord knows, working for James Norman, you're going to need it.'* The meaning of those words was clear—Brewer was in great danger. Norman would certainly suspect that the ambassador had told him the full story of what happened on HMS *Victory* and fear Brewer would use his knowledge to undermine his authority and possibly even speak to Admiral Hornblower to have him removed from command. How long would it take for the captain to trump up some charges and have Brewer arrested and transferred? Brewer frowned at the thought; he had no doubt this was well within Norman's capabilities. Brewer decided his best course of action was to keep the information to himself for the foreseeable future. The only problem with the plan was, what would he do if the captain asked him a direct question?

As soon as he set foot back aboard *Defiant,* Brewer headed straight for the captain's cabin. Captain Norman listened in silence as Brewer relayed the ambassador's instructions for delivering the packet to Bermuda without delay. When he finished, Norman looked at the packet that lay on his desk.

"Do you know what's in here?" he asked.

"The ambassador said it contains a copy of what we brought to him along with an addendum he composed."

Norman looked at his first officer. “But you have no idea what is in this so-called addendum?”

“No, sir.”

Norman sighed. “Stratford is up to his usual tricks. He’ll do anything in his power to inconvenience me whenever possible, and now he intends to make me late for my rendezvous with Hornblower’s squadron.” He paused to look out the stern windows at British merchantman unloading cargo in the distance. He sighed and turned back to Brewer.

“What else did the ambassador talk about?”

Brewer shifted uncomfortably. “Not very much, sir. He made a few disparaging remarks about your service in HMS *Victory*, which I put down to petty jealousy on his part.”

Norman’s eyes narrowed. “William,” he said softly, “I know Stratford Canning. If he mentioned anything regarding our time on HMS *Victory*, he told the story of the death of Lord Nelson. Is that correct?”

Brewer frowned and looked out the stern windows for a moment. What was he to do? Norman’s error fifteen years ago was one of character; was he any better if he lied now?

Brewer turned back to his captain. “Yes, sir, he did.”

Norman nodded. “I thought so. What did he say?”

Brewer sighed and looked at his hands, folded in his lap. “He said that you did not avenge Nelson, sir. He said it was a marine beside you that did it, who was immediately gunned down by the French. According to the ambassador, you picked up the marine’s musket, and Captain Hardy looked up and mistakenly credited you with the kill.”

“I see,” Norman said. His eyes were lowered for several moments, and then he looked back up at Brewer. “And do you believe him?”

Brewer leaned forward, his eyes holding Norman’s. “Sir, if you tell me that you were the man who gunned down the Frog, then I will believe you.”

Norman nodded and lowered his eyes again. Brewer

hoped he would confess and tell him the truth, but the years of playing a part proved too much, and Norman remained silent. After a few minutes, he rose from his desk and went to look out the stern windows, hands clasped behind his back. Hope rose again in Brewer's heart, but the captain's first words crushed it.

"You may return to your duties, Mr. Brewer," he said. "Make preparations to sail in the morning for Bermuda."

Brewer rose sadly. "Aye aye, sir."

He left the cabin without a word.

CHAPTER 13

A strong wind out of the southwest blew HMS *Defiant* down the Potomac, away from Washington City and out into the Chesapeake Bay. The pilot they took on board guided them down the winding river, slowly but efficiently. Brewer glanced at the passing shore as they coasted down the Potomac toward the open sea. It was studded with onlookers, turned out to watch a warship head downriver. A couple of the younger ones actually waved as the ship glided past, and one little lad even saluted as he sucked his thumb. Brewer waved back, remembering how the sight of a warship when he was a boy turned him toward a life at sea and wondering if it would do the same for any of these boys.

They dropped the pilot off with their thanks before making their way toward the mouth of the bay and the Atlantic Ocean. Captain Norman appeared on deck, but only long enough to give the order to sail. He acknowledged the salute of his officers, but he ignored Brewer completely.

"Mr. Greene," he said, "Once clear of the bay, make your course for Bermuda. All possible sail."

Greene cast a quick glance at Brewer before replying. "Aye aye, sir," and dashing off, bellowing orders as he went.

Norman watched him go. "I shall be in my quarters if I am needed."

"Aye aye, sir," they said as they saluted. Brewer, Phillips, and Sweeney watched the captain walk back to the stairway, his head down, whether against the wind or for some other reason, Brewer couldn't tell. Brewer turned to find the other two looking to him for an explanation.

"It seems that the ambassador is no friend of the captain's," he said, "and the captain believes this trip is simply a device to make us late to rendezvous with the squadron."

Sweeney grunted and turned to Brewer. "Well, I can tell you, Mr. Brewer, I'm not happy about being thrown out into the middle of the Atlantic in the midst of hurricane season. If we get caught by one of them, we'd be in for a very rough ride."

"It would be the same in the Caribbean," Brewer shrugged. "In any case, I don't think the ambassador cares about hurricanes, Mr. Sweeney."

The sailing master glowered. "Let him sail through one once. That'll change his mind, if he survives it."

"The ambassador has served at sea," Brewer said.

Sweeney looked at him. "Really? Where?"

"He said he was on HMS *Victory* with Captain Norman at Trafalgar. Norman confirmed it to me. He said the ambassador resigned his commission and went into the Foreign Service when Norman was given command of *Defiant* over him."

Sweeney narrowed his eyes as though he were processing this information, and then he looked at Brewer thoughtfully. Brewer thought for a moment he was going to say something to him, but the sailing master seemed to change his mind at the last second. Instead, Sweeney just grunted.

"Apparently, if he ever experienced one, he's forgotten how unpleasant hurricanes can be. I should welcome a chance to help him get his sea legs again."

Brewer and Phillips grinned along with the master, each enjoying the thought of the diplomat on a heaving deck. Brewer excused himself and stepped away to study the waves passing by. He allowed his eyes to follow a bird aloft, where the sails caught his eye, and he took a moment to admire the sight of sails at work.

When he looked around the deck again, he spotted the sailing master studying the log, and he headed aft. Sweeney glanced up and nodded to him before looking back to the log again.

"Mr. Sweeney," Brewer said, "got a minute?"

Sweeney looked up at the first lieutenant and nodded. He closed the logbook and handed it to one of his mates and followed Brewer to the fantail. Brewer glanced at the deck to make sure the captain's skylight was closed. Sweeney nodded his approval at the younger man's caution.

They leaned on the railing and looked out over *Defiant's* wake. Brewer just leaned there and studied the waves. Sweeney said nothing, determined to wait the first lieutenant out.

Brewer sighed and looked out at the retreating sea. "What do you know about the captain's time on HMS *Victory*?"

Sweeney shot a look at his friend. "A little. You mean about the captain avenging Nelson after Trafalgar?"

Brewer nodded.

Sweeney shrugged, his eyes scanning the waves. "I know what most everyone else knows, that's all."

Brewer nodded. "That's what I thought, too. Norman picked up a musket and shot the Frog that got Nelson."

Sweeney turned and leaned in close. "And as long as we are on this ship, Mr. Brewer, that's the way it will stay."

The look in Sweeney's eye was unmistakable. Brewer nodded and looked back out over the sea. Nothing could be gained by sharing what the ambassador had said; the captain's reaction confirmed the truth of it, and that was enough. Perhaps he could talk to the admiral when they reached the squadron about being transferred off *Defiant*—before something happened.

Mr. Sweeney changed the subject and spoke about the danger areas of the American coast just to the south of where they would reenter the Atlantic Ocean. Brewer was listening only half-heartedly until one particular word caught his attention.

"Excuse me?" he said. "What was that?"

"Ah," said Mr. Sweeney with a smile, "I thought that might get your attention. You heard me right, Lieutenant, I said *Blackbeard*. 'Twas nought but a short jump south of here that the dread pirate was caught by the good Lt. Maynard and lost his head in North Carolina's Outer Banks. That was back in 1718. I bet we'll be chasing his great-grandson soon enough."

"Who knows, Mr. Sweeney?" Brewer said. "Maybe it's his ghost that's been raiding off Boston. That reminds me: I wonder what they'll be able to tell us about this pirate activity when we reach Bermuda?"

Sweeney shrugged. "Who knows? What do they have for ships?"

Brewer shook his head.

"We'll see when we get there," Sweeney said. He searched the sky and said, "I'm much more concerned about the weather."

Brewer looked up, but the sky was clear at the moment. "Hopefully, the sun will smile on our journey, Mr. Sweeney."

The sailing master snorted loudly and muttered something about pigs flying. Brewer laughed and slapped him on the back before heading forward to watch Mr. Phillips conduct gun drills.

The favorable winds held, pushing the big frigate more

than halfway to Bermuda before the lookout cried out.

"Deck there! Sail off the larboard beam!"

Brewer, Greene, and Sweeney rushed to the railing, each with a glass ready to his eye. They quickly focused on the growing patch of white on the horizon. Sweeney lowered his glass and looked at Brewer.

"Think it might be an American frigate?" he asked. "Maybe one of the big ones? *Constitution*, maybe. Didn't we just miss her at Boston?"

Brewer nodded. "Mr. Sweeney, alter course to intercept. Mr. Greene, my respects to the captain. Please inform him we've sighted a sail on the horizon and that I've altered course to intercept."

Both men rushed off to carry out their assignments while Brewer continued to study the new arrival. Even at this distance, Brewer could tell this was no small ship. The cut of her sails soon marked the newcomer as a member of the fledgling United States Navy. Once held in derision by the Royal Navy, American victories in several one-on-one frigate actions during the War of 1812 had sobered the Navy's regard. Now any sane captain looked at engaging the Americans as his last resort rather than his first.

The sound of footsteps attracted his attention, and Brewer turned to see Captain Norman approaching. A midshipman handed his captain a glass and stepped back, ready to do his bidding.

"Where away, Mr. Brewer?" the captain asked.

Brewer pointed to a spot on the horizon. "There, sir. Two points forward of the beam,"

"I've got her," Norman said. Just as he said it, *Defiant* swung around as Mr. Sweeney altered course. Norman and Brewer rushed forward to watch as the British ship closed the gap. "She's American, all right."

"I thought so," Brewer said. "Mr. Sweeney thinks it may be one of their big frigates, possibly *Constitution*."

Norman lowered his glass and stared at the horizon. His eyes narrowed for a moment, and then he sighed.

"Resume course for Bermuda."

Brewer lowered his glass and stared at his captain. "Bermuda, sir?"

Norman nodded. "Most ships in this part of the Atlantic stop there anyway for water or mail, so perhaps we'll see them there. I also do not want to give them a chance to gauge our speed if I can help it."

Brewer nodded to himself. He'd forgotten that *Defiant* and the others of her class were still supposedly a mystery to the Americans. He put the glass to his eye again and focused in on the strange sail. He would dearly love to get a close look at an American of the *Constitution's* class. Those big frigates had routinely savaged the British thirty-six gunners during the recent war, and they were the direct reason for *Defiant* and her sisters.

Brewer left the captain and went aft as *Defiant* swung around and resumed her heading for Bermuda. When he got to the fantail, he put the glass to his eye again. Sure enough, the stranger had swung around to the same course and was now heading for Bermuda as well. *Well,* he thought, *it looks like the captain might get to host his dinner for the Americans after all.*

Dawn had not yet broken when Brewer came up on deck for the morning watch, but the first lieutenant could tell from the pitching of the deck that they were in for a rough ride. He made his way aft to the quarterdeck and found Lieutenant Phillips.

"I'm here to relieve you," Brewer said.

Phillips saluted. "Thank you, sir. Wind picked up about an hour ago, and I ordered a reef taken. Right now we are running under double-reefed tops'ls and the main course, sir. Our speed's picked up as well, but at the last cast we were making five knots."

Brewer nodded, knowing it was time to check their speed again. He looked around and saw Mr. Tyler standing by.

"Cast the log," Brewer said, and the midshipman grabbed the device and cast it.

After Brewer finished his business with Mr. Phillips, the younger man made his way below decks, and Brewer turned to look for Tyler, but the swinging of *Defiant's* aft light made it hard, and the howling wind stole any sound that tried to travel more than an arm's length or so. Brewer made his way aft and came upon Tyler and the mate helping him just as they were pulling the log back on board.

"Sorry it took so long, sir," Tyler said, "but we had a bit of trouble making a proper cast. Just bringing it back aboard now. Looks like nigh on to eight knots, sir."

"Very good, Mr. Tyler," Brewer said. "Make sure you note it in the book and secure the log." Brewer made his way back to the wheel and found that Mr. Sweeney had now come up on deck. It was obvious, once Brewer got close enough to see him clearly in the fading darkness, that he was worried.

"Good morning, Mr. Sweeney," Brewer said. "Anything wrong?"

Sweeney saluted. "Mr. Brewer. I'm not sure I like the sound of this wind."

Brewer looked around into the darkness. "How long do you think until daylight?"

Sweeney looked at the sky, and then at the compass. He thought for a moment, then he looked at Brewer. "An hour," he said. "Maybe less."

Brewer nodded. "What do you recommend?"

Sweeney looked as though he was reviewing a list in his mind, then he looked back at Brewer. He stepped close against the wind and said, "Take in all sails until daylight."

Brewer considered this. He looked over his shoulder and saw Mr. Tyler. "Mr. Tyler, my respects to the captain. Tell him the wind is up, and I would like to take in all sails until daylight."

Tyler saluted and rushed off to deliver his message. Brewer turned back to Sweeney.

"What do you think?"

"I'll know more when I can see the clouds, but I don't like it one bit."

"I was afraid you'd say that. I don't like the swells I've been feeling."

The two men hung on to the wheel in an effort to steady themselves against the heaving of the deck. Brewer was just beginning to wonder what was taking Mr. Tyler so long when he was surprised to see Captain Norman emerge from the darkness and grab hold of the wheel as well. The two saluted as best they could without being thrown from their feet.

"I was coming on deck to discuss your request, Mr. Brewer," Norman said, "but I can see that, as usual, you and Mr. Sweeney know what you're doing." He turned to Tyler. "Call all hands to take in sails."

Tyler rushed off, shouting orders man to man over the roar of the wind. Presently *Defiant* looked like an anthill during an earthquake as her crew emerged from the comparative dryness of the lower deck and began to carefully climb the treacherous shrouds and accomplish their tasks. The ship was rolling and pitching the whole time, which meant that the higher the crew climbed, the more dangerous it became for them. Brewer watched the men ascending into the darkness and prayed that no-one missed a hold. Presently, Mr. Tyler returned to report.

He saluted the captain. "All sails taken in, sir!"

"Well done, Mr. Tyler!" Norman said. "Mr. Brewer, dismiss the watch below, and send the hands to breakfast."

"Aye aye, sir."

Norman nodded and made his way below decks again. Brewer looked over at Sweeney and raised his eyebrows. The sailing master shrugged.

"Just remember," he said, "don't lower your guard."

Dawn came, and with it the first look at the sky. Sweeney did not like the look of the clouds to the south. Brewer requested the captain to come on deck, and Sweeney presented his case.

"Sir," he said as they all hung on the wheel again, "we need to decide if we are going to try to beat the storm across to Bermuda or if you want to turn north or northwest and run before it."

Norman studied the sky to the south before looking back at his sailing master. "How much worse do you think it will get?"

Sweeney looked again to the south and nodded to himself. "I think we got ourselves a hurricane coming, Captain. Not a real big one, I don't think, but nothing to sneeze at, even for a fifty gunner."

Norman nodded. "Do you think we can beat it?"

Sweeney looked south again and shook his head. "I dunno, Captain."

Norman looked at Brewer, then turned to study the southern sky. He turned back and looked Sweeney hard in the eye. "Mr. Sweeney," he said, "let's try to beat the storm. Best sail for Bermuda, if you please!"

"Aye aye, sir," the sailing master said, but Brewer doubted he was happy with the captain's decision.

Norman didn't seem to notice Sweeney's disapproval. He turned to his first lieutenant. "Mr. Brewer, call the hands to make sail. Just be careful not to roll her over."

"Aye aye, sir," Brewer said, and he left his captain to issue his orders. He didn't like the captain's decision, either, but there was nothing he or Sweeney could do to show displeasure. "All hands on deck to make sail! Hands to braces!"

Once more *Defiant* exploded as men seemed to erupt from below decks and ascend the rigging to their assigned spots on the yardarms. In his mind, Brewer had often likened them to so many spiders; he was amazed that most of them weren't thrown by the pitching and swaying of the ship.

Defiant leaped forward like a racehorse under the jockey's whip as the wind took up the new sail. Brewer also noticed that she was slowly rolling over on her beam end. He looked back to the captain standing there on the quarterdeck. Norman was watching the seas and the sails but made no effort to interfere with Brewer's handling of the ship. Brewer turned to Greene, who had come up alongside him.

"Make sure all the guns are secure!" he shouted to be heard above the wind. "The last thing we need right now is for one of those monsters to break free and go careening down the deck!"

Greene nodded and saluted before he staggered off. Brewer watched him until he was safely below deck, then he headed over to the captain.

"I think we need to ease her a bit, sir," Brewer said. "She's rolling awfully far."

Norman looked around again before leaning in toward Brewer. "Yes, I think you're right," he shouted. "Better take in a reef and see if that brings her back enough!"

Brewer saluted. "Aye aye, sir!" He turned to see Mr. Tyler standing ready. "Mr. Tyler, pass the word—all hands take in one reef! Have them stay there aloft until we see how she handles."

Tyler nodded and moved off. Speaking trumpets were useless in a wind this strong, and anyone trying to wave a signal would likely be blown down the deck if not actually overboard. The only way to pass orders was man to man. Brewer noted the messengers begin climbing up the shrouds, pausing at each yardarm to pass the message, which was then passed from man to man. Brewer hoped they finished the maneuver quickly, and that the reef allowed *Defiant* to straighten up enough to make sailing safe for a speed run to Bermuda.

Brewer felt *Defiant's* speed slow when the reef was taken in, but the wind picked up and the ship shot forward again. Fortunately, the deck rolled back, and when Brewer looked over at the captain, the latter smiled and nodded. Brewer sighed in relief and ordered the hands out of the yards to safety.

A couple of hours later, Brewer was in his cabin trying desperately not to be thrown from his bunk while reading *Ivanhoe* when there was a knock at his door, and Mr. Short stuck his head in. Brewer noticed that he was looking decidedly seasick. Brewer sympathized; truth be told, he was not far from it himself.

"Mr. Sweeney's respects," the peaked midshipman said, "and he has sent for the captain to come up on deck. Would you please come as well?"

"Yes, I'll come," Brewer said as he climbed out of his bunk, and he immediately regretted his decision. As soon as he stood, he discovered it was much harder to keep his footing on the pitching deck than it was to stay in his bunk that hung from the beams in his cabin. He was immediately thrown against the far wall of his cabin and was dazed for a moment, but he shook his head clear and made it up on deck without injury. He saw Mr. Sweeney hanging on to the wheel and made his way over. The sky, he noticed, was full of fast-moving, angry dark clouds.

"Well, Mr. Sweeney?" Brewer shouted when he reached the wheel.

"Came up on us sudden, sir," the sailing master shouted back. "I don't think we can beat it now. Do you want to try to run before it?"

"Where's the Captain?"

"I sent for him, but he did not answer so I sent Mr. Short for you! But I don't like it, Mr. Brewer! Indeed, I don't!"

"Let me go ask the captain!" Brewer shouted. Sweeney nodded, and Brewer turned to make his way below deck.

The sentry was trying his best to stay on his feet, finally having to brace his feet and forearms against the walls of the passageway. Brewer knocked on the captain's door; receiving no answer he knocked again. He looked at the sentry and was assured that the captain was indeed in there, so he decided to chance the captain's anger and opened the door to let himself in.

He found Captain Norman sitting at his desk, one arm holding the desk and the other on the arm of the chair to brace himself, looking toward the stern windows. Brewer noted that someone—probably Mr. Sweeney—had ordered the deadlights rigged to protect the windows from the stormy seas. The captain did not appear to notice Brewer's entrance.

"Sir!" Brewer said, as he staggered over to the desk. He was almost thrown across it at the last moment by the pitching deck. "Sir!"

Captain Norman looked at him. "What is it, Mr. Brewer?"

Brewer could hardly believe his ears. "Sir! You must come on deck! Mr. Sweeney says the sea has come up suddenly, and he now believes we cannot outrun the storm to Bermuda! Do you want to turn and run before it?"

Norman looked at him without saying a word, cold eyes staring from under hooded eyelids. Brewer thought for a moment his captain didn't hear him, but Norman finally spoke.

"Are you happy now, Mr. Brewer?" he said. "I'm sure you and your friend, the ambassador, talked all about me while you were having tea with him, didn't you? I'm sure he told you all about what happened with Nelson, didn't he? Did you come down here to gloat?"

Brewer was astounded at what he heard. First he wondered if his captain was drunk, then he wondered if he was insane.

"Sir!" Brewer tried again. "You must come up on deck! The storm—"

Norman pounded on the desk. "Curse you, Mr. Brewer!" he screamed hysterically. "You think you're something just because of a chance meeting with a blowhard who once frightened all those cowards who sit on the thrones of Europe! And you were nothing but a secretary! A glorified *clerk!*" Norman stood up as best he could. "You are nothing, *Mr*. Brewer! *Nothing!*"

Brewer stood erect and faced his captain, his face firm and his mouth closed. Norman was panting, his eyes wild and daring Brewer to act. Without a word, Brewer came to attention, picked up his hat, and left the captain's quarters.

When he stepped out on the deck again, Brewer could see immediately that the situation had grown worse. If a massive wave hit the ship broadside, it could easily roll *Defiant* over on its beam ends, and the entire crew would die. He made his way carefully over to the wheel and found Mr. Sweeney there, hanging on for dear life along with two of his mates.

"Well?" Sweeney shouted.

Brewer shook his head. "The captain is... indisposed."

Brewer thought he heard Sweeney curse at the news.

"What do you recommend?" Brewer asked.

"Turn," Sweeney shouted. "Run before it."

Brewer cast a quick glance aloft, and then at the raging sea, and nodded.

"I agree," he shouted. He turned to see Mr. Greene and motioned to him. "Mr. Greene, turn the ship away from the wind! We're going to run before it!"

Greene nodded and ran off to give the orders that would alter course and hopefully save the ship from disaster. Brewer turned back to help Sweeney and his mates with the wheel, and when the time came, it took all five of them to get it to turn over against the raging sea. The trouble was not getting the wheel to turn, for it turned freely enough when a trough in the waves exposed the rudder. It was when the ship came down into the sea again, and the waves hit the rudder that the muscle was needed to keep it turned the way they wanted it to be.

They finally got the ship turned to run before the storm, which gave it a much better chance of surviving the heavy seas. They let the wheel come back, and then they fought to keep it on this course. Brewer was about to order the hands aloft again to set more sail when Mr. Sweeney's eyes grew wide at something behind Brewer, and he cried out a warning.

Brewer turned to see Captain Norman on deck with no hat or overcoat, a pistol in his hand. Brewer turned to face the captain and keep Sweeney behind him.

"Mutiny!" Norman screamed as he raised the pistol. "You have defied me for the last time, sir!" He aimed the pistol at Brewer's chest.

Just at that moment, the *Defiant* got "pooped" as a huge wave broke over the rear of the ship and swept down the deck like a tidal wave. Both Brewer and Norman saw it at the last minute, and Brewer made a dive for the wheel to try to hang on and outlast the wave. He felt the water hit him just as the wooden base of the wheel brushed his fingers, and Brewer felt himself being swept away and down the deck. All at once something grabbed his arm and held on. As soon as the wave passed, he looked up to see the face of Mr. Sweeney, who was hanging on to Brewer's arm with one hand and the wheel with the other. Both men stood carefully and clung to the wheel.

"Thank you, Mr. Sweeney," Brewer gasped. "I believe I owe you my life."

"Yes," Sweeney grinned. "You do."

Brewer nodded, still gasping for breath. Suddenly, it hit

him.

"The captain!" He said, standing so quickly that he nearly lost his footing. Sweeney gripped him by the arm and shook his head.

"He's gone."

CHAPTER 14

It was too sudden and terrible to comprehend. Brewer looked at Sweeney as though he were speaking a foreign language.

Sweeney said, "The wave took him over the side. I was barely able to reach you."

Brewer leaned against the wheel and looked around the deck. He felt lost, as though he were in a fog. He turned when he heard Sweeney call his name.

"Mr. Brewer!" he said. "What are your orders?"

Sweeney reached over and took Brewer by the arm and shook him. He leaned in close and said, "You are in command now, Captain!"

Brewer shook his head to regain his focus and nodded. "Thank you, Mr. Sweeney."

The sailing master stood before him expectantly. Brewer looked around the deck again, but this time it was with a trained, appraising eye that missed nothing of the ship's condition. He saw Mr. Short in the shrouds, and he was pleased to see that the young midshipman had the presence of mind to avoid the wave that had claimed Captain Norman.

"Mr. Short! Take some hands and search the deck for

anyone incapacitated by the wave. Take any injured to Dr. Spinelli in the sick bay."

"Look out!"

Brewer spun to see another wave about to crash over *Defiant*'s poop. He dove for the wheel and barely managed to grip it before he felt the wave crash into him. His arms ached with the impact, and he prayed his finger hold was good enough. The wave washed over him, and Lieutenant Brewer was pleasantly surprised to discover he could still breathe.

Suddenly, Brewer was aware of several things happening at once. The wave that broke over *Defiant*'s poop caused her to broach, meaning the wave turned the ship sideways, putting her in great danger of being rolled over and sinking. At almost the same instant, Brewer and Sweeney turned to watch helplessly as first *Defiant*'s foremast and then her main topmast toppled into the sea. Fortunately, the shrouds held, causing the fallen masts to act as a sea anchor and pulled the bow around to straighten out the ship.

"Mr. Greene," Brewer shouted. "Get some hands to cut away that wreckage!"

Brewer looked in desperation at the tattered rags left on the sticks and knew *Defiant* was in trouble. There was no way those sails could catch enough wind to drive *Defiant* in front of the storm, and setting any other sails would increase their chances of rolling over into the sea.

Brewer turned to ask Mr. Sweeney his opinion of the sails when a midshipman ran up to him and practically jumped into his arms in order to make himself heard.

"Sail off the larboard quarter, sir!"

Brewer and Sweeney peered in the direction indicated. They were just able to make out a patch of towering white sails growing larger as the *USS Constitution* approached through the storm. Brewer thought he saw someone gesturing wildly on the other ship and quickly called for a glass. He put it to his eye and saw a young officer waving his hat with one arm and holding up a towing cable with the other. Brewer waved an acknowledgment and pointed toward the bow. The American officer waved again and dashed off to inform his captain.

"Mr. Greene!" Brewer shouted, "Make ready to be taken in tow. Send a party to the bows to receive the line. And make sure that wreckage is cut away in time!"

"Aye aye, sir!" Greene shouted. He ran forward, shouting for Mr. Short and several hands to follow him.

Brewer handed the glass to a waiting midshipman just as Mr. Sweeney joined him at the rail. Both men admired the American frigate as she swept past. An officer—Brewer supposed him to be the captain—saluted, and Brewer automatically returned the gesture. He went forward through the driving rain to watch as the tow cable was passed, concerned that a wave might heave their would-be rescuer into them. He arrived just as the thrown line dropped onto *Defiant's* deck. Greene and his party grabbed it and hauled for all they were worth. Soon Brewer saw what he was looking for, the thicker 3-inch cable, bent on the heaving line, coming from one of the American's after gunports. He was pleased to see that the American captain had the same concerns as he himself did, for he saw two spars were out from the American's stern gallery to boom *Defiant* off if necessary. Brewer turned back to see his men hauling in the thick cable now, and Mr. Greene himself supervised the securing of it before reporting to his captain. Brewer could hardly hear him over the storm, but he nodded his acknowledgement. *Constitution* turned and ran before the storm, pulling *Defiant* in her wake.

Mr. Sweeney caught up to him as *Defiant* swung into line behind their American savior. "That should do nicely," he said, nodding his approval. "We should be safe enough now, as long as our friend doesn't lose any sticks.

Brewer nodded. "I agree. Mr. Greene, detail a

midshipman to watch the American for any signals. I'm going below to check in with Dr. Spinelli."

Sweeney acknowledged, and Brewer made his way below to the sickbay. He found the surgeon setting the dislocated shoulder of young Mr. Short. Brewer noticed the boy was trying not to cry.

"Well, Mr. Short," Brewer said, "What seems to be the trouble?"

The midshipman winced as the surgeon adjusted his shoulder. "Bit of a bump, sir."

Mr. Spinelli looked at Brewer. "That 'bump' happened when our young midshipman tried to topple the mainmast. Assisted by the wave, of course."

Brewer looked at the boy with a mock frown. "Don't overstep yourself, Mr. Short," he said. "Leave that to the officers."

The boy tried to chuckle, but ended up crying out in pain.

Brewer patted him gently on his good shoulder. “Let that be a lesson to you, Mr. Short. Never laugh at your officers.”

Short looked up to make sure he wasn’t in trouble and was rewarded by the two officers’ laughter. He blushed and smiled and tried not to move.

“He’s very lucky,” the surgeon said quietly. “You sent him forward just before the wave hit, and it swept poor Short right off his feet and down the deck. We *think* he slammed into the mainmast and dislocated his shoulder. He’d have been lost over the side for sure if it hadn’t been for McCleary there grabbing him.” The doctor pointed to the big Cornishman who was standing against the bulkhead.

“Well, Mr. McCleary,” Brewer said, “thank you for saving Mr. Short’s life.”

McCleary blushed and shrugged. “Just sort of bumped into each other, sir.”

Brewer smiled and nodded. “You’re a good man,

McCleary. I'm glad you're on this ship."

McCleary smiled. "Thank you, sir."

Brewer turned back to the surgeon. "How bad is it?"

Spinelli shook his head. "I don't know yet. I was about to send McCleary to complete Mr. Short's sweep of the deck."

Brewer nodded and looked at the big seaman. "Go." McCleary nodded and was gone.

"I must return to the deck," Brewer said. "Keep me informed."

The surgeon said he would, and Brewer left the sickbay.

"Sir?"

Spinelli turned. "Yes, Mr. Short?"

"Is Mr. Brewer the captain now?"

The surgeon paused, struck by the thought. "Yes," he said, "I suppose he must be."

"I'm glad," Short said.

Spinelli looked back to the door. "So am I."

Back on the deck, Brewer found Mr. Sweeney and two mates manning the wheel. A quick look at the sky told him that they weren't out of danger just yet.

"What do you think?" Brewer asked Mr. Sweeney.

"We should weather it," the sailing master replied, "as long as it doesn't get any worse. If I'm reading this right, I think we might be clear of it by morning."

"Let's hope you're right. What's our situation?"

Sweeney shrugged. "I'm not sure. Mr. Greene and Mr. Phillips went forward about ten minutes ago."

Brewer nodded and headed forward himself. He passed the stump of the mainmast, still standing about ten feet high. The sight of it made Brewer shiver, and he hurried forward. He found Greene and Phillips at the tow cable. *Constitution* was barely visible through the rain and haze, about thirty yards out in front.

"How goes it?" Brewer asked as he joined the other

officers.

Greene and Phillips saluted. “We almost lost the tow,” Greene said. “We were able to get it secured in time. It won’t come loose again, sir.”

Brewer peered out at the American in front. “Any word from our friend?”

“Nothing, sir,” Phillips said. “But I’ll make sure we keep a watch, in case he has to cut us loose.”

“Thank you, Mr. Phillips,” Brewer said. “Have a sea anchor made up, just in case we need it. I’ll leave you in charge here, then. Mr. Greene, let’s go aft and see to the rest of *Defiant*.”

As they made their way aft, Greene leaned in close and said, “Is it true, sir? About the captain, I mean.”

Brewer stopped and looked at him. “Yes,” he said simply. “But we can’t think about that now. We’ve got a wounded ship to look after, if we want to survive this. Find the carpenter. I want to know how it looks below.”

“Aye aye, sir!” Greene saluted and was gone. Brewer turned and looked nervously at *Defiant’s* lone remaining mizzenmast. He noted that someone—probably Mr. Sweeney—had “goose-winged” the mizzen topsail, pulling down the lower corners while leaving the center still furled. This exposed enough sail to give the ship some forward motion without taking a chance of a sudden gust of wind laying her over on her beam ends.

Brewer turned and hurried aft to find Mr. Sweeney. He had barely arrived when Mr. Greene reappeared.

“Mr. Wayne’s respects, sir,” Greene said. “He said to tell you some of the lower gun ports are leaking, but so far it’s nothing the pumps can’t handle. He also said the deadlights are holding across the stern windows, but he can’t say for how long.”

Brewer nodded and turned to see Mr. Sweeney with a smile on his face, and for the first time he thought they just might survive the night.

The storm blew itself out just after dawn. Brewer and Sweeney, still on deck and manning the wheel by themselves, welcomed the sunlight.

"Well," Sweeney said, "looks like we made it."

"Yes," Brewer said. "Now we can take stock and look to putting the old girl back together again. By the way, Mr. Sweeney, I will need a report from you regarding the loss of Captain Norman."

Sweeney nodded, taking the liberty since they were alone. He leaned in close. "And you, sir? What is your view of the matter?"

Brewer shrugged. "Not a death I'd wish on anyone."

"Timely, though," Sweeney said. "He was about to shoot you."

"Yes," Brewer said as he looked away.

"No telling the ways of Providence," Sweeney said. "I wonder what made him do it?"

Brewer looked back at the sailing master, ready to tell him, but he looked away again without saying anything. Sweeney nodded to himself, looking at Brewer's back.

"I'm going below to the cap— to the captain's cabin," Brewer said. "I want to go through our orders, in case there was something Captain Norman didn't disclose. Mr. Greene has the deck."

"Aye aye, sir," Sweeney said.

Brewer walked solemnly down the passageway to what would soon be his new home. He knew this was what he had worked for his whole life, command of a King's ship, but this first time, under these circumstances, it was eerie to nod to the sentry and let himself in. He put his hat down on the desk and looked around. He was surprised at how little storm damage there was, but then he remembered that Jenkins had probably already cleaned most of it up.

"Jenkins?" he called.

Captain Norman's valet appeared in the doorway to the pantry. He stood erect, but his face was a mask of sadness. Brewer thought he might have been crying.

"Is it true, Mr. Brewer?" he asked.

"Yes," Brewer said. "I'm afraid it is."

Jenkins bowed his head for a moment, then looked up. "How?"

"A wave broke over the poop. The captain was caught out in the open, and he didn't have a chance to grab hold of anything. The wave swept him over the side."

Jenkins looked Brewer full in the face. "I don't know about the rest of the crew," he said, "but the captain was good to me."

"Yes," Brewer said. "Jenkins, I need to get into the dispatch box to look at the ship's orders. Can you find something to break the lock open?"

"Yes, sir," Jenkins said. He disappeared for a few moments and returned with a hammer. He handed it to Brewer. "Is there something I can do for you, Mr. Brewer?"

"Yes," Brewer said. "Please sit down. I need you to pack up Captain Norman's belongings and stow them below. Did he have any relatives?"

Jenkins looked off into the distance for just a moment. "Yes, sir, a sister. I believe she lives in Lancashire."

"Good. We'll forward his belongings to her. I'll write a letter to be included. Thank you, Jenkins." The servant rose and returned to the pantry. Brewer broke the lock on the dispatch box and found it contained only the ship's orders (confirmed by the broken Admiralty seal), the packet Brewer himself had signed for and received from the ambassador in Washington City, and the ambassador's written sailing orders. Brewer heard a noise and looked up to see Jenkins had returned with a pot of coffee. He set the service on the corner of the desk and poured a cup for his new captain before silently retiring back to the pantry. Brewer hoped that was a good sign.

He opened the Admiralty orders and read them. He discovered nothing more than Captain Norman had told them. Their destination was the Caribbean to join Admiral Hornblower's squadron, after gathering what information they could along the American coast. Brewer wondered what the Admiral would say when *Defiant* arrived at Jamaica with him in command. He would report Norman's death to the admiral in charge at Bermuda, but it would be highly unusual for him to do anything about replacing Brewer. That would be left to Hornblower, since the ship was to be under his command.

Brewer shook his head and chided himself for daydreaming. He replaced the orders and closed the dispatch box. He eyed the broken lock and thought he couldn't just leave it lying around, so he took it to Jenkins and asked him to secure it until he could get the lock repaired. Just as he was about to leave, it occurred to him that if he was going to deal with the question of Jenkins' position, it ought to be done before they reach Bermuda. *Well,* Brewer thought, *no time like the present*. "Jenkins?"

The servant appeared at the pantry door. "Sir?"

Brewer indicated the chair in front of the desk. "Please, sit down. I need to speak with you."

Jenkins sat. Brewer cleared his throat. "I know this may not be the right time, Jenkins, but I have a proposition for you. Obviously, I cannot pay you what Captain Norman did above your regular Navy pay, but I hope you will consider staying on board *Defiant* and serving me as you served him. If you don't wish to, I will understand. We should be in Bermuda in two or three days. I will sign your discharge from the service there, if you wish, and we can make arrangements to get you passage back to England.

Jenkins looked down at his hands. "Thank you, Mr. Brewer. I'll let you know." Without another word, he rose and retreated to the pantry. Brewer watched him go, wondering what he would decide to do. He left the cabin to allow Jenkins to pack up.

On deck, Brewer found Mr. Greene speaking to Sweeney and walked up to them. Both saluted.

"We have begun stepping the temporary masts, sir," Greene said, "and the sailmaker and his mates are busy getting some sails ready. We should be able to let go of the tow by this evening and make our own way to Bermuda. I've taken the liberty of sending Mr. Phillips below to get some sleep. I told him to relieve me at the first dog watch."

Brewer nodded. "And the butcher's bill?"

"Don't know yet, sir."

"Very good, Mr. Greene," Brewer said. "Carry on. Mr. Sweeney, may I speak to you for a moment?"

The two men left Mr. Greene and moved to the aft railing of the ship for some privacy. Brewer leaned against the rail and crossed his arms. Taking his cue, Mr. Sweeney did the same.

"I spoke to Jenkins," Brewer said. "He is packing up Captain Norman's belongings. I'll write a letter to be included, and once we reach Bermuda, we'll ship them to his sister in Lancashire."

"Do you think Jenkins will stay?" Sweeney asked.

"I don't know," Brewer said. "I hope he does. I did ask him to stay. He's supposed to let us know by the time we reach Bermuda."

"Are you sure you want him to stay?"

Brewer looked at his friend. "Why not? He's the best shipboard cook I've ever seen."

Sweeney shrugged. "He might feel a bit more loyalty to his old captain than to his new one."

Brewer wondered if that would prove to be the case.

"Will you move into the cabin before Bermuda?" Sweeney asked.

"I don't know."

Sweeney shrugged. "No sense in waiting. It's not like you won't get confirmed, especially if the commander at Bermuda leaves it up to Admiral Hornblower."

It was Brewer's turn to shrug.

Sweeney chuckled. "Don't worry, you'll get used to it. All the great ones were once where you are right now: Nelson, Cornwallis, Jervis, Morgan, Hornblower, all of them. You can do it."

Brewer looked at him. "Do you really think so?"

Sweeney smiled and nodded. "Yes! I've seen many first officers in my time, Mr. Brewer. You rank right there with the best of them. Keep your nerve, do what you know to be right to do, and you'll do fine."

Brewer sighed and hoped the sailing master was right.

The surgeon reported that Mr. Short's was the only serious injury. Mr. Greene reported that, beside Captain Norman, there were two seamen missing and presumed lost over the side in the storm. Brewer was pleased with that number; he'd expected it to be much higher due to the loss of the two masts.

Repairs proceeded on the *Defiant*, and they were able to cast off the tow during the second dog watch. Brewer and Sweeney had to keep the speed down with the makeshift masts, but they made it safely, crawling into Bermuda's harbor only two days after bidding their American savior goodbye. They were amazed to discover upon making the harbor that the American frigate had already put in and left. Brewer went ashore immediately and made arrangements with the harbor master to make the final repairs the ship needed. From there, he made his way to the commander's office, where he was shown into the presence of Admiral Sir Jonathan Morgan himself.

Brewer had never met the legendary sailor, but he had heard plenty about him from Hornblower and Bush. He was not a large man, but he carried an air of command about him like nobody Brewer had ever known, save Horatio Hornblower himself.

"Ah, Lieutenant Brewer!" Morgan said. "Good to finally meet you at last! I've heard a great deal about you from Hornblower, of course. Where's Captain..." Morgan looked at his notes. "Norman?"

"Lost at sea, I'm afraid, sir," Brewer said. He gave Morgan a verbal account of the report he'd written and rewritten the night before. Morgan listened without interrupting, peering at Brewer from under furrowed brows that Brewer found more than slightly unnerving. When he finished, he stood silently while Morgan stared into space for a few minutes, his brow furrowed even deeper, lost in thought. Finally, Brewer heard the admiral sigh and saw him shake his head.

"Too bad," the admiral said. "James Norman was a good captain. You were his First Lieutenant, Mr. Brewer, so you will carry on in command of *Defiant* until you report to Admiral Hornblower in the Caribbean. Although, from what he's told me in the past, there's not much doubt about your future. May I offer you my congratulations, *Captain*, premature though they may be?"

Brewer was thrilled by the admiral's praise, and he had to try very hard not to babble like an idiot. He shook the admiral's hand and nodded. Morgan ordered luncheon for two, and Brewer spent the next two hours hearing new Hornblower stories told from the point of view of a first worried, then grateful, commander.

Lunch was cleared away, and a servant brought a silver tray bearing the coffee service and two cups. Morgan poured Brewer a cup and then another for himself.

"This packet you brought from America," Morgan said as he sat back and sipped his coffee, "contains your former captain's intelligence report on pirate activity, along with a note from our ambassador in Washington City insisting I personally do something about it. Well, we both know how far that will get him, eh, Mr. Brewer?"

Brewer smiled but said nothing. He was picturing the look on Canning's face if he heard the admiral say that.

"Unfortunately," Morgan said with a sigh, "I cannot disagree with his sentiments. If piracy *is* on the rise, it must be dealt with immediately. How soon can *Defiant* sail?"

Brewer took a deep breath and let it out slowly while he considered. "We need a new mainmast, new foremast, sails are being made.... If we have dockyard help, a week; if not, closer to two."

Morgan nodded. "Get to work at once. I'll send you all the help I can. Come see me again before you sail. We'll go over any new information, and I'll write you a letter to take to Admiral Hornblower. Good Morning, Captain!"

Brewer came to attention, pleased at the admiral's use of his new—if nominal—rank. "Aye aye, sir!"

Brewer walked out of Morgan's office feeling rather pleased with himself. What could be better than having command of a King's ship? It's the only thing he ever wanted to do.

There is an old saying: Be careful what you wish for....

Chapter 15

Brewer made it back to his ship, and work began in earnest to repair the severe damage caused by the storm and put her back in fighting trim. Word quickly spread that they would probably be going out after pirates when they sailed, and every hand aboard was counting the prize money they would receive for each pirate ship they captured.

Brewer took Mr. Sweeney's advice and moved into the captain's cabin on *Defiant* as soon as he returned to the ship. Captain Norman's things were packed, and he wrote a letter of condolence to the captain's sister and placed it in the sea chest. Lt. Phillips and two ratings took the trunks ashore and shipped them back to England.

Jenkins stood silently as Phillips and his crew removed the late captain's belongings. After they were gone, Brewer asked, "Well, Jenkins, have you made up your mind?"

The servant turned and said, "Yes, sir. I've thought long and hard about it, Mr. Brewer, and I'd like to stay, if you'll have me. I've been on *Defiant* a long time, and I just think I'd like to stay."

"Then I'm glad to have you." Brewer stuck out his hand, and, after a moment, Jenkins took it. Brewer wondered what kind of a relationship they would have. Jenkins knew a lot about the ship and her crew, but would he feel that he could talk to his new master?

"I'll have the rest of your things brought up from below, sir," Jenkins said, "and I'll make sure it's all stowed away. Is there anything I can do for you just now, sir?"

"No, thank you, Jenkins. You may carry on."

The servant nodded and retreated to the pantry, closing the door behind him. Brewer took the opportunity to look over his new quarters. He was standing in the large day cabin, nicely furnished but not extravagantly so; this was where he would conduct ship's business. There was a desk up against the partition to the right, with bookshelves above. Across the cabin was his bunk, suspended from the deck above and looking almost like a coffin. On the far wall was a door leading to the captain's private head. Brewer thought he was fortunate to have such a large frigate; Captain Bush didn't have nearly so much room on *Lydia*.

Yes, Brewer thought as he walked back into the day cabin, *this will do nicely. Now to put the ship back in order!*

As far as the ship went, the admiral was as good as his word. New masts (and dockyard hands to help install them) arrived on *Defiant*, and within the week new sails were being rigged on the yards. The stepping of the new masts took some doing, but all in all *Defiant* seemed to have weathered the storm fairly well. The hull suffered some cosmetic damage that was easily put to rights, and in no time at all, Brewer found himself back in Morgan's office to report that HMS *Defiant* was ready for sea.

"You've done well, Captain," the admiral said as he read Brewer's report on the repairs.

"Thank you, sir," Brewer said, "but we couldn't have done it without the extra help you sent out. You don't imagine any of them would like to sign on, do you?"

Morgan looked up at that. "Why? Are you down?"

Brewer shrugged. "We lost our gunner and a couple of topmen overboard in the storm, sir."

Morgan grunted and went back to the report. "That's right, I remember seeing that in your report. I doubt they'd sign if you were offering a first-class berth on an East Indiaman." The admiral looked down at his report again. "But I'll do my best for you."

"Thank you, sir."

Morgan set the report down and sat back in his chair. "Your orders are to sail with the morning tide. My clerk will present you with the written copy, as well as a letter for Admiral Hornblower. As for news, I'm afraid there is very little to add to what you already know. There have been no sightings of pirates for the last several weeks, and I have not heard of any missing ships in that time, either.

"However, there is something you should know, Captain. We have recently received intelligence that indicates the pirates have become much better armed than was previously thought. We know that, back in 1815 when the Corsican was finally defeated for the second and last time, several ships of the French navy deserted."

"Mutinied, sir?" Brewer asked.

"No," Morgan said. "Our information is that they deserted, officers and all. They simply refused to serve under the Bourbons again. We could never get a count of the deserters from the French, but our best estimate is that around ten vessels were involved, one or two frigates and the rest smaller ships."

Brewer thought it over and was astounded. "How did they get past our blockade, sir?"

Morgan shrugged. "France was our ally again after King Louis resumed the throne, Captain, and you don't blockade your allies. Our best guess is that the desertions took place in the spring of 1816. It seems the ships sailed on routine missions and simply never returned to France. Instead they showed up in several South American ports, offering their services to Bernard O'Higgins and his ilk. Still fighting to throw off the monarchy, don't you see? Still fighting for the principles of the revolution."

"I see, sir."

Morgan sighed. "Of immediate concern to you, Captain, is the French frigate and the two smaller ships that sailed to the Caribbean to join the so-called Venezuelan navy fighting for Simon Bolivar. We now believe that at least the frigate has gone rogue and joined the pirates operating in the area, complete with the French crew. That means there may now be a military-quality ship and crew preying on merchant shipping."

Brewer nodded as he considered what that might mean.

"Be on your guard, Captain." Morgan rose. "You are to make directly for Jamaica to join Admiral Hornblower. Any questions?"

Brewer rose as well, tucking his hat under his left arm out of habit. "None, sir."

"Then good luck," Morgan said, as the two men shook hands, "and good hunting."

"Thank you, sir," Brewer said. He saluted and left the office. He signed for his orders and the letter to Hornblower at the clerk's desk and stepped out into the street. The cool sea breeze blunted the sun's warmth. Bermuda is a little too far north to take advantage of the tropical sunlight. Brewer shivered and put his head down against the wind as he made his way to the dock. While he walked, he thought about the turn his life had taken.

From the first time he saw a King's ship, he wanted to be the captain and lead the ship into battle. He'd seen plenty of action in his career, but never as the captain. Now he had the responsibility of safeguarding the lives of his crew and his ship, and to make sure he did not waste them. Brewer shivered again; this time it wasn't from the cold.

He found his gig waiting for him at the end of the wharf. As he stepped down to his place in the stern sheets, he noticed the gun batteries that guarded the harbor entrance and kept the pirates from dropping in. It was another sobering reminder that very soon he would probably have to lead *Defiant* into battle against the pirate menace. He swallowed hard and hoped he was good enough.

When he arrived back aboard *Defiant*, Brewer invited Mr. Greene, Mr. Phillips, Dr. Spinelli, and Mr. Sweeney to dine with him. He felt a little awkward about it at first, and he wasn't sure why. Part of him said it was because Captain Norman had only been dead a short time, but the fact was that Norman was gone, and Morgan *had* ordered him to assume command. Another part wondered whether Jenkins, despite what he said earlier, would be either willing or able to serve his new captain as well as he had his old one. But when Brewer informed him of the dinner party, Jenkins merely nodded and asked permission to go ashore to pick up a few items for the meal.

Brewer spent the time before the gathering catching up his log. He wondered how his guests would react to his being captain now. After all, being the first lieutenant was one thing, but being the captain of a King's ship was something else entirely. A captain wasn't allowed to have friends, especially among his own crew. He could show no favoritism to any sailor or officer who got into trouble. Brewer hoped he wouldn't have to mete out discipline for a while.

His guests arrived right on time, and while they waited for dinner, they chatted amiably and enjoyed the Madeira that Jenkins and his mates served. Brewer mingled with his officers—it struck him as strange to think of these men as *his* officers—and wondered just how a captain was supposed to act. For now, he tried to think of what Captain Bush would do.

Jenkins stepped out of the pantry and announced that

dinner was served. That was how he had done it under Captain Norman, and Brewer decided he didn't mind the practice. They found their seats, and the stewards served the feast. A duck, roasted golden brown, was placed on the table, followed by a mutton ham whose aroma evoked the finest restaurants in London. Large bowls filled with carrots and peas were brought, along with a small plate bearing several varieties of cheese. The meal was excellent, every bit as good as those Jenkins had made for Norman. Everyone dug in, and Brewer didn't hear anyone of his companions complaining! Brewer looked over his shoulder at Jenkins, standing just outside the pantry door as he always did during one of these events, and gave him a nod and a smile. Jenkins simply nodded once, discreetly, in acknowledgment, and Brewer found himself liking the man more and more.

Brewer waited until the supper dishes were cleared away and the coffee was served before clearing his throat and launching into the business portion of the evening.

"Thank you all for coming," he said. "I wanted to bring you up to date. Admiral Morgan has approved my taking temporary command of *Defiant*, pending confirmation by Admiral Hornblower. Mr. Greene, Mr. Phillips," he said, gesturing to them, "I will do my best for you, of course, but I will have to speak to the admiral when we join the squadron. For now, Mr. Greene, you will be acting first lieutenant; feel free to move into the cabin, if you wish, but I'm afraid I must ask you to continue standing watch for the time being."

"Aye aye, sir," Greene said. "Will you grant a temporary promotion to Mr. Tyler until we reach the squadron?"

Brewer thought for a moment. "Do you think he's ready?"

Greene nodded. "Yes, sir, I believe he is. He knows how to handle a ship in all but the most extreme or unusual circumstances, and the men respect him."

Brewer glanced at Mr. Sweeney, who smiled and nodded.

"Very well," Brewer said. "We will take care of that in the morning."

"Aye aye, sir," Greene said.

Brewer sat back in his chair. "Our orders are to proceed directly to the Caribbean. Admiral Morgan thinks it is better that we join the squadron immediately than to visit any more American ports."

"Too bad," Mr. Sweeney said. "Charleston and Savannah are nice towns."

The three officers smiled. "We'll just have to take your word for it this time, Mr. Sweeney," Brewer said. "Mr. Greene, once we sail, I want emphasis put on gun drill. We may well meet one of these pirates during our trip south, and I want to be ready. I also wanted to let you know what we might be coming up against. The admiral has intelligence that suggests that a French frigate has gone rogue and joined the pirates, complete with her French crew."

They looked puzzled at this, but Greene spoke for them all. "A French frigate, sir?"

"Yes. The admiral told me that in the spring of 1816, approximately ten French warships, estimated to be two or three frigates and the rest smaller craft, defected from the French navy. It seems they wanted nothing to do with the Bourbons, so they more or less stole their ships and sailed for South America."

"Do you mean they mutinied, sir?" asked Phillips.

Brewer smiled; he was glad that they were as confused at the strangeness of the situation as he had been. "No, Mr. Phillips, I mean they *defected*, captain, crews, and ships. They went out on routine patrols and simply never returned to France. Most of them ended up with Cochrane serving Bernard O'Higgins in the Chilean navy, but three ships, one of them a frigate, went to Venezuela to fight with Simon Bolivar. Now that frigate has gone missing, and the admiral believes it has gone rogue and taken up piracy. To our knowledge, it still possesses its wartime-trained French captain and crew , and it's weapons. If we run into them, it'll be just like old times."

Brewer thought for a moment. "What else? Oh, yes, now I remember. I noticed that Captain Norman was content to stay in his cabin and let his officers run the ship for him. From now on, I want to be called whenever there's a need. Mr. Greene, Mr. Phillips, just remember how you did it on your last ship. Well, I think that's it for now. Any questions?"

Mr. Sweeney spoke up. "Are we still going to stop at Newfoundland?"

Brewer smiled. "As often as possible." This was greeted by general laughter. "That's it, then, gentlemen. I will see you in the morning. We sail with the morning tide. Good night."

The two lieutenants and the good doctor saluted and bid their captain good night, but Mr. Sweeney remained and retook his seat after the others had left.

"Well, Mr. Sweeney?" Brewer said, as he got out a bottle of port and two glasses.

Sweeney accepted his glass and saluted his captain. "To Captain Brewer."

"Only until we reach the Caribbean," Brewer replied, "then it's up to the admiral."

Sweeney laughed. "They may as well give it to you right now, then. Hornblower's not going to turn you down."

"I pray you're right," Brewer conceded. "What do you think of Mr. Greene as a first lieutenant?"

Sweeney considered for a moment. "I think he'll work out fine. He'll have to learn to do one or two things differently, but all new first lieutenants do. Yes, I think he'll do nicely."

Brewer looked at the sailing master over his glass. "I am going to watch him closely during the voyage south, and if he works out, I may ask the admiral to confirm him as first lieutenant. I'm afraid Mr. Phillips will remain as third lieutenant, wouldn't you say?"

Sweeney smiled and nodded. "I doubt we will pick up a replacement with less time than he has."

Brewer took a sip of his port, and then contemplated his glass as though deep in thought. "Mr. Sweeney," he said, "let me ask you something."

Sweeney sat back in his chair to listen.

"You've been on this ship longer than I have," Brewer said quietly. "What kind of damage did Norman do to this crew? I know what I've seen these past months, and I can well imagine that what I saw done to Mr. Phillips was merely the tip of the iceberg. How do you think they'll respond to a... *different* hand when it comes to discipline?"

Sweeney narrowed his eyes as he considered his captain's question. Not quite what he expected from Brewer, but he could understand it. Sweeney knew that Brewer's mentor, Hornblower, was noted for winning crews over and getting them to follow him to hell and back with a bare minimum of flogging. *A rare thing,* Sweeney thought, *and one that our young captain would like to emulate, no doubt.*

Sweeney took another sip of port and leaned forward. "Mr. Brewer," he said softly, "I think they'll do you proud, as long as you do right by them. Captain Norman had his faults, but he knew how to take care of his crew, and that's why they put up with him like they did." Sweeney leaned back again. "You've had good training, Mr. Brewer, and you know how to run a ship. You've been a first lieutenant long enough that you know how to command. The only difference now is that the responsibility will be on *your* shoulders. For what it's worth, I think you'll do just fine."

Brewer sat back in his chair while Mr. Sweeney spoke, and now he merely nodded his thanks and turned to look out the stern window at the open sea. He was still uneasy as to whether or not the crew would try to test him, but, in the end, it really didn't matter. He was the captain of *HMS*

Defiant, and he would follow the good examples set for him by Hornblower, Bush, and Morgan.

"Thank you, Mr. Sweeney," he said. "I'll see you tomorrow."

Sweeney stood and drained his port. "Aye aye, sir," he said, and he left the cabin.

Brewer stared out the stern window for a while, allowing his eyes to become lost in the vast openness of the sea beyond the harbor's mouth. That was partly what drew him to the sea as a boy, getting lost in that vast expanse. Brewer was pleased to see that it held him still. But could he command?

Finally, his distraction with that question drove him up on deck, and he began to pace as he'd seen Hornblower do in his office on St. Helena. To his surprise and relief, no one bothered him as long as he kept his head down and paced the quarterdeck. Seven steps forward, and seven steps back. Brewer made a mental note to have Mr. Greene ensure this part of the deck was holystoned early enough so as not to interfere with his exercise. All at once he stopped and stared at one of the batteries.

Mr. Sweeney walked up to him. "May I ask what you're thinking, Captain?"

"Mr. Sweeney," Brewer said softly, "I've just remembered something the Corsican told me just before I left St. Helena. He said, 'You must be ready to seize the day when it presents itself. Half measures will not do; you must be ruthless and go for the throat like the wolf.' That's what I intend to do, Mr. Sweeney. I will make the most of this opportunity."

"Glad to hear it, Captain."

Brewer looked at him. "You had doubts, I take it?"

Sweeney shrugged but said nothing.

Brewer clapped him on the shoulder as he walked past. "Quite all right, Mr. Sweeney; so did I. Good night."

That night, Brewer was shocked to find that he could not

sleep. Part of the problem, he realized, was the responsibility and having to account officially for every action and every life on board *Defiant*. Well, that just went with command of a King's ship. But what really surprised him was the realization that he was simply anxious to get under way. He *wanted* to go out after these pirates, wanted to fight alongside his mentor.

Brewer finally gave up all ideas of sleep in favor of writing one last letter to his sister. True, he had just posted one to her the day before while on his way to see the admiral, but he needed to fill the time until dawn somehow, and he didn't want his crew to think he was nervous.

He went to his new desk, the captain's private desk, and pulled out paper, quill, and ink. Just as he was about to put pen to paper, a thought occurred to him, and he smiled as he wrote.

My Dear Captain Bush,

I am writing you as the new Captain of the Defiant. *Norman was lost overboard in a hurricane. He and I were swept up in the same wave, but fortunately the sailing master was able to grab me and prevent my being carried over the side as well.*

We were heading for Bermuda to deliver a packet from our ambassador in Washington City. I took the packet to the commanding admiral, and who do you suppose it was? Your old friend, Sir Jonathan Morgan! He told me all sorts of interesting stories about you and your adventures with Lord Hornblower. I must say, he tells them a little differently than you!

Captain, I wish you were here right now. I

have spent most of this, our last day at Bermuda, pacing the quarterdeck (sound familiar?) and trying to remember all that you have taught me. I wish I had taken better notes!

I hope you do not mind if, when we next call in England, I come round to Smallbridge to exchange notes and stories on how to be a successful captain. You learned from a good man, and so did I. Until then, sir, I have the honor of being

Your Obedient Servant,

William Brewer,
Captain, HMS Defiant

CHAPTER 16

In the morning, Brewer went up on deck and arranged with Mr. Phillips to have his letter put aboard the mail boat before they sailed. He was about to return to his cabin when Mr. Greene caught his attention and gestured toward Mr. Tyler, who at that moment was standing by the mizzenmast in conversation with Mr. Peters and Mr. Short. Brewer nodded in understanding.

"Mr. Tyler!" he called.

The midshipman jumped at hearing his name, then hurried over and saluted.

"You called, Captain?" he asked.

"Yes, Mr. Tyler," Brewer said. "I want to know why you are out of uniform."

"Sir?"

The boy was confused, and Brewer had to remind himself not to play this too heavily.

"Yes, Mr. Tyler, I said out of uniform. Let me ask you, Mr. Tyler. Would you say it is the job of a good lieutenant on a King's ship to learn to anticipate his captain's wishes?"

"Anticipate?" he said. "Ah, anticipate... why, yes, sir."

"I see," Brewer said. He turned to his first lieutenant. "Mr. Greene!"

Greene came over and saluted. "Sir?"

"You told me Mr. Tyler was ready for a promotion to acting-lieutenant. How is it he did not anticipate I would grant it?"

Greene feigned confusion. "I'm not sure, Captain... I was sure he would know."

Both men peeked sideways at young Tyler and were rewarded by the look of astonishment on his face. Both men laughed, as did Mr. Sweeney.

Tyler looked from one to the other. "Promotion?"

Brewer patted him on the shoulder. "Yes, Mr. Tyler. With the loss of Captain Norman overboard, *Defiant* needs another officer. Think you can handle it?"

Tyler's face beamed. "Oh, yes sir!"

"So does Mr. Greene," Brewer said, "and so do I. Now, Mr. Greene, kindly take our new lieutenant below and get him into a proper uniform!"

"Aye aye, sir!" Greene said, and the two officers went below. Brewer watched them go. He looked at Sweeney, feeling extraordinarily pleased with himself, before he went below to his cabin.

He sat at the desk in his day cabin and pulled out the captain's log. He spent much of the next hour going through the log, reviewing what Captain Norman had written, and he was amazed by what he read. Every entry looked normal and factual; apparently the man's mental problems did not extend to log entries. He was so caught up in what he was reading that he had no idea he wasn't alone until he heard someone clearing their throat. He started and turned to find Jenkins standing a discreet distance behind him, holding a tray with a cup of coffee on it.

"Coffee, sir?" the servant said.

"Yes, thank you, Jenkins," Brewer said as he sat back.

"Sorry I jumped; I didn't hear you come in."

"Quite all right, sir. It happened to Captain Norman frequently. In fact, it's the reason I began disarming him whenever he entered the room."

Brewer looked to the servant's face to see if he was joking, but Jenkins' face wore its usual imperturbable expression. He was about to ask him about it, when Jenkins cleared his throat again.

"What would you like for breakfast, sir?"

Brewer blinked. Food had been the farthest thing from his mind, but now that Jenkins mentioned it, he felt his stomach tell him it was a good idea. He thought about it for a moment, then finally sighed. "What would you suggest?"

Jenkins coughed into his fist. "I picked up some very nice mutton chops ashore, sir, along with a dozen or so fresh eggs. I could fry you a couple eggs alongside a broiled mutton chop, or perhaps you'd rather have an omelet?"

Brewer smiled. "Fried eggs and a mutton chop will do nicely, Jenkins. Thank you."

Jenkins bowed. "My pleasure, Captain." Something about the way Jenkins said that word made Brewer feel like he belonged here.

Jenkins continued, "I hope you won't mind, sir, but when I packed Captain Norman's belongings for shipment to his sister, I kept behind all the provisions—food stuffs and wines—he stocked in the pantry. I honestly did not think they would survive all the way to England in usable condition. If you'd like, I can prepare an inventory for your inspection."

"Yes, please do that, Jenkins," Brewer said. "I don't fault you for not shipping the provisions. They probably would have been stolen by the dock hands in any case."

"Thank you, sir," Jenkins bowed and retreated to the pantry to prepare his captain's breakfast. Brewer was learning this was Jenkins' habit of dismissing himself, and he let it ride. Brewer went back to reviewing the log until Jenkins returned with his breakfast. Brewer sat back and allowed Jenkins to lay out the dishes. In front of him now was a large platter with two fried eggs, a thick chop of mutton with a sauce on it that smelled absolutely heavenly, and two pieces of toast. Jenkins also refilled his coffee and placed a glass of lime juice on the table before standing back.

"This looks fabulous, Jenkins!" Brewer said as he dug in. It was every bit as good as it looked! When sated, he sat back and wiped his mouth. "Excellent! Let me ask you a question, Jenkins. Before I do, let me say this: anything you and I talk about in this room is just between us and will be held in the strictest confidence. Is that understood?"

"Very good, sir."

"Good. My question is this: what do you think of the sailing master, Mr. Sweeney?"

Jenkins' eyes widened a fraction, and his left eyebrow edged up ever so slightly. "Mr. Sweeney, sir? A very competent navigator, to be sure. I believe he learned his craft under Captain Cook himself."

Brewer nodded. "Do you think him personable? Trustworthy?"

Jenkins' brow furled slightly as he considered. "I really couldn't say, sir. Personable? I suppose so. I've never seen him act rudely to anyone, if that's any indication. As for his being trustworthy, I'm afraid I have no way to judge that, Captain."

Brewer leaned forward and looked into Jenkins' eyes. "What does your gut tell you?"

Jenkins actually blinked. "My *gut*, sir?"

"Yes. What do your insides tell you? Maybe you don't understand it, and maybe you didn't think about it. Some people call it instinct, and some call it something else, but I just call it a 'gut feeling'. What does yours tell you about Mr. Sweeney?"

Jenkins' face broke into the closest thing to a smile that Brewer had yet seen. Jenkins cleared his throat again and lowered his eyes for a moment while he considered. "My 'gut', as you call it, sir," he said with a sigh, "tells me that Mr. Sweeney usually knows more than he tells. Unquestionably a competent seaman, and a good man to have at your side during a fight."

"That is my estimation as well. Thank you, Jenkins."

His servant bowed and retreated to the safety of his pantry, and Brewer was left alone to consider what he had heard. Jenkins was proving to be every bit as perceptive as Brewer thought him to be. That could be a real asset to him in the future. Brewer hoped that Jenkins would prove to be someone he could trust in implicitly, but only time would tell.

There was a knock at the door, and the first lieutenant entered.

“Sorry to disturb you, Captain,” he said. “The guard boat is alongside, and there’s a man here who has a note for you from Admiral Morgan. Says he’s supposed to give it directly to you.”

“Oh? Well, let’s have him in.”

Greene beckoned for the man, who was standing outside the doorway. Brewer was surprised to see an old, grizzled tar enter his cabin. The man walked directly to his desk, saluted, and handed him a letter. Brewer acknowledged the salute and broke the seal on the letter.

Captain Brewer,

I am sending you the bearer of this note, Mr. Mosley, to you as a replacement for your gunner. He is experienced in his craft, and I think he will be a great benefit to your ship.

Jonathan Morgan
Admiral commanding

Brewer handed the letter to Mr. Greene and looked again at his new gunner. Mr. Mosley looked as though he had entered the navy with Drake or Morgan, but Brewer noted his eye seemed clear and his hand was steady.

"Welcome aboard, Mr. Mosley," he said.

"Thank'ee, sir," the gunner said. "It's good to be back aboard *Defiant*."

Brewer looked up. "You've served in *Defiant* before?" He looked at Mr. Greene, who was equally confused. Like carpenters and boatswains, gunners were standing officers who usually stayed with the ship instead of transferring like other crew members.

"Aye, sir," Mosley said. "I was gunner when Captain Norman took command, sir. Before we sailed from Portsmouth, I came down sick with a stomach fever, and the captain and his surgeon had me transferred to the hospital ashore. By the time I recovered, the ship had sailed without me."

"I see," Brewer said. "Well, it's good to have you back, Mr. Mosley. Tell me, where have you fought?"

"I was with Nelson at Copenhagen, the Nile, and Trafalgar, sir."

Brewer stood. "Very well, Mr. Mosley. I trust you can impart your experience to *Defiant's* gunners in short order. We may encounter pirates on the way to join Admiral Hornblower. Mr. Greene will take you below and introduce you to your mates."

Mosley saluted. "Aye aye, sir." He followed Greene out of the cabin. Brewer sat down for a moment and considered this new fortune. For Morgan to send him a gunner with a personal note indicated that the man was special. Brewer looked forward to observing Mr. Mosley in action.

Brewer made his way up on deck. The wind was fresh and the sky was blue as far as the eye could see. He walked over to join his officers by the lee rail.

"Good morning, sir," they said in unison as they saluted. Brewer smiled when Mr. Short, who was standing there as well, saluted with the wrong hand, as the proper hand was still in a sling from the separated shoulder.

"Good morning," he said as he returned their salute. "Are we ready to move, Mr. Greene?"

"Yes, sir," the acting first lieutenant said, "any time you like. All the crew are present and accounted for."

"Very well," Brewer said. "And has Mr. Barton finished his shopping?"

"Yes, sir," Greene said, "he finished last night. Everything is stowed and secured."

"Very well, Mr. Greene," Brewer said as he clasped his hands behind his back to conceal his nervousness, "Warp the ship out of the harbor, if you please."

Greene smiled and saluted. "Aye aye, *Captain*!" He went off, bellowing orders and gesturing at various petty officers and crew. Within minutes, *Defiant* was working her way across the smooth surface of the harbor.

"Signal from the shore, sir!"

Brewer turned. "What is it, Mr. Short?"

"Good luck, *Defiant*. Good hunting."

"Acknowledge." Brewer turned to Mr. Sweeney and grinned. "It seems the admiral is keeping an eye on us, Mr. Sweeney."

"That it does, Captain, that it does." Sweeney leaned in close. "Let's not embarrass ourselves then, eh?"

Brewer turned and looked at his sailing master. He saw immediately the man was not joking. Brewer looked at the shoreline as it glided past his view, but his mind was on his sailing master. Sweeney had taken him under his wing, so to speak, especially when it came to his dealings with Norman.

He wondered now whether or not the nature of their relationship would have to be reexamined, now that he was captain. He sighed and looked aloft at the men who were putting Mr. Greene's orders into action.

"An excellent idea, Mr. Sweeney."

Fortunately, they had nothing to fear. Lieutenant Greene's seamanship was nothing less than exceptional as he conned the ship out of the harbor and set her on a course bound for the Caribbean Sea. Brewer looked over his shoulder at Mr. Sweeney as Mr. Greene was giving the final orders that would point *Defiant* toward Windward Passage and smiled. Mr. Sweeney smiled and nodded as well.

Lt. Greene came up and saluted. "Ship on course for the Caribbean, Captain."

"Well done, Mr. Greene," Brewer said, trying his best to sound like a captain. "Dismiss the watch below. Hands to breakfast."

"Aye aye, sir," Greene said. He saluted and was off again.

"Mr. Sweeney," Brewer said, "walk with me, if you please." The two men fell in step along the rail. "I want to continue with Mr. Phillips' education," Brewer said as they reached the first turn. "How do you think he's doing?"

Sweeney looked at the deck for a moment. "I think he's coming along, Mr. Brewer, but I don't know that he's anywhere near ready for a commissioning board, even if it is a pretend one."

Brewer was surprised. "Oh?"

Sweeney looked straight ahead and spoke in a low voice. "Something's not right with the lad, but I can't quite put my finger on what. Care to guess what happened when I told him that Norman had gone over the side?"

Brewer's brow furrowed. "I imagine he was pleased, on the inside, at least."

Sweeney stopped and turned toward his captain. "His eyes got wide open, and he was terrified, Captain. It took him nearly a full minute to regain control and say how awful that was."

Brewer's left eyebrow rose as he digested the sailing master's words. He was not pleased by the news, which pointed to an unsteadiness that still had not been addressed. Brewer sighed in exasperation and looked first at the deck and then out over the passing sea. Sweeney thought he heard a muttered curse. After a moment, Brewer turned back and surveyed the waves that drove *Defiant* southward.

"Well," he said at last, "keep an eye on him. It's all we can do for now. It may be that what happened on *Retribution* ruined him for the King's service. I hope not, but we have to watch out for the possibility."

Sweeney could only nod in agreement.

Brewer sighed again and looked at the deck. Suddenly, he looked up and signaled for a midshipman. "Pass the word for Mr. Greene."

The midshipman saluted and went in search of *Defiant's* new first lieutenant. In less than a minute, Greene presented himself before his captain.

"Mr. Greene," Brewer said, "declare a make-and-mend day. Pass the word for Mr. Barton and Dr. Spinelli to report to my cabin, please."

"Aye aye, sir," Greene said, his surprise showing on his face. New captains didn't usually give the crew the day off, but now no work would be done aboard *Defiant*, other than necessary changes to the sails. He quickly pulled himself together and saluted before rushing off to fulfill his captain's wishes.

Greene wasn't the only one startled by the new captain's orders. Mr. Sweeney stood by the wheel and watched his captain retreat below deck, and he wondered if young Mr. Brewer would be able to make the adjustment to being in command. Sweeney had watched many men try and fail during his long career, and once he had asked his mentor, Captain Cook, about it.

"It's really quite simple, Sweeney," the great explorer had said. "Captains are born to it. They are not made, taught, or trained, they have to be *born* to command. There's something inside them that accepts the responsibility and authority without being corrupted. It's those that *aren't* born to it that turn out to be despots who make life hell for their crews. Take my word for it, Sweeney, when you find one who *is* born to it, stick with him, for he is a rare commodity."

Sweeney watched Captain Brewer's head disappear below the deck, and he wondered just how rare a commodity William Brewer would prove to be.

Brewer barely had time to reach his day room and take his hat off when a knock at the cabin door heralded the arrival of Mr. Barton. This was Brewer's first meeting with the purser since assuming command; Brewer hoped Mr. Barton would do as well for the new command as he had for the old.

"Reporting as ordered, Captain," the purser said.

"Mr. Barton," Brewer greeted him as he moved behind his desk, "please, have a seat." He indicated the chair in front of the desk. When the purser was seated, he went on. "I wanted to talk to you so I could get an idea of just how you do your job. I know from my time here on *Defiant* that you are very good at it; the crew is certainly very happy with you."

"Thank you, sir."

"I also know that you sailed long enough with Captain Norman that he was content to give you a free hand to do your job as you wished. But I'm just getting started at the job, you see, and I want to do things a little differently. I'm not trying to tell you *how* to do your job, Mr. Barton, but I am going to ask you to keep me informed. For example, I understand you went ashore yesterday? What did you find for us?"

Barton pulled out his notebook and began flipping through the pages. Brewer was pleased that he didn't seem to mind Brewer's questions in the least.

"Let me see, sir," Barton said. "I'm sorry to have rushed ashore without speaking to you first, Captain, but I heard a rumor from one of the supply boats and had to act at once. You were still ashore at the time, but I did clear it with Mr. Greene before I left. I just managed to reach the dock office in time."

Brewer leaned forward in anticipation. "And?"

The purser looked up from his notebook and smiled. "Well, Captain, for starters, I got us an extra half-ton of tobacco for next to nothing."

"Tobacco!" The weed was worth more than gold when a ship was at sea.

"Yes, sir!" said the purser, obviously pleased with himself. "I got there just ahead of two Indiamen. Let me tell you, they were not very happy when I bought up the last the dock office had. I also got us six dozen eggs. No chickens—they refused to part with any of them—but at least we got the eggs." Another flip of a page. "I tried to get us some fresh beef or pork, but the dock office master claimed they had none to spare—for the navy, at least. I think the Indiamen pay too good a price, that's the real reason. I was also able to get three-quarters of a ton of coffee, a ton of potatoes, and two thousand lemons."

"Excellent, Mr. Barton!" Brewer exclaimed. He rose to signal the interview was over. "Please keep me informed about stores. I know you didn't do that with Captain Norman, but I want you to do it for me."

Barton stood as well. "Aye aye, sir." He saluted and left the cabin. As he was going out, Dr. Spinelli arrived and was shown in.

"Come in, Adam," Brewer said. "Did you bring your chess set?"

Spinelli smiled. "Just happen to have it with me, Captain." They sat down at the desk and began to set up the pieces. "You know, sir," the doctor said, "I thought it would be difficult to get used to calling you that—*Captain*—but it seems to fit you somehow. I believe in time you'll come to wear it well."

Brewer smiled. "Thank you, Adam. And in here, when we're alone, 'William' is still appropriate."

The surgeon looked up and smiled. "Does that mean I don't have to let you win?"

Brewer laughed, and the game was on. They played for hours. Jenkins learned something about how he would have to adjust to his new captain; when he stepped out of his pantry to announce lunch, Brewer said, "Make it for two, will you please, Jenkins?" without even looking up. Jenkins merely raised his eyebrow fractionally and brought two plates, and he took them away again when they were empty. Neither combatant seemed to notice him in the least, although they were glad enough for the coffee and biscuits he provided.

They finally called a truce, as it were, with Brewer winning three games to his surgeon's two. Both men sat back, feeling refreshed by the game, and Brewer took the opportunity to study the doctor. Certain aspects of Mr. Spinelli's appearance still led Brewer to believe he loved his whiskey a bit too much, although Brewer could not remember seeing him drunk since *Defiant* left England. When Brewer had dealt with him, and the surgeon's mind had obviously been clear, he liked what he heard and thought the doctor might be able to provide an impartial sounding board, especially over a chessboard.

"Captain," the doctor said, "if you need someone to talk to, I'm always available."

Brewer looked at his friend in surprise and wondered if the doctor was reading his mind. Or maybe just his job description?

"Thank you, Adam," Brewer said as they packed up the chess set. "I will certainly keep your offer in mind. I have no doubt that I shall want to bounce my thoughts off of someone. I remember, when I was on the *Lydia* with Captain Bush, going against the Barbary pirates, there was an old captain in our squadron named Macpherson. He commanded the *Brutus*, an old sixty-four gun two-decker that looked to be nearly a hundred years old. Captain Bush went over for supper one evening, and when he came back, he told me a fascinating tale of a large, potted coffee plant that Captain Macpherson had in his day cabin. Bush said that Macpherson claimed the plant was his best friend! He said he talked over all ship's business with the plant. According to Bush, Captain Macpherson claimed that not only did the plant never argue with anything he said, but it also smelled better than any first lieutenant he had ever known!"

Dr. Spinelli laughed at that. "But could the plant play chess?"

Brewer laughed. "From what I remember of old Macpherson, the plant could probably beat him. Speaking of chess, I must remember to pick up a good, portable set when we reach the Caribbean."

"I highly recommend it," Dr. Spinelli said.

Brewer rose, and Spinelli followed suit. "Let's take a turn on deck, shall we?" Brewer said.

"Delighted," the doctor replied.

Together the two men ascended the companionway to the main deck of the *Defiant*. Here the doctor excused himself and walked over to speak to one of the petty officers who was making some rope on the forecastle. Brewer watched him go, and he wondered again if he had found his half, as Bush had been for Hornblower, and he had tried to be for Bush, especially after Gerard was wounded. Brewer sighed; he knew that time would tell, he just didn't want to wait.

CHAPTER 17

For the next several days, *HMS Defiant* cruised steadily south-southwest under pristine skies. Captain William Brewer had a chance to settle in to his new job and adjust to the subtle differences between being the first lieutenant of a King's ship and being the captain. Mr. Sweeney was a great help during this transition, and, to Brewer's surprise, the sailing master proved to be the soul of discretion. Not that Brewer was surprised that Sweeney could be discreet, but it was the tact with which corrections were delivered that got his attention—never in public, always a suggestion. Brewer found himself reminded of how fortunate he was to inherit such a crew.

Brewer had several conversations with Mr. Greene or with the wardroom as a whole on the ship's condition and what had to be done to ensure they would be ready for the inevitable battle with the pirates.

"Mr. Greene," Brewer asked, "how's Mr. Mosley getting along?"

"Splendidly, Captain. Reload times are already coming down for the crews he is working with."

"Excellent! I expect ship's gunnery to be brought up to

the wartime standard of three salvos to two. I want to overwhelm any pirates we meet before they can get away. Pass that along, if you please."

Greene smiled. "Aye aye, Captain."

It was a cool evening about twelve days out of Bermuda when Brewer came up on deck to take in Carslake's and Miller's weekly concert. He found a likely spot on the lee rail alongside Mr. Sweeney and settled in to enjoy the concert. After they played several tunes, the musicians opened up the concert to requests, and Sergeant O'Bannon was quickly summoned to sing an old Irish ballad. As he listened to the singing, Brewer took the opportunity to look around at his crew. In this relaxed atmosphere, they all looked fit and happy, enjoying to a man the diversion that peacetime allowed them.

His opinion changed suddenly when his eyes fell on Mr. Phillips, who was just aft of the wheel. The young lieutenant was standing with Mr. Tyler and Mr. Short, the latter's arm finally allowed out of the sling and recovering nicely. But it was clear from the look on Phillips' face that his mind was not on the evening's entertainment. His face had a haunted look on it, and his eyes drifted over the calm seas. Brewer's mind went back to the comment Phillips made to Mr. Sweeney regarding the death of Captain Norman. *Poor John,* he wondered. *What is going on inside your head?*

Just then, Dr. Spinelli joined him. The doctor was looking pleased with himself.

"Good evening, Doctor," the captain said. "Enjoying the music?"

"Yes, Captain," the surgeon replied. "I've been on many ships in my career in the King's service, but I don't believe I've heard a better melody than that put out by Carslake and Miller. And Sergeant O'Bannon, he should be on the stage in London!"

Captain Brewer laughed, but then he leaned in close to get the doctor's attention. "Adam, look over your shoulder, and tell me what you make of that."

The surgeon turned his head and saw Lieutenant Phillips staring out over the waves, his face devoid of all expression. "You mean Mr. Phillips? Interesting. I wonder what's on his mind."

Spinelli stared in wonder as Brewer whispered in his ear, repeating the story of the young lieutenant's comments when told of the death of Captain Norman. Brewer stepped back and asked, "What do you think, Doctor?"

Spinelli looked at his captain. *Maybe he is making too much of this,* he thought. *It is one of the marks of a new captain, taking everything as a matter of life or death. I hope Captain Brewer settles in soon. So far, he's been doing well, but what happens when a crisis comes?*

"Captain," Spinelli said, "I'm sure it's probably nothing. I'm sure you would agree that Mr. Phillips is a sensitive lad; it's possible that the death of Captain Norman—a man who persecuted him, don't forget—might have shaken him badly, especially considering the manner in which Norman died. Why don't you let me talk to him? Maybe I can find out what is bothering him."

Brewer glanced at Mr. Sweeney before nodding to the doctor. "A good idea, Doctor. Come and see me after you've talked to him."

Spinelli nodded and moved off to talk to some more of the crew. Mr. Sweeney pushed himself off the rail and stepped up to stand beside his captain.

"Do you think that's a good idea, Captain?" Sweeney said.

"I hope so, Mr. Sweeney. One thing I learned a while back is that it is an entirely different thing to speak to a first lieutenant than it is to speak to a captain, even when the two are the same person. Mr. Phillips may have opened up to me before, but now I fear he would be intimidated by my office. He has to talk to someone, perhaps he will to the doctor."

Sweeney nodded; the wisdom of the captain's argument was undeniable. He hoped that the doctor could get Phillips to confide in him; he had grown fond of the lad during the voyage, and, with Brewer in command, he was not scared to admit it, even to himself. If Phillips could keep his head on his shoulders, Sweeney thought he would make a very good officer. He was certainly coming along nicely when it came to navigation and ship handling, and from what he saw, Mr. Brewer was just as successful in teaching him to lead men. Sweeney shook his head. *If only the boy keeps his head.*

Brewer strolled forward toward the forecastle, where Sergeant O'Bannon was finishing up a request. As soon as the ballad ended, Brewer strode out in front of the startled entertainers.

"Gentlemen," the captain addressed the performers but spoke loudly enough to be heard by all, "you have outdone yourselves! I have never heard the like, on this or any other ship! And now, I would like to make a request. In honor of our American cousins who rescued us from the storm, could we please hear 'Shannon and Chesapeake'?" The crew laughed and cheered, and the musicians willingly complied. When the ballad of British victory ended, Brewer turned to the crowd. "What better way to end the night, than with an extra ration of grog for everyone!" The cheers could almost be heard back in London. Brewer smiled and turned to the three performers behind him. "And you three get an extra tobacco ration as well."

Only one man aboard did not join in the revelry. Back on the quarterdeck, Mr. Sweeney leaned silently back against the rail and looked around at his shipmates. He wore a grim expression on his face as he wondered if this night would be an omen of good or evil for the future.

Two full days passed before Captain Brewer was interrupted in his cabin by a knock at the door. He sighed to himself and frowned; he had just finished his log entry and was hoping for a few moments of peace to write a letter to his mother. He set the quill down and shook his head. Some things just aren't meant to be, apparently.

"Enter," he said.

The door opened, and Dr. Spinelli came in. The doctor seems particularly pleased with himself.

"Good morning, Captain!" he said as he rubbed his hands together.

"Good morning, Doctor," Brewer said. "You look like the cat who has eaten the canary. Have you been digging up new victims to beat at chess?"

"Yes, indeed," the doctor said as he sat down across the desk from his captain. "One *victim*, as you say, in particular."

Brewer's interest was piqued. "Mr. Phillips?"

Spinelli smiled and sat back. "Mr. Phillips."

A grin broke over Brewer's face, and he turned and shouted over his shoulder. "Jenkins!"

The pantry door opened, revealing the steward.

"Coffee for two, if you please."

"Aye aye, sir."

Brewer turned back to his friend and leaned on the desk in anticipation. "Alright, Adam," he said, "tell me."

"Well, sir, I..." he paused while Jenkins brought the coffee. As soon as the pantry door closed again, he looked to his captain and smiled. "I told a falsehood. I approached our young lieutenant as he got off watch and told him it was part of your training program that he learn the game."

Brewer laughed. "You didn't!"

Spinelli gave an exaggerated nod. "I did indeed. And you'd be surprised how quickly he picked up the game. I tell you, William, with a little practice, he may end up as the ship's champion."

Brewer snorted. "Just because he may be able to beat you hardly qualifies him as ship's champion. Were you able to get the boy to open up at all?"

"Of course, Captain," Spinelli said. "You know how talkative people can be when their mind is distracted by a good game."

Brewer's eyebrow inched up slightly, and the doctor hurried on.

"Basically, Captain, it seems that our young midshipman is afraid of you."

Brewer felt like he'd been hit with an electric shock. "Afraid? *Of me?*"

"Yes, sir," the doctor said calmly. "It seems he's sure that your attitude toward him will change, you being the captain now."

Brewer could only stare out into space, his mouth hanging open in shock. Of all the ridiculous.... "What have I done to bring *this* on?" he asked helplessly.

"Got promoted, I'm afraid," the doctor said with a sympathetic look. "Remember, beneath that uniform, he's still just a boy. His fear is, now that you're captain, you will be required by your office to treat him differently. He's afraid that he can't come to you now when he has a problem, that you may be forced to look upon it as a weakness."

Brewer sat back for a moment before leaning toward his friend. "He's afraid I'm going to turn into Norman somehow?"

Spinelli sighed and raised his eyebrows in helplessness, and then he nodded.

Brewer exhaled loudly and sat back in his chair. He closed his eyes and rubbed the bridge of his nose as he sat silently in thought. Jenkins came to refill the coffee, but upon seeing the condition of his master, he looked to the doctor to see if something stronger was required. The doctor merely shook his head, and the superb servant silently bowed his head and retired. The doctor looked again at his friend and decided to settle back to wait. It was several minutes before Brewer sighed again and opened his eyes.

"What can I do, Adam?" he asked.

Now it was the doctor's turn to sigh. "Nothing, really, I'm afraid," he said. "It will take time for Phillips to see that you are not Norman and are not going to become Norman. It will take time, but it *will* happen eventually. The question is whether Mr. Phillips can hang on long enough for him to realize it."

The frustration got to Brewer as he pushed his chair back from the desk and rose. He began to pace back and forth before the great stern windows. "This is a ship of war, Adam, not a nursery," he vented as he went. "We will in all probability be in action against pirates in the next few days, and I need officers, not children I have to coddle!"

Spinelli didn't see it that way, but he let his friend vent. Brewer was still new to command, and he had to work his way through this. But he had also asked for advice. "William," he said, as calmly and objectively as he could, "Phillips has been through events that would absolutely shatter lesser men, let alone a boy. Overcoming public humiliation to kill two mutineers in a standoff, saving not only his captain's life but also the ship! Then he joins a ship with a captain who seems to be a father figure one minute and a sadistic tormenter the next. In the middle of it all, he finds a first lieutenant who not only befriends him but actually takes him under his wing, as it were, and promises to help him become the kind of officer his first captain would be proud of. Now, all of a sudden, fate has removed the tyrant and elevated the mentor, and his confused mind is wondering whether the mentor will be able to keep his promise."

The captain stopped his pacing and listened to his friend.

When he finished, Brewer stared out the stern windows, hoping he could live up to his promise. He sighed as he felt the frustration drain from him, and he sat down again.

"Very well, Adam," he said with a smile, "let us hope Mr. Phillips does not take too long to make up his mind about me. In the meantime, I would appreciate it if you would make yourself as available as possible, just in case the lad needs to talk."

There was a knock at the door, and Mr. Tyler entered.

"Begging your pardon, sir," he said. "Mr. Greene's respects, and would you please come on deck? A sail has been sighted, two points off the starboard bow, course north-northeast, sir, coming right at us."

"Yes, I'll come," Brewer said as he rose. He retrieved his hat, and he and the doctor followed the senior midshipman up onto the quarterdeck. Mr. Greene handed him a glass.

"Still hull down, sir," Greene said. "As of now, it doesn't look like a British ship."

"Thank you, Mr. Greene," Brewer said as he studied the white dot on the horizon. "Mr. Tyler, get a glass, and into the tops with you. I want to know what she is."

"Aye aye, sir!" the lieutenant said, and he scurried off to take his post.

Brewer kept an eye on the growing speck. Mr. Greene's voice reached his ear.

"Think it could be a pirate, sir? We're within two or three days of Cuba."

"We certainly need to keep it in mind, Mr. Greene," Brewer said. He lowered the glass and looked up to the main top. "Well, Mr. Tyler? Let's hear you!"

Tyler lowered his glass. "Looks like a brig, sir! Not familiar with the cut of her sails, but she's not carrying enough sail for anything larger."

"Very good, Mr. Tyler!" Brewer shouted. "Keep me informed! Mr. Short! What's our speed?"

Tyler waved his acknowledgment and went back to studying the approaching ship. Short ran to the log book and returned.

"Last reading was nearly twenty minutes ago, sir. Five knots, sir."

Brewer lowered his glass and looked at the horizon. The stranger's sails were barely visible now, even without the glass. He estimated that time to intercept would be around three hours.

"Mr. Greene, we shall keep to our present course for now."

"Aye aye, sir!" Greene said.

"And what do you think, Mr. Sweeney?" Brewer asked.

The sailing master shrugged. "Don't rightly know, Captain, but I think we're about to find out."

"Any experience with these pirates, Mr. Sweeney?" Brewer asked.

"None, sir. Fought the Frogs a few times in these waters, but never any pirates."

Brewer nodded. "I see. Any advice?"

Sweeney looked at his captain, and he smiled. "Hit them first, sir."

Brewer swallowed hard and nodded. He handed his glass to Mr. Short and returned to his quarters. As he entered, Jenkins came out of his pantry, seemingly startled at the captain's appearance in the cabin.

"Something wrong, Jenkins?" Brewer asked.

"No, sir," Jenkins replied. "Just a little surprised to see you, sir. I suppose I'm still getting used to your ways, sir, that's all. Is there something I can get you, Captain?"

"A glass of port, if you please, Jenkins."

The servant lifted his eyebrow just a fraction. "As you wish, sir."

Brewer removed his sword and set it on the desk. He

looked out the stern windows for a moment, wishing they could show him the stranger's approach, then he sat down wearily.

Jenkins returned and set the port on the desk. He stepped back and stood off to the side, hands clasped behind his back. Brewer took a sip from the glass absently, aware of the servant's presence, but his mind occupied by other matters. For his part, the servant seemed to know what was happening and was content to wait until he was needed. It did not turn out to be long.

"Jenkins," the captain said, "did Captain Norman ever encounter pirates in these waters?"

"I don't believe so, sir," Jenkins said. "French warships, of course, and some privateers from several nationalities, but no actual pirates as such."

Brewer nodded. "I should have known. In wartime, there's no need for piracy. One can always purchase a letter of marque from some government or other to legitimize the activities." Brewer put his hand to his chin and thought for a minute, then looked up at the sound of a knock on his door.

"Enter," he said. The door opened to reveal Mr. Short.

"Mr. Phillips' respects, Captain," the midshipman said. "We are approaching the Windward Passage, and there appears to be fog off the larboard bow."

"Very well, I'll come," Brewer said. He picked up his hat and headed out the door and on to the deck, Mr. Tyler two steps behind him the whole way.

As he stepped up on the quarterdeck, Brewer saw Mr. Phillips standing beside the wheel in deep conversation with Mr. Sweeney. It was Sweeney who first noticed the captain and drew Phillips' attention to his presence.

"Windward Passage dead ahead, sir," the lieutenant said with a salute. "There's fog approaching from the southwest, off the larboard bow."

"So I see, Mr. Phillips," The captain said. He accepted a

glass from Mr. Tyler with a nod of thanks and nonchalantly began to study the approaching fog-bank. "What do you make of it?"

"I was just discussing that with the sailing master, sir," Phillips said. "It seemed to come up suddenly. We'll be in it within the hour—two at the most—if we don't alter course. I've already taken the precaution of ordering extra lookouts, sir."

Brewer lowered his glass and turned to his lieutenant. Phillips looked confident in what he was saying, but Brewer thought he heard a hint of hesitation in the young officer's voice. He glanced past the lieutenant to catch the eye of the sailing master.

Brewer looked back to his lieutenant. "What do you propose, Mr. Phillips?"

"Well, sir, we can alter course to the southwest and try to sail down the west side of the passage before the fog overtakes us."

Brewer glanced quickly to Mr. Sweeney, and the old veteran nodded.

"Very well, Mr. Phillips," he said. "You may call the hands to alter course. Give her as much sail as she'll take."

"Aye aye, sir!" Phillips saluted and turned to begin issuing his orders.

Brewer watched him for a moment and smiled to himself before turning his attention back to the fog bank. He hated fog and hoped they could beat it through the passage. Something caught his eye: several points of light that seemed to flicker just inside the edge of the fog. His eyes grew wide as he realized what was happening.

He turned and shouted, "Down! All hands! Down! Get down!"

He saw Sweeney, Phillips, and those on the quarterdeck drop, and he looked forward to see a group of seamen stare at him in uncomprehending disbelief.

"You men!" he screamed. "Get—"

Brewer felt a body slam into him, driving him to the deck and covering him, shielding him, really. Above them the deck erupted as shot tore into *Defiant's* timbers and upper works. Brewer tried to rise but was pushed back to the deck as the remainder of the broadside did its work. Only when he was sure it was safe did the captain's savior stand and help his captain to his feet.

Brewer's head was still ringing from striking the deck, but his eyes slowly cleared to see the face of the man standing before him.

"McCleary?" he said.

The Cornishman nodded. "Aye, sir."

Brewer looked around as his head cleared. *Defiant's* upper works were a shambles, sails shredded and several lines cut. He looked forward for the group of men he was trying to warn, but all he saw was mangled remains of bodies that had been torn apart by shot and splinters. The blood was running into the scuppers; there were at least a half-dozen others who were cut down or dismembered lying about the deck. The sight galvanized his emotions into a rage the spurred him to action.

He turned to look for his glass, only to have it handed to him by Mr. Short. Brewer raised the glass to his eye in time to see a large warship emerge from the fog.

"Mr. Phillips!" he cried. "Clear for action! Have the guns loaded and run out!"

"Aye, sir!"

Brewer turned to his sailing master, now back on his feet as well. "Mr. Sweeney! Steer for the enemy!"

"Aye, Captain!"

Mr. Greene appeared at his side, commenting, "It looks as though the Admiral was correct, sir. That's definitely a French frigate, and no pirate crew could fire so effective a broadside.

"Make sure the gun crews are ready, Mr. Greene. We shall try to cross her stern and rake her, but if we cannot do that, I want to lay alongside her within pistol shot. We'll show them that British broadsides haven't changed!"

"Aye aye, sir!" The first lieutenant saluted and was gone.

Brewer turned his attention back to the enemy frigate, now fully exposed from the fog. A quick count showed her to be a thirty-six gunner, probably (judging from damage done to *Defiant's* sails and rigging) armed with eighteen-pounders.

The damaged sails and rigging prevented *Defiant* from coming around as fast or as smartly as Brewer would have liked. Worse, the wind shifted, so that the enemy ship was able to cross *Defiant's* bow and rake them with another broadside. Brewer recoiled when he saw a seaman standing just ten feet from him smashed to pulp when a ball hit him squarely in the chest. He closed his eyes against the blood that sprayed him, and the next instant he felt something hit him in the arm. When he opened his eyes and looked down, he saw it was the bloody stump of the seaman's arm that had struck him. The man had never had a chance to scream, and all that was left of him now was a pool of blood and some strewn body parts.

Now Mr. Sweeney was at his side. "Captain!" he shouted as he pointed forward. "The foremast!"

With mounting horror Brewer watched the foremast slowly topple over, cut by the enemy's broadsides about twenty feet above the deck, taking the main topmast with it.

"That does it!" Sweeney lamented loudly. "We're fish in a barrel!"

There was a sick feeling in the pit of his stomach, and he was appalled by *Defiant*'s bad luck. "Mr. Short!" Brewer cried. "Tell Mr. Greene to get that wreckage cut away!"

"Aye aye, sir!"

Brewer saw what the pirate was up to. “Mr. Phillips! The enemy will pass down our starboard side. Ready the guns!”

“Aye, sir!”

Brewer watched the enemy frigate and noted that she was sailing very well.

“Stand by!” Brewer called, and he heard Phillips repeating the order to his crews.

“Ready, men! Fire!”

The two ships’ guns erupted almost simultaneously, Brewer managing to get the first shots in by a split second. The combined roar left his ears ringing, and the roiling smoke, combined with the fog, completely obscured the frigate. When they sailed out of it, he was disagreeably surprised to see that *Defiant’s* broadside had had little effect.

Mr. Tyler appeared and saluted. “Captain!” he said as he turned and pointed behind them. “Sail on the starboard quarter!”

Brewer turned. "Where away?"

"Two points off the larboard stern!"

Brewer grabbed a glass and ran to the rail. The newcomer was definitely a ship of war—Brewer could see her gun ports were open and the guns run out—and she was heading straight for *Defiant*. The question was, whose side was she on? If it was another pirate, *Defiant* may well be finished. Brewer resolved that he and *Defiant* would sell themselves dearly, taking as many pirates with them as they could.

"Sir!" Mr. Tyler called out. "It’s American!"

Brewer raised his glass to look again at the newcomer. She had tacked to put herself between *Defiant* and the pirate, and Brewer could now plainly see her colors flying from her stern.

"Rig our colors, Mr. Tyler!" Brewer ordered. "We don't

want them to have any doubt who the enemy is!"

"Aye aye, sir!"

The pirate also saw the American tack, and he turned in the general direction of Cuba and raised all sail. The American—it was a brig, Brewer now saw—swept past *Defiant* in pursuit. An officer on the quarterdeck waved at Brewer as they passed, and Brewer waved back. The American sailed on for a few miles before abandoning the chase and tacking back to *Defiant*. They hove to about two hundred yards away and quickly lowered a boat.

Brewer met the vessel as an officer climbed aboard. The two saluted.

"I am Commander Lindsey of the brig USS *Enterprise*," the American said.

Brewer shook his hand. "William Brewer, acting captain of His Majesty's frigate *Defiant*. Commander, I'm glad you showed up when you did. Things were just about to get a bit hot for us."

Commander Lindsey looked around. "Looks like they got the drop on you."

"Yes," Brewer admitted. "They used the fog as cover for a stealth approach. It was very effective."

Lindsey nodded. "How may we be of service?"

"I'm just finding out, Commander," Brewer said. "Come to my cabin—if it's still in one piece—and we'll find out together. Mr. Tyler, pass the word for Mr. Greene to bring his damage report to my cabin. If you'll follow me, Commander?"

The damage to *Defiant* was confined mostly to the upper deck and the rigging. His cabin, Brewer was relieved to find, was intact, and Jenkins proved equal to the task of providing lunch on very short notice, served with the best wine and followed by excellent coffee. Brewer described the strange vessel with the hidden thirty-two pounders, and Commander Lindsey nodded.

"We have received reports of sightings of this ship," he said as he drank his coffee, "but we have never managed to bring it to battle. They are pirates, based out of the north coast of Cuba, we believe. I personally think it could be the pirate Jean Lafitte, who disappeared after our attack on the pirate forces at Galveston. Either him, or one of his lieutenants."

Brewer swallowed some coffee. "Well, I intend to have my revenge, Commander. You say these pirates operate out of Cuba?"

"Yes," Lindsey said, with undisguised disgust in his voice, "but we can't go after them there because they've bought off the local Spanish authorities for protection. Unless we can catch them at sea and bring them to battle, our hands are diplomatically tied."

Brewer snorted. "I still say the best diplomat is a loaded thirty-two pounder."

Lindsey raised his cup in salute. "My friend, we speak the same language."

Brewer acknowledged the salute, and they drank to the death of pirates everywhere.

There was a knock at the door, and Mr. Greene entered the room. Brewer made the introductions, and Jenkins brought more coffee and a cup for Greene.

"Well, Benjamin," Brewer said, "what's the damage?"

Greene gratefully drank the coffee. "Not as bad as it might have been, Captain. Aside from the masts, the wheel needs to be replaced and the line rerun to the auxiliary steering. Mr. Sweeney discovered almost at once that the line was gone. He has no idea what happened to it. Two guns were put out of action, but both should be repaired by the second dogwatch. Our casualties were seven dead and thirty wounded. Dr. Spinelli said he expects to lose three of those."

Brewer stared at the table with a cold fury in his eyes. *Those men are dead because of me,* he thought. *I was surprised by the pirate, not they by us.*

Commander Lindsey read on Brewer's face what was going through his mind. He cleared his throat to get the Captain's attention. "Captain, please do not distress yourself with recriminations. You could not have known what was coming under cover of the fog. I agree it was an expensive lesson to learn, but your task now is to make sure your men did not die in vain. Do you require assistance in making your repairs?"

Brewer looked up. "I don't think so, Commander, but I would appreciate your presence at least until we regain rudder control."

"Happy to oblige, Captain," the commander replied with a smile.

"Mr. Sweeney is already working on the steering, sir," Mr. Greene reported, "and we are rigging the gallows for stepping a temporary foremast. That should see us to Jamaica."

Brewer nodded. "Did Mr. Sweeney have an idea when repairs would be completed?"

"He didn't say, sir."

"Find out, Mr. Greene, if you please."

Greene saluted and left on his errand, and Brewer and Commander Lindsey returned to the quarterdeck. Brewer escorted his guest to the gangway, and the two men saluted and shook hands.

“Thank you,” Brewer said.

“Our pleasure,” Lindsey replied. “Please keep me informed.”

Brewer nodded, and Commander Lindsey climbed down into his boat and was rowed back to *Enterprise.* Brewer watched him go and wondered if they would be fighting alongside each other one day soon.

Brewer turned and surveyed the deck of his ship. Burial parties were gathering the dead and lining them up on the deck before sewing them into their hammocks with the customary two rounds of shot each at their feet. The sight hurt him deep inside, and like most fighting men, he turned the pain to anger.

Just then, Mr. Wayne, the carpenter, came up and knuckled his forehead.

"I've completed my inspection of the inside of the hull, sir," he said. "There's no holes in it anywhere. Looks like the damage was pretty well confined topside, with them aiming at our sails and guns. With your permission, sir, I'll get started on the repairs."

Brewer looked around at the disabled guns on the deck. "I want these carronades made ready for action first, Mr. Wayne. After that, you may attend to your other duties."

The carpenter saluted and mumbled an "Aye aye, sir." He immediately began measuring the nearest splintered battery and making notes in a notebook his pulled from inside his shirt. When he was satisfied, he moved on to the next and did the same. Brewer watched him for a moment with an approving eye before nodding to himself and turning to the next task.

"Mr. Phillips!" he called. The lieutenant left off supervising the burial parties and rushed to his captain's side.

"Sir?" Phillips said as he saluted.

"Let's get *Defiant* organized again, shall we?" Brewer said, a little more angrily than he would have liked. "Run below and check on the sailmaker. Make sure he and his mates are on their way up with fresh canvas. Have them start repairs immediately on anything we can't replace."

"Mr. Moran and his mates," Phillips said. "Aye aye, sir."

"Next, I want you to see the bosun and tell him we need a detail to clean up the deck."

"Aye aye, sir," the lieutenant said.

Brewer was about to add something else when he saw

Mr. Sweeney emerge from the aft companionway. Brewer beckoned to the sailing master, who headed his direction.

"Very well, Mr. Phillips," the captain said, "that will do for now. Report back when those tasks are under way."

"Aye aye, sir," the young lieutenant saluted and went off.

Mr. Sweeney approached and saluted. "We'll have the steering repaired in an hour or so, sir. The hands are stringing the new lines now. We'll need to keep it at the auxiliary until we can make a new wheel in Jamaica."

"Very well, Mr. Sweeney," Brewer said. "I want to get under way again as soon as we have steering control restored. I don't like waiting around for those pirates to come back any more than I like being babysat by the Americans."

Sweeney grunted. *He doesn't like it either,* Brewer realized. He could only smile as he watched the master return below.

Two hours later, *Defiant* bade farewell to her American guardian and set sail for her destination. Brewer stood on the quarterdeck and watched with pride as the sails bent on the new mast. His crew had worked miracles to get the new stick up and crossed. He turned to look north where the American had disappeared over the horizon, and he wondered what they thought of the repairs that had once more made *Defiant* ready for action. He grimaced and blushed; whatever they thought, he hoped it swept away the fact that he had allowed his ship to be crippled like that in the first place.

Defiant swept southward over calm seas, passing east of Puerto Rico and then south of Hispaniola as she approached Jamaica. As he'd hoped, they sighted no shipping whatsoever on their way. This gave him the time he needed to restore his men's confidence, not only in him but in themselves as well. He was on deck as much as possible, mingling with the men and letting them take his measure. He always said the same thing to them.

"Rest easy, lads," he said. "They surprised us once. I promise you, it won't happen again. I'll get us into position, and then you men will pound them to sticks!"

To his relief, the men believed him, and his officers began to report that the men's morale was slowly rising. More and more of them were expressing confidence in Brewer, as a man, if not yet as a captain. Brewer wondered about that, but Mr. Sweeney brushed it off.

"Don't worry about it, Captain," he said in Brewer's cabin when the two were discussing the crew. "You know sailors to be a superstitious lot. Well, you took command when the captain was washed overboard, and then in our first action we were surprised and bad luck put us out of action. We had to be rescued by the Americans! There's a couple of the thicker ones below that have started wondering aloud about this being a bad luck ship now, but Peters and a couple of his mates shut them up right enough."

Brewer nodded even as his brows furrowed. How he could fix this?

CHAPTER 18

By the time HMS *Defiant* slid into the harbor at Port Royal, Jamaica, acting Captain William Brewer felt better in every way, not only about his ship and her fighting capabilities, but also about himself and his ability to command.

He had intensified the training routine for the men, and it soon bore fruit. Mr. Mosley, under the watchful eye of the first lieutenant, went about his job with a relish Brewer had never before seen in a gunner. The crew knew him well and responded both to his training methods and to his starter, when he was forced to use it. Once during the voyage, after Mosley had been back on the job for a week, Brewer pulled him aside to question him regarding the slow rate of fire at which the men were practicing.

"Beggin' yer pardon, Captain," the old man said, "but it's accuracy before speed every time. Do it any other way, and you'll have the fastest broadside in the world, but you won't do anything but waste powder and shot. They won't hit a thing. But if we teach them accuracy first, then we can speed up the rate of fire with practice and get that three-to-two ratio you want, *and* blow them pirates to blazes in the bargain!"

Brewer minded his place after that, and Mr. Mosley was as good as his word. *Defiant's* gunnery steadily improved until it was better than anything Brewer himself had ever achieved in *Lydia*. Once Brewer tried to congratulate Greene on the improvement, but his first lieutenant blushed and brushed it aside.

"It's all Mr. Mosley, Captain," the first lieutenant said. "He gets more out of the men than I thought possible."

Brewer could scarcely believe his luck at finding such an artisan in his crew. It also made him wonder just what Norman had been thinking when he demoted Mosley rather than take advantage of his talents.

Twice during the voyage, *Defiant* sighted a strange sail on the horizon. Both times Brewer altered course without hesitation to intercept the stranger, but both times the newcomer disappeared over the horizon and was lost. The second time, darkness aided the enemy's escape. Brewer remained in the area all night and cleared the deck for action just as dawn broke, hoping to find the pirate and bring him to battle. Their hopes were dashed, however, when *Defiant* found herself alone on a painted ocean.

And yet, it wasn't all for naught. Both Mr. Sweeney and Dr. Spinelli brought the captain word that the crew were talking of nothing else but how "their captain" took off after those pirates and made them turn tail and run for safer waters! Brewer was surprised to see the men turn in his favor so quickly, but Mr. Sweeney scoffed.

"Bah!" he said when Brewer had voiced his surprise. "The men *want* to love you! They've been waiting, and now you finally gave them a reason to love you!"

Thus it was a more confident Captain Brewer that stood alongside his sailing master as they entered the harbor. Brewer called for a glass and scanned the waters. He saw two frigates under repair, one undergoing a general refit and the other getting a new mast stepped in, probably due to a lightning strike from the look of it. There was also a cutter anchored in the harbor, but precious little else of the West Indies Squadron was in evidence. Brewer handed his telescope to Mr. Short and the *Defiant* hove to and waited for the harbor master to send out a pilot. Sweeney chaffed at the idea of being guided to an anchorage "like a garbage scow"; Brewer smiled at the way the sailing master made himself scarce while the pilot was aboard.

As soon as they were anchored, a guard boat pulled out from the wharf and made its way to *Defiant's* lee. A lieutenant came aboard and was escorted to the quarterdeck.

"Lieutenant Rodney, sir," the lieutenant said as he saluted.

Brewer saluted. "Any relation to the Duke of Norfolk?"

The lieutenant blushed. "Yes, I'm afraid. He's my uncle. I came out with Admiral Hornblower when he took command. I am the admiral's aide-de-camp. Is Captain Norman aboard, sir?"

"I am the acting captain," Brewer answered. "Lieutenant William Brewer. We lost Captain Norman overboard in a storm, and Admiral Morgan confirmed my acting-captaincy while we put in at Bermuda."

"I'm sorry for your loss," Rodney said. "Did you say Brewer? Were you with the admiral on St. Helena? Of course! I knew it! Admiral Hornblower's told me many tales of your adventures with the Corsican. I must say, it's a pleasure to meet you, sir!"

Now it was Brewer who blushed. "What can I do for you, Lieutenant?"

"Oh, yes," Rodney said as he cleared his throat. "The admiral is at his residence ashore. When we were notified that *Defiant* was entering the harbor, I was sent out to bring the captain ashore to dine with the admiral. As you are the acting captain, I suppose that means you, sir."

"Very well," Brewer said. He signaled for a midshipman. "Pass the word for Mr. Greene to report to my quarters. Lieutenant, please give me ten minutes to change into something more suitable, and then I will be at your disposal."

Brewer hurried below, shouting for Jenkins to get his best uniform out. Mr. Greene was admitted while he was in the middle of changing.

"Ah! There you are, Benjamin," Brewer said as he pulled on a clean shirt. "I am going ashore to dine with Admiral Hornblower. You will be in command. Make arrangements for repairs on the masts to begin at once. If anyone asks about shore leave, you can tell them no one sets foot ashore until *Defiant* is ready for sea again. Once the work is completed, we can authorize shore leave for those guns crews that won their divisional contests last week. I believe the prize was twenty-four hours' liberty at our next friendly port, was it not? They can be the first to go ashore, but not until the work is done."

"Aye aye, sir," Greene said. "You're going alone, sir?"

Brewer nodded as Jenkins helped him into his best coat. It was the new one he had purchased in London with Hornblower's help before he came to *Defiant*. Ironically, this was the first occasion he had had to wear it since then. "The admiral was expecting Captain Norman. I'll send you a note as soon as I know what the situation is ashore and with the squadron." Brewer stood tall and raised his arms to allow Jenkins to buckle on his sword, then he stood back.

"How do I look?" he asked.

Greene looked him over. "If you'll pardon me, sir," he said, as he leaned in to fix the collar. "Perfect now, sir."

"Thank you, Benjamin." He retrieved his reports and the dispatches he was to deliver to the admiral, picked up his hat, and headed for the door.

"Good luck, sir," Greene said as he followed his captain

from the room.

Brewer followed the young Lieutenant Rodney down into the waiting boat and took his place in the stern, the packet of dispatches from Admiral Morgan held tightly in his lap. He was excited at the prospect of seeing Admiral Hornblower again, but he was also nervous about what Hornblower would do regarding his current position. Yes, Hornblower was his mentor, but he was an admiral first, and Brewer did not think it an automatic thing that he would approve Brewer's promotion to post rank and hand him the only fifty-gun frigate in the entire Caribbean. He'd already been taken by surprise once by the pirates, and although Brewer knew he would never let it happen again, he wasn't so sure Hornblower would see it that way.

The boat reached the wharf, and Brewer led the way up and out of the boat. He waited for Rodney to step up on the wharf and followed him.

"The admiral's residence is just up the road," Rodney explained. "I hope you don't mind walking?"

"Not at all," Brewer replied, and the two men set off. Brewer was surprised that the young lieutenant didn't seem to be in a hurry, but he clasped his hands behind his back and walked beside the young officer.

"The admiral speaks very highly of you," Rodney said.

Brewer could only stare at the cobblestones passing beneath him. "He is too kind."

Rodney looked around at the town as he spoke. "May I ask, just how did you get into the admiral's good graces?"

Brewer smiled. *Just as I thought,* he said to himself, *another aristocrat trying to take a short cut to the top.* He shook his head and tried his best to look innocent.

"It's very simple, Mr. Rodney," he said as they arrived at the door of Hornblower's residence. "I did my duty."

"Of course," Rodney said, looking suitably chastised as he opened the door and led the way inside. He indicated a door to the right of the foyer. "If you'll be kind enough to wait in the library, sir, I'll inform the admiral that you're here."

Rodney bowed and left without waiting for Brewer to answer. Brewer watched him go; he silently feared for the future of the Royal Navy.

Brewer opened the door to the library and found it to be a typical waiting room. A small, unused fireplace on the wall was opposite the door, with a portrait of the king mounted over the mantle. In front were two small settees facing each other with a low table between. On the table, Brewer noticed several copies of the *Naval Gazette*. He wandered over to look out a window at the townsfolk walking past. He almost ignored the footsteps he heard coming down the hall.

"William?"

Brewer spun to see his mentor standing in the doorway. He looked exactly as Brewer remembered him from their last meeting in London, before Hornblower left to take command of the West Indies Squadron and Brewer left to take up his post in *Defiant*. Tall and lean, and now graying at the temples, Hornblower had an aura of competency and command about him that Brewer, at this stage of his career, could only marvel at.

"William!" Hornblower cried as he entered the room and grasped the startled lieutenant by both shoulders before he could even salute. "It *is* you! I thought Rodney was joking when he said he brought *Defiant's* commanding lieutenant!"

Brewer struggled to keep his composure. "Greetings, milord. It's wonderful to see you again. I have my reports and dispatches here for you from Admiral Morgan on Bermuda."

Hornblower took the packet and handed it to Rodney, who was standing in the doorway. Hornblower shook Brewer's hand. "It's good to see you again, William. Come, we can sit in my study. You can have something to drink while I go over these, and then we can talk. Have you heard from Bush lately?"

The two men talked of their old friend as Hornblower led the way out into the hall and up the stairs to his private study. Considerably larger than the library he'd just left, Brewer thought it to be the perfect room for an admiral, with a large oak desk at one end, and an empty fireplace with two overstuffed high backed leather chairs in front dominating the far wall. Brewer was surprised to see so many fireplaces in the Caribbean, and he wondered if it ever got cold enough to use them. Then he turned to see over in the far corner of the room a bust of Napoleon Bonaparte. Brewer couldn't help himself; he took two steps toward the bust and stared.

Hornblower noticed his friend's surprise. "A good likeness, don't you think?"

"Quite good, milord," Brewer said when he found his voice again. "I wonder how he's doing?"

Hornblower looked up in surprise. "Oh, that's right. You wouldn't have heard. I'm afraid our friend is no longer with us, William."

Brewer turned in surprise. "What? Bonaparte dead? When? How?"

Hornblower sat down behind his oak desk and began to open the packet of dispatches. "About three months ago now, if my figuring is correct. As to how, I have no idea. They buried him on St. Helena."

Brewer turned silently and stared at the bust in the corner, remembering his time on the island with the man who came closer than anyone since Alexander the Great to conquering the world, and they were fond memories. He turned when he heard a servant enter the room and accepted a glass or port from the admiral. By unspoken agreement, both men raised their glasses.

"A toast," Hornblower said, "to Napoleon Bonaparte, Emperor of the French. Sworn enemy of England, and a man

I am proud to have called my friend. May he rest in peace. To Bonaparte!"

"To Bonaparte!" Brewer echoed, and both men tasted their port.

Brewer looked back at the bust. "I wonder if they got him."

Hornblower looked up. "What?"

Brewer turned to him. "I was wondering if they got him. I remember him saying something to the effect that, after we left, he expected his enemies in the English government to arrange for his death."

Hornblower stared contemplatively at the bust and said nothing. That more or less settled the question for Brewer; he just nodded and turned back to the bust. He shook his head. It didn't seem right, somehow. Wasn't St. Helena bad enough? Was it really necessary to kill him? *Well,* he thought, *a man like that makes enemies.*

Brewer sighed and turned away from the bust, putting that part of his life behind him. He wandered over and sat down in a chair in front of the admiral's desk. He savored his port as he watched Hornblower set his reports aside and read Morgan's dispatches. His admiral made no sound as he absorbed the information, and Brewer wondered what Hornblower knew that he didn't.

Finally, Hornblower sighed and dropped the last sheet onto his desk. He sat back in his high backed chair and stared out into space. Brewer sat back and waited, and before long he saw his mentor blink and lean forward in his chair.

"Very well, William," Hornblower said, "I will read your reports later. For now, I want to hear from you firsthand what happened to Captain Norman. Then I want to hear what happened to *Defiant.*"

Brewer took about ten minutes to describe the hurricane and Captain Norman's decision to try to sail to Bermuda ahead of it, concluding with how the Captain was swept overboard by the wave. He did not include any information on his former captain's mental state in his report. When Hornblower had no questions, he went on to describe the appearance of the formerly French frigate from the fog bank and *Defiant's* subsequent rescue by the American brig. Hornblower listened with hooded eyes; Brewer found it disconcerting not knowing what his mentor was thinking.

"What do you estimate the repair time to be?" Hornblower asked.

"Not more than a week, my lord, if we can get some help stepping the new foremast."

Hornblower nodded and made himself a note. Finally, he put his pen down and mused.

"Well, William," he said at length, "you have brought me the information I've been lacking. I begin to see a pattern now in the pirates' movements, and with luck I think we can anticipate where they may strike next and be ready for them."

"That's good news, my lord."

"Yes, indeed, but we have matters to tend to before we can settle with them, the first of which is your status as captain of the *Defiant*. Admiral Morgan confirmed you as acting captain, but he quite rightly left the final disposition of your case to me as the admiral commanding the squadron. I will be honest with you, William; I will have a hard time justifying handing over a fifty-gun frigate to a lieutenant, however senior or qualified he may be. There are simply too many senior captains on the beach with influence in the Admiralty."

Brewer fought hard to control his emotions. "I understand, my lord."

Hornblower stood and refilled their glasses. "That being said, I don't happen to have any of those senior captains in port at the moment, so I can afford to take my time in making my decision. Therefore, William, you shall continue as acting captain of the *Defiant* for the time being."

Brewer relaxed, even if only a little. "Thank you, my lord."

Hornblower sat behind his desk. "Not at all. Also, since *Defiant* is the most powerful warship in the squadron, I will hoist my flag in her when we go out after the pirates."

"Yes, my lord," Brewer said. So, there it was. Brewer would keep his command, but under Hornblower's watchful eye. *Very well,* he thought. *I must use this opportunity to convince the admiral that I can handle commanding a ship. All I can do after that is to hope for the best.*

Brewer turned back to Hornblower and noticed that the admiral had been watching him. Brewer held his mentor's gaze as he wondered what his face had given away. Brewer relaxed when he saw a twinkle in Hornblower's eye and a smile creep into the corner of his mouth.

At that moment, there was a knock at the door, and Gerard entered the room. The admiral's flag lieutenant, Gerard had been Captain Bush's first lieutenant on the old *Lydia* when Brewer was the second. The two had also served together under Bush in the *Agamemnon* at St. Helena. Brewer had saved Gerard's life during the action against the Barbary Coast pirates, but Gerard wasn't aware of that, and Brewer was happy to keep it that way.

"Begging your pardon, my lord," Gerard said as he entered the room without looking, "but you wanted to know when the Americans arrived in the harbor. I've sent Mr. Rodney to—Good heavens! William? Is that you?"

Brewer rose and shook his friend's hand. "It's good to see you, Gerard."

Gerard took the seat beside Brewer, across the desk from his chief. "I was sorry to hear about Captain Norman, William. I trust you're adjusting well to your new responsibilities?"

Hornblower interrupted. "You'll get a chance to see for

yourself, Mr. Gerard. We're going out in HMS *Defiant* when we go after the pirates. Now, what were you saying about the Americans?"

Gerard became all business before his chief. "Yes, my lord. USS *Congress* is entering the harbor with Commodore Porter aboard. I have taken the liberty of sending Mr. Rodney out to bring the commodore to Admiralty House."

Hornblower nodded. "Good! The American's timing couldn't be better. Now that *Defiant* has arrived, we can coordinate a plan to go after the pirates."

"That was my thinking as well, my lord," Gerard said. "By the way, William, I believe there is some mail for you downstairs. With your permission, Admiral, I shall step out and retrieve it."

"By all means," Hornblower said, and Gerard left on his errand.

"So, William," Hornblower said as he leaned back in his chair, "tell me, have you had a difficult time since you assumed command?"

Brewer hesitated. He wondered whether he was addressing his old friend and mentor or the admiral commanding the squadron, and he knew it was not a question he could ask. He sighed and decided honesty was the best policy.

"Nothing that I couldn't handle, my lord," he said calmly. "I merely tried to remember everything that Captain Bush said you taught him."

"Ha!" Hornblower said as he leaned forward and slapped the desk with the palm of his hand. "If that is your only guide, my young friend, it is a wonder you were not hanged!"

Both men laughed. "There is one matter where I could use your help. I have a very young third lieutenant whom I am trying to mold into something."

Hornblower looked up. "That would be Mr. Phillips?"

Brewer was surprised. "You know of him?"

The admiral smiled. "Of course. I was in London when his captain made his plea to the lords of the admiralty. I was there to hear him make his case, in fact. Remarkable man; I have never been moved so by another's words. Mr. Phillips must be a extraordinary young man."

"Too young, perhaps," Brewer said softly. "Do you know what he did to make his captain so powerful an advocate?"

Hornblower shook his head, and Brewer told his mentor the whole story of the mutiny aboard the *Retribution*. Hornblower listened without comment. Brewer followed this tale with an account of incidents involving Mr. Phillips aboard the *Defiant* and sat back in his chair. He watched his mentor turn and stare out the office window. Hornblower's hand went to his chin and rubbed it gently in thought, his brows knit together in concentration. Hornblower nodded slightly, and he turned back to his young protégé.

"This explains much, Mr. Brewer. When Captain Styles made his plea for the lad before their lordships of the admiralty, he declined to state his specifics publicly, as was his right. The board members had the captain's written report, which, naturally, contained every detail. But it was Styles' impassioned plea that got Mr. Phillips his commission. I wish you could have heard it, William. It was incredible."

"Mr. Phillips is an exceptional individual, my lord. My concern is that his young mind may not be able to make the adjustment to his new responsibilities."

Hornblower shrugged. "That is for Mr. Phillips to show us. He has every advantage of support and opportunity, but he must ultimately decide whether or not His Majesty's Navy is for him."

There was a knock at the door, and Gerard entered. He was followed by an American officer. The two came to attention before Hornblower.

"Commodore! How good to see you again," Hornblower

said. Not standing on ceremony, the admiral came around his desk and shook the Commodore's hand heartily. He turned to Brewer, had stood immediately. "Allow me to make the introductions: Commodore Porter, United States Navy, allow me to present Lieutenant William Brewer, currently commanding His Majesty's frigate *Defiant*."

Brewer shook hands with the American before all three men took their seats around Hornblower's great desk. The admiral addressed Brewer.

"The commodore is in command of the American squadron in the West Indies. His current job is hunting pirates."

CHAPTER 19

The admiral's steward entered the room and announced that dinner was served, so Hornblower led his guests downstairs to the dining room. Brewer was surprised to see that the four of them were the only attendees, and he shot a questioning look at Gerard as he was shown to his place on the admiral's right. Commodore Porter sat across from him, on the admiral's left, while Gerard sat next to Brewer. Gerard just smiled reassuringly, and Brewer hoped he could take that as a good sign. Brewer wondered what the American's appearance in Kingston meant. He took the opportunity before dinner to send a message to Mr. Greene, telling him that the admiral intended to sail on *Defiant* and to rearrange accommodations accordingly.

The table was already laid with the fare. Brewer's eyes widened at the sight of it all.

"Mr. Brewer," Hornblower said, indicating a bowl on the table, "that is land crab salad. The land crab that went into this were coconut-fed; some prefer the meat to good English pork. Commodore, before you is a saddle of fresh lamb, and the bowl next to it contains yams. Oh, Mr. Brewer! I particularly want to bring to your attention the steaming dish before Mr. Gerard. It is a West Indian pepper pot: a Caribbean delicacy with which these other gentlemen are already familiar. Be sure to avail yourself—I assure you, there is nothing like it in all Europe!"

The food was delicious, and Brewer dug in for all he was worth. A discreet nudge from Gerard under the table reminded him to show proper restraint. Brewer caught his eye to convey his thanks, and Gerard winked at him and smiled.

As the third course arrived, Hornblower spoke up. "William, the commodore was just telling me on his last visit of a great victory his squadron obtained against the pirates."

"Oh?" Brewer said.

"Yes," said the commodore, taking his cue from the admiral and taking up the tale. "It was just before I took command, actually. Lieutenant Biddle led the force that attacked the pirate stronghold at Galveston, in Texas, near the Mexican border. We destroyed several ships without losing any of our own."

"And what about Lafitte?" Brewer asked. Jean Lafitte was the most famous pirate still alive, and Brewer remembered he was known to frequent the waters from New Orleans to the Mexican border.

Porter's brows rose slightly. "Unfortunately, we do not know. Prisoners we questioned said he was in the city when the attack began, but none knew what happened to him, and we were not able to identify any of the bodies as his. Lafitte's own men burned his house, and the fortress exploded, taking most of the settlement with it. I suppose it's possible that Lafitte was inside when the citadel went up, but we found no one who could confirm that."

Hornblower said, "The commodore's squadron is currently patrolling off the Yucatan, making it ideally placed to prevent any pirates coming out of the Gulf of Mexico, or any slavers going in. I intend to take *Defiant* and a few smaller ships and circle east around Cuba and up her northern coast. My hope is that this will either bring the pirates out to fight, or else drive them westward into the waiting arms of Commodore Porter's squadron. I will leave two frigates here to patrol the waters off Kingston, in case any manage to slip past us and head south. If that indeed turns out to be the case, we will join with the Americans and proceed south as quickly as possible to catch these monsters by the rear."

Brewer nodded, chewing his turkey slowly to give himself time to think. It sounded like a good plan, at least on the surface. "And slavers?" he asked. He had already heard several of his crew discussing the possibility of head money, which was the reward paid for each slave freed from a slave ship.

Hornblower turned to face Brewer but remained silent, and Commodore Porter sighed in exasperation. "That is a bit more difficult," he said, "because the slavers frequently pay off the local Spanish authorities to give them sanctuary. It's happening all over the Caribbean, and neither our navy nor yours has enough ships that are both big enough to defeat the slavers if they decide to come out, and fast enough to catch them, should they decide to make a run for it. Slave ships built in our southern ports were purposefully designed long and lean to transport a large number of bodies swiftly. Some of the best slavers can do seventeen or eighteen knots."

"Good lord!" Brewer exclaimed. He looked to Gerard, who merely nodded confirmation.

The admiral took up from here. "The best strategy we have developed so far is to fire at the slavers at long range and hope to slow them enough to bring them into close range. *Defiant*, with her 24-pounders and faster speed, will give us an advantage there. How is your gunnery?"

"Getting better every day, my lord," Brewer said. "We acquired a new gunner at Bermuda named Mosley, and he has worked miracles since coming aboard."

"Mosley?" Hornblower said. "He's your gunner?"

"Yes, my lord. I don't know much about him, other than he was with Nelson at some of his biggest victories. I am pleased to say that *Defiant's* gunnery has vastly improved on our trip south from Bermuda."

Hornblower smiled and leaned back in his seat as his steward brought their coffee while his mates cleared their dishes. "I'm glad to hear it. Mr. Mosley, Commodore, is a minor legend in the Royal Navy for his skill as a gunner, especially to those who were at the Nile and Trafalgar. We are most fortunate to have his services available to us."

"Thank you, my lord," Brewer said.

Dinner was over, and the three officers stepped out on the balcony to smoke cigars in the cool Caribbean evening. Gerard excused himself to attend to other duties, and Brewer bade his friend good night.

Hornblower turned to Brewer. "Lieutenant, I want you to tell the Commodore about your encounter with the pirate frigate."

"Yes, my lord," Brewer said, and he repeated the verbal report he had given earlier to his admiral. To his credit, Porter listened without interrupting, saving his questions until the moment after Brewer finished.

"So the first indication you had of the pirate's presence was when you saw his muzzle flashes?" the Commodore asked.

"Yes, Commodore."

The Commodore's brow wrinkled as he puffed his cigar and considered what he had heard.

"This is a troubling event, Admiral," the Commodore said. "To our knowledge, the frigate has never attacked a warship before."

Hornblower shook his head. "I have had no such reports either."

Porter addressed the two British officers. "This means the pirates are becoming more aggressive. With their French training, they could devastate the commerce of the area. We would be forced to have ships travel in convoy, escorted by heavy warships." He turned to Hornblower. "We must hunt them down now."

"I agree, Commodore," Hornblower said, "I intend to sail on *Defiant* in a week. It will take that long to step a new mast and make necessary repairs. I have no idea how long it will take us to work our way up the northern coast of Cuba, but if we are delayed, I will send word by a packet boat to the waters off the Yucatan."

Porter puffed on his cigar as he considered the timetable. "Very well, Admiral. My ship will sail on the morning tide, just as soon as we have finished watering. We will be waiting off the Northwest coast of Cuba for anything you chase our way."

The American saluted Hornblower and nodded to Brewer before marching out of the room. The two British officers watched him go, and then Hornblower turned to his young officer.

"What do you think of him, William?" the admiral asked.

"Hard for me to judge, my lord, after meeting him so briefly and under such circumstances," Brewer said automatically. He turned to see Hornblower looking at him with his one brow raised and remembered it as a sign of incredulity. Brewer smiled slightly. "All right, but you know I had to try."

Hornblower smiled.

Brewer considered. "He seemed a little... embarrassed, I suppose would be the word."

"About the question over slavers?"

Brewer nodded.

"Yes," Hornblower said as he puffed his cigar. "It seems that lately certain charges have been leveled against

American naval officers of southern birth, to the effect that they were not doing all in their power to capture slavers. I'm afraid Porter takes it as a slight against all naval officers."

"I take it then the commodore is not of southern birth?"

Hornblower smiled. "A Yankee from Connecticut."

Brewer smiled as he enjoyed his cigar and the cool night air. It was almost enough to make him forget his problems. He was still standing there some minutes later when Gerard silently appeared at Hornblower's elbow, and he did not notice the two whisper together.

"Well, William," Hornblower said, interrupting his reverie, "I must ask you to excuse me. I have some work to do before I turn in for the night. Thank you for an excellent evening." Brewer saluted, left the house, and returned to the *Defiant*.

Work proceeded on the new mast, and on the fifth day Brewer found himself back in the admiral's office to report the ship ready for sea.

"Well done, Captain," Hornblower said. "I shall join you tomorrow in time for the first dog watch, so *Defiant* may sail with the morning tide the following day, if the winds will cooperate."

"Very good, my lord. Would you do me the honor of dining with me and my officers tomorrow night? Along with Mr. Gerard, of course. My officers have been looking forward to it."

"Excellent idea, William," Hornblower said. "Coordinate with Gerard. Good afternoon, Captain; I shall see you tomorrow."

Brewer bowed. "Good afternoon, my lord."

Brewer watched his mentor retreat from the room and then turned to Gerard, who had remained.

"He hasn't changed a bit," Brewer said, nodding toward the door.

Gerard followed his friend's eyes to the door. "He has,

William, but not in any way that matters." Gerard seemed to consider something before continuing. "If you don't mind, sir, I will accompany you back to *Defiant.*"

Brewer thought this a bit strange, but decided to let events reveal what they would. "A pleasure, sir. Shall we go?"

The two officers were soon on the street walking toward the dock. "I'm sorry we can't present you to the governor," Gerard said. "He was recalled to England with some sort of family emergency."

"Quite all right," Brewer replied. "I'm glad to see you so well, Gerard. I was afraid for you when I left you on *Lydia*."

"Yes," Gerard said with his trademark smile, "it was touch and go for a while there, wasn't it? Well, after you left us in Gibraltar, I was transferred to *Zeus*, which was supposed to have this genius of a surgeon. I was only half conscious at the time, but let me tell you, the work he did on me was nothing short of a miracle."

Brewer smiled. "And just who was this miracle worker?"

Gerard shrugged. "Some chap named... Spinelli, I think."

Brewer hesitated for just a moment before falling into step again beside his old friend. He wore a smile on his face all the way to the dock.

Gerard led the way down into the gig, and the two men were soon settled into the stern sheets and on their way out to *Defiant*. Gerard's eye ran over the ship from stem to stern and from main top to the waterline; Brewer guessed it was his first time getting a look at the fifty gun frigates that were built to go toe-to-toe with the American giants.

Lieutenant Greene was present to welcome them on board. Officers normally did not stand watch while the ship was in port, but Brewer put it down to Greene being anxious that the Admiral would be sailing with them. Greene had taken it upon himself to oversee the preparations. Brewer approved; he would expect nothing less from his first lieutenant.

"Welcome aboard, Captain," Greene said formally, after saluting.

"Thank you, Mr. Greene," Brewer said. "Mr. Greene, may I present Lieutenant Gerard, Flag Lieutenant to Admiral Hornblower. Mr. Gerard, this is Lieutenant Greene, my first lieutenant."

Both men shook hands.

Greene turned to Brewer. "All is in readiness, Captain. I had Jenkins move your things into the chart room, and the main cabin has been rearranged to accommodate the admiral. Lieutenant Gerard can use the spare room in the ward room."

"Very good, Mr. Greene," Brewer said. "The admiral will arrive in time to dine with me tomorrow evening. Please alert Jenkins, in case he needs to go ashore tomorrow to make ready. The purser has permission to go ashore as well."

"Aye aye, sir."

"I hope you will be available to dine with the admiral and myself, Mr. Greene?"

"Oh, indeed sir! Thank you!"

"Think nothing of it. I also want to invite Mr. Phillips, Mr. Sweeney, the surgeon, and Mr. Moseley as well. See to it, please."

Greene looked surprised. "Mr. Moseley, sir?"

Brewer smiled. "Yes. It seems Mr. Moseley's fame and reputation have reached the admiral's ears."

Greene whistled low in surprise. "Exactly," Brewer said softly. "See to the invitations, if you please, and have the surgeon report to me in the main cabin."

"Aye aye, sir," Greene saluted and ran off.

"Now, Gerard, if you'll follow me?" Gerard fell into step behind him, and Brewer led the way below decks and to the main cabin.

Gerard examined the appointments before turning to speak to Brewer. "I must say, I'm surprised at the size,

William. It looks like they gave it the full size of a two-decker cabin."

"They did," Brewer smiled. "It seems Captain Norman had a good deal of influence with certain portions of the refit."

Gerard nodded in appreciation. He was about to say something, but he was interrupted by a knock at the door.

"Enter," Brewer called, and Mr. Spinelli walked in.

"Ah, doctor!" Brewer said. "Allow me to present an old patient of yours. This is Lieutenant Gerard, flag lieutenant to Admiral Hornblower. Mr. Gerard, my ship's surgeon, Dr. Spinelli."

Gerard stepped forward quickly. "Doctor! How good it is to see you again! I never got the chance to thank you properly for patching me up so well at Gibraltar. How have you been?"

Spinelli looked bemused for a moment, then his face cleared. "Gerard? Oh, yes! You were brought aboard *Zeus* in a bad way, right? I thought I remembered you! That was a near-run thing, let me tell you. Captain, I was afraid for a while there that I would have to take a leg and maybe an arm off this man here. Fortunately, the good Lord blessed him with the constitution of an ox. He refused to quit! I've never seen anything like it! Are you doing well now, Lieutenant?"

"Very well, thank you, Doctor," Gerard said as the two shook hands.

Jenkins appeared with glasses of wine for the officers, and each man took one. They drank toast after toast, until finally they were seated around the table in the cabin, each man content and leaning back in their chair.

Brewer leaned forward. "Tell me truly, Gerard, how bad is it?"

Gerard looked from Brewer to the doctor and back again, then he searched the swirls in his drink for a moment before speaking. "Several months ago, the pirate activity suddenly increased all across the Caribbean and the Gulf of Mexico. That raid Commodore Porter told you about at Galveston seems to have calmed the Gulf for the most part, but those murderous swine are still pillaging from the Bahamas and Cuba down as far south as Venezuela. We believe the same ship that ambushed you is responsible for at least ten missing merchantmen in the last four months, and that's not counting any American merchantmen."

Brewer and Spinelli exchanged a long look. Neither man had a doubt now as to why the Admiralty wanted *Defiant's* firepower in the Caribbean.

Gerard took a long draft of his wine, and then he spoke over his glass. "William, do you remember how it was when we had to fight the pirates off the Barbary Coast a few years back? Some of the most desperate fighting I've ever seen. These pirates are a whole other breed. Far more vicious, far more blood thirsty, than the ones off the Barbary Coast. It's almost as if they had no fear... I'm not sure how to describe it. I understand the ship that got the drop on you was alone? That explains why it broke off when the American brig showed up. Usually, these devils are wolves, attacking in packs, swarming over their prey from several directions at once. We've encountered tactics like these before, but never with the drive to press home the attack like we've seen lately. It's as though these were professional, veteran seamen turned to piracy."

Dr. Spinelli looked up. "Well, isn't that what we expected?"

The doctor cleared his throat and went on. "I mean, I seem to remember hearing that there were whole crews in the French navy that were so loyal to Napoleon that they defected when he abdicated after Waterloo. Just took their ships and left France. Now, if that's true, isn't it possible they went to the Caribbean and became pirates, keeping their military discipline?"

The flag lieutenant sighed. "That scenario is exactly what the admiral feared is happening. A couple of the larger pirate ships look an awful lot like the French sloops and frigates we fought during the war, only modified to make them more effective for piracy." Gerard noticed the interested looks on the faces of his listeners and explained. "They've been stripped down to give them extra speed. The larger, heavier cannons have been removed; pirates want to loot ships, not sink them on sight. They generally tend to carry larger crews for boarding ships and crewing any prizes they decide to keep."

"Well," Brewer said, "I hope we get to do something about that. Gerard, thank you for coming. I understand better now what we are up against. Well, as you have seen, we are ready to sail at the admiral's convenience. Dinner will be served at the turn of the first dog watch tomorrow."

Gerard rose. "Thank you, Captain. No, no, there's no need to escort me, I can find the way. The admiral and I will not be late, I assure you." Gerard headed toward the door, but he stopped with his hand on the knob and turned back. "I must warn you," he said with a smile, "it seems the admiral has heard of your Mr. Jenkins and is looking forward to the meal. Good day, gentlemen."

Brewer could only stare at the door after his friend had gone. Was there anything that Hornblower did not know?

CHAPTER 20

Acting Captain William Brewer was never as nervous in his life as the moment the lookout announced that the admiral's barge was approaching. Gerard had sent the admiral's things ahead earlier in the day, and Brewer had seen to it that they were stowed in the admiral's cabin. Now, standing with Lt. Greene on one side of him and Mr. Sweeney on the other, he waited at the end of the honor guard for his mentor to appear. He must have fidgeted more than he thought he realized, for Sweeney leaned in and spoke in a soft voice that nevertheless shook Brewer to his core.

"Steady, Captain."

Brewer blinked and regarded his sailing master, amazed at the calming power of two little words. Sweeney winked just as the bosun's whistle reclaimed their attention. The honor guard snapped to attention, and Admiral Lord Horatio Hornblower stepped onto the deck.

The admiral saluted the quarterdeck and then held the salute as he walked in review past the honor guard. He halted three feet in front of Brewer. The captain saluted smartly.

"Welcome aboard HMS *Defiant*, my lord."

"Thank you, Captain," the admiral replied.

"May I present my officers? This is my first lieutenant, Mr. Greene, and my sailing master, Mr. Sweeney."

Hornblower nodded at the salutes. "Gentlemen."

Brewer led him to the side. "My second lieutenant, Mr. Phillips, acting-third lieutenant Mr. Tyler, and midshipmen Mr. Short, Mr. Ross, and Mr. MacDonald."

Hornblower nodded to Phillips and Tyler, smiled at the midshipmen. "I look forward to sailing with you young gentlemen."

Brewer saw the smiles on the midshipmen's faces, and he realized Hornblower had lost none of his ability to win the hearts of his crew. He was determined to gain the skill himself before the voyage was over.

"And now, my lord, Jenkins awaits us. Mr. Greene, dismiss the men, if you please."

"Aye aye, sir," Greene said.

Brewer nodded turned back to the admiral. "My lord, Mr. Gerard, if you'll follow me?"

Hornblower acquiesced, and Brewer led his guests below to the admiral's cabin. Jenkins met them inside the door.

"Admiral, may I present Mr. Jenkins, the architect of the feast we are about to enjoy."

Jenkins bowed. "An honor, my lord."

Hornblower nodded. "Thank you, Jenkins. I must warn you, your reputation has preceded you to this part of the world."

Jenkins smiled and bowed again. "I'm gratified, my lord."

Jenkins withdrew to the pantry, and Brewer got his first look at the transformed cabin. The table was set and looked more resplendent than Brewer had ever seen it. A knock at the door announced the arrival of the other guests, and Mr. Mosley was presented to the admiral. Brewer tasked Mr. Greene to pour the wine, and the admiral took the opportunity to chat a bit with each man present.

Very soon, the assemblage broke up into small groups. Brewer stood in the midst of it all, nursing his glass and observing what developed. He was amused to see Mr. Phillips and Mr. Tyler corner Gerard, intent on getting him to relate some stories about the admiral. He glanced to the side and was surprised to see Mr. Sweeney talking to the admiral, and he wondered for a moment if Hornblower was trying to get Sweeney to tell him stories of what it was like to sail with Captain Cook. The thought made Brewer chuckle.

Brewer studied how his mentor conducted himself, and presently Mr. Sweeney came over and stood beside him. He followed his captain's eyes to where Hornblower was talking to Mr. Phillips.

"Trying to pick up a few pointers? Or just observing the master in action?"

Brewer glanced at his friend and smiled. He shrugged and said, "A little of both, I guess. How does he do it, Sweeney? How did Morgan? Or Cochrane? Or Nelson, for that matter? How did they inspire such loyalty from their crews? How did they get their crews to *love* them?"

Sweeney chuckled and sipped his drink. "Aye, that's the question, now, isn't it, Captain? Captain Cook used to say he'd seen two kinds of crews, those who would die for their captain, and those who wanted to kill him. Don't worry, Captain, you'll be fine; all you have to do is live those fine words I've heard you pour into young Mr. Phillips these past several months."

Brewer looked at his sailing master, but Sweeney only smiled. Brewer sighed. Sweeney laughed and saluted his captain with his glass. He was about to say something more, but he was prevented by the arrival of Jenkins and the announcement that supper was served.

The assembled officers migrated to the table and took their seats, Brewer at the head of the table with Hornblower at his right hand and Greene to his left. Next to Greene sat Mr. Sweeney, with Phillips next to him, and Mr. Tyler next to Phillips. Lieutenant Johnson of the marines sat at the end. On the other side, Mr. Gerard was next to the admiral, with Dr. Spinelli next and Mr. Mosley on the end.

Brewer turned to see Jenkins and his stewards bring the first course, a steaming turtle soup. The officers tucked in and sipped and slurped to their hearts' content, and Jenkins took the silence in the room as the supreme compliment that it was.

The soup bowls were cleared away, and the stewards brought in the feast. One platter piled high with chops covered in a steaming gravy, and another with a clove-studded ham dominated the center of the table, filling the cabin with their aromas. Tureens were set out filled with steaming, butter-drenched mashed potatoes, frenched green beans, and steamed broccoli. Mr. Phillips smiled at the memory the feast evoked.

Brewer smiled and rose. "With your permission, my lord. My lord, I hope you'll pardon the unusual selections made for our feast; they were mine, and I'll tell you why. After crossing the Atlantic, our first port of call was Boston. Ever been there, my lord? No? I highly recommend it. Very near the wharf, you will find a tavern called The Red Lion Inn. I must confess that Mr. Phillips and I were rather hungry when we went ashore, and we stepped inside. The innkeeper was kind enough to prepare us a feast very similar to what you see in front of you. Now, I will admit that I have no idea how to make any of this, but I described them as best as I could to Jenkins, and fortunately for us, he knew exactly what I was talking about. Pray, try the chops in front of you, my lord. I'm sure you'll think you were dining in heaven itself. Mr. Greene, will you carve the ham in front of you? The roast we had in Boston was beef, I believe, wasn't it, Mr. Phillips? Yes, I thought so. However, this wonderful ham will do as a substitute. Mr. Mosley, feel free to help yourself to whatever's in front of you, then pass it around. Excellent! Dig in, Mr. Phillips, and see if Jenkins isn't every bit as good as the Yankee was!"

"Excellent!" Hornblower said after taking a bite of his chop.

"The gravy on the chops works excellently on the potatoes as well, my lord," Brewer said as he helped himself to some broccoli and passed it to the admiral.

The men ate their fill and then some, and compliments were thrown both at Jenkins for the feast and Brewer for the idea. After the plates were cleared, Jenkins poured more wine, and Mr. Tyler, as the youngest officer present, toasted the health of the king. Hornblower leaned back in his chair.

"Thank you, Captain Brewer, an excellent meal! My compliments to Mr. Jenkins, and you may tell him I am gratified to find that his reputation is fully deserved."

"Thank you, my lord."

"Now, gentlemen," Hornblower said as he sat forward, gathering the attention of every man at the table, "on to business. Mr. Mosley," the admiral queried, "how's the gunnery on *Defiant*?"

"Very good, yer lordship," Mosley spoke up, "and getting better every day. The captain has allowed me to use a training system Lord Nelson had me use before the Nile, and it's brought the gunnery almost up to wartime standards of speed and accuracy."

"Yes, Admiral," Brewer said, "Lt. Greene and Mr. Mosley have been working with each division in turn, and to date every gun crew has dropped their reload time by at least thirty seconds while improving their accuracy."

"Superb," Hornblower said. "You'll soon have the chance to prove it. We sail on the morning tide, and our mission is to find and capture or destroy as many pirates as possible. We sail with *Defiant* and *Crab*. *Roebuck* is still off Curacao, and I will leave *Phoebe* and *Clorinda* to protect Jamaica. The remainder of the squadron is out on patrol guarding our possessions in the Caribbean or escorting our ships in and out of the area. We will sail around the eastern tip of Cuba and then head up her northern coast, checking every harbor we find along the way for pirates or slavers. We will most likely have to engage them at extreme range, in order to slow them down enough to board them. That's where you come in, Mr. Mosley; we shall have need of your particular long-range talents. The Americans are moving to a position off the northernmost tip of the island. We hope to chase any ships that escape us right into their arms. We shall proceed with *Crab* working inshore and *Defiant* placed well out to sea. I hope this will tempt some of the enemy to come out from their hiding places for the prospect of an easy prize. *Crab* will fly out to sea, leading the pirates into range of Mr. Mosley and *Defiant's* 32-pounders."

"Will *Crab* engage the enemy, my lord?" Mr. Greene asked.

"No," Hornblower answered. "*Crab* will be ordered to sail right past *Defiant* and place herself well out to sea. Her mission in such cases is to watch what happens. If we need help, *Crab* will sail at top speed either for our frigates at Jamaica or the Americans and bring them to our aid. Our mission will be to hold on to the pirates until then."

Every man at the table knew the near-impossibility of the mission, but they also knew there was no other way to do it, not with the ships they had available to them.

Hornblower looked around the table. "As you may have heard, we have reason to believe many of these pirates are expatriate French who deserted their navy, taking with them their ships, when Bonaparte was defeated in 1815. That means they are professionally trained seamen, not the typical pirates who turn tail at the first broadside. Their sailing prowess has enabled them to surprise many ships, but this time we will be ready for them!" Hornblower paused and smiled. "I don't need to tell you gentlemen that we have the chance here to pick up a good amount of prize money or head money on this voyage. I know you shall do your best and make your captain, myself, and all England proud of you. And now, gentlemen, if you will excuse me, I shall say goodnight. Captain, if you and Mr. Greene will remain for a moment, I would appreciate it."

Every man rose and bid their admiral goodnight. As they made their way to the door, Brewer heard Mr. Phillips and Mr. Tyler anxiously debating how much prize money they could earn, and whether it were more profitable to capture pirate ships or slavers, and he smiled to himself. Once the room emptied, Hornblower turned to Gerard and nodded, and the flag lieutenant retreated into the sleeping quarters for a moment and returned with a satchel. Hornblower opened the case and motioned for them all to be seated again at the table as he removed the papers from within. This time, Mr. Greene took his place at his captain's right hand.

"Captain," Hornblower said, "I have just this afternoon received this packet from Admiral Morgan in Bermuda. It details recent pirate attacks in the Bahamas, along with a request for the *Defiant* to be sent to Bermuda as soon as she can be released from operations here. It seems that several pirate vessels have been reported in the vicinity lately, most heading north, presumably to raid the New England coast before the rough winter seas set in. Naturally, we shall have to settle your status permanently before that can happen."

"Of course, my lord," Brewer said. He felt Greene tense a bit at his elbow, but he did his best to ignore it.

"Admiral Morgan also states that he advises me to think carefully regarding your present position aboard *Defiant*." Hornblower lowered the papers and looked at Brewer. "William, the admiral makes it clear that the decision is mine, and mine alone, as befits an admiral commanding a foreign station. He merely reminds me of the status accorded the command of a ship of *Defiant's* size and power, and he begs me to consider carefully before confirming any commander." Hornblower raised the paper again, muttering under his breath, "As though I wouldn't do that anyway! I think the good Sir Edward sometimes forgets I'm not one of his midshipmen anymore!"

Brewer tried his best not to laugh. He felt Greene shiver beside him with the strain of holding his mirth, and he gently kicked his first lieutenant under the table. Hornblower appropriately pretended not to notice.

"Now," Hornblower continued, "Where was I? Oh, yes, the dispatching of the *Defiant* northward. As I said, it will have to wait until our operations are completed here. Our plan will be as I have laid it out. The best outcome is for the pirates to run *en masse* before us, thereby giving us the chance to play the hammer to the Americans' anvil. I think that, with some good fortune—and Mr. Mosley's gunnery—we may be able to end the pirate threat in the Caribbean once and for all."

The admiral returned the reports to the satchel, then he looked at Brewer and Greene. "Do either of you gentlemen have any questions?"

Brewer glanced at Greene and then faced Hornblower. "No, my lord."

Admiral Hornblower nodded and rose. "Excellent. Now, if you gentlemen will excuse me, I shall retire early. I look forward to the hunt tomorrow."

The *Defiant* officers rose and bade their admiral a good night. Gerard lead the way to the door, and just before he left, Brewer turned to the flag lieutenant and smiled.

"No whist tonight?"

Gerard smiled. "Don't worry, William. I'm sure you'll get your chance."

Brewer went up on deck to make sure everything was in

good order before retiring to the wardroom. He was just turning to head below when he heard his name called. He turned to see Mr. Short running up to catch him before he could descend the companionway.

"Yes, Mr. Short?" Brewer said.

The midshipman ran up and saluted. "Begging your pardon, sir, but there was a letter for you in today's mail. Seeing as how the admiral is in your cabin, well, I wasn't sure what to do with it." He handed the letter over, and Brewer put it in his pocket without looking at it. He thanked Mr. Short and went below to the wardroom. He was surprised to find Dr. Spinelli waiting for him.

"Good evening, Captain."

"Good evening, Doctor," Brewer replied. "Can't you sleep?"

"Very funny," the doctor said. "So, has it been decided?"

Brewer sat down and sighed. "Has what been decided?"

"Ahh," Spinelli said with a knowing nod. "I take it the admiral did not ask you to stay to confirm your appointment as captain of the *Defiant*?"

Brewer smiled tightly. "No, he did not. There are some... concerns that I may not be senior enough for a ship of the size and power of *Defian*t. Too many senior captains available in peacetime. I think he is testing me by using *Defiant* as his flagship, hoping I'll do something good enough for him to justify confirming both myself and Mr. Greene."

Spinelli drummed his fingers on the tabletop as he gazed into the distance, concentrating. After a few moments, he shook his head and leaned forward, resting a forearm on the table.

"One of the problems of the peacetime navy, I'm afraid, probably the biggest problem. The war brought the best officers to command, but peace brings the best politicians, those who can work the system or have influence. Still, there's a chance that you can prove yourself on this voyage. And, it may be that the admiral will be able to give you command of something smaller than *Defiant*, a sloop, perhaps, or a brigantine, which would allow you to build your reputation."

Brewer rubbed the bridge of his nose to try to ease the tension he felt creeping into his temples and forehead. Spinelli watched his friend closely. "Well," Brewer said as he picked up his hat, "I suppose all I can do is my duty, and do it to the best of my ability. I don't want a ship I didn't earn, Adam, whether it's a fifty-gun frigate or a twenty-gun sloop. And whatever I'm given, it will be enough. I know the admiral will do what he feels is best for the navy and for me, and I trust him enough to leave it at that."

The doctor smiled and nodded his approval. "Well said, Captain! Are you up for a game of chess tonight?"

Brewer smiled and shook his head. "Not tonight, I'm afraid. I've got too much on my mind to give you a good game, Adam. Perhaps after we've been at sea a day or two, and we settle into our routine. By the way, do you play whist?"

"Whist?" Spinelli said. "Yes, but not for years. Why?"

"It's a favorite of the admiral's. He often plays it to relax while at sea. If he finds out you play, you may not have as much free time in the evening as you anticipate."

"Ah," the doctor smiled, "I see. And do you play, Captain?"

"After a year with him on the *Agamemnon* and St. Helena? What do you think, doctor?"

Spinelli laughed. "Yes. Good night, Captain."

"Good night, Doctor."

Inside his cabin, Brewer tossed his hat on his bunk and looked around. He was pleased to see that Mr. Greene had detailed someone put up a shelf on the wall for him to have his books out. He turned to see his writing case on the desk.

All the comforts of home, he thought. He was just taking off his coat when he remembered the letter Mr. Short had given him, and he reached into the pocket and pulled it out. He laid the coat on the bunk and broke the seal on the letter. He was delighted to see it was from his old friend Bush. He had written Bush when they first put in at Bermuda, but even so, he was surprised to get a letter back so quickly. Bush must have been in London when the letter arrived and written back immediately. Brewer sat at his desk and read.

> *Dear William,*
>
> *I have just received your letter detailing the death of Captain Norman and your taking command of the* Defiant. *I congratulate you on the command, but I, too, wish it were under better circumstances. I know you, William, and right now I imagine you may be confused about one or two things, and I want to give you some advice that a favorite captain of mine (whom we both know) gave to me.*
>
> *Lord Horatio told me once that a captain is put in place by God and confirmed by the King, and those are the only two personages to whom he is responsible. He does, however, have much to answer for, including how he treats his crew, their health and welfare, and their morale, too. If you treat them rightly, they will follow you through the very gates of Hell and bring you back out again. The lash is a poor reason for obedience, and it always fails under the worst conditions. The men under such compulsion will always choose to save their own skins rather than to sacrifice them for the King and Country of a*

sadistic captain.

William, I believe you have it in you to be a great captain. I have taught you faithfully what I learned from the man I consider to be the greatest captain and leader of men in the history of the King's Navy, Lord Nelson included! Just remember what you have been taught, and be sure to put it into action for Defiant's *crew, and you will be fine. You are not alone: seek out advice from those you trust, and then make your decision. That's what it means to be a Captain. I know you can do it.*

I must close, William, so this can get back to you without any delay. Take care, and give my best to Lord Horatio when you see him.

Your Obedient Servant,
William Bush

Brewer read the letter twice before putting it down on the desk. He looked at the letter again and shook his head in wonder. *How does he do it,* he wondered. *Thousands of miles away, and Bush still manages to give me just the right advice at the very moment I need it.* He smiled. *It seems I still have much to learn, Bush. Thank you.*

A knock at the door interrupted his thoughts, and Jenkins came in to help him with his things. Brewer folded the letter and put it in his writing case until he could answer it. The steward wondered why his captain was smiling as he hung up his coat.

CHAPTER 21

Brewer was on deck before the dawn, just to make sure everything was in readiness for *Defiant* to depart on the morning tide. Mr. Greene and Mr. Sweeney, he was pleased to see, had matters well in hand.

"Good morning, sir," Greene said, as both men saluted.

"Good morning, gentlemen." Brewer returned the salute. "Is all in readiness?"

"Yes, sir," Sweeney replied. "All the sheets and lines were checked over the past two days. Two lines were replaced. We should be seaworthy now."

Greene nodded. "The ship is ready for sea in all respects, Captain."

Brewer nodded a little stiffly. He knew he had to control himself and not allow his nerves to show in front of the crew, or especially the admiral, but he feared he was losing the battle.

"Very good, Mr. Greene," he said. "How long until high tide?"

"About three hours, sir."

"Excellent. Please make sure the hands have breakfast before we set sail."

"Aye aye, sir."

As Greene set about his business, Admiral Hornblower appeared on deck.

"Good morning, sir," Brewer saluted.

"Good morning, Captain," Hornblower replied. "I see that you are ready for sea. If you have nothing pressing, Captain, would you breakfast with me?"

Brewer hoped he sounded assured as he said, "I would be honored, my lord."

"Good. Let's go." Hornblower wasted no time heading for the companionway stairs. Brewer was a little surprised at his mentor's brusqueness, but he did his best to keep up.

As they entered the cabin, Gerard looked up from the paperwork he had spread over the table. Hornblower nodded to him, and he immediately set about picking it up and placing it in the portable file where the admiral's correspondence was kept. The moment he was done, Jenkins appeared and set the table for three. The officers sat down, and Jenkins served them scrambled eggs, crisp bacon, sliced tomatoes, kidneys, and toast with marmalade. The coffee was piping hot, and the three of them were digging in before Hornblower spoke.

"Tell me, William, have you chosen a coxswain yet?" Hornblower asked, before raising a spoonful of eggs to his mouth.

"Coxswain, my lord?" Brewer asked.

"Yes," Hornblower paused to drink some coffee, "a coxswain. A petty officer you would trust to pilot your gig." Brewer detected the sarcasm in his mentor's voice and blushed. "If you find a good one, he would also double as a sort of personal servant, bodyguard, and troubleshooter. Mine was named Brown; you might remember him from St. Helena. He escorted my wife and son back to England when the boy fell ill. When I moved to Smallbridge with Barbara, Brown went with me. Believe it or not, he said I would have to try a lot harder if I wanted to get rid of him! Brown and his wife run my household in Smallbridge now."

Brewer and Gerard smiled. Brewer remembered him now. Brown had always hovered in the background, never far away from his master, but never in the way, either, like the Rock of Gibraltar, standing silently behind Hornblower in solid support. Was there anyone like that for him, especially here on *Defiant*?

"I highly recommend you choose one, if there's anyone aboard whom you think qualified," Hornblower dished himself more kidneys and some bacon. "Brown saved my life more than once." Hornblower shrugged. "Just something for you to consider, William."

Brewer drained his coffee and called for a refill. "I shall, my lord; I confess that it's something I hadn't considered. I don't believe Captain Bush had anyone that close to him, nor did Captain Norman."

"Not every captain does," said Gerard. "Just the lucky ones."

Hornblower smiled. "Yes, well, as I said, just something for you to think about. Now, Captain, if you're finished, shall we see if the winds are favorable?"

Brewer stood and picked up his hat. "Of course, my lord, at your service."

"Excellent," Hornblower said, and Brewer led the way back on deck. Brewer gazed at the towering masts and spars overhead, and his gaze was drawn to the admiral's flag flapping in the stiff breeze. He looked around and saw Mr. Greene and Mr. Sweeney standing by the wheel.

"Mr. Greene?"

"Ready for sea, Captain."

Brewer turned to the admiral. "HMS *Defiant* ready for sea, my lord."

"Very good, Captain," Hornblower said as he looked around. "You may warp the ship out when ready. Notify *Crab* to make sail."

"Yes, my lord." Brewer saluted and turned from the admiral. "Mr. Greene, take us out, if you please. Mr. Tyler, notify *Crab* to make sail!"

"Aye aye, sir!" Greene said. "Rig the capstan! Move, you men! Bring the messenger!"

HMS *Defiant* exploded into action. Orders to heave round the capstan echoed across the deck, and soon the anchor was rung up and made secure.

"*Crab* acknowledges, Captain!" Tyler said.

"Very good!"

Brewer stood beside the admiral and tried to look like he was master of the raging din that was erupting on the deck. Hornblower was watching, and Brewer was anxious for everything to go well. Somehow, he managed to restrain himself from following Greene all over the deck. Brewer relaxed as he heard the report come in that the anchor was loose, and Greene ordered the men into the yards to loose topsails and jib. *Defiant* began to glide across the waves toward the harbor mouth. He looked over his shoulder and saw *Crab* beginning to move as well, and he relaxed just a little. *So far, so good.*

Hornblower turned to Brewer. "Once clear of the harbor, you may set your course for the Windward Passage. Please inform *Crab* of our intentions and have her take up position on our port quarter."

Brewer saluted. "Aye aye, my lord. Mr. Sweeney, steer southeast to clear the island, then plot us a course to clear Jamaica and on for the Windward Passage. Mr. Tyler, signal *Crab* to take station on our port quarter, course southeast!"

"Aye aye, Captain!"

"Aye aye, sir!"

"*Crab* acknowledges, sir!"

"Very good!"

Hornblower watched the activity and nodded in satisfaction. "Very good, Captain. I will be in my cabin.

Please call me when we reach the Passage, or sooner if anything requires my attention."

"Aye aye, my lord," Brewer said. "I estimate forty-eight hours to the Passage." He saluted, and Hornblower went below.

Brewer was still standing there, gazing at the companionway where the admiral had descended, when Sweeney and Greene came up and stood beside him.

"What did the admiral say, sir?" Greene asked. "Was he pleased?"

"Yes, Mr. Greene," Brewer said, without taking his eyes from the companionway. "The admiral complimented us on *Defiant's* performance so far."

"What did the admiral say at breakfast?" Mr. Sweeney asked.

Brewer sighed and turned. "He said I should consider appointing a coxswain for myself."

Sweeney beamed and nodded, but Greene looked puzzled.

"I don't see the significance of it," Greene said.

It was Sweeney who answered him. "Mr. Greene, only a captain needs a coxswain. An acting captain soon to be replaced has no such need."

Greene's eyebrows rose as realization dawned upon him, and a smile broke across his face.

"Yes, well," Brewer said, "let's not get ahead of ourselves, gentlemen. For now, Mr. Sweeney, I think we must continue Mr. Phillips' education. I want him to plot our course for the Windward Passage, and our position before we enter. Make sure you are watching his work, Mr. Sweeney; we don't want to end up off Venezuela with the admiral on board."

Sweeney grinned at that. "Aye aye, sir."

"Mr. Greene, I want you and Mr. Mosley to exercise the gun crews this afternoon. We need to keep our men sharp and ready. Concentrate on gunnery at long range."

Greene saluted. “Aye aye, sir.”

“You may carry on, Mr. Greene,” Brewer said.

Greene hesitated for only a moment before saluting again. “Aye aye, sir.” He went forward to find Mr. Phillips.

Sweeney took a step closer to his captain, and both men watched the first lieutenant walk forward. Sweeney turned to his captain. “A coxswain, eh?”

Brewer nodded, a hopeful look edging on to his features. “That’s what he said, believe it or not. Why didn’t Captain Norman make use of his?”

Sweeney shrugged. “I don’t know. I could say he didn’t want anyone to be able to exert influence or give an order in his name, as a coxswain would, but I’d only be guessing. Does anyone really know what went on in Norman’s mind? By the way, do you know why Norman got rid of Mr. Mosley when he took command?”

Brewer looked sharply at him and shook his head. perhaps now that particular mystery would be solved, confirming his suspicion that Sweeney knew far more than he generally let on.

“Mr. Mosley was the gunner on HMS *Victory* at Trafalgar.”

The pieces fell into place for Brewer. “Mr. Mosley was on *Victory* when Nelson was shot.”

Sweeney nodded.

Brewer sighed. “And he knew the truth about who actually shot the frog who killed Nelson.”

Another nod.

Brewer lowered his voice. “And it wasn’t James Norman.”

This time, the sailing master shook his head.

Brewer exhaled through pursed lips and nodded. “Well. I’m glad we’ve set things right, Mr. Sweeney. Have Mr. Phillips report to me when we’re ready to alter course.”

Sweeney nodded. “Aye aye, sir.”

Brewer started to turn away, but stopped short. “Mr. Sweeney, any thoughts on who would make a good coxswain?”

Sweeney looked at the mountain of sails filling with wind above their heads for a minute or two before looking down again. “I think perhaps Mr. McCleary, sir.”

“McCleary?” Brewer said. “Are you serious?”

Sweeney shrugged. “Don’t let his outward demeanor fool you. He knows how to handle a barge, and he has the kind of bulldog loyalty you want in a coxswain. He’s not as dumb as you might think by looking at him. Remember how he subdued Johnston? Quick and efficient. He also did a good job when you sent him to search the ship after the storm, remember?”

When his captain looked uncertain, Sweeney shrugged again. “Well, you did ask for my recommendation, Captain.”

Brewer sighed. “Yes. Yes, I did. Well, I thank you, Mr. Sweeney.”

Sweeney looked up to see Phillips approaching. “If you’ll excuse me, Captain?” He saluted and went off to give Mr. Phillips his orders.

Brewer strolled over to the lee rail and began to pace. McCleary? He wasn’t someone Brewer would have picked himself, but his was the only name that Sweeney had given him. Brewer had to admit, Sweeney was correct when he pointed out how well McCleary had carried out his assignments before and during the storm. And he certainly seemed to fit the mold of the silent support, the Rock of Gibraltar that a captain could rely upon when necessary. Brewer nodded to himself; McCleary was on Lieutenant Phillips’ watch; when Phillips reported to him, Brewer would ask his opinion of the man and his ability.

Brewer went to his cabin and started a letter to Bush. He hadn’t been at it for fifteen minutes when there was a knock at the door, and Mr. Short entered.

"Begging your pardon, Captain," the midshipman said formally. "Mr. Phillips' respects, we are ready to alter course."

"Thank you, Mr. Short. I'll come up directly." Brewer picked up his hat and followed the midshipman up and on to the deck.

Phillips reported immediately and saluted his captain. "Course plotted and approved by Mr. Sweeney, Captain. East to the tip of Jamaica, then northeast to the Passage."

"Very good, Mr. Phillips," Brewer said. "You may proceed. Inform *Crab* of our course and instruct them to follow."

"Aye aye, sir," Phillips said. Brewer let Phillips issue his orders before calling him back.

"Mr. Phillips," Brewer said, "walk with me for a moment. I have a question for you."

"Yes, sir."

"The admiral has suggested that I need to appoint a coxswain for myself."

Phillips nodded. "Captain Styles had one, sir."

"I asked Mr. Sweeney for his recommendation, and the only name he gave me was that of McCleary."

Phillips was surprised. "Really, sir?"

"Yes. As he is in your watch, I wanted to ask your opinion. Do you think he could handle the job?"

"Without a doubt, sir," Phillips said without hesitation. "He knows small boats as well as anyone on the ship, sir, and he's got something... a competence, I think is the word. You just naturally trust him to get the job done. He does good work, Captain. I think he'd do you good."

Brewer stopped and faced his lieutenant. "Thank you, Mr. Phillips. Pass the word for McCleary to report to me in the wardroom. Keep an eye on the course; we don't want to look bad before the admiral. Ross has a good set of eyes, doesn't he? Send him to the main top with a glass then, if you please. We don't want to be surprised again. At the first sight of a strange sail, beat to quarters and call me immediately."

Phillips saluted. "Aye aye, sir." Brewer nodded and went below decks.

In the wardroom, Brewer poured himself a cup of coffee and sat down to wait for McCleary. He didn't have to wait long. Within a couple of minutes there was a knock on the door.

"Enter," Brewer said, and the big Cornishman made his appearance.

"Sorry I'm late, sir," he said in his thick accent, "I got here as quick as I could."

Brewer rose. "Welcome, McCleary. Sit down, please."

McCleary looked around before finally settling on the chair next to the captain's. Brewer silently approved of the choice and took his own seat.

"Let me come straight to the point, McCleary," Brewer said. "I need to appoint a captain's coxswain, and your name was suggested. Do you think you could handle the job?"

The big face brightened. "Yes, sir. I could do it fine."

Brewer thought for a moment, and he decided to go with his gut. "Alright, McCleary, we'll give it a try on this voyage and see how it works out. Any questions?"

The big Cornishman rose. "No, sir. But at home, sir, folks just called me Mac."

Brewer smiled. "Very well, Mac. Carry on."

"Thank you, sir!" the seaman saluted and was gone.

Brewer chuckled to himself as he watched his new coxswain go. He had a good feeling about this.

Brewer came on deck just as *Defiant* was making its turn to the northeast. The seas were calm and the winds were favorable, so Brewer was hoping for a swift ride through the Passage and along the northern coast of Cuba. He paused to smell the sea breeze and also to meditate a bit on the admiral's plan. He could only find one flaw in it; what would they do if *Crab* was not enough to induce the pirates to come out of a Spanish port? She was a fine ship, but no pirate in his right mind would confuse *Crab* for an Indiaman. Brewer made a mental note to ask the admiral about this at his next opportunity.

Mr. Sweeney strolled over. "Mind if I join you, Captain?"

Brewer smiled. "Not at all, Mr. Sweeney. I was just thinking about the admiral's plan, and I think I've found a flaw."

Sweeney grinned. "What do we do if *Crab* isn't a tempting enough bait to draw the pirates out?"

“Exactly,” Brewer said.

Sweeney grunted and looked out over the rolling waves. "I thought of that last night. Have you asked him yet?"

Brewer shook his head with a sigh. "I've just thought of it myself. Perhaps you should be captain, Mr. Sweeney."

The sailing master recoiled in mock horror. "No, thank you, Captain. I don't want your job. I'm happy in my little corner of the world."

Brewer laughed. He looked up to see Gerard come on deck, and he waved the flag lieutenant over. Gerard was all smiles as usual when he approached.

"Good morning Captain, Mr. Sweeney," he said. "Captain, might I have a word with you?"

"Of course, Mr. Gerard. Would you excuse us, please, Mr. Sweeney?"

"Of course, Captain," Sweeney said as he saluted. "Mr. Gerard."

"Thank you, Mr. Sweeney," Gerard answered. The sailing master returned to the wheel. Gerard watched him go and shook his head in wonder. "Is it true he learned his trade from Captain Cook? My God, I warrant he's got some stories to tell."

"Yes," Brewer said. "I wager the two of you could

entertain the crew, swapping a Hornblower story for every one he told of Cook. Now, what can I do for you, Lieutenant?"

The two men fell into step, strolling toward the fantail. "I wish to speak to you about the admiral. I don't know if Captain Bush ever told you any stories, but for years it has been the admiral's custom to pace the quarterdeck in the morning."

"I remember him doing the same thing in his office on St. Helena."

"Then you know what I speak of. While we are at sea, the admiral would like to begin his exercise again. He will appear on deck at four bells of the morning watch. Will you please give orders to have this portion of the quarterdeck holystoning complete by then? Also, please ask your officers not to speak to the admiral during this time, unless he speaks to them first. It has happened, once or twice, that the admiral would invite someone to walk with him, if he needs to talk over an issue. Did that ever happen on St. Helena?"

Brewer thought for a moment and shook his head. "Not to my knowledge."

Gerard nodded. "I thought not. As I said, it is rare, but it does happen occasionally."

"I will give orders to ensure the quarterdeck is prepared and the admiral's privacy is ensured."

"Thank you, Captain."

Brewer smiled. "Will he be taking his baths under the deck pump as well?"

Gerard looked up in surprise and then chuckled. "You know about that, eh?"

Brewer shrugged. "Captain Bush may have told some stories on the way to St. Helena."

"Yes, well, if the admiral mentions it, I shall let you know. If you'll excuse me, Captain?"

Brewer watched Gerard descend before walking over to

where Mr. Greene and Mr. Phillips were talking with Mr. Sweeney.

"Mr. Greene," Brewer said, "the admiral will come on deck daily at four bells of the morning watch to take his exercise. Please ensure that holystoning is completed on the quarterdeck by then. Also, please pass the word that nobody is to speak to the Admiral until his exercise is completed. For now, let's note it in the standing orders, just to make sure."

Greene nodded. "Aye aye, sir."

Brewer turned and strolled forward. He was smiling at the prospect of sharing this deck with Admiral Hornblower.

CHAPTER 22

Brewer came on deck at three bells of the morning watch, a half hour before the admiral was due to make his appearance. His intention had been to ensure that all was in readiness for the admiral (Bush had told a story once of Hornblower's temper when his exercise was interrupted), but he saw at once that he needn't have bothered. Mr. Greene was personally supervising the watch detail that was finishing the holystoning. Mr. Phillips and Mr. Sweeney were leaning on the lee rail, deep in conversation. *Probably talking about the change of course,* Brewer thought. Today was the day that Phillips would have to fix *Defiant's* position and swing her around to the northwest, up the northern coast of Cuba.

Brewer turned back to see that the watch detail had finished their work. In the half-light of the breaking dawn, Brewer thought it looked good enough to eat off of. He heard a whisper behind him, and when he turned around he saw every midshipman *Defiant* possessed clinging to the rigging on the lee side, obviously waiting to see an admiral walking up and down on the quarterdeck. He was just about to tell them this wasn't a spectator sport when he saw Mr. Sweeney detail one of his mates to the ship's bell. The admiral would make his appearance momentarily, so Brewer left the young gentlemen where they were and strolled over to where Sweeney was standing to observe as well.

The ship's bell rang two times, and the sound did not have a chance to die before Admiral Lord Horatio Hornblower ascended the companionway steps and made his way directly aft to the quarterdeck. His hands were clasped behind his back, and his chin was down on his chest as he fell into step along the weather rail. Seven strong steps to the aft railing, then he turned and made seven strong steps back. Brewer glanced up at the midshipmen, and he smiled when he saw every one of them staring wide-eyed at the admiral. He laughed when he realized that Mr. Short was actually counting the number of steps that Hornblower took!

The admiral kept up his pace for exactly one hour, and during the entire time not one spectator left. Hornblower never seemed to take any notice of the fact that he was being watched by so many of the officers and crew, but when six bells rang out, it was as if he roused from sleepwalking. He finished the leg he was on and heaved a great sigh. Then he looked around and saw the captain and his officers, still standing by the lee rail.

"Good morning, Captain, gentlemen," Hornblower said as he came over. Salutes were exchanged, and Mr. Sweeney went off with Lieutenant Phillips to begin working out the ship's position.

"Mr. Greene," Brewer said, "please take in a reef while Mr. Phillips figures out exactly where we are."

"Aye aye, sir," Greene said. He went forward, bellowing orders and sending men skyward.

Hornblower and Brewer watched him go before turning to stroll slowly aft. Hornblower breathed in deeply and turned his face toward the sun.

"I love it every time I get away from the land," he said.

"Did you enjoy your exercise, my lord?" Brewer asked.

Hornblower turned to him. "You were watching? Well, yes, Captain, I did. I don't get to do that often in Kingston, and I find that I miss it. The pacing gives me a good chance to clear my mind and order my thoughts. I highly recommend it."

Brewer smiled. "I remember you doing it on St. Helena. Perhaps I should say, I remember *hearing* you do it on St. Helena. Come to think of it, it usually happened after Bonaparte left the office."

Hornblower laughed. "Well, he did give me quite a bit to think about."

"Tell, me, Admiral," Brewer said, "do you prefer pacing in an office, or on the moving deck of a ship?"

Hornblower raised one eyebrow. "Captain, if you are asking whether I prefer to be at sea or land locked..."

"No, my lord," Brewer hastened to say, "but I was wondering whether you found any difference in the efficacy of the practice."

Before Hornblower could reply Sweeney and Phillips approached with a chart.

"Yes, Mr. Sweeney?" Brewer asked.

It was Phillips who answered. "Begging your pardon, Admiral; Captain, I plotted *Defiant's* position. Mr. Sweeney concurs with my findings."

"That was fast work, Mr. Phillips," Brewer said. "So, where are we?"

Phillips held out the chart and pointed to a spot that was below and slightly to the right of the entrance to the Windward Passage. "I place us about here, Captain. I figure we can make the Passage by heading two points west of north for near six hours, then turning northwest to head up the coast of Cuba."

Brewer studied the chart for a moment, then he turned to Hornblower. "With your permission, my lord?"

Hornblower nodded. "Granted, Captain. Well done, Mr. Phillips."

The young lieutenant beamed. "Thank you, my lord!"

Brewer smiled. "Very well, Mr. Phillips, report to Mr. Greene and put us over on the new course. Two points west of north. And signal *Crab* we are about to change course."

Phillips saluted. "Aye aye, sir!"

"Captain," Hornblower said, "from this moment on, I want the lookouts doubled. *Crab* will take her inshore station when we make our turn northwest."

"Aye aye, sir," Brewer said. "Do you expect action immediately?"

Hornblower looked up at the rigging. "I think we would do well to expect action at any time. Any ship we sight could be a pirate. We will beat to quarters as soon as we are approaching another vessel. Is that clear?"

"Yes, my lord," Brewer said. "I shall enter it in the standing orders, along with the requirement for the lookouts to be doubled. I assume you want to be called for every sighting?"

Hornblower thought for a moment. "Yes, that might be best, seeing that I'm more familiar with the shipping of this region than you are."

"Very good, my lord," Brewer said. He saluted and went to make the entries in the standing orders.

Mr. Sweeney stepped up and read over his captain's shoulder. "Ah, I was just wondering when the admiral would order the extra lookouts. I imagine we're going to be chasing down almost everything with sails on this voyage. I wager the old man's counting on Mr. Mosley to outgun anything that *Defiant* can't overtake."

Brewer finished his writing and turned to look at his sailing master. He had never known Mr. Sweeney to be so free with his words. Usually, getting Mr. Sweeney to comment on anything was like pulling teeth, but here he was behaving just the opposite.

"Is everything all right, Mr. Sweeney?" Brewer asked.

"Aye, Captain," Sweeney said.

Brewer nodded and looked out over the waves. "Mr. Phillips did rather well. Is he getting that good at it, or was he lucky this time?"

Sweeney caught the question underneath and grinned. "Well, Captain, he got no help from me, I can tell you that. No, he's actually picking it up faster than anyone I've ever seen."

"And have we seen any more of the behavior he exhibited during the incident with Johnston? Has he mentioned it at all?"

Sweeney shook his head. "Not a word to me, Captain. As far as I can tell, he's put the whole incident behind him."

Brewer nodded. "Thank you, Mr. Sweeney. Carry on."

Sweeney saluted. "Aye aye, Captain."

Brewer strolled forward and made his way below to the sickbay, where he found Dr. Spinelli reading a medical text.

"Oh, hello, Captain," the doctor said as he marked his place and closed the book. "What can I do for you?"

"Nothing for me, Adam," Brewer said as he sat down, "I actually came down to ask you about Mr. Phillips."

"Oh? Is something wrong?"

"No, no, nothing like that," Brewer said. "I want to make sure of him, that's all. Has he spoken to you lately?"

Spinelli regarded his friend thoughtfully before answering. "We played chess just yesterday, as a matter of fact. He is getting better and better at the game, William; he is even attacking in combination now. You would not find him an easy win, I assure you. But to answer your question, no, he did not confide in me during the game. Come to think of it, I don't believe he has said anything to me on that subject since that first game when he admitted to being afraid of you. Since then, all his conversations have been about the ship's routine or the game itself. I haven't noticed anything odd about his manner, if that helps at all. Why the sudden interest?"

"We may be going into action, doctor, probably within the next forty-eight hours. I was going over preparations in my head, and Mr. Phillips' name rose to the top of my list. So, I thought I'd better check up on him."

The doctor nodded. "Sounds reasonable, Captain. Well, as I said, from what I can tell, he seems to be doing well since the specter of Captain Norman was removed from the equation. But if you're not sure, might I suggest you play chess with the boy and see for yourself? Don't I remember your purchasing that chess set we talked about while we were at Kingston? Have you broken it in yet?"

"Now that you mention it, I haven't! So, Doctor, you think that Mr. Phillips would be a worthy opponent with whom to break in my new set?"

Spinelli smiled. "I do indeed, Captain."

"Very well, doctor," Brewer said, "I shall catch him tonight when he comes off watch."

"Good, William. Now, what else is happening outside of my little cubbyhole?"

"I have a new coxswain."

"Indeed? Who?"

"McCleary."

"Excellent choice. I remember when he was down here after the storm, before you sent him out to search for additional injured, he never faltered. Just stood up against the wall, doing whatever was asked of him. Nothing seemed to turn his stomach, and he never hesitated when given a task. I think he'll make you an excellent coxswain."

"Thank you, Doctor. I—"

Brewer was interrupted by a knock at the door. Mr. Short entered the sick bay and saluted.

"Begging your pardon, Captain," he said. "The admiral

presents his compliments; would you dine with him, sir?"

Brewer rose. "My respects to the Admiral; I shall attend him immediately."

Short saluted and was gone. Brewer turned to the doctor. "Thank you for your help, Adam."

Spinelli nodded. "Any time, Captain."

Brewer went up the stairs and hurried aft to the main cabin. He wondered what could be the cause of such an abrupt summons, but he couldn't come up with a single reason. He reached the cabin door and knocked. He would find out soon enough.

Brewer entered the cabin with his hat under his left arm as was customary. The table was set for two, and Hornblower was standing with his back to the door, looking out the stern windows at the ship's wake, his hands clasped behind his back. He turned when he heard Brewer enter the room.

"Ah, there you are, William," Hornblower moved to the desk and poured each of them a glass of wine. He handed Brewer one, then he raised his glass in a silent toast. Brewer responded, and both men drank. Hornblower set his glass on the table and said, "I must apologize for the sudden summons, William, but it occurred to me that you and I haven't had much of a chance to talk. Tell me, how are you adjusting to your first command?"

Brewer hesitated, not sure what to make of all this. Perhaps he hesitated a moment too long, for his mentor noticed.

Hornblower smiled. "Never fear, William, it is your friend and mentor who asks, not the admiral commanding the squadron."

Brewer relaxed without realizing he had tensed and let out the breath he was holding. "Better than I'd hoped, my lord. Mr. Sweeney has been so good as to offer advice when asked, and that has been an immense help."

"Good," Hornblower responded. "I was hoping you

would be able to avail yourself of Mr. Sweeney's experience. His presence was one reason I steered you toward *Defiant* when the *Lydia* was decommissioned. In the peacetime navy, most men his age retire or are put on the beach, but Sweeney is simply too good at his job to let him go. And how are the crew adjusting to the change in command?"

"Better and better as time goes on, sir. I am taking every chance I have to interact with the men and show them that I am still the same man I was when I was the first lieutenant."

Hornblower looked pensive, as though remembering experiences Brewer could only guess at. "Be careful with that, William. You *are* different now; you're the captain. A lieutenant, even a first lieutenant, can have a personal intimacy with the crew that the captain is denied by his very position. Hence the importance of a good coxswain. Have you seen to that as yet?"

"Yes, my lord, I have appointed a seaman by the name of McCleary. I thought to have Mr. Phillips and Mr. Sweeney instruct him in his duties."

Hornblower nodded approval. "The ship seems to be in good shape. I understand you took a pounding between the damage from the storm and then being surprised by that pirate."

Brewer paused as Jenkins brought their dinner. Brewer was pleasantly surprised to see a good roast of beef, along with some stewed tomatoes, cauliflower, and baby carrots.

"I hope you don't mind, Captain," Hornblower said, "but I brought some provisions along."

"Not at all, my lord, not at all!"

Hornblower stood. "Then allow me to slice you some of this beef, William, and we can indulge ourselves. Help yourself to the carrots or anything else you wish."

Brewer helped himself to the tomatoes and the carrots before Hornblower laid two thick slices of beef on his plate. Brewer waited until his chief was seated and served before tucking in himself. Everything tasted even better than it looked!

When the edge was off his appetite, Brewer took up the thread of conversation again. "To answer your original question, my lord, yes, we took significant damage. The storm that washed Captain Norman overboard took the main and fore masts at almost the same instant. We would have been in grave peril if the Americans hadn't shown up when they did."

Hornblower looked up. "Americans?"

"Yes, my lord. The USS *Constitution*, one of their large frigates. She appeared out of the storm just after we lost the sticks and took us in tow. Apparently, she was on a course for Bermuda herself when the storm hit. She towed us clear and gave us some assistance with rigging the temporary masts to get us to Bermuda, where we had new ones stepped. We were lucky when we ran into that pirate. Those thirty-two pounders were fired at nearly point-blank range, two of the three loaded with grape. Fortunately for us, they were aimed high to take out spars and rigging, so our casualties were light."

"And the Americans came to your rescue yet again, is that right?"

"Yes, my lord. The American brig USS *Enterprise*, a Commander Lindsey was in command. The pirates fled at their approach. Our rigging was too badly damaged to pursue. We made repairs and headed for Kingston."

"I see," Hornblower said as he took a sip of wine. Brewer wondered what was going on in his mentor's mind, but before he could ask they were interrupted by the cry they had been waiting for.

"Sail ho!"

Both men were on their feet before the sound faded. Brewer beat his chief to the door by a full step and led the way up on deck. He saw Greene, Phillips, Sweeney, and Tyler on the weather rail, all with telescopes to their eyes, observing the new arrival.

"Report, Mr. Greene!" Brewer bellowed.

Greene lowered his glass and offered it to his captain. "She appears to be a sloop, sir. Her hull just now appeared over the horizon."

"She's raising sail!" Tyler cried.

Brewer raised the glass to his eye. The stranger was indeed crowding on full sail, and she appeared to be turning away from *Defiant*. He lowered the glass and turned quickly to Hornblower.

"Sir, with your permission?"

Hornblower studied the newcomer for only a moment before lowering his glass and nodding.

"Mr. Greene," Brewer said, "call all hands! Make all sail! Mr. Tyler, signal *Crab* we are closing on an unidentified ship. Both ships, beat to quarters! Mr. Sweeney, point us right at her!"

"Aye aye, Captain!" Sweeney said.

Tyler lowered his glass. "*Crab* acknowledges, Captain!"

"Very good!"

Hornblower stood back and watched the speed with which the *Defiant's* crew reacted to their orders. Sails were unfurled faster than he had seen on any peacetime ship—nearly as fast as on the old *Lydia* during the wars—and the ship was cleared for action in under eight minutes. Hornblower approved; Captain Brewer seemed to have his ship well drilled.

"Captain," the admiral said, "load the guns but don't run them out. Speed is what we need right now."

"Aye aye, sir!" Brewer answered. He signaled to Mr. Short. "My compliments to Mr. Phillips and Mr. Mosley. Load the guns, but don't run them out. Wait for the word."

"Aye aye, sir!" Short answered.

The *Defiant* leaned to one side as she picked up speed. Brewer could see Mr. Sweeney and his mate keeping one eye on the sails and the other on the listing deck. Brewer could well imagine that the gun ports on the low side of the ship were practically at the waterline.

"Fourteen knots, sir!" came the cry.

"That's got her!" Brewer heard Mr. Sweeney say. "A sloop like that can't do more than ten or so."

"Captain," Hornblower said as he lowered his glass again, "my compliments to Mr. Mosley. I want to know the moment he thinks he can hit that ship with a thirty-two pounder."

"Aye aye, my lord," Brewer said. He turned and nodded to Mr. Short, who ran the message to the gunner.

The sloop turned out to be faster than Mr. Sweeney's expectations, and after three hours *Defiant* had only managed to cut the gap between the ships in half. Both ships had made minute adjustments in their courses to try to get every scrap of advantage out of the wind, and very quickly *Crab* fell behind. Hornblower saw what was happening, and he knew there was nothing to be done about it. He just hoped they could bring the sloop to heel before *Crab* disappeared over the horizon.

A runner from Mr. Mosley warned that it wouldn't be too much longer. Hornblower's eyes were like fire. Brewer ordered Mr. Sweeney to lay *Defiant* one point off to starboard. The change would bring *Defiant* up along the side of the sloop and give her an easier shot when Mr. Mosley gave the word.

Brewer walked forward after the change of course. He wanted to be present when the guns fired. As he passed the foremast, he saw Mr. Mosley staring intently through his glass, trying his best to judge the distance and muttering to himself the whole time.

"God!" he exclaimed, half under his breath. He looked

around desperately. When he saw the captain, he exclaimed, "By God, Captain, if I ever catch up to the bloody fool who ordered all the long-nines removed from frigates, I'll castrate the bugger meself!"

Brewer forced his face to remain still, despite his urge to grin. "Yes, well, what about that ship, Mr. Mosley?"

Mosley turned back to the fleeing sloop. "I'd like to turn one more point to starboard, Captain. That will let me make a ranging shot with the number one gun. If it's on, another point will allow us to get a full broadside off within thirty seconds. If we land a broadside of twenty-four pounders on a sloop, anything that's left of it will have to surrender."

Brewer looked ahead to their fleeing quarry. It seemed incredible to hope for a hit at this distance, but Mosley thought it possible, and that was good enough for Brewer. At that moment, the admiral arrived, and Brewer quickly explained Mr. Mosley's plan. Hornblower looked at the sloop for only a moment, then lowered his glass.

"Agreed," he said.

"Mr. Greene!" Brewer called. "Run out the larboard battery. Send a messenger to Mr. Sweeney. Tell him every time he sees me wave my arms, he is to turn us one point to starboard. One point only, Mr. Greene, and I want him to bring us back on course after every broadside. That's all."

"Aye aye, Captain!" he said. "Mr. Phillips, run out the larboard battery! Mr. Ross! Message to Mr. Sweeney!"

Brewer turned away to stand beside Hornblower as they watched Mosley. The gunner was squatting behind number one gun, a twenty-four pounder that would fire the ranging shot. Brewer looked down the side of the ship at the entire battery loaded and now run out, ready to fire. The eager expressions of the gun captains and of Mr. Phillips, commanding the battery, needed no interpretation. Brewer turned back just in time to see Mr. Mosley nod to himself, straighten up, and turn to him.

"Now, sir, if you please."

Brewer cast a glance at Hornblower, who merely nodded. Brewer turned and waved his hat to Mr. Sweeney, who waved back in acknowledgment. Brewer could hardly contain his excitement as he faced Mosley.

"You may fire as your gun bears, Mr. Mosley."

The old gunner nodded once and sighted down the long barrel of the cannon. Brewer shared a brief glance with his admiral of satisfaction mingled with hope before they both raised their telescopes and focused on their quarry.

Brewer could feel *Defiant* turning slightly to starboard, and then thirty seconds later came the roar of Mr. Mosley's gun. The ball took several seconds to reach the target, and cheers rang out when they saw a waterspout rise at the sloop's waterline, aft of midships. Brewer turned again and waved his hat to Mr. Sweeney, who acknowledged as before. Brewer looked over to Hornblower. The admiral was smiling and merely nodded, not wishing to deprive his young protégé of his moment.

Brewer turned to the battery. "Mr. Phillips! You may fire as your guns bear. Make every shot count!"

"Aye aye, sir!" Phillips shouted. Brewer and Hornblower were amused to hear the young lieutenant's voice crack in the excitement. "Larboard battery! Stand by to fire!"

Brewer, Hornblower, and Mosley all turned with their glasses raised to watch the effect of a long range broadside on so small a target. They heard Mr. Phillips shout "Fire!" and felt the massive *whoosh!* of air. They waited for the smoke to clear, hoping for a good view. Their patience was rewarded when, even through the drifting haze, they could see shot after shot strike home. Cheers went up all along the deck.

“Well done, Captain!” Hornblower shouted. “Please have Mr. Sweeney plot a course straight for the sloop.”

“There’s no hurry, Admiral,” Mr. Mosley said. “Look!”

Hornblower and Brewer barely got their glasses to their eyes in time to see the sloop's mainmast topple over.

Hornblower turned to the gunner. "Fine shooting, Mr. Mosley! Lord Nelson would be proud!"

The gunner nodded his thanks and turned back to survey the results of his work. Without the mainmast, the sloop's speed had fallen off drastically. Hornblower and Brewer lowered their telescopes and looked at each other with satisfaction.

"With your permission, my lord," Brewer said, "I will close with that ship."

"Agreed, Captain."

Brewer went aft. "Mr. Sweeney! Set course for that ship! Take me to within pistol shot. We'll see if there's any fight left in them."

"Aye aye, Captain."

Defiant swung around and closed on the unknown vessel. Just as Brewer was about to order a turn to fire a broadside, a white flag was run up at the stern.

"Splendid, Captain!" the admiral said, loud enough for the crew to hear. "Your plan worked to perfection!"

"Thank you, sir." Brewer turned to the battery behind him. "Mr. Phillips, Very well done! An extra ration of grog for the entire battery!" Cheers went up from the gun crews. "And you, Mr. Phillips, will you join the admiral and myself for supper tonight?"

Phillips blushed and beamed all at the same time. "Thank you, sir!"

"Send a boat over, Captain," Hornblower said. "Find out what they're carrying, and bring the officers back here."

"At once, my lord," Brewer said. "Mr. Greene, take the cutter."

"Aye aye, sir," Greene said. "Bosun! Call away the cutter's crew! Marines! Boarding party!"

The cutter was soon rowing across the two hundred

yards of empty ocean between *Defiant* and the damaged sloop. Brewer stood on the quarterdeck beside the admiral and watched its progress carefully.

"This was always the hard part," Hornblower said. "I always hated the waiting while Bush was off boarding the enemy. Well, we'll see what Mr. Greene brings back. In the meantime, be sure to keep a sharp eye on that ship. If they give Greene any trouble, blow her out of the water."

Brewer thought his mentor was joking, but one look at the hard gleam in the admiral's eye was enough to convince him otherwise. He saluted.

"Aye aye, my lord."

Hornblower nodded. "Call me when Mr. Greene returns."

"Aye aye, my lord."

Brewer watched his mentor descend the companionway stairs and wondered what Bush would say about Hornblower's last order.

An hour later, Mr. Ross ran up to where Brewer was talking to Mr. Mosley.

"Cutter's returning, sir."

"Excellent! Notify the admiral. I'm coming at once."

"Aye aye, sir."

Brewer headed to the waist where the cutter's crew would board. He was joined there by Admiral Hornblower just as Lieutenant Greene was stepping up on the deck. He saluted the admiral and handed a satchel to Brewer.

"Sloop's called the *El Dorado*, sir. Papers in that satchel claim she's a merchantman out of San Juan."

"Why did they run?" Hornblower asked.

"They said they thought we might be pirates," Greene said.

The remaining members of the boarding party now came on board, along with a prisoner taken from the sloop. Greene presented him to Hornblower and Brewer.

"Admiral, Captain," Greene said, "may I present the captain of the *El Dorado*?"

Hornblower and Brewer turned to the newcomer. He was swarthy, with long dark hair and a long, droopy moustache that made him look almost like a pirate himself. He carried himself with a defiant manner that Brewer did not fail to notice.

Hornblower, however, seemed to overlook it, and he addressed the man courteously. "What is your name, Captain?"

The newcomer's eyes narrowed briefly before he sighed. "My name is Jean Lafitte."

Brewer stared at the man before turning to Hornblower.

"The pirate?"

CHAPTER 23

"I am not a pirate," Lafitte said coldly. "I hold a valid privateering license from the government of Spain through the Viceroy of Mexico."

"Purchased at great cost, I'm sure," Hornblower said. Lafitte stared at him through hooded eyes but said nothing. "What was your destination and cargo, Captain?"

"Foodstuffs and oats," Lafitte said quietly, "bound for Havana."

"I see," said Hornblower. "And your privateering activities?"

"Are no concern of yours, Admiral," Lafitte said with an arrogant tilt of his head. "I am answerable to the Viceroy only."

"Not if we find any evidence of an English cargo in your hold," Brewer said.

Lafitte smiled. "Search to your heart's content, Captain."

"So we will," Brewer said. "Sergeant at arms! Take this man below and clap him in irons."

Lafitte exploded. "This is how you treat a fellow captain? We are a merchant vessel flying the flag of a friendly power!

This is outrageous!"

"Yours is an identified sloop, not merchantman, that ran from a Royal Navy frigate. On top of that, you, Captain, are wanted by the Americans for piracy. We will hold you below until we can turn you over to them. Take him away, Sergeant."

"Let's go, sir," the Sergeant said, placing his pistol in the small of Lafitte's back. "No tricks, if you please."

Lafitte looked over his shoulder and saw blood in his captor's eyes, and the two mates with their cutlasses at the ready just beyond, and quickly decided this was not the time for heroics. He turned back and smiled.

"Not today, Sergeant."

The guards led the privateer below, and the admiral and the captain turned back to Mr. Greene.

Greene continued his report. "If that's a merchie, Captain, it's a strange one. I counted sixteen twelve-pounders on the gun deck. The marines and Mr. Tyler are searching the ship as we speak, Captain. Will we keep her as a prize?"

Brewer looked over to Hornblower, but the Admiral only raised his eyebrows. Clearly, the decision was being left to him. Brewer turned back to Mr. Greene and nodded.

"Once we're through searching her, detail a master's mate to lead a prize crew and take *El Dorado* back to Kingston."

“Mr. Gerard will write the orders for my signature, Lieutenant,” Hornblower said to Greene.

"Aye aye, sir!" Greene saluted.

"This is a day the prize captain will remember the rest of his life," Hornblower said. "You never commanded a prize, did you, William? No, I thought not. Nothing tops the feeling of bringing an enemy ship into harbor. I wonder what we'll get for her from the prize court?"

"Depends on the cargo, I imagine, sir," Brewer said. "I'd

wager somewhere between £20,000 and £30,000?"

"Hardly that," Hornblower said with a sad shake of his head. "We're not at war anymore, Captain, and like every other part of the Navy, the prize court rulings aren't what they once were. If we get £20,000 out of her, we shall be very fortunate indeed." Hornblower considered for a moment. "Still, Captain, she looks in good condition, don't you think? I could certainly use another cruiser for patrols."

"You're going to take her in, my lord?" Brewer asked in surprise.

"Why not?" the admiral replied. "She should make a noteworthy first command for a young officer, don't you think?"

Not as noteworthy as Defiant, Brewer thought. Wisely, he said nothing.

It took the rest of the day and into the next morning to jury rig a mast on *El Dorado* so she could raise sail and steer a course south-southwest toward Jamaica. Brewer was proud of the way his men worked to get the job done quickly and well.

Greene detailed the hands that would comprise the crew. Brewer looked over his selections and gave his approval. The cutter returned again, and Mr. Tyler reported that their search revealed no British cargo aboard.

"Don't take any chances," Brewer instructed the prize captain, a petty officer named Evers. "If the wind holds, you should be back in Kingston by late tomorrow."

"When you arrive," Hornblower said, "you will report to Captain Fell aboard the frigate *Clorinda*. He may make use of you in his patrols, but that is his decision."

"Aye, sir," Evers said. He saluted the admiral first, and then the captain, and turned and walked smartly to where the boat was waiting for him. Hornblower and Brewer watched him as he sat in the stern sheets of the cutter as it rowed across to his first, albeit temporary, command.

"I hope he'll be all right," Brewer said.

"He'll be fine," Hornblower answered.

"Mr. Evers knows his way about a ship, Captain," Greene said, "and the sergeant of marines and his men will keep that crew of pirates in line until they reach Jamaica."

Hornblower crossed his arms and leaned against the rail. "I'm more interested in what our friend down below can tell us."

Brewer turned to lean on the rail as well. "Didn't Commodore Porter say the Americans suspected Lafitte died in the attack on Galveston?"

"He did indeed. But... Lafitte might not know that. And I particularly want to know the whereabouts of that frigate that waylaid you on your way here."

Evers waved from the quarterdeck, and Hornblower and Brewer waved back. Brewer turned and saw Mr. Short.

"Captain," Hornblower said, "I shall be in my cabin. Kindly have Mr. Sweeney resume our course up the northern coast of Cuba, and signal *Crab* to take her station inshore. When you've seen to your duties, come along to my cabin and we'll have a talk with our friend Lafitte."

"Aye aye, sir," Brewer saluted. It took him about ten minutes to set things aright on deck. He was just going below when he ran into the doctor.

Brewer said. "I am on my way to the admiral now. He wants to interrogate the prisoner Jean Lafitte."

"Indeed?"

"It should be quite a show. He thinks the Americans want him for piracy, but the Americans believe he died in their attack on Galveston. It will be interesting to see the look on his face when we inform him of that fact."

Spinelli leaned forward, suddenly interested. "Do you mean that the admiral may allow Lafitte to trade information for not turning him over to the Americans?"

Brewer sighed. "I'm afraid the admiral has not seen fit to

share his plans with me. But I'm sure it will make an interesting tale over chess tonight."

Spinelli bowed. "At your command, my captain."

Brewer clapped him on the arm and went below. He ran into McCleary, his new coxswain, cleaning his pistols.

"Hello, Mac," he said. "Making sure I stay alive? I like that sentiment!"

The big Cornishman smiled. "Can't be too careful, can we, Cap'n?"

"Have you picked out a cutlass for yourself?"

"Not yet, sir."

"Well, get down to the armory and pick yourself out a good one, and a brace of pistols as well. Then make sure your cutlass and my sword are ready. I'm pretty sure we'll be needing them."

When Brewer made his way to the admiral's cabin and knocked, Gerard opened the door and let him in.

"Ah, there you are, Captain," Hornblower said. "I was just beginning to wonder if I'd lost you overboard as well."

"My apologies, my lord," Brewer said.

"No matter, Captain. It seems you and I will have a lot on our plates for this voyage, eh? Well, whatever it takes. Shall we have Lafitte in and see what he knows? Mr. Gerard, if you please?"

Gerard opened the door and addressed the sentry. "Pass the word for the sergeant at arms to bring the prisoner to the admiral's cabin."

"Aye, sir."

Gerard shut the door and moved to stand by the admiral.

"My lord," Brewer said, "do you really intend to let this pirate go if he gives you information on where the other pirate ships are located?"

"My dear captain," Hornblower chided, "that does not sound ethical! I believe that according to international law,

Lafitte has violated the terms of his letter of marque from the Spanish government, so it is up to them to punish him. I simply intend to give him the choice of being turned over to the Spanish, or to the Americans."

Brewer smiled. "I see."

The door opened, and Jean Lafitte was marched in by the sergeant of the guard. His hands and ankles were shackled.

"Sit down, Captain," Hornblower said. Gerard took his place at the door, and Brewer stood behind the admiral. Lafitte was led to his chair and made to sit. The guards stood directly behind him on either side.

"I must protest my treatment, Admiral," the bound man said. "I have not been charged with piracy, and yet I am chained like a pirate."

"Yes," Hornblower said, "well, that's what I want to talk to you about. As the Admiral commanding the West Indies Squadron of His Majesty's navy, I am prepared to charge you with violation of this letter of marque you claim to have from the Spanish government. Also, as I said, the Americans want you for piracy in the Gulf of Mexico. So, my problem is, to whom do I turn you over for prosecution? To the Spanish, or to the Americans?"

Brewer watched Lafitte and couldn't help but admire the villain's calm. He said nothing, merely watching the admiral through hooded eyes.

Hornblower leaned forward, resting his forearm on his desk. "I want to know where your pirate ships are."

Lafitte smiled. "I don't know."

Hornblower sat back and smiled. "That's what I thought you would say. There's something else you ought to know. Commodore Porter of the American West Indies Squadron was my guest just before we sailed from Kingston. Mr. Brewer here and Mr. Gerard were present at the dinner. Commodore Porter told us that the Americans believe you may have perished when the citadel blew up during their attack on Galveston."

The pirate was surprised by that one. His brows rose and he straightened. "How do I know you speak the truth?"

Hornblower sat back and relaxed, now totally in control of the conversation. "As I said, both these officers were present and will gladly attest to the truth of what I have told you. If you question their honor, then you will find out the truth of what I say when we present you alive before Commodore Porter."

Lafitte's eyes narrowed as he considered the choice before him. Briefly his eyes shot to Brewer and then over his shoulder in Gerard's direction, but he said nothing to either officer. Hornblower sat quietly, waiting his prisoner out. Brewer saw Lafitte's eyes stare out into the distance and then begin darting from one point to the next as his mind went through the options open to him. Finally, he blinked and looked at Hornblower.

"And how can I influence your choice?"

Hornblower's gaze never wavered. "I want to know where the pirate ships are."

Brewer saw the pirate lower his eyes and purse his lips as he considered the choice. Brewer wondered whether he would really betray his comrades; a King's man would never do so, but a pirate?

Lafitte finally nodded to himself and raised his eyes to meet Hornblower's. Brewer could see his decision was made.

"Last I heard, they were at Cardenas."

"How long ago?"

Lafitte shrugged. "Perhaps a month."

"Under whose command?"

Lafitte raised his eyes again. "El Diabolito."

Hornblower tapped his finger on the desk, never taking his eyes from his prisoner.

"Thank you, Captain," the admiral said. "Sergeant, take

him away."

Lafitte rose. "And what of me?"

Hornblower looked up. "We shall verify your information first. If it is accurate, I will turn you over to the Spanish authorities for what I imagine will be a very short trial and an even shorter sentence. If you have lied, we shall turn you over to Commodore Porter for what will no doubt be a short trial followed by your swinging from the end of a hangman's noose."

The guards took Lafitte out. After Gerard closed the door behind them, he went to retrieve the maps of the north Cuba coastline again. He spread them out before Hornblower and Brewer and stood back. The two officers poured over the close-scale maps and soon located Cardenas, just a short distance east along the coast from Havana. Hornblower rubbed his chin as he considered this new information.

"Two days at full sail," he said. "That would mean an engagement shortly after dawn of the third day." His hand swept past Havana toward the Florida Keys. "It would also mean the Americans would be much closer to the scene of the action. Hmm..."

"And what of Lafitte, my lord?" Brewer asked.

"All in good time, Captain. I am considering altering our strategy a bit, in light of this new intelligence. Heave to, please, William, and signal for Lieutenant Morgan to come aboard."

"Aye, sir," Brewer said. He went to the door and passed the word for the midshipman of the watch. Mr. Short reported to the cabin.

"Mr. Short," Brewer said, "my compliments to Mr. Phillips. He is to heave to and make signal to *Crab, 'Captain to report on board.'*"

"Aye aye, sir," Short said. He saluted and departed on his mission.

Within the hour, Lt. Morgan, who was in command of

the *Crab*, was standing beside Brewer in the cabin.

“Mr. Morgan,” Hornblower said as they bent over the map, “I am changing our plan in light of new information we obtained from a prisoner taken from the prize. The pirates are reported to be at Cardenas, here.” He pointed to it on the map. “We shall proceed directly there, before the pirates can disappear, with *Crab* running inshore to draw the pirates out. You will run out to sea as before and take station well out to sea from *Defiant*. I fully expect more than one ship to be located there. If they come out in such numbers that the ship seems to be in danger, *Defiant* will hoist a green pennant, and you will set your course under all sail for this area northwest of Cuba to find the American squadron and bring them running. *Defiant* will keep the pirates engaged and draw them in that general direction.”

“Aye aye, my lord,” Morgan said.

“If we play this right, gentlemen, there will be prize money for all.”

The next evening, Brewer again dined with the admiral. *Defiant* had been gliding along under full sail for most of the day, and Mr. Sweeney was confident they would be off Cardenas shortly after dawn. For some reason, Brewer gauged the temperature of the room as rather cold, and he wondered just what was going through Hornblower's mind. Gerard was no help; Brewer thought the flag lieutenant was deliberately avoiding his gaze.

"So, my lord," Brewer said after downing a mouthful of Jenkins' delicious beef-and-kidney pie, "we hope that we shall soon be in action against the pirates. What do you think our friend from St. Helena would say, were he seated at this table with us?"

For the first time, Gerard's eyes flashed to Brewer's, but whether in surprise or warning, Brewer could not tell. Unfortunately, Gerard's eyes dropped as quickly as they had risen, so Brewer turned back to Hornblower.

The admiral was munching on a broccoli floret, his eyes seeming to burn through Brewer. And yet, Brewer did not see hostility in his mentor's eyes; rather, he saw an interest, as though Brewer had suggested something that Hornblower had not considered. Hornblower finished his broccoli and set his fork down. He wiped his mouth with his linen napkin, leaned back in his chair, and sighed. Brewer saw Gerard relax a bit, and he wondered what had gone on before his arrival.

"What would our friend say?" Hornblower mused aloud. "I have been wondering that very thing, William. What do you think?"

Brewer sat back and thought a bit. "I remember one thing he told me during that last interview: Go for the throat."

Hornblower nodded. "I remember several times when he was a guest at Governor's House. Barbara and I would watch as he crawled around on the floor with Richard, re-fighting many of his battles. I remember now, he told Richard he always tried to isolate a portion of the enemy line, and then he would hit it with overwhelming force. I wonder if we could do the same thing with *Defiant* somehow?"

Brewer smiled. "What do you have in mind, my lord?"

Hornblower leaned forward. "I plan on Mr. Mosley repeating his feat of the other day. If we pick the closest one and get a broadside or two into her at long range, then we might be able to turn on the next before they scurry around and get a broadside in our stern."

Brewer nodded. "I agree, my lord. Do you know, I never could see Bonaparte dancing to someone else's tune."

Hornblower laughed. "You're right there, Captain. He always wanted to lead, and that's what we're going to do. I want those butchers to dance to our tune."

CHAPTER 24

Captain William Brewer stepped on out on the deck of *HMS Defiant* at four bells of the morning watch. The warm Caribbean Sea breeze felt good in his lungs. He looked to the south, but he saw nothing but ocean; the coast of Cuba was below the horizon, making *Defiant* invisible to any on the land or in a harbor. He glanced up at the main top, all but hidden in the predawn gloom. They would need several sets of very good eyes up there today, if they were going to put the admiral's plan into action.

On the quarterdeck, acting-Lieutenant Tyler was supervising a party while they finished holystoning the deck in preparation for the admiral's exercise.

Brewer strolled over to the other side of the deck where Lieutenant Greene was speaking to Mr. Sweeney. The two men saluted as the captain came near.

"Good morning, Captain," Greene said.

"Good morning, gentlemen," Brewer said. "What's our status, Mr. Greene?"

Greene answered readily. "We're primed, Captain. As soon as it gets light, I'll send Mr. Tyler and Jeremiah into the tops with a good glass each."

Brewer nodded his approval. Tyler and Jeremiah had the best eyes on the ship.

Sweeney stepped up. "Captain, by my calculations, we're moving a bit faster than we anticipated. I recommend we shorten sail, at least until we sight *Crab*."

Brewer looked up at the mountain of sail that floated over the *Defiant's* deck as he considered his sailing master's request. He looked around until he saw what he was looking for.

"Mr. Short! My respects to the admiral. Inform him we are nearly off Cardenas and I am shortening sail."

Short saluted and scampered off. Brewer looked at Sweeney and nodded. The old sailing master smiled and turned his attention to the sails overhead.

Brewer heard something and turned to see Hornblower himself ascend the companionway stairs. Brewer turned and saluted.

"Good morning, my lord."

"Good morning," Hornblower said, a little gruffly to Brewer's ears. "Well?"

Brewer smiled to himself, suddenly remembering the stories Captain Bush used to tell on *Lydia* about how gruff Hornblower could be before he took his exercise and had his morning coffee.

"I was about to shorten sail, my lord," Brewer explained. "Mr. Sweeney believes we are moving too quickly to give *Crab* adequate cover, and I agree with him."

The admiral looked at the billowing sails above, and then looked to the south, as though *Crab* were visible from the deck. He turned back to Brewer and Sweeney.

"Agreed," he said. "Slow us down, Captain. I assume you will have some sharp eyes in the tops to keep an eye on *Crab*?"

Brewer assured him they did, and soon both officers observed the two men scrambling up the shrouds to the main top. It was nearly an hour before they called down the report that *Crab* was in sight, hull down, just over the horizon. By this time, Brewer noticed, Tyler's crew had completed their morning's work.

"Now comes the hard part, William," Hornblower said, "the waiting. This was the hardest thing for me to get used to when it came to fighting pirates. I was used to sighting the enemy, closing with him, and then fighting until someone emerged as the victor. Pirates will scurry away if they don't feel they have the advantage. We have to make it worth their while, and then we have to snare them."

"Yes, my lord," Brewer said.

Hornblower looked down at his young captain and sensed his unease. He turned and handed his telescope to Mr. Short.

"Captain, will you join me this morning?" Hornblower gestured toward the quarterdeck.

"An honor, my lord."

Brewer fell into step alongside his mentor. He knew from Captain Bush how rarely Hornblower invited anyone to share his exercise, and he made a mental note to include a full account in his next letter to his former captain.

"Was it the same fighting the Barbary pirates?" Hornblower asked.

"No, my lord," Brewer said. "There was no waiting with them. According to Captain Bush, they were even more aggressive than the French."

Hornblower nodded. "I thought as much. I've never fought them, but I have heard similar accounts from brother officers at the Admiralty."

Brewer paused for just a second before he asked, "My lord, is this very different from going out after the *Natividad*? I recall Captain Bush saying they were a Dago crew under the madman's admiral."

Hornblower gazed out over the sea for a moment as he

considered. "No," he said. "Left to themselves, the Dagos would run from a stiff fight. I knew Crespo would have none of that." Hornblower paused, and Brewer noticed a darkness t in his eyes. "Crespo would drive them to destruction."

Brewer kept silent as they paced back and forth. He knew enough to tread lightly. Bush had only spoken of the *Natividad* fight sparingly, and even then he would only say it had been a hard fight and that Hornblower had won them the day. The two men paced the remainder of the admiral's exercise back and forth in silence, then Hornblower stopped and looked south over the waves, lost in thought. Brewer saw him blink and turn to look up at the main top, where Tyler and Jeremiah were busily scanning the horizon. Then Hornblower met Brewer's gaze.

"Thank you, Captain," he said. "I am returning to my cabin. Call me if I'm needed or if *Crab* heads out to sea."

"Aye, aye, my lord."

Brewer stood and watched his mentor descend below decks and wondered what was going through his mind. He glanced to the south himself, and saw exactly what his admiral had seen—nothing. Brewer remembered what Hornblower had said about waiting and realized that there was absolutely nothing he or Hornblower could do now. The plan had been set in motion; all they could do was wait to see whether or not the pirates were willing to take the bait.

He crossed his arms and stood against the rail, still looking to the south, toward Cuba over the horizon, knowing that somewhere along this coastline there were pirate ships waiting, safe in Spanish ports, for some unsuspecting ship to pass by. Even if *Defiant* found them, there was nothing they could do about it, so long as the pirates stayed in port. That was why Hornblower decided to dangle the *Crab,* seemingly alone, as bait to draw them from their lair. Despite his confidence in Hornblower, Brewer wondered if such a fantastic plan had any chance at all of working. Wouldn't the pirates think such a ship that close to shore was a trap?

Brewer sensed he was not alone and glanced over his shoulder to see Mr. Sweeney standing silently beside him. He turned back to his study of the empty sea.

"Don't worry, Captain," Sweeney said. "It'll work."

"How can you be so sure?" Brewer whispered.

"If for no other reason than it is Hornblower's plan. You don't rise as he has without having an instinct inside you that tells you what to do. You don't understand it, but you learn to listen to it. Hornblower has. That's why we'll win."

Brewer turned and looked hard at his sailing master. Sweeney stared serenely over the waves, a confidence on his face Brewer could only envy.

He turned toward the fantail. "Walk with me, Mr. Sweeney, if you please."

Sweeney obediently fell into step beside his captain, and they retraced the path that Brewer and the admiral had paced shortly before. Neither man said anything, step following step in utter silence. Finally, without looking up, Brewer asked in a low voice, "Mr. Sweeney, am I the first new captain that you've tried to take under your wing, so to speak?"

The master walked on for several steps before answering. "No," he said. "The second."

They made another three complete circuits in silence before Brewer spoke. "Who was the first?"

Sweeney walked on without answering, and Brewer suddenly knew why.

"It was James Norman, wasn't it?"

The sailing master nodded a single time, and both men continued to pace in silence. Brewer wasn't sure he wanted to ask any more questions, but as they made the next turn, Sweeney looked at the deck and spoke softly.

"He came aboard after a short time as first lieutenant of HMS *Standard*, a sloop that'd had good luck against

Bonaparte's forces in the Mediterranean. He had Hardy's backing, even then, and that was enough to get him the command. He seemed full of confidence when he came aboard, but something seemed odd, not quite right, I should say. Then Mr. Mosley got sick and was quickly moved ashore, and the ship sailed without him. That should have told me something was wrong, but it didn't. We escorted a convoy to Newfoundland during the height of the last American war, but we never ran into any of their frigates. Looking back, I'm not sure if Norman went looking for them or tried his best to stay out of their way. At first he seemed to welcome my help, but then he turned on me while on deck, same as he did you. He might have tried to get rid of me like he did Mosley, except that one night in St. John's I had some drinks with some mates who told me the whole story of what happened on the deck of HMS *Victory* that black day in 1805 when England won her greatest victory and lost her greatest hero."

They made the next turn, and Brewer waited for the sailing master to continue, but Sweeney remained silent for the next three turns. Brewer had resigned himself to the silence when Sweeney suddenly resumed his tale.

"Well, the next time he went for me, I let him know that I knew the truth about him and his precious reputation, and for a while he left everyone alone. After that, I was untouchable. Soon we settled into a strange relationship in which he left me alone and I left him alone. The one thing I could not do was help any of his... victims, shall we say? The best I could do was to train them, as we did with Mr. Phillips, and then try to pick up the pieces after the captain ripped one to shreds. Some of them recovered, but many more didn't. Sometimes an officer or the first lieutenant would try to intervene, or at least shield the fellow, try to deflect some of Norman's fury. Usually the captain found an excuse to get rid of them, as he did with your predecessor.

"Then you came aboard, along with Greene and young

Mr. Phillips. It was easy to see that Phillips would be the next target; Greene seemed too competent for Norman's games, and you had a reputation from St. Helena and the Med. I think that's what made you a little different than all the other first lieutenants in Norman's eyes. You knew Bonaparte. Your reputation was earned, and the captain's was forged. That's one reason I was reluctant to help you at first, because I had no idea what the captain would do with someone like you. You wouldn't be intimidated easily, and you weren't going to turn a blind eye to what the captain was doing to Mr. Phillips. Then you helped him on deck, in obvious defiance of the captain, and you took the captain's punishment without complaint." Sweeney stopped and turned to his captain. "That's when I knew you were real, Captain."

Brewer nodded his thanks, and the two men resumed their pacing. "I think that's when the captain began to... fall apart, I guess you could say. Did he ever ask you about Bonaparte?"

"Once," Brewer said, "but I gave him the standard answer I give everyone, which didn't satisfy him at all." Brewer shrugged at the memory. "It's not something I like to talk about with just anyone, because it usually leads to a lot of questions that I don't like to answer anymore."

Sweeney went on. "Normally, he would have found an excuse to get you off the ship at the first opportunity, but he knew Hornblower backed you and would ask questions if something were to happen and you weren't on the ship when she reached Jamaica. Thwarted, I do believe the captain lost his mind and went insane, and it was left to Providence to take a hand and save your life during the storm." Sweeney shook his head. "Damn shame. I think there was a time when James Norman could have been a great officer, but his weakness back in 1805 cost him, not his career, but his soul."

They made another turn at the fantail. "And what would

you have done, were it you on *Victory* in 1805, Mr. Sweeney?" Brewer asked at last.

"The same as you, I expect," the master said sadly. "Told Hardy the truth as soon as possible, and let events take their course. Pity Norman chose not to do it."

"Yes," Brewer said. "Well, thank you, Mr. Sweeney. That answers many questions I've had in the back of my mind."

"Pardon me, Captain."

Brewer turned to see the flag lieutenant approaching.

"Yes, Mr. Gerard?"

"The admiral's compliments, Captain. Would you take an early meal with the admiral now, sir?"

"Of course," Brewer said. "I shall come immediately. Mr. Phillips! You have the deck. I shall be with the admiral."

"Aye aye, sir!" Phillips acknowledged.

Brewer followed the flag lieutenant do the admiral's cabin. He paused before entering the day cabin to allow Gerard to announce him, and when he crossed the threshold he found his mentor sitting on the settee under the stern windows, a cup of coffee in his hand.

"Ah, there you are, Captain," he said without rising. "I hope you don't mind my sending Mr. Gerard after you, but I wanted to talk to you before we engaged the pirates. And since I have deprived you of your chambers and usurped your cook, I thought to make amends. Let us hope that Jenkins is up to his usual standards."

"He has yet to be otherwise."

"Then let us partake."

The two men sat at the table, and Jenkins appeared and served them a feast of salt pork, stewed potatoes, gravy, and fresh baked bread—not ship's biscuit! Brewer was astonished and looked at Jenkins.

"The admiral brought the ingredients with him, sir," the servant explained. "He even went to great lengths to swear the ship's cook to secrecy when it was baked."

"I had to," Hornblower said between mouthfuls. "Didn't want a mutiny on our hands, now, did we?"

"No, my lord," Brewer said.

"Never fear, William," Hornblower consoled his captain. "After we've bagged these pirates, I'll make sure the entire ship's company gets fresh baked bread!"

The two officers finished their dinner, and Jenkins brought out hot coffee. The two men sat back in their chairs and wondered aloud how long they would have to wait.

Just then, Mr. Tyler burst through the admiral's door. "Beg pardon, sir!" he said to Brewer. "My lord, *Crab* has gone to full sail and is approaching!"

CHAPTER 25

Admiral Horatio Lord Hornblower grabbed his hat and hastened past the startled acting-lieutenant with Brewer hard on his heels. When the officers reached the main deck, they were met by McCleary, who handed each of them a telescope and pointed.

"A point or two east of south, my lord."

Hornblower nodded his thanks and hurriedly raised the glass to his eye. Brewer paused to direct a smile at his coxswain before joining his admiral.

"There!" Hornblower cried. Brewer soon found the growing speck of white-over-brown, southeast of them and running out to sea. There was no sign yet of whom or what she was running from.

"Call the hands, Captain," Hornblower said calmly. "Course east-southeast. We need to pass between *Crab* and her pursuers."

"Aye aye, my lord," Brewer said. "Mr. Phillips! All hands wear ship! New course east-southeast! Clear for action and beat to quarters!"

HMS Defiant exploded in activity, some men manning the braces, others racing to their guns to get them ready for action. Brewer could see Mr. Sweeney ensuring his mates were holding the wheel over hard to larboard, swinging the big frigate around to save their comrade. The new course allowed *Defiant* to sail at her swiftest before the wind, and Brewer could tell the gap between the two ships was going to close very rapidly.

"Pardon me, sir."

Brewer turned to see McCleary standing beside him with Brewer's sword and two pistols in his hands. Brewer smiled as he took the sword belt and buckled it on. The coxswain held out the pistols; Brewer checked each one before tucking it in his belt. He saw that McCleary had a cutlass on already.

"Fresh flints in each pistol, sir," the coxswain said.

"Thanks, Mac," Brewer said. The big Cornishman grinned as he stood back a couple steps. He would stay within striking distance until the fight was over and his captain was safe.

Within minutes, *Crab* was visible from the deck, but there was still no sign of her pursuer.

"Mr. Tyler!" Brewer called to the maintop. "Can you see the enemy?"

Hornblower and Brewer could see the acting lieutenant scanning the horizon to their south before suddenly steadying on a bearing and pointing. His cries were lost, carried away by the wind, but Brewer and Hornblower followed his direction. They soon caught the speck of white on the horizon.

"Begging your pardon, Captain."

Brewer turned to see Jeremiah, who had been sent to the main top with Mr. Tyler.

"Mr. Tyler's compliments," Jeremiah said between gasps for air, "but we couldn't make you understand, sir."

"It's alright, Jeremiah," Brewer said. "We see him."

"But that's just it, sir! It isn't just one! Mr. Tyler says there's three!"

"Three!" Brewer exclaimed.

"Aye, sir!"

"Very well, Jeremiah," Brewer said. "Report to Mr. Tyler. As soon as they're hull up, return to the deck."

"Aye, sir," Jeremiah stumbled off and began climbing again.

"Well, well. Three," Gerard said. Brewer hadn't heard him come on deck.

"They must be in single file," Brewer said. "That would explain why *Crab* only reported one originally." Hornblower lowered his glass and frowned, then handed the glass to Gerard as he went off to pace while he considered his options.

Brewer looked at Gerard, who had Hornblower's glass to his eye and was using the opportunity to study the situation for himself. Brewer wanted to ask him what Hornblower would do, but he didn't want to look like a wet-behind-the-ears midshipman. He looked over his shoulder again to see his mentor still pacing the quarterdeck, his chin on his breast, his mind probably racing like the wind.

"Captain, sir!"

Brewer turned to see Tyler followed by Jeremiah.

"They should be visible any minute now, Captain," Tyler said, pointing to the southeast. "It looks like the lead ship is pulling away from the other two."

Brewer nodded. "Trying to get to *Crab* quickly."

"Aye, sir," Tyler agreed. "And, Captain, it looks like the third pirate may be the one who ambushed us."

Brewer raised his glass to his eye and stared out to sea, focusing on the third and most distant speck of white, first wondering and then hoping he would get his chance to pay the pirate back. He snapped the glass shut; his decision was made. Before Gerard could stop him, Brewer turned and went over to interrupt Hornblower's pacing.

"What is it, Captain?" the admiral snapped.

"Mr. Tyler has returned to the deck, my lord," Brewer said. "He reports the lead pirate is pulling away from the other two."

"Excellent!" Hornblower cried. "May I borrow your glass, Captain?"

Brewer handed over the glass and stood back as Hornblower scanned the horizon, and he was suddenly struck by the scene. All the stories he heard from Captain Bush since they left St. Helena now came back to him, and he could almost see himself on the deck of the *Lydia* as she approached the *Natividad* in the Pacific, or on the *Sutherland* as she took on four French ships of the line.

He also recalled something the Corsican once said to him, something about Brewer being Hornblower's Berthier, referring to his own invaluable chief-of-staff. Brewer wondered if this was how Berthier felt as he watched his emperor survey the battlefield before Austerlitz, his greatest victory, or Waterloo. No, Berthier wasn't at Waterloo; some said he lost his mind and threw himself out of his window to his death just as Napoleon was beginning his Hundred Days. Regardless of whether it was true or not, the fact remained that Napoleon lost at Waterloo without Berthier to manage matters for him. The thought fell heavy on Brewer's shoulders, and it gave him a new appreciation for just how well Bush did his job during the Napoleonic Wars, and also how valuable Bush actually was to Hornblower's success. Brewer also knew something else: it was his turn now.

"Captain," Hornblower said, "kindly have Mr. Sweeney alter our course two—no, make that *one* point to starboard. I want to hit that gap in the pirate line. We'll blast both sides as we punch through. Pass the word for Mr. Mosley."

"Aye, my lord," Brewer said. "Mr. Sweeney! One point to starboard, if you please! Pass the word for Mr. Mosley!"

"We'll have the guns loaded and run out, if you please, Captain," Hornblower said.

"Aye, my lord. Mr. Phillips, have both batteries loaded and run out!" Brewer called.

Brewer reclaimed and raised the glass to his eye again. *Crab* had already passed *Defiant* on her way out to sea. The lead pirate ship, Brewer now confirmed, was a cutter as well, one which, although only slightly larger than *Crab*, was surely carrying three times *Crab's* numbers. The cutter was closing, slowly but surely, and pulling away from its consorts, creating the gap into which Hornblower was even now throwing the *Defiant*.

"Now," Hornblower said, "I expect the two to our starboard to come after us. I hope Mr. Mosley will be able to repeat his miracle of the other day—ah, there you are, Mr. Mosley." Brewer turned to see the old gunner scurry up to the admiral.

"Here's the situation, Mr. Mosley. You see the cutter to port, closing in on *Crab*? We are going to pass to her stern, through this gap in the line you see ahead of us. I need you to sink the cutter with the first broadside. I shall have Mr. Sweeney turn a point or two to starboard if you like, but we must sink that ship to take the pressure off *Crab*. Mr. Phillips will command the starboard battery to keep those two ships to starboard busy until we're ready to come around and deal with them. Do you have any questions?"

The old gunner took the glass offered by his captain with a nod of thanks and quickly surveyed the situation. After a bit he lowered the telescope and looked at Hornblower.

"None, my lord."

"Very good, Mr. Mosley," Hornblower said, "assume your station. We'll be in range soon."

Brewer watched as Mosley went forward and walked behind the first several guns, speaking to each gun captain, gesticulating to make sure his intentions were understood. Once he was satisfied, the gunner stood back and signaled that all was ready.

Brewer acknowledged silently with a nod.

Hornblower took another look, and Brewer thought he could feel the tension radiating from him. Off to his left, Brewer could now see the pirate cutter adjusting its course to give *Defiant* a smaller profile. He saw a small puff of smoke as the cutter fired on *Crab*, and he turned in time to see the shot fall astern. He turned back to see that Hornblower, too, had taken notice. Without a word, the admiral lowered his telescope and turned toward Mosley. He nodded once.

"First section!" Mr. Mosley called, “Fire!"

Brewer was staggered by the concussive force of six 32-pounders going off simultaneously right next to him. He noticed that the admiral was better prepared, bracing himself against the railing. Brewer recovered his footing quickly and raised his glass to his eye just in time to see the cutter erupt and then disintegrate as five of *Defiant's* 32-pound shells struck the hull and the sixth splintered the pirate's mainmast. The cheering that rang out on *Defiant* was deafening. Overwhelming force indeed!

Brewer saw the the pirate cutter begin to flounder. *Crab* continued out to sea. Brewer saw Hornblower's attention turned back to the south. The captain of the *Defiant* quickly followed suit.

The southern ships were still a good ways off; that made sense to Brewer, as these larger ships would take longer to warp out of the harbor than the cutter. The first ship was the ex-French frigate that had greeted them on their arrival in Caribbean waters, and the second looked fast and formidable as well. Brewer identified it as a barque.

Brewer lowered his telescope and frowned. He turned to see Hornblower looking up at *Defiant's* sails, gauging the wind. He looked at the approaching ships, and then back to the sails billowing overhead.

Brewer looked again at the approaching ships. The frigate was steering an intercept course for *Defiant*, probably intending to occupy their attention while the other ship slipped around their stern for an "up the kilt" shot that could devastate them.

"Mr. Phillips!" Brewer cried. "Stand by! Prepare to fire on the leading ship!"

"Aye aye, sir!"

"My lord," Brewer asked his admiral, "during the wars, how do you think a ship like that would have been armed? Eighteen pounders, or twenty-four?"

Hornblower thought for a moment. "Eighteens, I should think."

Brewer nodded. "Then we might be able to get two salvos off before she comes within range. Permission to open fire, my lord?"

Hornblower looked at his friend and smiled. "Agreed."

"Mr. Mosley! Mr. Phillips!" Brewer cried. "Prepare to fire! Mr. Sweeney! Two points to larboard, if you please!"

"Aye aye, Captain!"

"Aye, sir!"

Defiant swung to port to give the starboard battery a better angle. Brewer waited for just the right moment.

"Mr. Phillips!" he called. "You may fire as your guns bear! Two broadsides, if you please! Mr. Sweeney, I want to swing hard to starboard as soon as the second broadside is loosed. We'll give her a dose of the larboard battery as we pass by!"

"Aye aye, Captain!"

Phillips and Mosley were running from gun to gun, making sure each crew knew what was expected of them. Brewer and Hornblower watched them step back, each at one end of the battery, and nod to each other.

"Fire!"

Brewer braced himself this time; even so the effect of the blast from *Defiant's* broadside nearly knocked him from his feet. He recovered in time to see debris erupting at several points along the enemy ship as the broadside struck home, but the French-built frigate kept coming. The second broadside a minute and twenty seconds later had a similar result.

Brewer turned to Sweeney. “Hard a starboard, Mr. Sweeney! Course south-southwest!”

“Aye, sir!” the sailing master called. “All hands! Tacks and sheets!"

Defiant swung sharply around just as the pirate ship let loose a ragged broadside. Brewer felt a couple of the enemy's shots strike home. *We’re lucky*, Brewer reflected. It might be a French ship, but their gunnery certainly wasn't up to the standards he remembered from the wars.

"Excellent work, Mr. Phillips, Mr. Mosley!" Hornblower called. "Now let's give him one more in passing!"

Mosley and Phillips were already at work, running from gun to gun along the larboard battery, checking that each was loaded properly with either grape, chain, or shot. Brewer stood by the admiral and watched his men work. Here is where all their hard work would bear fruit.

Defiant steadied up on her new course, and Brewer saw that they would pass well within range of the pirate frigate. He raised his telescope to his eye and could see the enemy's ports open and their guns run out. Judging from the differing muzzle sizes, Brewer thought the enemy ship was armed with a mixture of twelve- and eighteen-pounders. Brewer lowered the glass, a grim smile on his face. *Good,* he thought. *Nothing to match Defiant's firepower.*

Brewer watched as *Defiant* straightened on her new course and approached the enemy. The pirate frigate looked ready for battle, Mr. Phillips’ broadside having failed to put any of the pirates’ guns out of action. The two ships were going to pass about twenty-five yards apart, and Brewer could see activity on the enemy’s deck. He remembered going into action beside Captain Bush against the Barbary pirates. It had been as near run a thing as he ever wished to experience; only the stalwart presence of Bush had brought HMS *Lydia* through with a victory.

Hornblower lowered his glass. "Captain, I believe we have an opportunity here, if we can react fast enough. We must reload in record time in order to get the second broadside into them as we pass."

"Aye, my lord," he said and turned to a midshipman. "Mr. Short, my compliments to Mr. Phillips. Remind him that a speedy reload is of the utmost importance. We won't get a second chance like this."

Short saluted and rushed off.

Next Brewer sought out the sailing master. "Mr. Sweeney, as soon as possible after we fire, the admiral wants to put the ship over on the larboard tack and rake the pirate's stern."

Sweeney acknowledged the order. He considered the sky and then *Defiant's* sails and was not happy at all with what he saw. The wind was slackening, but they could manage if it didn't fall away any further.

Brewer rejoin Hornblower and both men watched the approach of the pirate. Brewer knew it would be only a matter of minutes before both ships opened fire. He looked to his admiral. Hornblower seemed impervious to it all, utterly calm and in control, measuring distances with his eye and calculating the closing rate. He remembered Bush telling him how Hornblower was very closed-mouthed before a battle, and he wondered how Bush endured it for so many battles. Finally, the admiral lowered his glass and nodded once. That was all Brewer needed.

"Mr. Phillips!" he called. "You may fire as your guns bear! Be ready to rake their stern as soon as we go about!"

"Aye, sir!"

The two ships began their dance of death. Bowsprits

passed each other, and as the foremasts came even, *Defiant's* guns roared. It puzzled and bothered Brewer that the enemy had not fired yet. Ordinarily, he would expect pirates to fire a ragged, undisciplined broadside with each gun loosed individually. Brewer glanced at the admiral and saw immediately that the same thought had occurred to him. Hornblower was looking hard at the pirate ship, his lips compressed into a hard, thin line.

"Interesting," he said. "Well, Captain, as a mutual friend used to say, for what we are about to receive—"

At that moment, the pirates fired. The enemy were shooting high, after the French manner, trying to dismast his ship. Even so, Brewer felt the deck shudder as rounds of 18-pound shot struck the hull. The broadside made havoc of *Defiant*'s upper works and rigging. Splinters, some of them long as a man and sharp as spears, rained down, causing men to dive for cover. The slower ones screamed in pain as they were struck down.

Defiant's broadside had done its work, and Brewer saw Phillips and Mosley urging their men on during the reload. Brewer wished he had been able to time it; he could not remember a faster one.

Brewer ran to the rail and tried to gauge his ship's position through the smoke. After a seeming eternity, he was able to peer through a gap in the smoke, and he turned to Sweeney.

"Mr. Sweeney! Now!"

"Aye, sir!" Sweeney replied. He began barking orders, setting into motion plans already communicated to the participants. In short order, *Defiant* swung around to port and crossed the frigate's unprotected stern.

Brewer turned. "Mr. Phillips! Fire!"

Defiant's broadside erupted again and sent death and destruction throughout the enemy frigate. Brewer was about to order a reload with grape when Hornblower appeared at his elbow.

"Now let's get after the other one," the admiral said. "Please put the ship about and head straight for the barque."

"Yes, my lord," Brewer said. "Mr. Sweeney, alter course for the barque."

"Aye, Captain!"

Brewer walked over to where Hornblower stood by the rail, feeling his ship come around to starboard and steady up on course.

"May I ask your plans, my lord?"

Hornblower lowered his glass. "We need to hit the barque and damage it before they can get that frigate back into action. If we can dismast the barque quickly, we can turn again and give the frigate our full attention."

"Aye aye, my lord," Brewer said. He remembered Bush telling him how Hornblower was very closed-mouthed before a battle, and he wondered now how Bush endured it for so many battles.

"We'll use the starboard battery, Captain," the admiral said, "to dismast her on the first pass, if we can, then swing around her stern. Tell Mr. Phillips to use the same plan as the last time. Once we cross her stern, we'll head back to deal with the frigate."

"Aye aye, my lord." Brewer saluted and went off to give Mr. Sweeney and Mr. Phillips their orders. He returned to find his admiral had not moved. Brewer took up position two steps away and wanted to study the enemy, but he discovered he had misplaced his telescope. He looked around him, but he turned when he heard someone discreetly clearing his throat. He turned to see McCleary standing two steps away, arm extended, telescope in hand. Brewer nodded his thanks as he took the glass, and it dawned on him that even though he hadn't noticed the coxswain since the engagement began, it was evident he had never been more than a step or two away. Brewer shook his head at how quickly Mac was learning.

Brewer studied the pirate ship as it approached down *Defiant's* starboard side. He wondered how many ships she had plundered, how many innocents murdered. He looked forward to blowing this ship out of the water.

Once again, Mr. Phillips waited until the two foremasts were even before he gave the order for *Defiant* to open fire. The carronades erupted, spewing metal across the enemy's deck, and the 24-pounders smashed the enemy's hull. Brewer again turned his attention to the timing of *Defiant's* turn, turning to the sailing master at the prime moment and nodding.

That was all Sweeney needed. He immediately gave the orders that swung the big frigate around to starboard and across the pirate's unprotected stern. This time, Phillips needed no order; he loosed his broadside just when it would inflict maximum damage to men, masts, and sails..

"Now, Captain," Hornblower called out, "back to the frigate!"

"Aye aye, my lord! Mr. Sweeney! Hard to starboard! Set your course for the pirate frigate!"

"Aye aye, Captain!"

Defiant swung around and began to sail up the port side of the barque. Brewer could see her men struggling to regain control of their ship. He was just turning to consult with Hornblower as to his plans for the next phase of the engagement when he heard Mr. Phillips' voice rise above the din of battle.

"Look out! All hands! Look out!"

Brewer spun and saw Phillips in the waist, a look of terror on his face, pointing at the barque, its larboard battery readied to fire. He hadn't expected the pirates to survive *Defiant's* broadside in any condition to fire a gun. Before he could react, he felt the rush of air as the enemy's guns fired, and he staggered backward.

He never heard the crack as the lower mizzen yard came apart and crashed to the deck, falling right on top of him.

CHAPTER 26

"Captain!"

McCleary cried out and ran towards his fallen master. Brewer was lying on the deck with a big yardarm across his neck and back. Hornblower felt a cold fist grab his heart and squeeze. The Admiral threw decorum to the wind and ran to his protégé's side. McCleary was already checking his Captain over and pulling away the debris.

"He's alive, my lord," the coxswain reported, "but we've got to get this wreckage off him."

McCleary bellowed for some hands to assist him with the Captain. Hornblower was silent as he watched them work; in truth, he did not trust himself to speak, remembering how devastated he'd felt when Bush had been lost and presumed dead, and now Brewer was down.

What happened next was worse.

A sailor's voice rose in a wail. "We're being boarded!"

The Admiral spun to see a sight he had never even imagined was possible—the pirate barque had closed with the *Defiant,* following its broadside, and was even now grappling her as screaming, blood-maddened pirates hauled the ropes that brought within their reach a prize that would allow them to dominate the Caribbean.

McCleary rose slowly, staring in disbelief. Greene shouted orders for the hands to repel boarders, but Mac looked from the pirates to the Admiral to the Captain.

"My lord, what do we do about the Captain? There's no time now to get him below!"

Hornblower drew his sword. "Captain Brewer is your responsibility, McCleary. Keep him safe!"

The Cornishman gazed into the Admiral's eyes and said simply, "I promise you, sir, that if he's dead when this is over, I will be, too."

Hornblower moved off to take his stand on the quarterdeck, and McCleary took charge of the situation.

"Smith, Jones, Davey, Douer—you make your stand here, with me. Two-toes, Youngblood—you cover our backs. Here comes Mr. Short with some weapons. Everybody ready? Here they come!"

They barely had time to come shoulder to shoulder before the pirates swarmed over the railing, screaming for blood.

Sweeney drew his sword just as the first wave of men came over the rail. He parried the first attack, sidestepped the second blow and brought his cutlass down on the back of the pirate's neck, feeling the jolt all the way up to his shoulder when his blade bit into bone. He jerked the cutlass free and recovered as the body fell to the deck. He stared at the blood that ran down his blade; he found the sight intoxicating.

"Lash the wheel!" he cried to the helmsmen. "Grab your cutlasses and fight for your ship!"

The Admiral was holding his own. He fired both his pistols and dropped two of the pirates, then readied his sword. Dodging an overhead blow, he swung his blade for all he was worth, severing his enemy's throat. Blood that gushed from the gaping wound and splattered over his coat. *Barbara is going to kill me! This coat will never come clean!* He blinked at how ridiculous the thought was, then with a great laugh he deflected a blow before plunging his sword into a pirate's chest. He ducked a blow aimed at his head and pulled a pistol from the dying pirate's belt and shot the pirate behind him with it, but then he slipped on the blood pooling on the deck and was barely able to parry a thrust at his own chest. The blade sliced through the side of his coat, and in a fury Hornblower dropped the man with a left uppercut to the chin. He did not hesitate before thrusting his blade into the unconscious man's chest. Hornblower slashed at a nearby pirate and severed his wrist, then ducked barely in time to keep his head, losing his hat instead. The Admiral looked past the man in front of him and saw the enemy still coming over *Defiant's* rails. He parried the next thrust and drove the hilt of his sword into the man's eye socket. As the man fell away, screaming with pain, Hornblower snatched up a pistol and shot one of the pirates trying to board; he took great satisfaction in watching the man fall into the sea between the two ships. Even so, he could tell that the numbers were tilting heavily in the attackers' favor, and he began to give ground.

Mr. Greene found himself by the mainmast when the pirates boarded. He looked up just in time to see a pirate turn a swivel gun in his direction, and he quickly ducked behind the mast as it fired, showering the area with pellets and mowing down a half-dozen seamen. He gave a great war cry and threw himself into the battle, giving ground deliberately to fall back towards the other officers. He struck at the back of the group attacking the Admiral, then rushed past to where two pirates had Mr. Sweeney pinned again the railing. He impaled one of them from the rear, which distraction allowed Sweeney to dispatch the other. The

Master went to help his mates, while Greene make a quick survey of the situation.

What he saw did not encourage him. There was fighting over the entire length of the deck, and Greene estimated that the pirates outnumbered the *Defiant's* deck crew two to one. He wondered who was still alive on the lower gun deck; if those men could be brought up, that would give them a chance. A small one, but still a chance.

On the lower gun deck, Tyler got slowly to his feet and leaned against an upturned gun carriage. He looked around the gun deck and was appalled by the carnage. More than one shot from that devastating broadside must have come through a gun port, for guns were disabled and their men crushed. He noticed Lieutenant Phillips groan and try to rise, and he ran over to help him.

"Lieutenant!" Tyler said as he grabbed him by the arm, "What are we to do?"

"Do? How should I know?" Phillips said as he rose. His eyes went up toward the sounds of the battle, and then he looked around the gun deck. Panic rose as he took in the destruction. It was worse than anything he had seen on *Retribution*. He felt the terror rising like bile in his throat and was nearly overwhelmed when he caught sight of the midshipman standing at his side, looking to him for direction. The boy's faith steadied him. He took hold of himself and swallowed hard.

"Mr. Tyler," he said, "we need to get some of these guns back in service."

Mac was covered in blood, none of it his own. He was on his second cutlass: the first had broken when he parried strikes from two cutlasses simultaneously. There was no retreat for Mac and his comrades, not protecting the Captain as they were. Twice during the fighting, there was a pause as the pirates regrouped for another charge. The first time, Mac took the opportunity to check on the Captain. Mac thought he could almost be asleep. *Too bad, Captain,* he thought, *you're missing all the fun.* The second time, he used the reprieve to pull *Defiant* shipmates to help protect the Captain. He only had trouble with one.

"Long Tom!" Mac bawled, "Where are you going? Get over here and help us protect the Captain until we can get him below!"

"Can't, McCleary. Mr. Greene sent me into the tops to help the marines pick off some pirates!"

Long Tom never saw Mac's fist as it connected with the side of his head. All he knew was there was a sudden explosion of pain and light, followed by finding himself on the deck looking up at the point of the coxswain's cutlass wavering inches from his throat. The look on McCleary's face needed no interpretation.

"You ain't going to the tops, Tom. You either fight here with me, or you die on this deck."

Tom stared the coxswain with fear and rage. "What about Greene?"

Mac edged the cutlass point closer to Tom's face. "If the Captain lives, I'll speak for you. If he doesn't, chances are we'll all be dead, too." The cutlass point waved menacingly. "What'll it be?"

Tom's eyes narrowed. "I won't forget this, McCleary."

The coxswain said nothing.

Tom sighed. "Okay, I'm in."

Mac helped him up, and Mr. Short gave him a cutlass.

The pirates charged again soon after. Mac's reinforced group held them off, but just barely. If Tom hadn't been part of the line, Mac doubted they'd have held.

On the quarterdeck, Hornblower and Greene were fighting side-by-side, Mr. Sweeney at their backs. Mr. Greene fought like a madman. Hornblower recognized the look in the lieutenant's eye, that look of blind terror that most have when they fight their first boarding action. Fortunately, Greene's terror manifested itself in furious action and determination to stay alive. Hornblower had seen men struck down when their terror froze them on their feet, leaving them unable even to defend themselves.

"It looks as though the ships are beginning to drift apart!" Mr. Sweeney cried from behind him. "It may be possible to pull away!"

"Any sign of *Clam*?" Hornblower demanded loudly, to be heard over the hoarse yells and screams all around them. He was busy fending off a ferocious attack by a man with a scarred face and black hair long enough to make a strike to the neck difficult.

Sweeney cried out as he ran a pirate through. "Haven't had the time to look for her, my lord."

Hornblower wondered desperately about the chances of firing off the signal that would send *Clam* looking for the American squadron, but the pirates were pressing far too closely. Another parry, now a thrust; he had to find a way to tip the balance in their favor, and he knew it had better be soon.

Mr. Phillips helped a gun crew maneuver one of the big guns into position. Even with ten of them throwing their full weight into the effort, it was almost more than they could handle. He stood and wiped his brow on his sleeve as Mr. Tyler came up and saluted.

"We have a total of four guns ready for action, sir," he said, "including this one."

Phillips looked out a gun port and saw the growing distance between the ships. An idea came to him, and he turned back to Tyler.

"Can any of them elevate?"

Tyler looked down the line and nodded. "One, sir, Number four."

"Load Number Four with double grape," Phillips said, "and the rest with shot. We'll use Four to try to rake the pirate's deck and upper works, and the other three to try to push them away from us."

"Aye aye, sir!"

Phillips wished he could take the larboard battery and use it to starboard. Since that was impossible, he decided to use their gun crews for something else.

"Listen to me, you men! Mr. Tyler is going to remain here with four gun crews. Tyler, fire into the pirate ship as long as you can. I want the rest of you men to come with me! We are going up to the main deck and fight for our ship! Ready, Mr. Tyler? Fire!"

The concussion was immense, even though it was only four guns that fired. *Defiant* rocked back, and continued a lesser rocking as the waters between the ships fought for space. Phillips headed for the companionway at the head of several dozen men. Mr. Tyler was feverishly working his crews to get the guns reloaded and run back out again.

"Come on, men! For *Defiant*!" And Phillips led them into the fight.

They spread out and attacked the pirates wherever they found them. Phillips himself led a half-dozen aft to struck down those attacking Hornblower and Greene.

"Mr. Phillips!" Hornblower said. "Report!"

"My lord," Phillips said, "the broadside did a lot of damage below. We managed to get four guns back into action, and Mr. Tyler has orders to fire as long as he can. I took most of the men from the larboard battery and brought them on deck to repel the boarders."

A new group of boarders rushed aft and attacked. Phillips and his squad jumped in front of the exhausted defenders and took up the fight. Just then, Mr. Tyler sent off another broadside, and the distance between the ships widened. Sweeney ran to the rail and Hornblower joined him, scanning the pirate's rigging to make sure no marksmen were targeting them.

"What do you think?" he asked the sailing master.

Sweeney considered the distance, and a glance aloft told him that enough rigging remained to catch the wind. "Not yet, my lord. If someone over there figures out what we're trying to do and turns their ship into ours, we could be in serious trouble."

Hornblower looked for himself, but he knew the sailing master was correct. They would only get one chance to pull away.

"Let's hope Mr. Tyler gets a few more broadsides off," the Admiral said, "and gets us the room we need."

The mass of fighting men shifted, and all at once the two men were set upon. Hornblower and Sweeney fought back as best they could, maneuvering toward the wheel so as not to be pressed against the rail. In the heat of battle, neither man noticed two pirates coming up behind them and raising their cutlasses.

Fortunately, someone else did. Without hesitation, Mr. Phillips threw himself between his Admiral and the pirates. He parried the blow from the first attacker, but the second brought his weapon down and deep into Phillips' right forearm. The Lieutenant screamed in pain and dropped his sword, clutching his wound in a futile attempt to stop the bleeding. Phillips waited for his life to end, thinking wretchedly that he had failed to save the Admiral. Suddenly, Mr. Greene was there, slashing the throat of the pirate who had wounded Phillips and then plunging a dagger into the chest of the other.

Seeing the blood and the shocked expression on young Phillip's face, Mr. Greene looked around for help. "You! Perkins! Come here! Take Mr. Phillips below to the surgeon!"

The seaman obeyed. "Aye aye, sir. Come along, Mr. Phillips!"

Greene spared a moment to watch them until they reached the companionway. He hoped Phillips would be all right. The lad had matured tremendously, especially since Captain Brewer took over command. Still saving your admiral's life isn't the worst way to go.

Greene took a deep breath and threw himself back into the fray, killing two pirates with bloody dispatch. Another broadside pushed the pirate barque a little farther away, but they still could not break away and cut off the pirates from reinforcement. Even with the force Phillips had brought from below deck, they were still heavily outnumbered. He glanced up and saw some of the marine sharpshooters were still there and doing their best to even the odds, but unless a miracle happened, he feared the pirates would carry the day.

"Mr. Greene! Mr. Greene! Deck there!"

Green looked up to see a topman hailing him.

"Sail to larboard! I think it's *Clam*, sir!"

Greene hastened to the rail to look for himself. Sure enough, *Clam* was approaching with all sail set. Greene admired Morgan's pluck, but wouldn't it be better if he went off in search of the Americans?

"Deck there! Two more ships approaching behind *Crab*!"

Greene could hardly believe it! Had Morgan actually taken it on his own initiative to go fetch the Americans? How had they arrived so quickly? He turned and found Hornblower.

"My lord! Did you hear? *Crab* is approaching from larboard, with two ships following her!"

Greene called to the masthead. "Can you identify the sails following *Crab*?"

The call they had hoped for came back. "I think they're Americans, sir!"

"That's it, gentlemen," Hornblower said firmly. "Now all we have to do is to hold on."

The end, when it came, was as sudden as it was decisive. *Crab* led the USS *Constitution* around the far side of the pirate barque. One broadside from each ship was sufficient to convince the pirates to haul down their flag. A party from the USS *Enterprise* boarded *Defiant* on her larboard side and compelled the pirates on board to surrender. Hornblower made his way over to check on Brewer and found McCleary directing four hands in lifting the captain's unconscious body.

"He's alive, my lord," the coxswain said, "but beyond that I can't say. We're carrying him down to the doctor now."

"Keep me informed, McCleary," Hornblower said.

"Aye aye, my lord," Mac saluted and followed his captain below.

CHAPTER 27

It was the gentle rocking that did it, that soft swaying back and forth that nudged him gently out of his cocoon of blackness and back into the world of the living. He didn't want to go; awareness brought with it the return of pain, which turned his gradual stroll toward consciousness into an uncontrolled, headlong, downhill rush. He tried to open his eyes, but the light blinded him and caused stabbing pain behind his eyes and across the back of his head. He thought he heard voices, but they faded into the distance as the darkness arrived and reclaimed his allegiance.

The next time the rocking woke him, he was more ready and willing to answer its call. He opened his mouth to draw a breath and was surprised to hear a loud moan escape. He was aware of feet scurrying about, and a voice that seemed to cut through the gloom.

"Captain? William? Can you hear me?"

Brewer struggled to open his eyes just a crack, half-expecting the blinding light and intense pain that had rewarded his previous attempts. When these didn't come—or at least not nearly to that degree of severity—he decided to throw caution to the wind and opened his eyes. A form swam before him, slowly coming into focus.

"Adam?" Brewer's words came out as a weak croak.

Dr. Spinelli smiled. "Yes, it's me, William."

Brewer turned his head gently to get a view of his surroundings. "Where am I?"

"On board *Defiant*," the doctor said, as he held open Brewer's eyes one at a time to check their reactions. "You're in sick bay. We're at anchor in Kingston harbor."

"What? The battle?" Brewer tried to raise his head, but he cried out in pain when his head revolted against the movement.

"Now, Captain," the doctor said, as he held his captain's head and gently lowered it back to his pillow, "you just lie there and rest. The admiral left orders to be notified when you regained consciousness, and I just sent your watchdog McCleary to fetch him."

"Mac?"

"Yes," Spinelli said as he wiped Brewer's head with a cool cloth. "He's hardly left your side since he brought you down here."

Brewer lay back and closed his eyes. The throbbing in his head was like a drum. All he wanted to do was sleep.

His eyes opened of their own accord later when he sensed someone was there. He leaned his head to one side and was greeted with a sight not seen in many sickbays: Admiral Sir Horatio Lord Hornblower asleep on the cot beside him. Brewer smiled to himself—he was surprised that it didn't hurt—and rolled his head slowly to the other side, pleased to see the occupant of the chair.

"Mac," Brewer croaked.

The big coxswain was at his side in an instant. "Sir! You're back! Yer lordship, he's awake!"

"Well, Captain," Hornblower said as he leaned over Brewer's cot. "I don't mind telling you, you had us worried. It wasn't until the doctor told me yesterday that you were finally awake that I began to relax."

"The battle?"

Hornblower smiled. "The battle was won. We ended up taking a prize, but I can tell you the whole story after you've gone ashore."

"Ashore?"

"Yes. *Defiant* was badly damaged, so I've ordered her in for a complete refit. She will be moved into the dockyard tomorrow."

Brewer felt crestfallen, even through his pain.

"All will be well, William," Hornblower said as he patted his young protégé gently on the shoulder and rose to go, "all will be well. You concentrate on getting better, and we'll talk again when you're up and around. I've given orders that Dr. Spinelli and this Cornish gorilla you call a coxswain are to look after you ashore. Keep me informed, Doctor."

"Aye, my lord," Spinelli said. Hornblower inclined his head and left the sickbay.

Brewer rolled his head to look at his coxswain. The big seaman smiled.

"*'Gorilla'?"*

The Cornishman grinned wider and shrugged his massive shoulders. "I guess he likes me, sir."

Brewer closed his eyes and laid back, whispering "Lord, help me." He could have sworn he heard snickering, but his head hurt too much to do anything about it. He heard someone approaching and turned his head to see Mr. Greene.

"Hello, Captain," Greene said. "The admiral told me you were awake, so I thought I'd stop by."

The doctor approached. "Mac, why don't you go get us something to eat? Bring back some broth for the Captain, will you? Don't worry, I'll watch him like a hawk while you're gone."

After his coxswain departed on his mission, Brewer

turned to the surgeon. "How badly were we hurt, Adam?"

"Sixty-five killed, nearly twice that number injured."

Brewer flinched at the steepness of the bill. "Any officers?"

Spinelli looked down. "Lieutenant Gerard was wounded. Mr. Phillips lost his right arm defending the ship against pirate boarders."

Brewer slowly rolled his head to face his first lieutenant. “Benjamin? *Defiant* was boarded?”

“Ah, yes, sir, she was,” Greene said slowly. “When you went down, the Admiral, Mac, and I, we all ran to you to see how badly you were hurt. While we were checking on you, the pirates changed course so as to grapple with us. My God, William, they came over the railing in wave after wave; I’ve never before seen so many from one ship. The Admiral took his stand by the wheel along with Mr. Sweeney and some hands. Mac grabbed a few hands and formed a barrier around your body to keep the pirates from finishing the job, as it were. I wonder how many he killed—he was covered in blood afterward, none of it his own. Mr. Phillips was injured protecting the Admiral’s back during the fighting, but he managed to stay on his feet until the day was ours.”

Brewer thought for a moment. “The frigate?”

Greene shook his head. “Got away while we were dealing with the boarders. Seems they had no stomach for any more fighting.”

Brewer closed his eyes at a spasm of pain. "Will John be alright?"

Spinelli heaved a sigh. "He developed an infection. I had to take the arm above the elbow."

"Does the Admiral know?"

Spinelli considered. "I'm not sure, but I doubt it."

"Where is Mr. Phillips?"

"Already gone ashore to the Naval Hospital. You will see him tomorrow. And now, your broth is here. See that he eats it, Mac."

The surgeon retreated, leaving Brewer at the mercy of his grinning nursemaid.

Captain Brewer left *Defiant* the next morning. He was lowered into his gig and, along with his surgeon and coxswain, was rowed ashore and taken to the Naval Hospital where he insisted on sharing his room with Lt. Phillips.

Two days later, the admiral came by for a visit. Brewer tried to sit up in his bed, but a lancing pain shot through his head and he lowered himself back on to his pillow.

“Let that be a lesson to you,” Hornblower said. “Lie still.”

“Aye aye, my lord,” Brewer said weakly, then promptly demanded. “What happened after I went down?”

Hornblower adjusted his seat a bit for comfort’s sake and launched into his tale. “When you were struck by that spar, William, I confess that my attention was... diverted from the battle. The pirate took advantage of my lapse to do something I have never seen pirates do before—*he closed on a King’s ship and grappled us*. We were boarded before I could rally the men to repel them. We were unable to fire off the warning rocket to send *Crab* after the Americans, but fortunately Captain Morgan saw our situation and sailed off on his own authority. Commodore Porter arrived in time to assure our victory. It seems that the Commodore hadn’t waited to be called; fortunately for us, he had set sail this morning to search us out. The Americans boarded the pirate from the other side and swept over her and on to *Defiant*. As soon as the deck was secured, you were carried below.”

Brewer closed his eyes. Even the effort of listening was exhausting. “What about Lafitte?”

“I kept my word to him. After the Americans departed, I sailed into Havana and turned him over to the Spanish authorities. I did warn him, however, that if our paths crossed again, he would not be so lucky.”

“Thank you, my lord,” Brewer whispered, “for saving my

ship."

"You have a good crew, Captain. They fought for you; it was all them."

Brewer drifted off to sleep, and Hornblower sat there for several minutes watching his young protégé. Finally, he wiped a tear from his eye and left the hospital.

Over the following weeks, Brewer slowly crawled toward the point where he might resume a normal life. A couple of different times, he was disabled almost completely by blinding headaches that seemingly came out of nowhere. Each time, McCleary helped him back to his bed and called for Spinelli.

"Adam," Brewer asked after one episode, "how long will I suffer from these headaches?"

Spinelli sighed. "There's no way to know, William. The yardarm that hit you struck across the back of your skull, your neck, and off toward your left shoulder. You suffered a concussion and it's possible that your brain was bruised. Unfortunately, medical science knows very little as yet about treating brain injuries of that sort. All we can do for now is treat those symptoms we can and hope for the best."

"Marvelous," Brewer said, as he closed his eyes and began hoping.

A few days later, Brewer was able to take a walk around the compound, albeit with the use of a cane and the ever-present McCleary along for support. To his great delight, Lieutenant Phillips was able to join him.

The three men walked slowly in the warm Caribbean sun, making small talk about the weather or the various birds that crossed their path. They stopped when they turned a corner which gave them an excellent view of *Defiant*. The ship was in dry dock now, and the dockyard workers were busy. In the distance, it looked like their ship was being consumed by a never-ending swarm of ants. Brewer saw the look of dismay that crossed Phillips' face, and he cleared his throat.

"Don't let it bother you, John," he said. "Think about what she'll look like when she's recommissioned. She'll dominate the Caribbean, that's for sure."

"But will we be on her, sir?" Phillips asked.

"I don't know," Brewer answered honestly. "I have a meeting with the admiral at the end of the week; no doubt I'll find out more then."

Phillips nodded, and the group set off again. Brewer raised his face to the sun, enjoying the sea breeze, but he noticed that his young companion was in desperate need of distraction.

"Tell me, John," he said, "will you stay in the Navy?"

The younger man—Brewer found he could no longer think of him as a boy—hung his head. "I don't know," he said. “Is it even still up to me? With only one arm, I mean?”

Brewer shrugged. “As much as it ever was, I imagine. I still think you’re worth having; if I get a ship, you’re welcome on my deck anytime, John.”

“Thank you, Captain.”

They finished the walk in silence, and Brewer bid farewell to his friend when they returned to their room. After Phillips had gone inside, Brewer turned to his coxswain.

“Mac, I need to find the doctor.”

McCleary looked up in surprise. “Is something amiss, Captain?”

Brewer sighed. “No, Mac, I’m fine. I just need to ask him a question, that’s all.”

McCleary led Brewer back out into the courtyard and made him sit on a bench while he went off in search of the good doctor. Brewer thought briefly about getting up and searching for the doctor himself, but something told him it would not be a good idea to run afoul of his powerful coxswain. In any case, Mac was back in less than five minutes with the good Dr. Spinelli quite literally in tow.

"Hello, Adam," Brewer said.

"Good afternoon, Captain. It is now quite clear to me that your coxswain has no earthly idea what the words 'Just a minute' mean."

Brewer laughed and looked past the doctor to the coxswain. Having released his prisoner, Mac had stepped back and was watching the birds, oblivious to the doctor's complaints.

"Tell me," Brewer said, "have you spoken to Mr. Phillips?"

Spinelli shook his head.

"I just took a walk with him," Brewer said. "Mac and I, I mean. He is understandably low in spirits."

The doctor nodded. "I can imagine."

"I told him he was welcome on my deck."

Spinelli smiled. "I'm sure that helped."

"Keep an eye on him, will you?" Brewer said. "I don't like the idea of his getting melancholy, not now. I'll speak to the admiral about him on Friday."

Spinelli nodded. "Will you call off your watchdog now, so I can return to my experiment?"

"Of course, my dear doctor," Brewer said with a smile. The doctor got up and stalked off, tossing a withering glance at McCleary, who was now innocently looking for a four-leaf clover in the grass.

There was nothing much to do until his meeting with Hornblower, so Brewer spent his time reading. He finally got a chance to finish the new biography of George Washington that he had picked up in Boston. He was somewhat dubious about a couple of parts, and he resolved, as soon as he was up to it, to get a letter off to John Adams to get his impressions of the book as a whole and these questionable passages in particular. He was even able to get Phillips interested in reading, and after a careful inspection, the lieutenant asked if he could borrow *Ivanhoe*.

Brewer soon began to have visitors. Jenkins was the first to see him, and Brewer asked him to sit for a moment.

"Oh, I'm sorry, sir," he said, "but I haven't time. I just wanted to let you know, Captain, that I've been offered a very good position by the governor, sir. It seems that Admiral Hornblower was far too kind in his appreciation, you see. Well, Captain, I've come to say that I've decided to accept the governor's offer, and I hope there won't be any hard feelings."

Brewer shook his hand in congratulations. "Of course not, Jenkins. I'm happy for you."

Jenkins bowed. "Thank you, sir."

Brewer walked him to the door. "May I ask a favor of you?"

"Of course, Captain."

"I was hoping that you would give some pointers to whomever I get to replace you."

"I'd be happy to oblige, Captain Brewer."

"Thank you, Jenkins."

"Well, I must be going," Jenkins said. He started out the door, but then stopped and looked back to his former captain. "May I say, sir, that I have seen quite a bit of naval service, and I consider my opinion in certain areas to be well informed."

"Yes?"

"I just wanted you to know, Mr. Brewer, I appreciate the fact that you took over in dire circumstances, and I don't just mean the weather. You did well, sir, in my opinion."

Brewer stood back. "Thank you, Jenkins."

The servant bowed and left his captain to think.

Mr. Greene and Mr. Sweeney came by later that afternoon.

"Glad to see you're up and about, Captain," Greene said.

"Did Evans have any trouble bringing our prize in?"

Brewer asked.

"Not a bit. Those Dagoes were meek as lambs once they understood that Mr. Ross could be a very intimidating young gentleman when the spirit moved him."

Brewer laughed at the thought of little Ross intimidating anyone. "As long as it worked. Have you heard anything about what you're to do next?"

Greene shook his head. "Not a word, any of us."

Sweeney spoke up. "We were hoping you might ask the admiral what his intentions are for us, while *Defiant's* getting her refit." He rubbed his hands together. "Personally, I wouldn't mind a little shore leave in Jamaica."

Brewer smiled. "I'll ask the admiral. I go to see him tomorrow, as a matter of fact."

Greene said, "Do you think he'll confirm you in *Defiant*?"

Brewer spread his hands in a gesture of uncertainty. "I honestly have no idea. There are any number of senior captains right here in this squadron who would consider themselves more deserving."

Sweeney smiled. "That's where you're wrong, Captain. No man deserves it more than you."

Friday came all too slowly. Brewer was scheduled to dine with the admiral at noon sharp, and he thought the hour would never arrive. Not even his favorite sonnets from Shakespeare could distract him. Finally, the time came, and Mac accompanied him on the walk to the admiral's residence. Young Mr. Rodney opened the door and greeted him formally, but not, Brewer thought, with any warmth.

"A pleasure to see you, Lieutenant," Rodney said. Brewer noted that, since he was no longer in command of *Defiant*, Rodney's use of 'lieutenant' was technically correct—but Brewer knew there was more behind the dig. "If you'll wait in the library, sir, I'll tell the admiral you're here. Shall I direct your servant to the kitchen for his dinner?"

"Mr. McCleary is not my servant, lieutenant," Brewer said. "He is my coxswain, and I owe him my life many times over. Remember that."

"Of course, sir," Rodney said. He turned to McCleary. "If you'll follow me?" and then left without looking back. Mac shrugged his shoulders and followed him out. Brewer sincerely hoped Rodney would keep his mouth shut.

Rodney was back in five minutes and showed Brewer up the same flight of stairs as before to the admiral's study. Hornblower was seated behind the huge oak desk, reading a letter.

"Come in, William," Hornblower said. "Give me a moment to finish this letter from my wife."

"I trust the Lady Barbara is well?" Brewer said.

"Yes," Hornblower said as he scanned the paper, "but my son Richard has discovered that cows are not to be trifled with. It seems that one chased him right out of a pasture and into a mud pit!"

Brewer smiled. "That's one hazard not encountered the navy, my lord."

"Quite so!" Hornblower said. He rose and poured them each a glass of port, and both men moved over to sit in the overstuffed leather chairs by the window.

"Are you quite recovered?" Hornblower asked.

"Well on the way, my lord. The stiffness eases daily, as long as I do what my coxswain tells me to. Was it like that for you? Did Brown run your life, or seem to, anyway?"

"Oh, yes," Hornblower said. "And I wouldn't have had it any other way."

Brewer raised his glass. "To coxswains," he said. "Our guardian angels."

Both men drank, and Hornblower set his glass down. Brewer steadied himself. *Here it comes,* he thought.

"William, let me be direct with you. I cannot confirm you as the captain of the *Defiant*. There are simply too many senior officers available in the peacetime navy for me to promote a lieutenant to the post."

"I understand, my lord."

"I want to make clear that my decision has nothing to do with your performance as acting captain. You took a ship in trouble and turned it into a fighting machine in very short order."

"I had very good help."

"Of course, of course. I understand you already know about Jenkins. I'm afraid I spoke a bit too highly of him in front of the governor. Not that he doesn't deserve the praise, but I'm afraid I made it impossible for you to keep him."

"Quite all right, my lord."

"Now, as for your next posting. I'll give you a choice. There will soon be an opening for a first lieutenant on the frigate *Clorinda*. Her captain will take over the *Defiant* when she's recommissioned, and he has made clear he will take his officers with him. I can offer you the first lieutenant's billet. Or... if you prefer, there is another post. As you know, I have taken into the King's service a prize recently captured. She's a sloop, already equipped with sixteen 12-pounders, to which we will add four 18-pound carronades."

"The *El Dorado*!"

"Yes, only now she will be known as HMS *Revenge*. She's perfect for me to promote a lieutenant to Master and Commander. Want the job?"

"Do I?" Brewer cried. "Thank you, my lord! I don't know what to say!"

Hornblower nodded. "Then don't say anything. As for your officers, you can have your pick. A barque is normally crewed by the captain: two lieutenants, a master, and three midshipmen, but I suppose you can take your doctor friend as well. Better that than leaving him here with me!"

"Thank you, my lord," Brewer said. "I was sorry to hear about Gerard."

"Yes," Hornblower said sadly. "It will take him a long time to recover, but eventually he'll be good as new. Or so the good doctor tells me."

"I'm pleased to hear it, my lord. I also wanted to thank you for suggesting I get a coxswain. Mac saved my life at least twice during the voyage."

Hornblower smiled. "I remember how Brown meant so much to me when I was at sea." The admiral sighed. "More than an admiral's aide, anyway."

"Have you thought about a replacement?"

"No," Hornblower said. "Have you anyone in mind?"

"Well, my lord, I happen to know of a young lieutenant who has proven himself in battle. He even lost an arm in the course of protecting his admiral's life. Might I suggest Mr. Phillips?"

Brewer could tell from the look on the admiral's face that he still did not know the circumstances of Phillips' injury. Nevertheless, a smile illuminated his mentor's face.

"An excellent idea, Commander," the admiral said. "Please have Mr. Phillips come and see me tomorrow morning at nine."

"Aye, my lord," Brewer said. "But... won't Mr. Rodney be disappointed?"

"Perhaps," Hornblower said, "but I've lately been thinking that Mr. Rodney needs some sea duty to season him. Don't you think he'd do well as the new third lieutenant on *Clorinda*?"

Brewer raised his glass. "I do indeed, my lord."

He went back to his room that day and told Phillips the admiral wanted him, but not the reason why. Brewer saw the crestfallen look on the lieutenant's face and knew he expected the admiral to dismiss him from the navy. The next morning, Brewer patted Phillips on the back and watched him leave the room like a man walking to his own execution. Brewer shook his head and chuckled. Poor John didn't realize that admirals don't dismiss lieutenants from the navy; that was what captains were paid for. He hated to put his friend through all this unnecessary grief, but it would all turn out for the best.

Mr. Phillips marched up the road from the hospital to the admiral's residence. He was sure his career in the Royal Navy was over. The admiral probably just wanted to offer his condolences and thank him for saving his life in the action on board *Defiant*. Phillips tried to stay positive; he was young, after all, with his whole life before him. There were many ships in the merchant service that would welcome an officer with naval experience, even a one-armed one; he might even catch on with an East India Company ship if he was lucky. His spirits perked up a bit at the thought—fortunes were made on HEIC voyages. But it was no good. No sooner had the prospect cheered him than he found himself miserable again. The problem was, he didn't *want* to be an officer in the merchant service or even on an HEIC ship. He wanted to be a King's officer. Phillips kicked at the road in frustration. Why did it have to happen like this? He finally settles on making the navy his career, and then he loses his arm in his first boarding action and is to be put ashore because of it. *Oh well*, he thought philosophically. The admiral's life was worth his arm.

He arrived at the admiral's residence and stood there for a moment, looking at the door. He inhaled deeply to steel himself for what lay ahead, then reached out and knocked on the door. A minute later it was opened by a lieutenant whom Phillips presumed to be the admiral's aide.

"Yes?" the officer said. "May I help you?"

"Lieutenant Phillips," he answered. "The Admiral asked me to come and see him."

The officer stepped back to allow Phillips' entrance. "Of course, Lieutenant, please come in." Phillips entered, and the officer closed the door. "I am Lieutenant Rodney, the admiral's aide. Will you please follow me?"

Phillips fell into step behind the aide. He kept his eyes lowered as the feeling of impending doom rose once again. Finally, Rodney stopped in front of a door and indicated that Phillips should wait outside. He knocked and entered the room. Phillips heard his name being announced, then Rodney emerged and said, "You may go in now, Lieutenant."

Phillips nodded his thanks and entered what turned out to be the admiral's study. He found Hornblower sitting behind a massive oak desk, reading a report. Phillips jumped a little when Rodney closed the door behind him.

Hornblower looked up. "Good to see you again, Mr. Phillips. Please give me one minute to finish reading this. Feel free to look around; I'll be with you shortly."

"Yes, my lord," Phillips said. He began to stroll around and examine the bookshelves that dominated one wall of the study, but he stopped when he came upon the bust of Napoleon Bonaparte. He was still looking at it when Hornblower joined him.

"Is that who I think it is?" Phillips asked.

"Yes," Hornblower said, "I'm afraid it is."

"You knew him, didn't you? On St. Helena. You and the Captain."

"Yes, Lieutenant."

Phillips turned to the admiral. "What was he like?"

Hornblower looked down at the smaller officer. "What did Captain Brewer say?"

Phillips looked down. "Not very much. He told me a story once about Bonaparte charging into the office looking for you and turning on him instead. He told it as an illustration about keeping control of your fear and not letting it show." Phillips looked at the bust again. "I never really asked him."

Hornblower considered for a moment. "Tell me,

Lieutenant, did Captain Brewer boast of facing down Bonaparte?"

Phillips turned again, a look of shock on his face. "Oh, no sir! He showed tremendous respect for the man. In fact, I made a remark about the Captain putting Boney in his place, and the Captain took me to task, right there in front of everyone! He said that, defeated or not, he was still Napoleon Bonaparte, Emperor of the French, and not a man to be trifled with."

Hornblower nodded in satisfaction and turned away from the bust. Phillips took one last look before following the admiral to his desk.

"Lieutenant," Hornblower said as he sat in his chair and indicated for Phillips to sit as well, "did Captain Brewer say why I wanted you?"

Phillips lowered his eyes. ""No, my lord," he said softly, "but I figured it had to do with my arm."

Hornblower leaned forward. "I think you should know, Lieutenant, that I only recently became aware of the circumstances under which you lost your arm."

Phillips' head snapped up, his eyes wide. He tried to say something, but Hornblower stopped him with a gesture.

"Let me simply say, Lieutenant, thank you for saving my life. When my wife hears of it, you will be practically a son to her."

Phillips looked embarrassed at the thought. Hornblower smiled and pressed on.

"Lieutenant, there are some who would say that your wound should disqualify you from further service in His Majesty's navy." Hornblower was pleased to note that Phillips was crestfallen at the prospect. "However, Mr. Phillips, I am not one of them. In fact, I find myself in need of a new aide, and your captain claims there is no one better suited to fill the position than yourself. What do you say?"

Phillips stared at the admiral like he'd grown another

head. "My lord! I... I don't know what to say. Is this because... because of my arm?"—

Hornblower rose from his seat and walked over to a table in the corner. Phillips watched him pour two glasses of wine and return, handing on to him. "Mr. Phillips, I can understand why you might think that. Let me assure you—and I believe Captain Brewer will tell you the same—that I do not make offers of this kind as rewards for doing your duty. I am offering a position of great importance and responsibility to an officer who has proven himself to me in battle and also has his captain's highest recommendation. The only question is, will you accept?"

Phillips felt a tear welling up in his eye so he turned away quickly and wiped the offending liquid away. He turned back to his admiral. "With pleasure, my lord."

Hornblower smiled and raised his glass, and the two men drank to the future.

The next time Brewer saw the young lieutenant was over a week later.

"Commander!" Phillips called as they passed on the street. "Thank you so much for your recommendation to the admiral!"

"Think nothing of it, John; you earned it. Just promise me that, when you're done with the admiral, you'll consider coming back to sea with me."

"Yes, sir!" Phillips hurried off. It seems that an admiral's aide is never idle.

The next few weeks flew by for Brewer. His first action was to meet with Greene and Sweeney. Because McCleary would not allow him to exert himself just yet, the meeting was held in his hospital room.

"I'm sorry we had to meet here," Brewer said after they came in and sat down, "but my nursemaid here"—pointing over his shoulder at the big coxswain—"was unyielding."

"We understand, sir," Greene said. Sweeney just nodded. McCleary glared at both of them.

"The admiral has decided not to confirm my commission as captain of the *Defiant*. There are simply too many post captains available on the navy list to justify his giving such a large ship to one as junior as myself. However, he has offered me command of the prize that Mr. Evers so kindly brought back. She already has sixteen 12-pounders on board, and the admiral said that those would be augmented with four 18-pound carronades. She will be taken into the navy and renamed *Revenge*. At my request, the admiral has confirmed Mr. Tyler's commission as lieutenant, and he has been assigned to *Revenge* as the second lieutenant. I have called you gentlemen here to ask you if you would consider signing on as well. Mr. Greene, I have need of an excellent first lieutenant, and I can think of none better than yourself. What do you say?"

Greene was grinning from ear to ear. "I would consider it an honor, Captain."

"Thank you. And you, Mr. Sweeney, well, I don't think I could navigate a ship around a bathtub anymore without you. What say you?"

Sweeney sat back and looked out the window for a moment before replying. "Mr. Brewer, I don't know," he said slowly. "I've been doing this for nearly forty years by now; I don't know if I want to go to sea again at my age in a ship as small as a rowboat to play nursemaid to a crew young enough to be my grandchildren."

"I understand completely, Mr. Sweeney," Brewer said, as seriously as he could. "Then you'll do it?"

Sweeney grinned. "I couldn't think of anything I'd rather do, Captain."

"Excellent!" Brewer said. "Dr. Spinelli will be coming along, if only because Admiral Hornblower said we are not permitted to leave him behind."

“What about your watchdog?” Sweeney asked, indicating McCleary.

“Oh, I think his feelings would be hurt if we went without him, wouldn’t they, Mac?”

“Yes, sir,” the big Cornishman replied.

“There you go,” Brewer said to Sweeney.

“Oh, well, I was just wondering,” Sweeney said with a shrug.

"Our crew is mainly from *Defiant*, although I'm sure the governor will try to get rid of a few undesirables by giving them to us, so we'll have to watch for those. Any questions?"

Sweeney shook his head and looked at Greene, who turned to Brewer and grinned. Brewer saw a glow in his first lieutenant's eye that made him smile himself.

"Just one, sir," Greene said. "When do we leave?"

THE END OF VOLUME ONE

About The Author

James Keffer

James Keffer was born September 9, 1963, in Youngstown, Ohio, the son of a city policeman and a nurse. He grew up loving basketball, baseball, tennis, and books. He graduated high school in 1981 and began attending Youngstown State University to study mechanical engineering.

He left college in 1984 to enter the U.S. Air Force. After basic training, he was posted to the 2143rd Communications Squadron at Zweibruecken Air Base, West Germany. While he was stationed there, he met and married his wife, Christine, whose father was also assigned to the base. When the base was closed in 1991, James and Christine were transferred up the road to Sembach Air Base, where he worked in communications for the 2134th Communications Squadron before becoming the LAN manager for HQ 17th Air Force.

James received an honorable discharge in 1995, and he and his wife moved to Jacksonville, Florida, to attend Trinity

Baptist College. He graduated with honors in 1998, earning a Bachelor of Arts degree. James and Christine have three children.

Hornblower and the Island is the first novel James wrote, and it is the first to be published by Fireship Press. He has self-published three other novels. He currently lives and works in Jacksonville, Florida, with his wife and three children.

If You Enjoyed This Book

Please write a review.
This is important to the author and helps to get the word out to others
Visit

PENMORE PRESS
www.penmorepress.com

All Penmore Press books are available directly through our website, amazon.com, Barnes and Noble and Nook, Apple iTunes, Kobo books and via leading bookshops across the United States, Canada, the UK, Australia and Europe.

The Lockwoods of Clonakilty

by

Mark Bois

Highly entertaining, well researched and original in thought. Lieutenant James Lockwood of the Inniskilling Regiment returns to his family in Clonakilty, Ireland, after being badly wounded at Waterloo. After three years on active service his return is a joyous occasion, but home is not the perfect refuge he craves.

Twenty years before, he had married Brigid O'Brian, a beautiful Irish Catholic woman of willful intelligence, an act that estranged him from his wealthy family. Their five children, especially their second daughter, Cissy, are especially and irritant to the other branches of the family, as the children balance their native Irish heritage against the expectations of the Anglo-Irish Lockwoods.

GREEK FIRE
BY
JAMES BOSCHERT

In the fourth book of Talon, James Boschert delivers fast-paced adventure, packed with violent confrontations and intrepid heroes up against hard odds.

Imprisoned for brawling in Acre, a coastal city in the Kingdom of Jerusalem, Talon and his longtime friend Max are freed by an old mentor from the Order of the Templars and offered a new mission in the fabled city of Constantinople. There Talon makes new friendships, but winning the Emperor's favor obligates him to follow Manuel to war in a willful expedition to free Byzantine lands from the Seljuk Turks. And beneath the pageantry of the great city, seditious plans are being fomented by disaffected aristocrats who have made a reckless deal to sell the one weapon the Byzantine Empire has to defend itself, *Greek fire*, to an implacable enemy bent upon the Empire's destruction.

Talon and Max find themselves sailing into perilous battles, and in the labyrinthine back streets of Constantinople Talon must outwit his own kind—assassins—in the pay of a treacherous alliance.

PENMORE PRESS
www.penmorepress.com

Penmore Press

Challenging, Intriguing, Adventurous, Historical and Imaginative

www.penmorepress.com

Lightning Source UK Ltd.
Milton Keynes UK
UKHW021006130819
347891UK00013B/931/P